DETECTIVE QUINN ISAACS:

ALMOST THE ^ PERFECT CRIME

JACQUE JACOBS

An imprint of
Drellag Press, LLC

Acknowledgements

Writing a novel is a solitary art which, if you're fortunate, exits the writer's computer with the encouragement and support of family and friends. Family is everything to me. I am lucky–Bonnie, Bob, Cheri, Jack, Amy, Billy, David, Tom, Nancy and Chuck are my cheerleaders. My friends and beta readers who read every word, and do not hesitate to give me honest feedback, make my writing better. I am grateful for Nancy Gill Gorneau, Susan Lovelace, Dondra Maney, PhD, Paula Van Hooser, Peggy Jones, EdD, and Ruth Jackson Johnston who have read every word. Donna Duffy, Sandra Council, PhD, Bonnie MacDougall, PhD, Catherine Richey, Jeanne Selander-Miller and members of the Tuesday Writers and Night Writers of the Laura (Riding) Jackson Foundation have given me feedback on sections and taught me a great deal about what makes a good story. Their willingness to read, talk with me, and point out how to make the work better is invaluable. My cousin, Becky Anderson Clark, talked me through what would capture her as a reader who loves detective stories. Thanks, Becky. I owe a special thanks to Michelle Wheeler who spent an afternoon with me imagining and discussing how to create a *raison d'être* for Quinn to be in law enforcement. Thank you so much, Michelle.

With a lifetime of reading and an academic life of writing and publishing, I still find it hard to believe that this is my seventh novel going to press in three years. Thanks to my parents, Richard Macklin Evans and Mary Elizabeth Anderson Evans, who taught me the value of education and encouraged me to always do my best. I hope these stories, set in the Smoky Mountains of our ancestors, would make you proud.

Dedication

To my grandson, Kristopher Ray Coats, who is on his own journey of self-expression. I'm proud of you and love you always.

Other Works of Fiction by Jacque Jacobs

Love is a Cabin Series

High on a Mountain – Book 1

Life on a Mountain – Book 2

Settled on a Mountain – Book 3

New Beginnings on a Mountain – Book 4

Community Unites on a Mountain – Book 5

Holidays on a Mountain – Book 6

Table of Contents

Part I
Crime Comes in Many Forms

Chapter 1

*Integrity is telling myself the truth, and honesty is telling
the truth to other people.*
Spencer Johnson

"You're Safe."

Quinn Isaacs couldn't force herself to get up from under her warm hand-quilted comforter. She burrowed into her pillow, the soft material forming earmuffs, as she tried to block out the nightmare she thought she had conquered. The January freeze coming to the Smoky Mountains in the next twenty-four hours was nothing compared to the chill in her bones. Her pulse raced as she struggled to pull the girl in her dream down behind the lab table—just as she had seventeen years before at the shooting her senior year in high school.

The science teacher and the other students had made it to the storage room at the far end of the classroom. Quinn had been headed there when she saw three girls crouched behind the lab table totally immobilized. She stopped and hunkered down with them. She had tried to console them—to stop their whimpering and occasional mutterings.

"We have to stop that drip!" Eliza hissed as she tried to stand up to turn off the dripping faucet on the lab sink.

Quinn had pulled her down and almost purred. "Eliza, the drip is loud to us, but you can't hear it outside the room."

"Yeah, how do *you* know that, Miss Rich Bitch?" There was fear and anger in her voice.

Quinn tried to rub Eliza's shoulder thinking it would calm her, but Eliza slapped Quinn's hand away as she stood to turn off the dripping faucet.

In that split second, bullets ripped through the door and across the top of the lab table—killing Eliza instantly.

Quinn grabbed Mary Sue and Tricia as the blood spattered over and around them. Using every bit of will she had to stop herself from trembling, Quinn steeled herself and whispered, "Quiet. Absolute quiet. Now!" The tone was as stern as any teacher the girls had ever heard. She turned to look at Eliza and whispered, "I only wanted to help." Then the silence in the room engulfed them.

This was always where Quinn's nightmare ended: Eliza limp on the floor while Quinn tried to protect and comfort the other two girls.

The blaring "Boogie Woogie Bugle Boy" ringtone on her phone startled her to full consciousness. She flung the pillow to the other side of her king size bed, sat up, grabbed her phone, and turned off the alarm. It was Monday morning—five-thirty a.m. *Arghhh...why did I think* that song *was the way to wake up?* She set the phone back on the night stand, pulled her knees up onto the edge of the bed and buried her face. Her hands involuntarily pulled her shoulder length hair into a ponytail and wrapped it into a knot—just as she had when they were rescued seventeen years ago. She heard herself whisper, "You're safe. You're safe."

She stood slowly and walked to the large wingback chair in her bedroom and sat down, planted her feet flat on the floor, and straightened her spine. She recalled what the counselor had told her to do. She controlled her thoughts. *It was seventeen years ago. You saved two lives—lives of your classmates. Now you work to save lives.* She took a long breath—let it out slowly through pursed lips being very careful not to make a whistling sound—*the sound of flying bullets*.

Her eyes fell on the exquisite painting on her wall by Frida Kahlo. She had spent hours looking at it when it hung in her grandmother's home. Quinn cherished receiving it as a housewarming gift when her grandmother bought this house for her. "My precious Quinn, Señora Kahlo expressed the utter femininity of woman while expressing her strength to defy convention and follow her passion. Always follow yours, my pet." She felt the nightmare fade and the confidence return—*I am, Grandmother. Thank you for knowing I had to be in law enforcement.* She undid the knot in her hair and headed for the shower.

At six-thirty-four a.m., she turned into the front parking lot of the Round City Police Station in the mountains of east Tennessee which she called home. Although she was born and raised thirty-five miles away in Knoxville and attended the University of Tennessee, she had moved here with her Immigration Enforcement job a decade earlier. Feeling the slight slide of her tires on the rapidly freezing slush, she pulled into the space marked: Lead Detective. It was her second week on the job. *Wonder why this space isn't in the secure parking lot at the back?* That concern was not the top of her to-do list today. She stepped carefully out of her SUV and headed towards the station door.

She walked toward the officer on duty.

"Morning, Detective Isaacs."

"Good morning, Officer Jamison. Looks like the worst of the blizzard missed us this time."

"Yes, ma'am. Makes the plowing easier and the crime fighting safer—hard to chase a crook on ice." Jamison stifled a laugh at his own attempt to joke with the new lead detective. He watched her face to see if she would at least smile.

She did.

He relaxed as he pushed the button to unlock the secure door for her to enter.

"Jamison," Quinn paused and looked into his dark brown eyes—the same deep brown of his skin, "ever wonder why crime fighters don't have the same motto as postal service workers: 'neither snow, nor rain, nor heat, nor gloom of night...?'" She smiled at him and didn't wait for an answer as she turned and started a slow walk to her office.

"No, ma'am..." he stopped himself as she turned away. *Best not to push it. I hear she's a lot tougher than she looks—she'd have to be.* He shifted his eyes from the monitors he should be scanning to watch her five-foot nine-inch frame move with purpose down the hall; her golden brown hair moved gently against her back revealing the highlights that made it shine.

Quinn opened the hall door and headed to her office in the crime lab. She wanted to read the report on the woman brought to the morgue over the weekend. *Did the call about the deceased woman trigger my nightmare?* She reached to pick up the phone buzzing on her desk.

"Isaacs, here."

"Detective?" The inquisitive tone conveyed surprise when Quinn answered.

Quinn rolled her eyes. *I was when I walked in the door.* She looked down at the caller ID and stood ramrod straight. "Chief Hansen, good morning. How may I be of service?"

"Detective, please stop by my office when you have a minute—something I'd like to run by you."

"Yes, ma'am. Be there in five. Soon enough?" She smiled hoping to make her voice sound more cheerful than she felt.

"Bring your coffee. 10-4." The chief hung up abruptly.

One week in and I don't even know everyone, much less how they operate—especially the chief. Quinn turned in the small office and placed her black cashmere coat on the old-fashioned coat tree which had belonged to her grandmother. It made her new office feel like hers without overly feminizing a space which still carried the scent of the man who had occupied it for the last ten years. *Detective Albright, where's your cheat sheet on employee personalities and quirks that every detective needs to know?* She shrugged her shoulders. *On the other hand you didn't work for the new chief.*

Stepping out of her boots, she slipped into fashionable, but practical, black Gucci loafers—another attempt on her mother's part to make sure

Quinn dressed in keeping with their wealth. Quinn straightened the front of the jacket on her black wool pant suit and checked that her sidearm was secure and her new gold shield attached to her belt. In a long practiced way, when she was stressed or problem-solving, she pulled her hair into a ponytail and tied it in a knot at the base of neck—just as she had the day of the shooting.

She grabbed her insulated mug and stopped to get coffee from the break room. Scanning the rooms along the hall as she tried to memorize the layout of the building, she reminded herself that the community was still reeling from the death of their beloved police chief last month and the abrupt resignation of the lead detective the next day. She was aware of the gossip in Round City about how quickly the Town Council had selected their new chief—and how quickly the Chief hired her.

"Detective." The Chief was standing in the doorway to her outer office.

Quinn turned at the calm feminine voice behind her.

"Chief." Quinn extended her hand to shake. She tried to ignore the fact that she was so lost in thought she walked right by the Chief.

"What's got your attention so early this morning?" Jill Hansen shook hands and then extended hers to point toward her office door.

Quinn gave a wan smile. "I'm still trying to learn the layout of the building."

"Ha. Me, too, and I've been here a month longer than you."

Drip, drip, drip. Quinn's eyes quickly scanned the ceiling. "Chief, is that the sound of water dripping?"

"No. There's no water dripping." Jill looked up to the ceiling. "Apparently, they did have a problem with water leaking in several office ceilings, but I was told that was fixed a couple of months back. I'll check into what caused the leak. Don't want more."

"Silly. Guess it will take me a while to learn the sounds of a new building." *There is no drip—that was a long time ago.*

"No problem." The chief, formerly a lead forensic detective in Atlanta, moved toward the table in her office. "Have a seat, Quinn."

"Yes, ma'am."

"I'll be interested in your follow-up on the female victim brought in over the weekend, but I'd like a quick review of a report I read this morning of an item left on the roof of a police officer's vehicle last night."

Quinn raised her eyebrows. *Detective Marshall didn't mention anything else when he called about the dead woman.* "Yes, ma'am. I had just walked in when you called."

"No problem. I had actually expected to leave you a message. Anyway, the forensic tech indicated he left everything on the lab table."

With Quinn's office immediately to the left inside the lab, she had not seen the lab tables when she went into her office. "Yes, ma'am. I'll get right on it. Detective Marshall and I will meet this morning on the female victim. It appears to be natural causes but we'll work with the Medical Examiner and be thorough. The male victim from Saturday night appears to be a straight forward bar fight, but we're on it. Everything else is either pretty routine or cold cases."

"The item on the police cruiser might be, too."

"Routine or a cold case?"

"I doubt it will be routine."

This woman doesn't mince words: short, sweet, and to the point. "Yes, ma'am. Anything else?"

"No. Please text me as soon as you've read the reports and reviewed the evidence."

Quinn stood. "Yes, ma'am."

"Oh, and Quinn...I hired you as Lead Detective because your reputation precedes you. We're both committed to this community, but there'll be no small number of people waiting for us both to fail."

"Sad to say, I'm not new to the expectation. I'll do my best."

Quinn looked into the blue-gray eyes of this woman who carried herself with the regal bearing of a queen, spoke with the softness of your closest confidante, and conveyed the toughness of the meanness street cop.

The chief stood and extended her hand. "I'm counting on it. Welcome aboard."

The Plumber

One thing Buddy hated about plumbing work was being called out late at night especially two nights in a row. *Oh, well, might just be worth it.* The traffic thinned out quickly as he drove under the interstate on Route 54 in east Tennessee headed toward County Road 12 which ran south off this road. *Where else could it go? Wall of rock to the north!* He shook his head to clear his vision in the deep blue-black night. He knew the darkness and the dropping temperatures were going to turn the slush to ice before long. *Nothing I can do about the road conditions—except not spin out if I can help it. Have to be extra careful on the side road.* He turned on his blinker for the left turn and saw a vehicle coming toward him with the right turn signal blinking. The driver was going much too fast for the road conditions, especially if he was turning right onto the county road. Buddy slowed for his left turn and saw the headlights behind him were a safe distance—unlike the crazy one coming toward him. He watched the oncoming driver as he took the turn much too fast. *Idiot. Now where are* you *headed? I thought the woman said it was a dead-end road.*

The woman who called him for a plumbing problem told him she lived in the middle of nowhere and gave specific directions. He set the trip odometer when he turned onto County Road 12 and watched for any sign of wildlife on the road—and watched more carefully for any surrounding houses to the place he was headed. So far, no evidence of life: wild or otherwise. In exactly 2.2 miles his headlights caught the red plastic disk nailed on the mailbox next to the driveway. There was no sign of the vehicle that had turned ahead of him. He glanced in the mirror thinking he saw headlights behind him, but it was pitch black.

His headlights hit the reflective letters "Summers" on the post of the mailbox. A sly smile crept onto his face as his right blinker winked. *No one on either side of the road. I'll find out from the woman if there are any houses beyond here. Where was that guy headed?* He didn't see the vehicle behind him turn onto the road too and turn off his headlights. Buddy drove the fifty feet off the highway and pulled right up in front of the steps to the porch. He let his eyes adjust to the night when he turned off the truck. The darkness surrounding the house didn't bother him. *That's just fine with me.* He often wondered why others weren't as attentive to detail as he was. *Idiots.* Unaware of his own soft maniacal laugh, he headed to the front door. He stopped in his tracks as the door flung open.

A short woman with long blond hair in a ponytail, who couldn't be more than thirty, called through the screen. "Hurry up! Colder than a witch's tit out there."

"I'm coming. Steps aren't cleared."

"Done told you on the phone my old man ain't here."

Buddy stepped through the door into a large living room with a raging wood fire. He always noticed details; he especially noticed unusual details. Most folks took in half-a-dozen pieces of cordwood at a time; the stack on the floor next to the fireplace was enough to last for weeks. The woman now stood in front of the flames and he couldn't help but see she didn't have on anything under her flimsy long-sleeved nightgown.

"Where's the problem, ma'am?"

"The problem—is most likely sitting on a bar stool in Maryville grinning from ear to ear 'cause he ain't made it home." Her hand rested on her right hip—slung out to make a statement. "The plumbing issue is in my bathroom. Come this way."

"Ma'am, on the phone I thought you said the kitchen sink." He watched her move down the hall and the sway of her hips did not escape him. *Normal walk or bait?* He looked at his watch. *Why the hell didn't I check the weather forecast before I left? I always do.* He rubbed his forehead with his gloved hand.

The woman stopped abruptly and turned around.

He almost ran into her.

"Did I say kitchen? Silly me! It's my bathroom. Right there. That toilet's about to flow over." Her mountain drawl was slow and sultry. Her eyes fluttered as she stood in the narrow doorway and pointed—she didn't move.

He watched her hand move slowly to turn on the light in the bathroom. *Pappy was right. Never know when details can matter.*

He tugged at the latex gloves which he had put on before he entered the house. "Uh, ma'am, if you don't mind, I need to get in there to check it out."

The woman still didn't move. "Go on then. I don't bite." She smiled and batted her eyes.

He turned sideways to move through the narrow opening. He felt her leg brush against his. Buddy wasn't unfamiliar with the come-on actions of some women. He knew his blue eyes and lean six-foot frame, not the stereo-typed butt-crack-showing plumber, seemed to have appeal to women: not all, but many. He reached for the handle on the toilet without lifting the closed lid.

The woman shrieked.

He jumped back.

"No, don't go flushing it. It'll run all over my floor and I just cleaned it. Don't you have one of those things that will unclog it?" She looked up at him from her five-foot two inches and pouted as she moved her hand up and down imitating a plunger—maybe.

"Be right back." He turned sideways facing the door frame away from her and felt her hand pinch his ass through his jeans. *Just be calm. Keep moving.* He rushed out to the truck to get the plunger. As he turned toward the front door, he thought he saw parking lights down the road to the east. *Is it that other truck or just a reflection? Maybe this woman was expecting someone.* He looked toward the porch; there was no light on. He stopped to consider his next steps. To most folks in these mountains, no porch light on meant: "Don't come calling." *Was the light on the porch earlier the glow from the burning fire coming through the window?* He felt a pain in his head, shook it from side to side, and reentered the house. He stepped into the hall now barely illuminated by the fireplace. He reached the bedroom door. The lights in the bedroom and the bathroom had been turned out. He stopped to listen.

Baptism by Fire

Quinn finished reading the report from the forensic tech written in the wee hours of Monday morning. She walked into the lab and examined the evidence spread out on several trays on the stainless steel workspace. Her right index finger stopped above a child's shoe covered in mud, the laces frayed and worn, and an unmistakable ragged tear in the cheap material bearing dark dried matter—likely blood.

Quinn noted the untouched areas of the shoe and was intrigued by the care the forensic tech had taken. The photographs on the table made it clear the tech had been careful to leave as much evidence intact as possible in scraping samples to examine.

"Morning, Detective." Chuck walked toward her. He was almost thirty, tall with a sturdy build, and deep-set eyes.

Quinn had not heard anyone enter the lab. She kept herself from jumping—a reaction she had worked to master after the school shooting. "Good morning. What are you doing back so early? I saw that it was after two when you finished the report on this evidence."

"Couldn't sleep. We need to figure this one out." Chuck stared at the table.

Quinn smiled at the inclusiveness of the word: "we."

"Bear?" Quinn looked at the tech.

"Probably." The tech turned to look at this new lead detective. He hadn't expected such a quick response. The word had spread that Quinn Isaacs came from a wealthy family in Knoxville but had earned her stripes as an immigration agent. *Maybe the new Chief* did *know what she was doing when she hired this woman.*

"Any reports from physicians? Or the hospital here or in Knoxville?" Quinn returned his close look.

"No, ma'am. No missing child reports; no warnings of bears."

"Although it doesn't look new, given the amount of wet weather we've had lately, you'd think it would be soaked. Where was it found?" Quinn waited.

The tech looked at Quinn. "That's curious, too."

Quinn waited.

Chuck dropped his voice to almost a whisper. "It was in that old plastic bag…" he pointed, "on the roof of a patrol car when the officer returned to his vehicle after answering a domestic abuse call on the edge of town."

"Chuck, did the officer take a picture of the bag on his roof?" Quinn scanned the photos looking for a photo of the police cruiser.

Chuck shook his head slowly. "No, Detective. I called and woke him up to ask. He apologized and said that he grabbed the bag without thinking. Almost threw it across the field." He saw the frown by his new boss. "Well, Ma'am, folks have been known to put bear scat on a cop's vehicle."

Tempted to laugh or make a joke, Quinn decided decorum was warranted given the actual evidence—and this her second week on the job. "Understood. Anything not in your report that has occurred to you in the night?"

"Ma'am?"

"Chuck, please call me Quinn. We're going to be working side-by-side and I am counting on our teamwork to solve these cases."

"Yes, ma'...Quinn." He smiled shyly and looked back at the table.

Quinn smiled. Then she held up her now empty mug. "Buy you a cup of coffee?"

Chuck's eyes shot up. "Ma'am? Uh...what?"

The surprise in Chuck's voice cautioned Quinn to be alert to relationships in her new organization.

"Coffee?" Quinn held up her mug. "Let's take a walk to the break room. I'll buy you a cup of coffee."

"Thanks. I'd like that." A smile started to creep across the face of a young man whose eyes showed the weariness of too much crime and not enough concern by others.

Getting the Lay of the Land

Quinn and Chuck walked toward the break room. "Is Round City your home, Chuck?"

"Yes...De..."

"Relax, you'll get used to it. Just say Quinn three times quickly. Then it'll come easily."

Chuck laughed. "Okay, Quinn, Quinn, Quinn."

"See. Was that so bad?" She smiled.

Now Chuck's laugh was from the belly.

The two officers passing in the hall glanced at them and nodded.

Chuck spoke quietly to Quinn. "I've had to mind my manners here. When I came out of college, I learned things were more formal than I was used to. Shoot, in college we called our professors by their first names. I've never called anyone here by their first name in the eight years I've been on this job."

"Where did you go to college?"

"Middle Tennessee State."

"Good program. I think the forensic tech over in the Valley went to MTSU, too."

"Elizabeth? Yeah, I know her, but she was at university after me."

"Always good to know folks with similar skills, don't you think?"

"Absolutely." He walked toward the coffee machine. "If I may be so bold, what made you choose Round City?"

Shifts hadn't changed yet, so there was no one in the break room.

Quinn smiled. *My decision to leave the Immigration Enforcement Agency is likely as curious to folks as the Chief's decision was to hire me.* "As I'm sure everyone knows, I was with the Immigration Enforcement Agency for more than a decade; all of it was here in Round City. This is my home; my parents live in Knoxville." She knew her response would matter in building a working relationship with this young man.

"Miss the big city?"

"Rarely. Each time I visit my parents, it generally cures me of any need for big city life." Quinn put money in the locked box for coffee donations. They walked back into the lab and Quinn nodded to a table. "Let's sit for a minute."

A smile spread across Chuck's face. He had never been asked to sit and talk to the former lead detective. "My time's your time, ma'am...Quinn."

She scanned the evidence on the lab table. "Have any thoughts on the shoe you might like to share: official or otherwise?"

"I try not to speculate, but this is so unusual—makes it hard not to wonder."

"Run it down for me." Quinn was direct but gave Chuck a slight nod and smile.

"The shoe is clearly old and the mud long since caked and cracking. It's the left foot, so where is the right? The plastic bag is thin and not one you can buy anymore—suggesting it might be decades old. Someone wanted it found, or why put it on the top of a police vehicle?"

"Good points. Go on."

"Unlikely any DNA will match up to anyone in our database..."

Quinn interrupted him. "What's your thinking on that?"

"It appears the blood soaked deep into the shoe. Suggests whatever grabbed the shoe and the foot in it, cut one of the two arteries in the foot—and the person likely bled out." Chuck couldn't bring himself to use the word—child. "Given the age..."

"Chuck, have you ever seen someone injured by a bear?"

"Yes…" His voice trailed off.

"Me, too." Quinn saw Chuck's face fade to an off-white.

"Quinn…" he tried not to stumble on her name. "I think that's why it's hard not to speculate about the shoe: Who was wearing it? When? How? Did he survive? Don't you think it's curious?"

Quinn gave him a reassuring smile and nodded. "I do. You've had a rough night and early morning. We'll work the case. If you need resources you don't have, let me know."

Chuck quickly turned his head to look at her. "I *will*. Thanks."

Quinn made a mental note of the implied message that the tech had not always had access to what he needed. *Lots to learn about the operations in this station.*

"Thanks for making the time to give me your thoughts. I'm going to reread the reports and I'll get back to you with any questions. In the meantime, feel free to let me know if you need anything." Quinn pushed back her chair.

Chuck did as well. "Will do, Quinn. Will do. Thanks for the coffee." He held up his mug.

"Anytime." Quinn headed for her office. She could swear Chuck stood a little straighter than when they left the lab.

More or less

Her personal mobile rang. She pulled it from the pocket of her slacks as she closed her office door, sat down, and loosened the knot in her hair. "Buenos dias."

"Buenos dias, mi hija."

"Papa. How are you? To what do I owe the honor this morning?" Quinn's eyes darted around her office and took in her framed family photos on the wall. She hoped there wasn't something bad in this phone call—it wasn't like her father to call during work hours.

"Just thought I'd give the first lead detective in the family a friendly start to her second week in her new job."

"Thanks, Daddy. That's really sweet." Even when the child is an adult many southerners still call their fathers "Daddy." She knew he wasn't overly fond of it, and was respectful enough *not* to call him "Daddy" in formal settings. Born into an aristocratic family in Madrid, Spain, he met her very proper, wealthy, Southern mother during university. Now both her parents taught at UT-Knoxville in the foreign language department: acceptable jobs for people who didn't need to earn money to live. "Hope you can make it to Round City one of these days and see my new office."

"Absolutely. Well, I know you're busy so I won't keep you. I hope you have a good week."

"Thanks. Tell mother I sent my love. Love you."

"I'll tell her. Take care, Quinn. Un abrazo, mi hija." And, with that, he hung up.

A soft smile crept onto her face. *Likely the closest I'll come to being congratulated by my parents on my new position.* She knew the hug he sent was sincere. Another glance at her wall and the pictures of her parents and grandmother caused her to pause. Her name was unusual and people often assumed she was male. Quinn was the name her parents had agreed upon when her father wanted to name her Quintessa: ancient Spanish for queen. Even more fascinating to her was their mutual decision to give Quinn her mother's maiden name which her father had taken when they married. *Challenging enough that Spaniards use the surnames of mother and father for female children, but a Spanish male would almost never take his wife's surname.* She smiled. *Mine did.* She pulled out her desk chair and logged into her computer. *Reports await.*

Quinn finished a review of the officer's report, checked the duty roster, and hoped to see the officer when he came in at four. She looked to the right of the duty roster and saw he was off today. *Well, I can call him if I need more information.*

She checked her watch, not wanting to miss her meeting with Detective Marshall at eight-thirty. She had time so she sent a text to the Chief: "Info when ur ready."

"My office in ten." The reply was swift.

Quinn walked into the Chief's outer office. The administrative assistant looked up from her computer.

"Morning, Detective." The smile on her lips appeared plastered on her face.

"Morning, Ms. Leonard. Have a nice weekend?"

"Yes, ma'am. Hope you did."

"I did. Thanks. Chief Hansen is expecting me."

"Oh?"

Quinn smiled at the woman whose tan skin and straight jet-black hair was lovely against the soft blue sweater she was wearing under her navy suit jacket. *Wonder if she's a member of a local tribe? Cherokee?*

The Chief stood in the open door to her office. Quinn felt the tension between Ms. Leonard and the Chief. "Come in, Detective. Ms. Leonard, hold my calls unless an emergency."

Ms. Leonard's smile was well practiced. "Yes, ma'am."

Quinn was already at the Chief's door and immediately Jill Hansen was closing it.

"As lead detective you'll be a member of my advisory team. My first need for advice may be on how to manage my administrative assistant."

Quinn listened without saying a word.

"I know you don't have the benefit of the actual exchange, but here's an example."

Quinn nodded.

"I excused myself from Ms. Leonard last week saying I needed to read reports. She said something on the order of, 'Oh, ma'am, you don't need to read them. Chief Nelson had me read everything. I'll just let you know if anything needs your attention.'" Jill paused and watched Quinn's totally impassive face. "I said, 'Thanks. I'm sure I'll benefit from your read and direction. Just want to get off on the right foot and try to gain an understanding of all the things that come into this office. I'm sure you understand.'" The Chief sighed. "This was her response. 'Oh, I understand, ma'am. After all, it's your neck on the chopping block...well, so to speak.'" Jill stopped.

Quinn smiled. "Maybe she's just not used to a different style of leadership?"

The Chief did not respond.

Quinn hoped her face showed empathy. "Wish there were a simple fix. Not sure if it's relevant, Chief, but I read a management article several years ago which suggested some women find it difficult to work for a woman boss."

Jill nodded. "Maybe that's it. Hadn't thought about that." She paused. "Most of us are taught how to respond to male authority figures, but few are taught the differences in female leadership." She lifted her hands and slightly waved them back and forth suggesting she was undecided. "Pretty sure I'll just wait to see how it goes. I'm sure she's trying to figure me out."

Quinn smiled. "Not sure how long Ms. Leonard worked for Chief Nelson, but she's been in this office all the time I've been in Round City. Hopefully, she'll adjust."

The Chief studied Quinn's face. She had been impressed in the interview with Quinn's maturity for leadership in her mid-thirties. A thorough check into the background around the school shooting and Quinn's efforts to protect the girls had convinced Chief Hansen that Quinn had been mature beyond her years for a long time. *Wonder how much the shooting accounted for her career choice?* She nodded. "I hope so, too, Quinn. I hope so, too."

Quinn smiled at the comfort of the mountain double-speak so common among folks who grew up here. She was startled when she realized the Chief was speaking to her.

"Quinn, something wrong?"

Quinn chuckled. "No, ma'am. I apologize. I was enjoying your mountain double-speak."

The Chief laughed. "Nice not to have to explain it. Seemed I was always explaining it in Atlanta." She rolled her eyes. "Always fun to see the look on their faces when I said, 'You know, it's the echo in the mountains.'" She smiled, sipped her coffee, and was immediately back on task. "You've been in Round City over a decade. Assume you like living here?"

"I do, Chief. I'm looking forward to being more involved in the day-to-day lives of our community. My work at Immigration kept me on the periphery of it."

"Lots to do. That's for sure."

"If it's not presumptuous, may I ask what brought you to Round City—besides the position, of course."

"My family's been here for several generations. I graduated from high school here, went to college, married, joined the big city police force, divorced, returned. You know—same ole story, different actors."

"Seems to me each of our lives has a story. Glad yours brought you back here." Quinn thought she was going to like this woman. She was witty without being disrespectful, and must have some good experience if her actions today were any indication.

"I was a lead forensic detective in Atlanta, so when the opening came up here, it just happened to be at the right time in my life. Happy to be home."

Quinn nodded her head. "Our good fortune, I'm sure."

"Now, tell me what you know about the shoe."

Chapter 2

It's not that I'm so smart, it's just that I stay with problems longer.
Albert Einstein

Problems to Solve

The medical examiner, a retired local physician, turned to his assistant, Tristan Doyle. "Might be a long day, Tristan, with our stabbing victim, the death of an otherwise healthy female, revisiting the drug overdose from last week, and those bones..."

"Any word on where those bones came from, Doc? Clearly not related to the homicide." Tristan's voice rose in pitch as he talked.

Dr. Walters shook his head. "Hardly! One of our fine officers was out checking on a group of teens drinking in that old shed off Route 54. When he returned to his SUV, the bones were on the hood." Doc loved the serenity of the Smoky Mountains and hated the continuing encroachment of the modern world.

"They sure look human, don't they? You planning to send them to the lab upstairs or are we gonna work on 'em?" Tristan's sardonic smile was often viewed as downright satanic by many folks around the station.

Doc Walters rarely looked at Tristan's face and would likely have shrugged his shoulders even if he had noticed the expression. "They'll go to the upstairs lab. Not sure why they didn't head there in the first place. Too old for our work. Do you mind taking them up?"

"No problem. No problem at all." Tristan moved the bones to a rolling stainless steel cart and headed out the locked door of the morgue. "I'm gonna stop and see if there are any muffins in the breakroom. Want one?"

"No, thanks. Ate breakfast. Don't dawdle now—got lots to do. Helps a lot when you're in on the autopsy from the beginning; you've got a good eye for the possibilities." Doc liked mentoring Tristan whose intellect for problem solving was far beyond his nineteen years. Doc hoped he would head off to university and do something with his brains.

"Thanks, Doc. Likely all those crime movies I watch." Tristan's raucous laugh was disarming.

The ME shook his head slightly as he ignored the behavior. He pulled the remains from the refrigerated unit to set up the work area to finish the required autopsy of the man stabbed in a bar fight Saturday night. It wouldn't take much more time and then he could focus on the woman brought in over the weekend. He and Tristan would work together to make sure they missed nothing. *Can be pretty easy to assume this is routine given the report from the officers, but I never want to in front of a judge as the ME who missed the not so obvious.*

Tristan left the morgue and took delight in rolling the rickety cart to the lab—the unbalanced wheels spun and hit the floor making enough noise to wake the dead. The noise didn't bother him, but he knew it was annoying to many of the people on the main floor. *Too bad the elevator is so noisy coming up from the basement. Be more fun to roll off onto the tile floor and wake 'em all up.* He was so caught up in his fantasy that he passed the lab door. He backed up and pushed the button on the intercom.

"Tristan here. Got something for you."

"Just a minute." Quinn's voice was clear and crisp.

Tristan blinked as Quinn opened the door. *Wonder why Chief Nelson changed the system so I have to buzz to get in the lab? Maybe the new Chief will change it back. I'll have to figure out how get her to do that.*

"How may I help you?" Quinn stood in the open doorway. She felt her wariness antennae surface as she studied the young man.

"ME said to bring these bones up to you. They were found..."

"Yes, the medical examiner sent me a text. He told me where they were found. Thank you." She gave him a polite nod as she used her right hand to pull a stainless steel cart up so she could move the bones without having him enter the lab. *Is this young man...She looked up when he interrupted her train of thought.

"Hey, do you want to know more about the bones?"

"Thanks all the same. I have the officer's report. I appreciate the delivery—saved us a trip. Have a good day." She gave the tech a polite nod, pushed the cart to the side, stepped back, and closed the door. As she backed up, she almost bumped into Chuck.

"I can take those." Chuck reached for the cart.

"I forgot to introduce myself to...I didn't quite catch his name."

"Tristan. I wouldn't worry about it. Tristan probably already figured out who you are." He waited a beat. "For all the horrible things I've seen, I don't think any of them have caused me to be uncomfortable the way that guy does."

Quinn studied Chuck's face and gave a slight nod and returned to her office. *Tristan is fit, leans toward handsome, but there's something...What is it about him? His eyes?*

Chuck pushed the cart with the bones to the side and went back to the analysis of the child's shoe.

Tristan shrugged as he turned the cart toward the elevator. He grinned as he thought about how much louder the cart would be with the wobbly wheels and no weight to push them down.

The Curious and the Mundane

Quinn's watch signaled seven-fifty-eight a.m. She raised her hands over her head, crossed her eyes, and squeezed her eyelids shut. More than a decade in law enforcement had presented daily opportunities for read-ing directives, reports, statistics on crime, and even some management reports on budgets and operations—*now I need to lead* and *direct investigations. May need to set up a lunch with Sheriff Oliver or Billy over in the Valley for some friendly advice. Hmmm...Billy is lead detective.*

Quinn picked up the phone on her desk. "Isaacs here."

"Detective. Officer Jamison on the desk. You're needed in roll-call." He hung up.

"10-..." She didn't get to finish the rest of the 10-4 code ending communication before the call was cut off.

She strode down the hall; the flat heels on her loafers made solid contact with the floor.

Quinn entered the roll call room and wondered if the entire force was there. She stood at the door and decided to step to the back left corner. She didn't know why she was needed, but she was glad for another opportunity to learn how things worked.

"Detective Isaacs, come on up." The morning shift sergeant was waving his arm to her.

Quinn gave a slight nod of her head, set her lips with a soft smile, and walked to the front. She was unaware she unbuttoned her suit jacket as she walked and adjusted her shield on the waistband of her slacks. She reached the front of the room and stopped at the side next to a young female officer who nodded at her.

"Morning, Detective."

"Good morning." Quinn waited on the shift sergeant.

"Come on over here." He patted the flat of his hand on the podium in front of him. "I don't bite." There were snickers throughout the group.

Quinn was well aware that at five-feet-nine she was taller than most women, which she knew intimidated some men—and women. She carried herself with the bearing of her upbringing and the experience of more than a decade in a man's world of law enforcement.

"Sergeant," she turned to look at the troops, "Officers." She looked back at the sergeant. "To what do I owe this pleasure?"

The words were no sooner out of her mouth than applause started in the back and quickly made its way to the front where Quinn stood with the sergeant.

"Well, ma'am, it's come to my attention that we have not given you a proper welcome as our new lead detective—not the usual way of mountain folks, as you know." The applause continued as the sergeant grinned at her.

Quinn nodded and raised her hands, palms out toward the officers. "Thank you. Thank you very much. I consider it a privilege to have been selected and I look forward to getting to know each of you. Several of us in the room have worked together on cases over the years and I look forward to our continuing work in all areas of law enforcement—not just immigration. As I try to learn the operations here, I hope you'll let me know if I can be of service in any way. We'll meet occasionally..." She stopped and smiled at them. "Thanks for the silent groans..." Laughter permeated the room. "but our time belongs to the citizens of our community and I need to be doing my job, not boring all of you. I want you to know I value the work you do. Thank you for protecting our community— and for the warm welcome." She extended her hand to shake with the shift sergeant, gave a friendly wave, and saw Chief Hansen, who had been standing by the back door, quickly exit the room. *Nice of them to invite me in. I guess time will tell how long the honeymoon lasts.*

Quinn stepped to the side and listened to the directions from the shift sergeant to the officers. She smiled at the occasional comment from someone in the room.

"Right, Sarge."

"You said it."

"Okay, officers," the sergeant said, "Let's go get them before they get us."

Quinn headed for her office.

Crime Comes Calling

"Isaacs." Quinn answered her secure phone line.

"Williams here." She smiled when she heard the voice of the lead detective from the sheriff's department in the Valley which was beyond the interstate. He was one of the few people, besides her parents, who had her private number. She liked their personal interactions when she was over in the Valley as an immigration agent, and she hoped to get to know him even better—much better. *The times we've been together outside of work have been more interesting than I've had with a man in a long time.* She smiled. *Yes, Billy Williams, I would like to get to know you very, very well.*

"Good morning, Detective. To what do I owe this honor?"

"No honor on my part. I call bearing crime news."

"Oh?" She tried to dampen her disappointment. She was walking a tightrope in her new role as she managed her professional life—and hoped to have a personal life. Previous cases worked with the detective, and the few times they had been together socially, had given her more than a little personal interest in him.

"Yep, sorry. I'll call you on your other number soon—I promise."

She heard the warmth in his voice.

He quickly outlined a homicide on Route 54 last night. "The car the victim was in appears to have been stolen from Round City."

"How do you know it was stolen?" She was scanning her computer screen looking for reports that carried any information on a stolen vehicle. Round City was far from a big city, but certainly much larger than the unincorporated Valley. She stopped herself. She did not need to look at this moment.

Billy was still talking, and she wasn't listening.

"Whoa, back up. Still getting accustomed to the systems here and my new role. I got distracted. Give that to me again, please."

"Quinn, sorry. I am thrilled to have you as lead detective in the big city."

"Ha. Hardly a big city. I haven't gotten used to my new role yet. Will you fax me the report?"

"Should already be in your secure email."

"Thanks. Truthfully, that's why I was distracted." She cleared her throat. "I thought I'd missed your message so I was trying to find it."

Billy laughed. "Fair enough. Fair enough."

Quinn grinned, again, at the easy mountain double speak she'd heard twice today. It added even more cheer to her morning than being welcomed by the officers. It reminded her of one of the reasons she loved living here. *It's hard to explain to people who aren't from here that the double speak can be a way of reassuring the other person that whatever you said was a fact, not important to the circumstance, or not offensive.* She looked at the pictures on the wall. *Yeah, it's a kind of mountain reassurance that's too deeply ingrained for most of us to break the habit.* Suddenly she realized she had gotten lost in thought again.

"So, how was your weekend, Billy?" The line abruptly cut off. Her personal phone rang. She laughed as she answered it. "Wow, when you say soon, you mean soon."

"Just wanted to keep my promise. My weekend was work. Yours?"

They chatted for two or three minutes.

"Let's get together for a drink soon." It was quiet. Billy wondered why she didn't respond. "You can still drink in public, right? I mean now that you're the lead detective."

"I'm well over twenty-one, have always limited my intake of alcohol and choose to believe having *a* single drink in public sets an example for others. Of course, if that makes *you* uncomfortable, we can have a drink at my home."

"Thought you'd never ask. Tell me when and I'll be there."

"Soon. Okay?" Her voice softened.

"Soon works. Call me back if you have any questions or leads on the stolen car." He paused. "Bye, Quinn. Hope to see you—really soon."

The tenderness in his voice made her smile. "I look forward to it. Bye, Billy." She ended the call.

She found the email from Billy and looked for any reports in the system on the stolen vehicle. Detective Marshall had flagged the report on the car. She decided to take a walk down to the bullpen where the other detectives were housed even through Marshall was due at eight-thirty.

Although she had led teams in Immigration Enforcement, she hadn't gotten used to actually being the supervisor of others who were regularly under her direct command—she needed to sort out how to make her role work. *Were any of the detectives in the briefing this morning?*

"Morning, Detective." She smiled as she stood at the partition separating the desks of the detectives.

"Morning." George Marshall, who was the senior detective, looked up at her, and smiled. "Is it eight-thirty, already?"

"No. Just decided to take a walk."

"Have a seat." He moved the stack of folders off the chair beside his desk.

"Thanks. Won't take but a minute."

"Glad for the distraction. What's up?"

Quinn sat and held out the printed report. "Any progress on this one?"

He took it from her and looked at the heading on the report. "No. I flagged it because he's my neighbor and thought if I could help out, I would. We don't usually get stolen vehicles to handle until the officers do some checking on them."

Quinn made a mental note to figure out when and why officers would do investigative work and when it involved detectives. "Any additional information not in the report?"

"Nope. Like the report says, the teenage son left the keys on the front seat when he got home from a pick-up basketball game. Nothing like an open invitation."

"Sad, but true. I just received the report from the lead detective in the Valley on the other side of the interstate."

"Billy Williams?"

"Yes. Know him?"

"Reputation only. Albright was a chain of command kind of guy." He waited to see if she had any reaction to that. "Kept interactions with lead detectives to himself."

Quinn nodded. "Glad you had the report flagged. Feel free to reach out to Detective Williams and see if you can wrap up our side of this case." She stood.

So did Marshall. "Thanks. I'll be up in a few minutes. Just rechecking the reports on the woman in the morgue."

"Sure. See you then."

He extended his hand. "Glad to have you on board."

"Privilege is mine. Look forward to working with you." She shook his hand and left.

Chapter 3

We will either find a way or make one.
Hannibal

Time Flies

Quinn hung up the phone with George Marshall who had called with the ME's report confirming the woman brought in over the weekend died of a heart-attack. *Sad, but at least it's not a murder.* Quinn was startled at the tap on her door. It opened slightly.

"Boss?"

She looked at her watch and saw it was four-thirty p.m. "Chuck, you're still here?"

"Yeah…" He hesitated. "About to leave, but I wanted to check in first."

"What's up?" She smiled.

He visibly relaxed into the door frame. "I've done some pretty extensive research on that child's shoe and the closest one of similar design is over thirty years old."

"Any way to tell when this one was last manufactured?"

"Getting close. I've reached out to the manufacturer and hope I'll hear back soon."

"Good."

"The plastic bag is probably newer than the shoe, but still pretty old. No identifying marks, which generally means it's a cheap brand. The zip lock bag was pretty popular by 1973 and knock offs were much thinner plastic than the name brands. Best guess at this point is the bag is thirty to forty years old—from the late 1980s or early 1990s."

"Good work, Chuck. I look forward to what you learn about the shoe. Now go get some rest."

"You, too, Quinn. Never know when our days can turn into nights."

"I'm sure. Had plenty of those in Immigration—won't come as a shock. Night."

Chuck gave her a wave and then stopped. "Assume you received the note that I'm in Knoxville tomorrow for training. My assigned days off are Tuesday and Thursday, so I'll take a comp day at some point if it's alright with you."

She studied his face. "Sure, Chuck. Hope the training goes well." She watched him walk out and turned to scribble a note to talk to him later about his days off. *Why not two days in a row? His choice? Or Albright's idea?*

She looked back at the computer screen and decided to reread the evidence reports on the shoe found on one police vehicle and the bones found on another. *Is there a connection?*

Early Evening

Buddy arrived home about twenty minutes after leaving yet another plumbing job—this one was new construction. *I need to slow down on taking these plumbing jobs—doesn't leave me much time to get my project done.* He was tired after a late night on Sunday and early day today, but exhilarated. His plan was coming together and he couldn't have expected a more opportune time than the arrival of a new chief of police: a woman. He walked to his fridge and pulled out a beer. He rarely drank, but this was a day he expected Albert Simmons to drop by—and he wanted to keep up appearances. He poured half the beer down the sink, threw some lemon peel he kept in the fridge into the garbage disposal, and ran it to get rid of the smell. *Maybe after Albert leaves, I'll do some more research on any new and improved ways to eliminate odors. I've managed to get rid of most of the smells so far, but you never know.* Just as he was about to head out to his workshop, there was a knock on his door: no doorbell for him on his non-descript white clapboard cottage on the back corner of an out of the way dead end street—he wanted his privacy.

"Hey, Albert. Come on in. You're early. Want a beer?"

"Sure, Buddy. Just had about the longest day I've had in a while. Grabbed something to eat and came straight away."

"Really? What's going on?" He walked to the fridge and took out a beer, popped the top, and handed it to one of the few people he let in his home.

"Beginning to wonder if police work is for me. Seven years on the force, doubt I'll ever make sergeant..."

"How about detective? Ever think of sitting for that exam? You're smart. I could help you study."

"Aw, I don't know. I think you have to play some suck-up even if you pass the exam. Just don't have it in me." Albert took a long swig of the beer, sat down in the chair opposite his friend, and both men put their feet on the battered old coffee table.

"Well, Albert, it might not be hard to suck-up to the new chief. Have you met her yet?"

"Met her? Ha! I'm so far down on the totem pole she'll be headed to greener pastures before I'd ever meet her person to person. And, guess what—there's a new lead detective, too."

Buddy didn't say anything. *A new lead detective. Well, well, well.* "Come on, Albert. You're good with folks—much better than me. I'll bet you ten bucks you *can* figure out a way to put yourself in the path of the new chief or the lead detective. What'd you say? Is it a bet?"

The two men had known each other since middle school. Albert always thought Buddy was different than most folks he knew, but he didn't seem to create problems, and had been friendly enough over the years. They had gone to a small school about twenty-five miles from Round City so they didn't know many of the folks their age here in town.

He'd been glad Buddy called to congratulate him when he got his police badge two days after his thirtieth birthday; no one else from their school days had. The two men had gotten into the habit of seeing each other once a week or so since then. They both liked video games and Buddy had an extensive subscription to games and a bookcase full of DVDs in his spare bedroom.

Albert looked at Buddy. "Any time limit on collecting on the bet?" They were accustomed to their penny ante bets on whose score would go up the most on whatever game they were playing.

"Well," Buddy stretched out the word, holding out his beer—not having had one drop of it. "Seems only fair to make it a little challenging. So, how about three weeks from today?"

"What? Are you crazy? You think I can manage to run into the chief or lead detective and meet one of them in the next three weeks? I didn't meet the old chief, God rest his soul, except when I took my oath and then about three years ago at a station party. And everyone stayed clear of the lead detective."

"I didn't say you had to have dinner with either one! Just manage to meet and make sure one of them knows your name."

Albert took another swig of his beer. "Okay, you're on." He never expected to collect on the bet. "Now let's go play something I know I can beat you at."

The two men stood and walked into Buddy's game room. There would be no more talking tonight.

Some Things Need Attention

"Hate to run, Buddy, but these feet have to hit the street tomorrow. Know what I mean?"

"No experience with that myself—but I get it. Thanks for stopping by. Later."

The two men never shook hands. Albert didn't care, he was used to Buddy's quirks. Buddy locked the front door, turned off the porch light and the lights in the living room. The beer bottles were carefully rinsed and gently placed in the recycle bin in his garage. He turned off the kitchen light and then followed his routine of making sure the light on a timer in his bedroom had come on before he headed out to his workshop. He never turned on the light on the back porch and the vines on the trellises along each side of the covered walkway had long since made it impossible to see any movement between the house and workshop. The windows in his workshop were painted with black paint on the inside covered by black-out material draped over them. He never turned on a light in his workshop until he was inside and the door securely locked. As far as his neighbors knew, he rarely, if ever, entered it. He didn't like thinking about his neighbors and preferred to assume that they never thought of him. *No one's close, thanks to Grammy, so how would they know my movements unless they came and stood in my back yard? Took years for all those bushes and trees Grammy planted to double the height of the brick and wood wall.*

His eyes adjusted to the dim light in his workshop—he had LED magnifiers for his more intricate work. Quietly and methodically, he moved from the row of storage cabinets on the south wall to the freezer. It was time to move some material from the freezer to the thaw cabinet. One of the large floor-to-ceiling metal cabinets which he'd had custom built at a metal shop in Memphis, over 400 miles from Round City, had slats for shelves to allow for the liquid from defrosting to drop to the bottom. The bottom of the cabinet was connected by a plumbing pipe to the drain pipe to his septic tank which he had cleaned out at regular intervals. *It's worked well for all these years. Why can't any of those cops work well? I keep giving them evidence.*

Once the material in the freezer thawed, he moved it to a sealed drying cabinet—to speed up the process. *Not much space in the freezer*. The remainder of the cabinets held his carefully dried and stored material. He applied the diligence to routine and detail that he always took with his work. *You'd be proud of my attention to detail, Pappy.* The workshop was quiet except for the soft hum of the electric running the freezer and drying cabinet. His mind rarely strayed from the task at hand until he was ready to acquire new material.

Wonder if I messed up putting out two sets of material in one night in one town—especially this town. He shook his head. *Will they ever figure it out?* He unlocked each cabinet and nodded his head at the neatness of his work. Each shelf in the cabinets was neatly labeled with a code for date, time, and place of acquisition and then the date and time of drying. He was a little sad about the child's shoe which was the beginning of his collection—from thirty years ago. The ringing of one of his phones in his pants pocket startled him. He knew by the ringtone it was his plumbing service phone.

"Yeah?"

"My toilet's backed up and my old man ain't home. The kids are hollering. Can you come fix it?" The woman's words were slurred.

He hated the real work that came with his different jobs but it had served him well over the years. He knew there was no one who cared where he was or what he did. These odd jobs didn't usually interfere with his project. *Besides it's the only way I meet women.*

"Address?"

"Know where the dirt road is just south of the old mill?"

"Yeah."

"Go one mile after you turn on the road and you'll see my front porch light. What time can you get here?"

He looked at his watch, looked around his workshop, and sighed. "Twenty to thirty minutes."

"Thanks. Thanks a lot. See you then." She hung up the phone with a bang in his ear. He wasn't surprised she wasn't calling on a mobile phone, probably no mobile service where she lived.

He double checked the locks on each cabinet, checked the temperature on the defrosting cabinet, and turned off the light. He stood inside the workshop for a minute to allow his eyes time to adjust to the total darkness. Then he opened the door, locked the double locks, walked to his house, and into the kitchen. First, he turned on the hall light—he always followed the same routine. If anyone were watching, it would appear he had come from his bedroom to the kitchen before heading out. He turned on the kitchen light, turned off the hall light, and opened the fridge. The paper bags with sandwiches from the local coffee shop were neatly dated and lined up on the shelf. He took the one for today's date and grabbed a bottle of water. He hadn't eaten in hours.

Just as he reached the kitchen door into the garage he stopped abruptly. *I didn't wash my hands.* He scrubbed his hands, as if preparing for surgery. He grabbed a paper towel and stopped—he knew it wasn't sufficient to wipe off the kitchen door knob with a paper towel. The alcohol wipes were in a jar by the door. He took several and wiped the outside and inside of the door and then walked over and wiped the light switches and the handle to the fridge. He pressed the foot release on the trash can and dropped the paper towel, alcohol wipes, and foil paper wrappers in the trash. He stood for a moment, closed his eyes, reviewed his actions of the last hour and was satisfied he could leave.

Backing out of his garage, he suddenly remembered he hadn't re-placed the plunger from the job last night. He never used the same plunger on two jobs. He pulled back into the garage, shut the door and then he saw he hadn't taken the "plumbing services" signs off the van when he got home. He always took them off. His head hurt. *Focus. You can't make mistakes.* He walked straight to the cabinet labeled plumbing—others were labelled carpentry, hand tools, saw blades, window glass, cleaning supplies, electrical, and rags. He took one of the new plungers, and put it inside his van. A quick scan of the side shelving in the van assured him he had what he would need for tonight—unless something unplanned came up—like last night.

Home Again

Quinn pulled into her garage, got out, took off her boots, left them by the door and entered the kitchen. She put her sidearm in the gun safe by her back door along with her badge. *Never want to be the poor law enforcement officer who has a break-in and someone steals your badge or worse yet your gun.* As she walked to the hall closet to hang up her coat, her house phone rang. She stopped in midstep and waited to see if it was a robo call. *I know Sheriff Oliver told me to keep a landline with my new job, but really? I only ever get robo calls.*

"Hey, Quinn. Home yet?"

She grabbed the phone. "Hey, Billy, long time no talk."

"Indeed. Seems like days and yet I find it was only about twelve hours ago."

"Seriously? 12 hours?" She took the cordless phone and continued toward the closet to hang up her coat. "Is it after eight already?"

"Yes, ma'am. Almost on the dot. What time did you go to work?"

"Got there at six-thirty this morning. Hold on a minute."

"Sure."

"Thanks. I needed to hang up my coat."

"Wow, you really did just get home. Oh, I get it. You had a hot date for supper!"

"Sir, if I had a hot date, I would *not* be talking to you on the phone."

"Got it! Sure hope that's because I'd be the hot date in the flesh."

"Play your cards right, it could happen. How was your day?"

"Busy. Just wanted to see if we could firm up a time for that drink? Does the big city detective have any personal time?"

"Not sure yet." She decided to ignore the 'big city' dig. "Seven days into the job, and all that. Tell me something happy—made any new furniture or turned any bowls lately?" She smiled thinking about the afternoon in his basement when he taught her to turn wood to make a goblet even though she had yet to finish it.

"I'm working on a special piece. I'll share it soon."

"I'd like that. Hey, listen, if my life has anything like normalcy this week, maybe I could drop by on Saturday afternoon. Some wood turning might be good for me and I want to finish that goblet. Who knows—I might even let you buy me a glass of wine." She smiled thinking about the flirtatious banter between them.

"The bottle will be chilled and waiting. Might even be able to rustle up some food."

"Then, all things being equal, I'll call you before I head over. Can't promise a time."

"I know. Things are a little slower on this side of the mountains, so I should be good. I'll let you know if something comes up for me."

"Thanks, Billy. I appreciate the call *and* something to look forward to at the end of the week."

"The pleasure is all mine. Have a good week, Quinn. Take care of yourself."

"Working on it. Night, Billy."

She set the phone in the cradle and decided on a protein shake for a very late supper. She washed her hands, fixed the shake, and headed to her bedroom to undress. *I forgot to put my slippers by the kitchen door. This floor is chilly in my stocking feet.* She stopped. Drip. Drip. Drip. She waited. Silence—absolute silence. She reached her bedroom and set her shake on a coaster on the table in her large bedroom. No sounds. *What is wrong with me? I need to remember to check outside tomorrow and see if there is ice melting and hitting a window pane or something.* She decided to let it go and walked into the bathroom to take a very hot shower.

Her mind wandered to the reports from the two police officers on the plastic bags left on the roofs of their official vehicles. The forensic report on the shoe was still not complete and Chuck had not begun work on the bones. She knew this was meticulous work and she didn't want it rushed. *I'll talk to the sergeant who was on duty that night and get his assessment.* She stepped out of the shower, wrapped her hair in a hand towel, and herself in her bathrobe, another gift from her mother—100% velour jacquard cotton. *I don't even want to know what she paid for it.* Her feet tucked under her in the comfortable leather arm chair next to the table. She sipped her shake. *Maybe I'm a hypocrite. I shun the wealth of my parents, but I accept the gifts they bestow upon me because they have that wealth.* She leaned her head against the back of the chair and closed her eyes. *Bigger problems to solve right here in Round City than my slightly askew moral compass when it comes to money.*

A review of the day left Quinn satisfied that she had made progress in establishing a routine. She was excited to do some field work, but she'd wait and see how tomorrow went. Marshall had handled notification on the deceased woman and was working the stolen car. Another detective was handling the bar fight that cost a man his life over the weekend. A smile spread across her face as she pictured the officers clapping a welcome to her—it was a good start. *I'm glad I learned in Immigration to put cases 'to bed in my head' so I don't take them into my sleep. Tomorrow is another day and there are good people working these cases. That's a plus.* She rinsed out the glass from her shake in her bathroom sink, brushed her teeth, pulled the towel off her hair and brushed it. She opened a drawer in her closet and pulled out a nightgown and slipped into it. *Cleaning team comes tomorrow.* She picked up the pencil and wrote a note on the paper she always had on the island in her large closet: "Mildred, please let me know if you hear anything dripping near or around my bedroom? Thanks. Quinn." *Maybe she'll help me figure it out.*

Tucked under the warm comforter on her bed, she closed her eyes. The velvet voice of her father replayed in her head as she thought of his call this morning. *The two men in my social world called today: Daddy and Billy. Hmmm.* Billy had gone to her parents' home with her at Christmas, but she was never quite sure if that could be considered a date, or just a friend responding to her need for a companion at her parents' fundraising event for local charity. She remained friends with her college love but mostly saw him when their respective jobs brought them together.

She'd been totally immersed in her work as an immigration agent, and it had been a very long time since she'd been in a relationship. *Wonder if I can find balance now? All I want to do is have an occasional night out and someone to talk to. Well, time will tell.* She reached over and turned off the light. She was sound asleep in minutes.

Chapter 4

The most common way people give up their power is by thinking they don't have any.
Alice Walker

Night into Morning

Buddy drove carefully to the edge of town and replayed the phone call in his head. *The kids are hollering. How many kids? Settle down.* He was always nervous around children. He kept his eyes on the road and tried to focus on getting this plumbing job done. He wanted to spend some time in his shed tonight. He needed to figure out how much material he had dried out. *Really need to figure out the rest of my plan. Not much time left. The finale is close at hand. Those cops need to figure this out. Now!*

He reached the end of the paved road just south of the old mill and set his mileage. *Lots of old roads, paths really, in these hills. Don't see any signs of houses yet.* Just as the mileage showed .9 of a mile, he saw a shoveled path ahead and then a light so bright on the porch it would blind anyone. He parked and looked around. *Are those lights down the road a house or a car?* He rubbed his eyes; then he headed up the steps. *Kids must be old enough to shovel. Willing to bet the woman who called didn't do it.* He looked down to keep from being blinded by the porch light and stomped his feet on the porch to get the snow and mud off. He was about to knock when the door opened.

"Ain't getting no warmer out there. Get in before the cold takes over inside."

Evening to you, too, ma'am. "Yes, ma'am. Sure is cold tonight." He held the plunger in his hand.

Two boys, who he thought looked to be ten or twelve, sat on the dilapidated plaid couch with their hands in their laps—they looked straight ahead. He always noticed details. *I'm betting those boys weren't hollerin' about anything. Might not live to tell about it if they did.* He was particularly observant about human behavior.

"Where's the plumbing problem?"

"That door over yonder." The woman, probably five feet seven inches tall and skinny as a rail, pointed. "Jason, get up and go show this here plumber."

"Yes, ma'am." The older of the two boys stood up. "This way, sir."

Buddy nodded. He didn't need a guide. He had seen where she pointed, but decided to see what happened.

The boy walked toward the door, turned on the light, pointed into the bathroom. "There, sir."

"Thanks. That's all I need." Buddy stepped into the room and hoped he wouldn't fall through the floor which was clearly rotting under the linoleum—there had been more than one overflowing toilet, tub, or sink.

First, he turned the faucet on the sink to see if the pipes were frozen. Water ran slowly, but it was flowing. *Glad for that one.* Then he lifted the seat with no lid and plunged the toilet. The refuse moved quickly and he flushed the handle, clear water filled the tank and bowl. He rinsed the plunger in the clean water and flushed again. He always left the plunger beside the toilet when he finished a job.

"Good to go, ma'am."

"How much you gonna charge me?"

Buddy looked at the boys. The older boy had returned to the sofa and both boys looked straight ahead. He knew something about the lives these boys must live.

"Five dollars, ma'am. I'll just charge you for the plunger this time."

The woman fumbled in her purse and pulled out a wadded up five-dollar bill and handed it to him. "Don't need no receipt." She turned to her sons.

"Jeremiah, what do you say to this man who saved your hide?"

The younger of the two boys stood up. "Thank you, sir. I'm sorry to cause a problem for my momma and to make you come out in the cold." He stood like a tin soldier.

"We're good." Buddy started to step away. "Know how to use a plunger?" He looked at Jeremiah and Jason.

"No, sir. Ain't never seen one til tonight." The boys said it almost in unison.

"Ma'am, okay if I show these boys how to do this. Then they can take care of it for you."

"Sure, sure. Get over there boys, now."

Buddy stepped ahead of the boys and stepped carefully on the rotting floor. "Nothing to it, really." He showed them how to make sure you had a seal with the plunger, push on the handle to get suction and then pull it back gently to see if the waste and water would flow out—only the water flowed this time because Buddy had already cleared it.

"Questions?"

"No, sir." Jason shook his head.

"No, sir. Thank you, sir." Jeremiah's eyes looked up at him.

He reached over and patted each boy on the shoulder with his gloved hand. "You're good boys. You'll do fine if you ever need this again." He stepped out the door and headed for the front door.

"Have a good evening, ma'am."

He pulled off the latex gloves, turning them into themselves before he reached his van and opened the door with his bare hand. He reached into the pocket on the driver's door and pulled out a small plastic bag. He put the gloves in and placed the plastic bag in the small plastic bin on the floor of the passenger's side. He'd put them in the trash when he got home and then wipe out the bin and replace it. He was very careful—just like his Pappy taught him.

Nights Drag On

Before he pulled out onto the main road, Buddy used the app on his phone to shut off the timer on his bedroom light. It was due to come on before he got home and he wanted it to coincide with a normal routine when he entered the house. As soon as he was home, he scrubbed his hands in the sink in the garage, placed a new plunger in his van, looked around and was satisfied everything was in order. He entered the house and turned on the kitchen light, crossed over and turned on the hall light. Then he used the phone app to turn on the bedroom light as soon as he turned off the kitchen light and just before he turned off the hall light. He would not be walking down the hall for a long time. He had work to do in the shed.

The lock on the inside of the door to the shed clicked, Buddy let his eyes adjust, and then he walked to the sink and scrubbed his hands again. He scrubbed them until they were almost raw. Visions of the two boys on the sofa interfered with his concentration. *Focus. There's work to do here.* He dried his hands, hung the towel neatly on the rack next to the sink and held his hands up and looked at both sides. *My hands are clean, Pappy. See?* He jerked his head up and turned to look at his cabinets. *Focus.*

He checked the timer on the thawing cabinet. *Won't be thawed for another twelve hours.* He was very careful in calculating the defrosting time so that he knew exactly when the material had to go in the drying cabinet. *Only one more bag of good material to thaw.* He turned to the three remaining cabinets which held the dried material. *Not much left there either.*

As he often did, Buddy was completely engrossed in reviewing the catalog of his material and shifting things from one cabinet to another in precise order. He stretched, yawned, and looked at his watch. It was almost three a.m. *I better get some sleep.* He knew the app on his phone had shut off the bedroom light so he would enter without turning on any lights. The shed was locked after he followed his ritualized routines for exiting. He entered the house, washed his hands, wiped off the door handles, and headed for the bedroom. *Short night tonight. It's almost dawn.*

Tuesday Dawns

"Morning, Jamison."

"Morning, Detective. Looking like some sun today to melt that snow."

"If you can believe the weather forecast. Sure hope they're right." She smiled and kept walking. "Have a good day."

"You, too, ma'am."

It was six-thirty-five a.m. when Quinn sat down at her desk and turned on her computer. She was hoping for some semblance of a routine that would let her catch up on the bigger issues that arose in Round City and surrounding communities. She sat back in her chair and then stood up. *Better to get in the habit of checking in and out with the shift sergeant and the detective bullpen.* She walked down the hall.

A soft knock on the open door caused the sergeant to look up. It was the same one who had called her down at shift change yesterday and would be ending his shift shortly. Before she could speak, he was on his feet.

"Morning, Detective. To what do I owe the pleasure?"

"Morning, Sergeant. Please, call me Quinn."

"Might take some getting used to. Chief Nelson always expected us to use titles."

"I know. He was a good man—may he rest in peace. Sit, sit. Just wanted to say good morning and thank you for the warm welcome yesterday."

"Pleasure's all mine, ma'am. It was Officer Simmons who brought our failure to welcome you to my attention. I'm rightly embarrassed. Guess we had so long with Detective…"

Quinn interrupted him. "No apologies needed, Sergeant. We're good." She made a mental note to find out who Officer Simmons was. "Quiet night?"

"Pretty much. Only thing unusual is confirming jurisdiction on a body picked up last night."

"Body where?" Quinn leaned against the door frame.

"On a dirt road off of Route 54."

"Route 54 toward the Valley community?"

"Yep. Our ME has the remains, but since the county line runs near there, we just need to make sure who has jurisdiction."

"Male or female? Who found the body?" Her voice was calm and steady. She reached back and put her hair in a knot at the base of her neck.

"Female. Her husband found her when he got home late Monday night. Morgue guys estimate the TOD as Sunday night."

Quinn listened attentively. *Time of death was Sunday night? Why did it take so long to find the body?* "Appear to be natural causes?" *Two women dying of natural causes in twenty-four hours? Could happen…*

"Not sure. ME is pretty thorough. He'll send a report as soon as he knows."

"Thanks, Sergeant, I'll read the officer's report."

"Sure thing. And, thanks for encouraging the troops yesterday. They mostly won't bother you, but I heard some folks saying it was good to have a friendly lead detective."

"We're a team, Sergeant. Each of us has a different job—but we're a team. Thanks for the update. You'll be headed home shortly, right?"

"Yes, *ma'am,* and I'm off for two days. So, guess I'll see you later in the week."

"I'll look forward to it." Quinn smiled at him, turned and headed to the break room to get coffee. She decided to see the detectives later in the morning. *I don't want them thinking I expect them here at the crack of dawn.*

Too soon to drop in on the ME? She stopped in front of the elevator across from the lab and pushed the down button. *How did I not notice the noise of this elevator last week when I got a tour of the building?* Then she remembered the captain had taken her down the stairs. *Glad I can't hear it inside the lab.*

Busy Day Ahead

Buddy was awake after only four hours sleep, dressed, and ready to head out. Tuesday was his day to do the tasks he had to do. The weather was cold, but the main roads were clear and the sun promised to keep the paved ones dry. *I'll make better time going the long way.* He took a sandwich from the fridge, put it in a small cooler and headed out to his van. *Should have taken those off last night.* He stopped to rub his head before he took off the magnetic signs that he used when he had a plumbing job. *I'm getting careless.* He wiped them off and placed them on the shelf. He put the "Cleaning Services" signs on the side of the front doors.

A little over thirty minutes later, he turned off the main highway southeast of town down the road that ran past the small brick building which had once been the four-room school he and Albert had attended. They had three grades in each of the elementary rooms and two teachers in the other two rooms for the middle and high school: one teacher taught English and social studies, the other one math and science. The building had been vacant for years and the grass was rarely cut anymore. Vines were growing over the wood framed windows. *Wonder if many kids even live out this way now.*

Buddy turned his concentration to the dirt road. There hadn't been much snow over the weekend. He had all-weather tires, but he knew it was still possible to get stuck if the ground underneath was still soft.

Another mile and I'll be there. It took him about ten minutes, driving slowly and carefully, as the overgrown trees provided cover from the distant farms. *You always counted on that distance, didn't you, Pappy? I learned from the best—but unlike you I can't live out here; I have to live in town.* Slowly the stone building appeared over the horizon: a building which had stood for a hundred years—maybe longer.

The van pulled up to the rusting gate and Buddy was careful on the frozen ground. He pulled his keys out as he fingered them for the one to open the padlock. He purposely left a rusted lock on the rusted chain; every year, he chemically rusted a new chain and a new padlock. If anyone bothered to look closely, they would see the locking mechanism in the padlock was clean and well oiled. Lucky for him, no one bothered to come down this road. The gate opened, he pulled his van in, got out and locked the gate, then drove into the darkness of the deep wooden shed structure on the north side of the stone house.

He took his cleaning supplies out of the van, set them down on top of the chest freezer which was perched on four concrete blocks to keep it off the ground, and entered through the kitchen. No one would see his van, or him, from the highway or the distant farms. The damp and the cold didn't bother him. Thirty-one years of cleaning the stone floors had made him indifferent to the cold. The man he called Pappy had given him time to heal after he brought him here, but it wasn't long before he was well-schooled in cleanliness being next to Godliness—even though he had figured out he was only six or seven at the time.

Pappy moved his experiments from the school where he taught math and science into the house. Buddy knew it was to protect his research and to train Buddy. After Buddy graduated from college, Pappy just disappeared. Buddy had no idea where his pappy went. *To this day everyone thinks he moved on cause the school had closed. I've done searches. I can't find him.*

Buddy wasn't really sure if the land belonged to him now. Pappy never said and Buddy had never bothered to find out. He just paid the paltry property taxes by money order and assumed the county thought it was Pappy paying them. He also paid the electric bill which he picked up from the mailbox on the highway once a month. Many years ago Pappy had made sure the mail carrier never left any mail that wasn't official first-class mail.

When Pappy's mother died, not long after Buddy finished high school, Pappy had put the house in town in Buddy's name. Buddy wondered why she had left it to him. It was Grammy's money that had paid for him to go to college where he majored in biology—Pappy would have it no other way. *Wish I could remember when I figured out that Pappy wasn't my daddy—leastways not the biological one.*

The floors mopped and the counters wiped down, Buddy didn't touch the windows, although Pappy had always insisted they get cleaned every other week. Nowadays he just partially closed the drapes so it'd look like someone lived here. *Never know when some drifter might come up on it.* After wiping the sink from the dirty water dumped down the drain, he put the cleaning equipment back in the van, went back in, checked the timer on the single lamp that came on every day at six p.m. and went off at nine p.m. He washed his hands, backed the van out of the drive and headed for town. Once he reached the highway, he turned on the radio.

"Mrs. Eugenia Summers was pronounced dead on Monday night when an ambulance responded to a call from her husband, Mr. Bobby Summers. Funeral arrangements will be announced. In other news…"

Yeah, what a surprise. She was dead long before her hubby got home. Eugenia? Don't think I ever met a Eugenia—Eugenia, Eugenia, who could have known, a call and a fall when your hubby ain't home. He chuckled at his silly rhyme. *Your husband should have come home on Sunday, Eugenia.* Buddy was pretty sure the headlights, which had passed him on Sunday evening at the Summers' residence, weren't the husband returning home. He turned off the radio and started whistling; cleaning the old stone floors always made him whistle.

The Medical Examiner

Quinn stepped off the elevator as soon as the doors opened. "Morning, Dr. Walters. Do I need a mask?"

"Only if the smell is a problem for you." The ME looked up from the stainless steel table and nodded at the new lead detective. "Nice to see you, Detective. Don't get many visitors here."

"Hope you won't consider me as a visitor." She smiled at him. "Didn't have time to get acquainted last week on my big tour. Thought I'd stop by and see if you had a minute."

"Yes, ma'am." He pulled the sheet up over the woman and turned to the counter behind him and threw away his gloves and washed his hands. "Might want to step over to my office—a little less disturbing to most folks. Although I have to say, my wife would be disturbed if she saw the disarray on my desk." He chuckled and pointed to the one empty chair—the other had books and journals stacked a foot high on it. "Have a seat."

Quinn sat opposite him at his desk. "I thought you had a forensic tech who worked with you." She looked around the room.

"Tristan is part-time. He never works on Tuesdays but he's pretty good about coming any other time I need him outside his normal work-days of Monday, Wednesday, Friday."

"Oh. May I assume you don't need full-time help?"

"Mostly not. Tristan only works six hours a day, three days a week, and that's more than we need most weeks. He keeps the place clean and Chief Nelson felt sorry for him—rough life that boy has had. Well, anyway, we aren't busy enough to need a full-time ME. I only come in when there's a body." He glanced at her to see if she reacted. She didn't. "Sad to say, the number of bodies has increased over the last year or two. Not a social scientist myself, but always curious about what drives folks to the things that cause them to end up on my table." He continued to watch the new detective carefully.

"Seems a full-time job just to figure out the cause of death, much less the reasons behind it." Quinn was curious about what was, and what might not be, evident in the determination of a cause of death. "I understand you were in general practice before you started as ME Have you always been in Round City?"

"No, ma'am." His warm smile and soft blue eyes looked at her across the desk. "I was born in Knoxville—believe you're from there, too."

"It's my family home. I was actually born in Spain—though I don't say that often."

He wiggled his bushy gray eyebrows. "Some reason?"

She laughed. "No, it's just most people aren't interested."

"Do tell."

"My father is from Spain and my mother from Knoxville. They met in college. I was born two years after they married while they were in graduate school in Madrid. My father wanted to be sure I would have both passports."

"Smart man. My dad always said, 'If you can't have two passports, then the next best thing is a passport in one country and a residency visa in another.'"

"Did he live abroad?" Quinn raised her left eyebrow.

"Strange as it seems for someone from the mountains, he was in the Navy and loved all the places he was able to visit. He always wanted to live abroad. He was a physician, too, so once you started practice in those days, you were pretty much settled in one place. Well, I'm sure you didn't come to hear my family history. How can I help you this fine day?"

"I understand that Ms. Summers, the woman on your table, was brought in last night."

"Yes, ma'am. Should have you a preliminary report in a couple of hours. I'm pretty methodical in my work. Don't ever want to miss anything, if I can help it."

"Does your assistant...Tristan...help you with autopsies?"

"Tristan it is. He doesn't do any of the hands-on work, but he has a pretty good eye and even though he's self-educated in these things, he's generally pretty spot on in his observations."

"That's good. I'm sure you're pleased to have such a competent assistant."

"It works—most of the time."

"Oh? When doesn't it work?" She smiled at him.

"Guess I should expect a detective to want more information." He chuckled. "He's a bit...well...eccentric: strange laugh. Doesn't bother me, but occasionally the gossip gets down the elevator shaft."

Chuck thought he was strange, too. Wonder why? Quinn smiled. "Well, strangeness comes in many forms."

"That it does. Anything else I can help you with?"

"The woman brought in over the weekend. Detective Marshall gave me the autopsy report. Any chance this one will be natural causes?"

"Don't know until I know." He smiled at her.

"Of course. Wrong question. Guess I just want to be sure the first woman was natural causes if this one isn't."

"Always willing to revisit a case, if warranted."

"Thanks, Doc. I promise, I'll get the hang of all this soon."

"No worries. Anything else?"

"Just want to get us on this case once jurisdiction has been sorted out."

"What?" His voice had a slight, but quiet, edge to it. "We don't have jurisdiction?"

"It's okay, Doc. I'll verify—but even if it turns out her house is in the other county, I know the sheriff in the Valley and I'm sure he'd be pleased to know you've done the work. Just can't investigate until we know for sure."

The ME looked at her. *I think I'm going to like this young woman: easygoing, open, but no nonsense.* "Glad to have you onboard, Detective. Don't be a stranger."

"Thank you for the time. Come up to the first floor sometime. My door is always open."

"Thanks. Appreciate the invitation."

Quinn was walking toward the exit to the stairs.

"Uh, Detective. The elevator is over there."

She nodded. "Actually, I prefer the stairs. Don't want to end up on your table from a heart attack." She smiled at him and headed up the stairs—glad for the exercise, but also glad to avoid the loud noise of the elevator banging.

Chapter 5

It is unwise to be too sure of one's own wisdom. It is healthy to be reminded that the strongest might weaken and the wisest might err.
Mahatma Ghandi

Routines

At the top stair, Quinn stopped and checked her heart rate on her watch. *Still pretty fit. Hope I don't end up having to put my fitness routine on my calendar like every other appointment that's likely to develop.* She pushed open the door and saw someone jump back. A man pulled the door open slowly.

"Sorry to startle you, Detective."

"I think it was I who startled you, Captain Brown. Good morning."

"Good morning to you, too. Get lost?" The chief administrative officer of the force smiled at her.

"No, just down for a brief morning visit with Dr. Walters."

"Haven't read reports yet this morning. Something new?"

"Woman brought in last night. Apparent TOD was Sunday night. He'll have a preliminary report for us soon."

"He's very thorough."

"That's a good thing for an ME, right?" She smiled at him. "Have a minute?"

They were approaching the breakroom door.

"Sure. Come on, I'll buy you a cup of coffee."

"Thanks. Mine is cold by now, I'm sure." They filled paper cups and sat down in the empty room.

"Captain, have you seen the report on the shoe that was left on the officer's car?"

"Yes."

The look of surprise on his face made her wonder what was behind it. "It looks pretty old. Anything over your time on the force that might give insight into where it came from?"

"Been pondering that one myself. We're accustomed to footprint evidence that leads to a shoe, but working from the shoe without any known crime scene is a different kettle of fish. Your forensic techs are pretty thorough. So I think we'll find out whatever can be learned from it."

"So, no missing child from ten, twenty years ago? Longer?"

"No unsolved child cases in this jurisdiction. One of your detectives can look into adjoining jurisdictions once there's verification on the age and model of the shoe."

Quinn nodded. They both stood. "Thanks, Captain. I appreciate your time and look forward to working with you. Don't hesitate to let me know how I can be of service."

"Likewise. Welcome, Detective. Glad you're with us."

She extended her hand. He shook it. "Glad to be here. Thanks for the coffee." She held up the cup.

They walked out the door together—she turned left and he headed toward the front of the station.

The District Attorney

Quinn no sooner walked in her office than the phone rang. "Isaacs."

"Hey, Detective. Peggy O'Haire here. Welcome to Round City policing."

"Quinn will do nicely, Peggy. Good to hear a familiar voice."

"Really just wanted to welcome you and decided a call I needed to make to your shop was as good a time as any to welcome you."

"You don't need a reason. I look forward to working with you."

"Quite sure you'll knock the socks off those folks. I liked the former chief, rest his soul, and his lead detective but they were old school for sure."

Quinn didn't respond to the comment. "Appreciate the welcome. Now what did you need to share with us?"

"The body your ME has on the slab is definitely in your jurisdiction. The back property line for that house runs along the county line. So, she's all yours."

"Summers is the name, right?"

"That's the one."

"Thanks, Peggy. I'll see that we're on it."

"I assume you'll be my contact as lead detective."

"That works til I figure out the routines here."

"Oh, you'll find out they're pretty accustomed to hierarchical. Look forward to the new chief—imagine two new women at the top right here in Round City law enforcement. Be nice to have some female leadership over there." Her tone was wistful. Then she spoke crisply, "Really did just want to say welcome and let you know to move ahead with Summers."

"Appreciate the call and if it doesn't violate some rule—one I haven't had time to learn about, let's have lunch one day soon."

"No conflict. We're on the same team. I'll look forward to lunch. Enjoy your day, *Detective*."

"You, too, *Madam* District Attorney." Quinn could give as good as she got.

Quinn leaned back in her chair, looked at the ceiling, loosened her hair from the knot, and let out a slow breath. *Time to figure out a system for handling cases.*

She clicked on the office message app on her desktop, found Detective George Marshall's name and sent a note to him, the shift sergeant, the ME, and the Chief: Notification from DA—jurisdiction is ours on Eugenia Summers.

Before she moved her hand from the keyboard, a message popped up: "Got it. Want to talk? GM"

Wonder if I'm in over my head?

She took her secure phone out of her pants pocket and set it on the desk. Then she picked it up and dialed Billy's number.

"Williams, here. Oh, hey!"

"Wow! He looks at the screen on that phone. Hey, yourself. Got a minute?"

"At your service."

"I'm calling you as a detective to ask for some advice."

"Oh." The disappointment was evident in Billy Williams voice. He'd much prefer it was a social call. "Still at your service. Whatcha need?"

"Don't have a lot of experience with the DA and was wondering how to avoid any major pitfalls."

"How much time do you have?"

"Can you give me the short course now and if I need more, I'll ask for a lesson on Saturday."

Billy smiled. *Okay, she hasn't forgotten the promise of a glass of wine on Saturday.* "Are you asking about district attorneys in general or our shared DA O'Haire?"

"Kinda both. I want to be able to support our detectives and officers when we deal with her."

"Just be yourself."

"What? How's that helpful?" She rolled her eyes.

"The DA is on *our* team—law enforcement. Our job is to get her all the evidence as cleanly as we can, hers is to use it to prosecute to the full extent of the law. That about sums it up."

"I may not have a lot of experience in the prosecution of cases, but something tells me it can't be that simple."

"Peggy O'Haire is about as good as they come. She's no nonsense, knows the law *and* the communities, and always tries to weigh the value of prosecutorial fairness to all parties."

"Alright then—sounds like a straight shooter."

"Yeah, sort of like you. Know the rules, enforce them, know when to use the stick and when to use the club."

Quinn laughed. "I could only hope I might gain that kind of wisdom. One more question."

"Sure."

"Tell me one thing that I should know about how law enforcement works with a DA—particularly Peggy O'Haire."

"I'll tell you two. One is specific to her: she's smart and don't ever forget it. Two: Law enforcement officers often struggle with what they view as leniency in the final prosecution of a case."

She was quiet for a few seconds. She had a flashback to Eliza dying next to her. *What justice was there for you, Eliza?*

She cleared her throat. "I've talked with her on several immigration cases before they shifted to federal court, so I've seen her in action; she is smart. The part about LEOs is new to me, but I've had what might be close to similar experiences with folks higher up in immigration enforcement taking over a case I've worked. So, I get it. Thanks for the heads-up."

"Detective Isaacs, you're going to do a great job for Round City. What else can I do for you?"

"Not sure if you were notified, but we picked up a deceased female, Eugenia Summers, last night. Her home borders your county line, but we've verified the property is in ours. So, we're on it."

"Need anything from me?"

"At the moment, nothing. Thanks for taking my call and for the lesson. See you soon."

"Great. Call anytime. Have a good day, Quinn. Later."

"Later." She held the phone as he hung up. *Something tells me I'm going to be grateful for a lifeline with Billy and probably the sheriff in the Valley.*

Searching for Evidence

"Marshall here."

"Hey. Quinn here. Thanks for your quick text response."

"What's up?"

"Have time to sit together for fifteen minutes or so on the Summers' case?"

"Absolutely. Your place or this bull pen?"

"Probably quieter over here. Bring your coffee and come when you can."

"See you in ten."

Quinn pulled up the report from the officers on the scene last night. They were still waiting on the autopsy. She focused on the words: house was like a refrigerator. She'd wait and see what George Marshall thought before they talked to the officers. She picked up her mug, washed it out and headed for the break room to get fresh coffee.

The door of the break room opened just as she reached it. She saw Chief Hansen through the glass.

Jill stepped back. "Fresh pot, it seems." She held up her mug and let Quinn enter.

"Good. Not a big fan of coffee made in the lab by our tech." She wrinkled her nose and stretched out her lips in an exaggerated downward arc.

"That bad?"

"Yes, ma'am. *That* bad."

Both women laughed.

"Thanks for letting me know about jurisdiction on Summers."

So, she's read my e-message already. "Detective Marshall is coming to the lab in a few minutes and we'll go over what we know at the moment. Still waiting on the autopsy on Ms. Summers. The other woman brought in over the weekend was a heart attack."

Jill nodded. "I've read the officers' report on Ms. Summers. I'll be interested to learn about the house being like a refrigerator."

"Me, too, Chief. Still plenty of houses here that totally rely on fireplace heat. If they burn wood and something happens that they can't add wood, inside temperatures can drop pretty fast."

"True. Fifty degrees inside can seem a lot colder than fifty degrees outside."

Quinn frowned as she remembered the immigrant family that almost froze because they left the windows open and didn't know how to turn on the heat in a rental house. "Absolutely. The effect of cold on the body is affected by radiant heat and air flow. If there is no heat source and no air movement your blood moves to protect your vital organs..." Quinn looked at her. "Of course, you already know that."

"Pretty much." Jill watched Quinn's facial expression. "I look forward to your report." She opened the door and headed toward her office. "Let me know if you need anything."

Quinn reviewed what she knew from the report as she walked down the hall: nothing in the home disturbed, no evidence of foul play, no known history of drug abuse, husband claimed to be out of town until just before he called 9-1-1. She shook her head. *Well, Mr. Summers, we'll just see about that.* She was almost to the lab when George Marshall fell in step with her.

"Coffee in the lab still bad? Or did you just need a break?"

"Yes and yes." She entered the code in the keypad on the door.

"Been meaning to ask about the new fancy access to the lab. Something go missing?"

"No." Her mother's admonishment to her when she was a child popped into her head: Don't lie, you just don't have to tell everything you know. "Seems the old one was malfunctioning and Chief Nelson had some tech money that could be used, Detective Albright had them put in a more modern system."

"Makes sense."

And it's mostly true. I just don't need to say it's also because Chuck told me Tristan Doyle made Detective Albright pretty uncomfortable.

She swept her arm in an arc and pointed toward a table with four chairs by a wall which was half covered with white board and half with cork board. "Enter at your own risk."

"That's ominous." He laughed. "How do you want to work this?"

She walked toward the white board. "Let's start with the questions each of us has. I'm hoping to have a preliminary autopsy report anytime now." She looked at her watch.

"Doc's usually pretty thorough—even before he gives a preliminary."

"So I've heard. It serves us well. What I don't want is to lose any evidence in the meantime."

"Quinn, the scene is secure and an officer is on duty there. The husband didn't even take his suitcase out of his car."

"Yeah, I read that he told the officers he was going to his mother's house."

"Can you believe he said that he was only at the house to tell Mrs. Summers he was filing for divorce?" George shook his head.

"May turn out to be some of the best information we have at this point. We'll talk with him and I have no doubt see through him, if he's guilty." She started a timeline on the white board.

"Yep. Once we have a plan, he'll be first on the list when we get the autopsy report."

They both looked up when the buzzer on the door sounded. Quinn stepped toward the door to see who it was.

"It's Doc Walters." She buzzed the door to open and walked toward it.

"Hey. Got up here to visit sooner than I thought." Then he saw George. The ME nodded. "Any chance this get together is about the Summers woman?"

"As a matter of fact, it is. Have any news for us?"

Home Again

Buddy pulled in his garage a little after nine-thirty a.m., took off the magnetic cleaning signs, wiped them down and put them away. He spent the next two hours in the garage doing an inventory of his plumbing supplies, cleaning supplies, and electrical equipment. *Need some new bulbs for my LED magnifiers.* He wrote everything down so he could get his supplies in Maryville. He'd be quick about his trip as he planned to spend the rest of this day finalizing the data on the material he had in the cabinets in the shed.

I should have gone back to the Summers' place to check. It might have given me more material. His hand shook as he opened the kitchen door. It was getting riskier to do follow-up and get material. The patterns of material to collect had become too random and the use of animal bones to keep the forensic techs busy was not going to help if he did too many. *How much material do they need?*

He dropped his head on his arms on the desktop. He was tired. Tired of death, tired of trying to make a point, and most of all tired of struggling with the early parts of his life where he couldn't fill the holes.

A timer emitted a low ping, barely audible, but enough for him to hear and check the thawing cabinet. *Won't be long now. Then this material goes into the drying cabinet.* He turned off the light in the thawing cabinet and opened the freezer—only one more package he dared use. It was a crucial. *If those high-fallutin techs can't figure it out from these samples, will I dare give them the others?*

Listen to the ME

"Have a seat, Doc. Fill us in." George Marshall was easy-going and his comfort with the ME was evident.

The ME sat down. "Not sure what I know at the moment is going to be much help." He looked at the two detectives.

"Anything you can share will be helpful, I'm sure." Quinn gave him a reassuring smile.

"It's Ms. Summers. I can't rule out murder...and I can't confirm natural causes."

Marshall let out a low whistle. "Drugs?"

"You know the toxicology can take hours to weeks. And, I'm suspecting there might be some chemicals involved, but not necessarily drugs in the traditional sense." He hesitated a moment..."and, there's bruise on her neck that doesn't make sense to me."

Quinn nodded her head slowly. "Okay. What's your best advice at this point?"

"I think we better get the lab at the State Bureau involved."

"What's the protocol for that?" Quinn looked from one man to the other.

"In the past, Detective Albright would have made the call." The ME looked at George and then shrugged. "I always suspected he cleared it through Chief Nelson."

"No problem." Quinn looked straight at him. "I'll check the files to see if there is any written protocol and then check with Chief Hansen for her preference."

Detective Marshall nodded his head. "Sounds like a plan." *And, this is why I did not apply for your job, Quinn.*

The ME stood up. "Thanks for letting me barge in."

"Not at all. You're welcome anytime. I'll let you know as soon as we have a plan." She walked him to the door.

"Whewee." George watched her walk back toward him. "Better you than me, Quinn. I *never* wanted the responsibility. Happy to be a foot slogging detective."

"Here's the good news, George. A week into the job, I can get forgiveness. A month, maybe not." She chuckled and he laughed with her. "Have time to take a ride out to the Summers' residence?"

"Sure thing." George's smile showed his surprise. "Want to go?"

"Counting on it. Let me do some quick research, check with the chief, and we'll head out. I'll give you a fifteen minutes heads-up if that works."

"Perfect. I'll be ready to roll when you are." He stood and walked to the door. He stopped and turned around. "Look forward to working with you, Quinn."

"Likewise." She smiled and nodded. "See you shortly."

She walked into her office and pulled the protocol manual off the shelf. She'd already determined last week that there wasn't an electronic copy. It didn't take her long to find it. "All requests for assistance by another agency, including State Bureau of Investigation, Federal Bureau of Investigation, Immigration Enforcement, Drug Enforcement or any local law enforcement must be approved by the Chief of Police."

She picked up the phone, then put it down. *Wonder if there's a reason that the Chief had me e-message her instead of calling her admin assistant?* Quinn sent an e-message: Need approval for SBI on Summers remains. *Wonder how long before I'll hear.* She walked out of her office to go to the restroom and wasn't two steps out when her phone rang.

"Isaacs."

"My office in five."

"10-4." She hung up the phone, looked at the large binder with policies and protocols, and shrugged her shoulders. *Still need to make a stop on my way down the hall.* She turned out the lights to the lab since Chuck was attending a training session in Knoxville today.

On the way down the hall, Quinn tried to reconcile the clipped command from the Chief with the soft-spoken woman earlier. *Glad she's the one dealing with the operations and policies and not me. I'm ready to dig into a real case.*

Police Policy

Quinn stopped by the restroom and then headed to Chief Hansen's outer office. The scowl from Ms. Leonard did not escape Quinn in spite of the unflattering smile she spread across her face.

"Need something, Detective?"

"Appointment with the Chief."

Ms. Leonard looked at her calendar. "Nothing scheduled."

The door to the Chief's office opened. "Come in, Detective. Hold any calls, Ms. Leonard." Jill had to catch the door to keep from slamming it.

Quinn stopped just inside the door to wait on the Chief.

"Sit. Sit." Jill Hansen pointed to a chair in front of her desk. Then she took the one beside it. "I assume you read the policy before you sent me an e-message?"

"Yes, ma'am."

Hansen ran her fingers through her short brown hair sprinkled with silver gray highlights. "Quinn, I hired you because your reputation is stellar. Sheriff Oliver gave you high praise, and even your boss at Immigration said you had promise." She gave a wan smile.

Quinn kept her face impassive. *Oh, I'm sure my reference from Immigration Enforcement was lukewarm. I didn't cause the problem or even contribute to the debacle my boss had with having a kid with his secretary and not finding out until the kid was grown and came to work for him.*

"Detective?" The Chief looked at Quinn.

"Sorry, Chief. I heard you. The policies are top heavy."

"Good." Jill continued. "It's going to take time to move people to a new way of doing things—to say nothing of changing policies. You can help by keeping me informed without asking permission. I trust you to make the decisions you need to make and do your job. If that changes, you'll be the first to know."

"Yes, ma'am. Anything else, ma'am?"

"Yes." Jill looked at Quinn. "We'll find a rhythm to our work, but in the meantime, when it's just you and me, please drop the ma'am."

"Yes, ma'..." Quinn caught herself. "Will do."

"You'll get the hang of it. Let me know what you learn from the SBI."

Chapter 6

Great people do things before they're ready.
Amy Poehler

Headed to the Scene

Lots to figure out in a new job. I was so naïve when I went to Immigration, it never occurred to me I needed to figure people out. Now I don't want to get lost in trying to figure folks out. Quinn dialed the number for Assistant Director Nelson of the State Bureau of Investigation. A few months back they had worked together on a case with Sheriff Oliver from the Valley.

"Quinn, how are you?"

"Well, thanks. Sorry for the circumstances the last time I saw you." She wondered what he thought about her now being with the police force where his brother had been chief.

"Been tough for the family. Although it's a big relief to me to hear that you took the lead detective job there. David would have been pleased to have you on his team."

Quinn had never called Chief Nelson by his first name. It sounded strange to hear it. "Honestly, I'm glad to have closer ties to serving the people of this community: it's home for me."

"Glad to hear that. How can I help you?"

"First, I'm thankful you know I'm new at the job." She hoped the warmth in her voice was evident. "Chief Hansen has asked me to serve as liaison to the SBI but I have no idea the chain of command in your shop. I tried to call Ralph Jackson, but was told he wasn't available."

She had also worked with Jackson, the Special-Agent-in-Charge directly under AD Nelson.

"He'll be a good contact for you and I'll let him know. In the meantime, how can we help?"

Quinn outlined the situation with determining the cause of death for Mrs. Summers. "Our ME believes we need your team's expertise to ensure we can verify the COD."

"Sure, no problem. Just send the remains. Hold on a minute." A few seconds later, he said, "Lawson is in charge in the lab until five. Think you can have her here by then?"

"We're on it. I'll tell the ME to contact Lawson and arrange it. Thanks, Director."

"Quinn, it's Elliott. Glad to be of help and thanks for joining the Round City team."

"My pleasure, Elliott. Stop in when you're in town."

"Will do. You do likewise. Have a good day."

"Ready in fifteen." Quinn sent the text to Detective Marshall. She had spoken with the ME to have the body of Mrs. Summers transported to SBI tech Lawson. She put on her boots and took the police issue parka off the coat rack. She turned it around and looked at the yellow lettering: DETECTIVE. A smile crept across her face. *I like the look of that.* In her former job, her parka simply read: IMMIGRATION. This one told her job. *New beginnings.* She saw the light on in the far corner and walked back to check. She and Chuck were the only people assigned to this space—he did the lab work on the more complex cases. The other techs were in a lab off of the morgue. *Wonder if the new Chief will keep it that way?*

She saw that the light was on a timer and had come on after she left the room earlier. It was a small lamp on the back counter. *Don't suppose it causes any harm. I'll have to ask Chuck why it's there.* She shrugged and headed back to her office to make sure she was signed out of her computer. The tap on the glass door startled her. She slipped on her parka and headed toward it.

"Ready, Quinn. Your vehicle or mine?" Detective Marshall held the door for her.

"Safe to assume you have a police issue vehicle?"

"Yep. Oh, yeah, I heard that they ordered a new one for you."

"Should be here any day. Apparently Detective Albright's was decommissioned when he retired last month."

"Ha! Needed to be. He insisted on driving that twenty-year-old piece of junk. Never did understand it. Never understood why he insisted on parking in front either."

"'Ours not to reason why'..." she smiled. *So, it was Albright who wanted to be in front.*

"Yeah, 'ours, but to do and die.' I've read Tennyson, too." He laughed. "Can't say I'm a fan, but I'm reasonably well educated for what most people expect from a cop."

"Ah, George. The beauty of our work is that too many people assume we do this work because we aren't smart enough to do anything else. Let's not let them figure out that we do it because there's nothing we'd rather do." *I have to do it. I have to protect others.* She reached to pull her hair back and put it in a knot.

George watched her. *Wonder why she pulls her hair back?* He shrugged and headed out of the back parking lot.

Quinn made a note to ask to have her parking space in the back when the new vehicle came.

"Tell me what you know about the area where Mrs. Summers lived."

He glanced over at her. "Rural—lots of that around here. Isolated."

"Lots of that around here, too."

"Yep. I've got some feelers out to see what I can learn about the family. The Summers bought that place about eight years ago. Title is in his name and her maiden name. Marriage license is dated two years after they bought it."

"Good to know. Any kids?"

"No evidence in the house according to the officer's report and no birth records I could find."

"Either of them employed?"

"Her: part-time hair stylist out of her home. Him: hardware salesman to small mom and pop stores."

"Do those still exist? How do they stay in business with all the big box hardware stores?" Quinn wondered when she would learn all the details that didn't come into play in immigration enforcement work.

"You'd be surprised at the number of small businesses that still survive. Lots of folks in these hills don't want to come into town to the big box stores, and more than that small communities usually have folks that have lived there for generations and they know everyone's survival depends on supporting each other."

Quinn thought about the Valley Store and The Corral Restaurant and Bar over in the Valley. She nodded her head. "Yeah, I can see that. Been to a few places like that myself."

"Might be interesting to see if Mrs. Summers was engaged in any other kind of work."

"Like?"

"Oh, let's just call it moonlighting."

"Detective—George. I've seen things in my time on this planet that I would never mention to my parents, but I can handle reality. You think she's engaged in prostitution?"

"Could be. Could just have some action on the side."

"Evidence of that on the scene?"

"Freshly used condom."

"Okay. I'm assuming that's been tagged and bagged."

"Yep. Probably in the downstairs lab." He stopped. "Well, it's in one of them, anyway."

"Speaking of labs, any explanation for why we have two labs plus the ME?"

George was quiet.

They turned left off Route 54 and down the road leading to the Summers' home. The yellow "Do not cross" tape was soon evident and George slowed before pulling into the driveway. He stopped on the deserted road and turned to look at Quinn.

"I don't want to speak ill of the dead—and more than that I liked Chief Nelson." He paused. "Let's just say, small towns and close relations can create situations that have to be addressed in ways that may not always look the same as every other place."

"10-4, George. Got it." *Score one for you for being diplomatic and respectful. Add one more question for me to figure out about where the rift is that created two labs and if it still exists.* She opened her door. "I'll get out here."

The Summers' Home

George waited until she was out and then pulled into the driveway. He looked in the rearview mirror and saw Quinn scanning the road and the house.

"Something catch your eye?"

Quinn nodded. "Don't look now but there's a police officer at your back."

George turned and almost knocked down the officer behind him. "Dammit, Simmons, how many times do I have to tell you that you can get killed that way?"

"You wouldn't kill me, Detective, even if you'd like to—Detective Isaacs would be too good a witness on the stand."

Quinn smiled and extended her hand. "Quinn Isaacs."

"Albert Simmons, ma'am. Pleased to meet you." *I did it. I won the bet. I met the lead detective. Buddy, this time you'll have to pay up. I met the new detective. Wow!*

"Officer Simmons." Quinn said his name a second time.

"Sorry, ma'am. Yes?"

"It's a pleasure to meet you. I heard you are responsible for the fine greeting I received yesterday from the troops."

The young officer blushed, turned red from ear to ear—all the way to the strawberry blond hair line that showed beneath his cap. "Have a mama who taught me to welcome folks new to our home. And, well, the station is a kinda home for all of us, too, right?"

"Please tell your mother I send my congratulations on raising a polite son. And, thank you for the welcome. Now, what do we have here?"

Simmons straightened his shoulders and looked at her and then glanced at Detective Marshall. "Ma'am. Sir. It's been pretty quiet here. Not even anyone on the road this morning. Any more work to be done in the house? The officers last night did a sweep and took some stuff into evidence."

Quinn looked at the officer and wondered how old he was. She was all business when she spoke. "Still working on COD. If it's not natural causes we'll be in there with a fine-tooth comb. Any evidence of tracks around the outside that might go somewhere other than the front door?"

"The back of the house is pretty close-up on a thick stand of trees. Don't know if the officers last night found anything. They said the woman had been dead for a while. The snow that fell the last couple of days likely hid anything that's there."

Quinn nodded. "Thanks. You can stay on your post." She turned to George Marshall. "Shall we?" She pointed to both sides of the house.

"Meet you in the back, ma'am."

Quinn made a mental note that George Marshall reverted to a formal exchange. She assumed it was because of the young officer. She headed around the right side of the house and Marshall moved to the left. She carefully scanned the tree line to the north of the property and watched for any evidence of indentations in the snow that would suggest footprints underneath. It was pristine.

As she turned the corner of the house, she heard Marshall call softly. "Quinn, over here."

Quinn moved carefully, still watching for the potential impact of footprints that might have been snowed on last night. *She died Sunday night. It's late Tuesday morning. Lots of opportunity for evidence to disappear out here.* She reached the spot where George was standing.

George pointed to the pristine snow which had dropped in places that were lower than others and had the appearance of footprints.

Quinn noted he had his camera around his neck. She hadn't noticed it when they were in the front of the house. *I'm supposed to notice and remember every detail. Focus.*

"Might have been a mistake to tuck my camera under my jacket. Now it's fogging up in this cold air." He reached in his pocket. Then he smiled as he pulled out a small cloth. "Ta da. I have my trusty cloth to clear the lens." He grinned from ear to ear.

"Always prepared, I see." *Okay, I can give myself a pass this time. He had the camera under his jacket.* "Happen to have a soft brush hidden away, too?"

"Nah, but I do have one in my kit in the car. I'll get photos of what we see here and then go get it. With any luck there might be footprints underneath in the ice or snow." He carefully straddled the indentations and took photos.

Quinn took out her phone and took photos of him taking photos and then a video of the area around the back of the house.

Never lifting his head, George focused on taking photographs. "Quinn, there have to be footprints underneath this snow. Look how flat the snow is everywhere around it." He gave a wide sweeping motion with his arm. "These indentations are regular—like footprints."

"If there's mud or ice underneath, we might find something on that step into the back door." She pointed toward the house. "Anything in the officer's report about mud being tracked into the kitchen?"

"No, that's why I'm surprised to find these indentations in the snow."

"Could have taken the boots off and left them on the step and gone inside in sock feet."

"Dam...sorry, ma'am. You're right. Guess I need another cup of coffee."

"That, Detective, is why two heads are better than one." She laughed. "No doubt the coffee helps, too!"

"I'll go get my bag. Let's dust off some of this snow and see what we can find."

The Beginning of Remembering

Buddy sat up and looked at the clock on the desk in the shed. He had fallen asleep. The dreams were becoming more vivid but still remained disjointed. He stretched his foot and then turned his chair and stretched it as far as he could in the small space. *I hate how cold makes my ankles hurt.* He twisted his feet left and right. Then he stood up. It was almost noon. He looked at his data sheet and was satisfied his plan was moving along and soon all this would end. He might even figure out the question that had haunted him for years: *Who am I?*

The shed in perfect order, Buddy took a small packet, locked the door, and headed into the kitchen. He wiped down the door knobs, threw away the alcohol wipes, and washed his hands. He had eaten his last sandwich on the way back from cleaning the old stone cabin. Now he'd go buy the next weeks' worth—that required a forty-five-minute drive each way this week. He never shopped in the same cafes or restaurants more often every two months. Today he'd go to Maryville and pick up the cleaning and plumbing supplies he needed, as well.

He had taken the cleaning signs off and double-checked there was nothing to make his van stand out. Then he headed out. Forty-three minutes later he was in the small hardware store on the edge of town. He parked and went in.

The Hardware Store

Two men were standing at the front door talking quietly, but that never dissuaded Buddy from eavesdropping. *Never know what you might learn.*

"Hey, Summers, sorry to hear about your ole lady. Must have been tough to find her yourself. You sure you don't need to take some time off?" The embroidered patch on the shirt of the man talking read: manager.

"Nah, customers come first in this business. You know that."

"Always appreciate you stopping in, but we'll call you if we need anything."

From behind his sunglasses, Buddy watched the man called Summers. He knew it could only be the husband of the woman on Sunday night. *Knew I should have gone back and got some material.* He made careful note of Summers' looks, but didn't want them to notice him. Before he could move on the manager spoke to him.

"Hey! Welcome. Help you with something? Happy to direct you to the right aisle."

Buddy turned his head to the other side and kept walking—he pretended he didn't hear the manager. He knew exactly where items were located in this store and was grateful for winter gloves so he didn't have to wear latex ones. It was in this store, five months and three weeks before, when a clerk had asked him why he forgot to take off his gloves. He'd bought paint that day so he assumed she had thought he was wearing them to paint. He'd just shrugged and kept looking down at the floor. He purposely didn't frequent any one store or shop regularly. He preferred to shop online when he could. He had online orders sent to his private mail box.

Maybe it was a mistake to come here today. He kept walking. *Nah, glad I heard that Summers guy talk. Guess he learned a lesson about leaving his wife home alone.* Buddy had to stop himself from letting out a loud guffaw. *Hah! Boy, did he did learn a lesson!* He quickly got the supplies he needed, checked out, and headed for the diner downtown.

Seven sandwiches in his cooler—he'd put the dates on them when he got home, Buddy decided to take the back roads out of town. *With any luck I'll find a police cruiser and get to leave the package on top.* He drove just below the speed limit, stopped at every light, and on the east edge of town smiled when he saw a police cruiser parked on the side of the road. He slowed down, reached over and picked up his binoculars. He looked to see if anyone was in the cruiser. It was empty. The cruiser was parked by a large hedge in front of a white Victorian house badly in need of paint. The hedge was so overgrown he couldn't see the front door or windows as he pulled in front of the cruiser.

He hopped out, placed the small plastic bag on top of the cruiser, and was back in his van in seconds and headed out of town. He watched his side view mirrors and saw no one come out to the cruiser and it was soon out of sight. He leaned back, smiled, and started laughing—his maniacal laugh filled the van and reverberated off the window. *Pappy, you just wait. I've done everything methodically—just like you taught me. Yes, I have.*

The Summers' Home

"Good work, George. Let's see what you were able to get with all that fine dusting."

"Just like doing fingerprints, Quinn. Ever dusted for prints before?"

"Only in training. I learned pretty quickly that it's best left to the professionals."

"I agree. If we find something under this bit of snow, we'll call in the professionals. Is Chuck in yet if we have something to analyze?"

"He's in training in Knoxville. The techs in the other lab...by the way do we have a designation for each of the labs?"

"Yep. 'The other lab.'"

"Ha. Ha. Anyway, as I was saying, the other techs there have good reputations, too. As soon as you give the word, I'll make the call to get someone out here." She waved her phone.

"Doubtful, boss. No signal out here."

She was surprised he addressed as her 'boss.' She let it go. "Of course. I'll just use the radio then."

"Yep. That's what we do." He never lifted his head from his work.

Quinn watched as he carefully dusted the snow from the first indentation. They both knew the ice underneath it could hold a clue. She squatted down being careful not to block the light from the sun sparkling off the snow. "Would the light from my phone help?"

"Think I'm good at the moment."

Slowly the fine snow drifted off on the slight breeze or settled on the snow beside it.

"Quinn, look." George Marshall's voice was quiet but distinctly held the promise of news.

Quinn leaned in. There in the ice, with tiny wisps of snow still lying in the deeper crevices, was a footprint. She spoke softly. "Headed away from the house, don't you think?"

"Looks that way. Better call the techs. Need to get what we can before it's lost."

"On it." Quinn stood up straight and headed for the front and the police cruiser to call for technicians. *Could be anyone's boots, but it is as important to eliminate someone as it is to find a potential suspect.*

"Hey, Detective. Find anything interesting?" Simmons had stepped out of his cruiser when he saw her come around the corner of the house.

"Need the radio, Officer." There was no mistaking the seriousness in her tone.

"All yours." He stepped aside.

She looked in the vehicle at the radio and realized it was nothing like the one she had in her official vehicle with Immigration Enforcement. *I'll get a lesson later.* "You can make the call. Tell dispatch we need a tech team here."

"10-4." He slipped past her into the cruiser.

"Simmons here. Detective Isaacs wants a tech team..." He gave the location.

Chapter 7

In a dark time, the eye begins to see.
Theodore Roethke

A Simple Clue

"Donna, it's great to see you again." Quinn extended her hand and also exchanged greetings with Frank, the other tech. She and Donna had worked together on an immigration case, but she had not met Frank before. Quinn knew she didn't need to stay at the scene, but she was smart enough to know she could always learn something. The techs started on their work—they were slow and methodical.

"Detective, are there..." She paused when she realized George had not heard her address him. She stepped closer to him.

"George."

"Yes?" He turned to look at her.

"Are there other houses along this road? Have they been canvassed? Does Mrs. Summers have any relatives in the area?"

"Closest house is two miles further down the road and it's a three-season cabin. No one there now."

"Are we sure about that?"

He stopped and looked at her. "Fair enough, boss. Shouldn't make assumptions. Want to take a drive while these folks work?"

"Sure, let's do it."

They were no more than a quarter mile down the road when it was evident there were no fresh tire marks in the snow beyond—it was totally undisturbed.

"We're good to navigate this if you want to continue, Quinn."

"Let's go."

George drove carefully and stayed to the center of the road. As they approached the cabin, there were no signs of smoke from the chimney and the gate was locked and no evidence of tire tracks approaching it. However, he noticed indentations on the sides of the road although covered with fresh snow. *How long ago? Lots of folks might turn around here.* "What do you think, boss?"

"I think I'm not accustomed to being called 'boss' and might actually prefer Quinn. That work for you?"

"Shirking your duties already, are you?" The lilt in his voice was suggestive of teasing, but with no disrespect.

"Ha! I'm still figuring out what my duties are." She watched him as he carefully drove to the dead-end past the cabin. "I've read the list and pretty sure I can do everything on it, but I prefer being part of a team."

"Afraid to make a decision?" His voice was even and more inquisitive than accusatory.

"Oh, trust me, I have no problem making decisions. But life has taught me that informed decisions are more likely to be productive than shooting from the hip." She paused. *Eliza, stay down.* She blinked several times. "However, never doubt that I know how to use this weapon on my hip—and I will when the situation requires it."

"Relax, Quinn. I'm pretty sure it will take a while to settle into your job and for us to get used to someone who isn't ruling with an iron fist, but it may take lots of questions—might want to get used to it."

"Have a few of my own, George." She smiled.

"I bet you do. Happy to help any time I can."

George carefully turned the car on the ice-packed road and headed back toward the Summer's house. He slowed and pointed. "Some tracks here recently. Covered with fresh snow."

"Stop, please." She got out and took pictures. "We'll get someone to come down—tread pattern might prove useful."

"Good point."

He pulled back into the driveway at the Summers' house and they both got out. One of the forensic techs was stepping out of the van and called to them.

"Sir. Ma'am. Got a minute?"

"Absolutely." Quinn moved quickly toward the van. "What's up, Donna?"

"Printed out the pictures for you. Easier to see than the camera."

George moved next to Quinn as Donna handed them the photos. He whistled.

Quinn turned to him and then back to the forensic tech. "Tell me about this."

"Well, ma'am, it's the strangest thing I've ever seen. Sure enough there are two footprints in a relatively normal gait, but as you can see, one goes forward and one goes backwards."

Quinn stared at the photos. She took one from Donna and looked carefully at the snow on either side of the prints.

"Ma'am, if you're wondering if there's a set of prints on either side of these—there isn't."

Quinn turned to George who had been studying the picture himself.

"Beats all I've ever seen." He shrugged.

"Thanks, Donna. Any more you can get back there?"

"We'll do as many sets as we can, but with the afternoon warming up, the best we might find is how far back in the woods they go. We have good enough marks to identify the soles and the boots once we get back to the station. I think we need to figure out where they came from and went to."

Quinn nodded. "Absolutely. I don't want too many people tramping around back there, but tell me if you need me to call in additional help."

"Might be a good plan to have two officers with us just in case there's someone hiding out in those woods. Not so sure we want to encounter someone on our own—Frank's topnotch at the forensics, but not so big on the bravery." She smiled slightly and looked in Quinn's eyes.

"Got it." Quinn saw that Officer Simmons was standing beside his cruiser.

"Officer Simmons, please call for two officers to come to the scene as soon as possible."

"10-4."

"I don't want to lose momentum, so Detective Marshall and I will work with you until we get some officers here. And, Donna, I'm sending you some pictures of a place down the road about a quarter of a mile on the left as you drive south. I'd like to see if we can get tread patterns under the snow." Quinn looked at George who nodded assent and they headed toward the back.

Whose Clues?

Buddy settled into the drive back to Round City using the old two-lane road which he knew would eventually wind back to the main highway and get him home. He couldn't believe his good fortune in finding a cruiser so easily on the outskirts of Maryville. *With all the technology today, why aren't these idiots making any connections? I'll have to find a way to ask Albert how much checking one police force does with another. I've done everything by the book—Pappy's book, anyway.* He carefully made the sweeping curve that would lead him back to the highway. Albert usually came over on Mondays and sometimes on Fridays, but Buddy decided to text him and see if he could come tonight.

He pulled into the gas station just off the highway and sent a text to Albert. "Up for losing again tonight?" He really didn't expect Albert to reply and he didn't. *Must be out in some godforsaken place. He'll see it sooner or later. Good ole Albert, he has no idea how much he has helped me along the way.* He pulled up to the pump filled up with gas and was back on the highway. He'd be home by four-thirty p.m. *Perfect. I can catch up on my research.*

The Dense Forest

Frank continued to brush snow off the indentations, mark them with numbered stakes, and take pictures. Donna, Quinn, and George walked four feet on either side of the path scanning the ground.

"Detective Isaacs, look." Donna pointed straight ahead.

"What's up?" George turned toward Donna and then Quinn.

Donna pointed to the line formed by the trees on the back edge of the Summers' property. "The snow isn't as deep back there. Even the light breeze we've had doesn't blow as much under the evergreens. See those indentations?"

Quinn and George followed the line of her finger. There, maybe five steps into the wooded area were tracks. They were covered from the light dusting of snow that fell during the night, but the tracks were clear.

"Hey Frank," Donna called. "Bring the kit here." She turned to Quinn. "Ma'am, we may need to get lights to get good enough range on these tracks. Look like all terrain by the width of tire tracks."

She walked over to the detective. "I'm going to go call for additional help. I want sweepers inside that house—top to bottom. Any names I should ask for?" She studied his face.

"Just tell dispatch to send the Alpha-team. That'll get our best out here even if they're off duty today."

She nodded. "Thanks." Quinn headed toward the front of the Summers' house. Simmons was standing on the front porch looking toward the road.

"Officer."

"Yes, ma'am." He came down the stairs quickly and almost slipped. He tried to recover and hoped she hadn't noticed.

Quinn ignored the near slip, but made a note to learn more about Albert Simmons. "I need to make this call. Please patch me through to dispatch."

"Ma'am. Yes, ma'am." He opened the driver's door to the cruiser as Quinn opened the passenger door. He called dispatch and handed the handset to Quinn. She took it, looked at him, and nodded. He exited the vehicle.

"Isaacs here, I need Officer Simmons relieved and the Alpha-team at the Summers residence..." she gave the directions and listened. "10-4."

She sat for a moment trying to decide if she needed to call back and inform the Chief. She decided against it. It was mid-afternoon and she would be back at the station shortly after the Alpha-team arrived and she'd text the chief then.

"Thanks, Simmons. Have some more folks on the way and you should be able to head back into town before the end of your shift. Appreciate your help."

"Happy to stay if you need me." He had a school-boy smile.

"I think we'll be fine, but I'll confirm once the other folks get here. I suspect we'll hear them, but if not..." she didn't finish because he interrupted her.

"I'll let you know, ma'am. Right away. Don't you worry about it."

"10-4." She turned and headed toward the back of the house.

Alpha Team

Thirty minutes later another forensic van and three cruisers pulled up in front of the Summers' home. Quinn heard the noise through the trees and headed to the front of the house.

"Afternoon, Detective Isaacs. We've met." The tall, muscular, hazel-eyed man extended his hand. "I'm Sergeant Clark, leader of the Alpha Team. Whatcha got here?"

Quinn recalled meeting him at the diner with Billy Williams right after Chief Nelson was killed. "Nice to see you again, Sergeant." Quinn gave him the run down on what they knew at this point: husband found body Monday night, remains now enroute to SBI lab. She walked to the other van and picked up the picture she had set on the passenger seat earlier. "This" she handed him the picture, "is why I called for you."

The sergeant looked carefully at the picture. "Well, that's a new one on me. More than one of these?"

"Yes. Marked, measured and photographed four sets, but I decided to send the techs and Detective Marshall to comb the woods while we waited on you."

Clark looked around at all the cops waiting for direction. "Has the house been swept?"

"As far as I'm aware just a cursory sweep last night as it was assumed to be a natural death."

"Was it? Cancel that—if so, you wouldn't have sent the body to the SBI lab."

"Right. Had hoped to get a COD before we put all the work into this place, but these prints and apparent ATV tracks in the woods suggest we need a thorough sweep of the place."

"On it. I'll send Simmons back, almost time for shift change. We can cover the techs in the woods and sweep the house. You and Marshall can stay or go—up to you."

"Sergeant, Detective Marshall has made clear you are not just the Alpha-team, but the best team. I'm sure the scene is in good hands. Feel free to call me anytime. I'll notify Chuck we may have new evidence soon. There was a used condom found last night that was tagged and bagged. I'll move it upstairs to Chuck's lab."

Clark looked at her his mouth set, but his eyes twinkling. "All the clues matter, right?"

"Yes. Yes, they do." *Did you really think I would take that bait, Sergeant?* She nodded her head and moved toward the back to get Marshall and tell the two forensic techs they were headed to town.

Clark assigned one of the first two officers that were called to cover the techs in the forest and one to cover the front. Then he dispersed his team in the house and the yard, and turned to speak to Officer Simmons.

"Simmons, looks like you've cut a break. Head on back. You'll get there a bit ahead of end of shift, but that'll give you plenty of time to write your report. Any problems, have your shift sarge contact me."

"10-4, Sarge." Simmons headed to his cruiser. He was glad to get out of the cold. *Buddy might be right. Maybe I should study for the detective exam. Seems a lot more interesting than sitting in a cruiser watching a house.*

Return Text

Buddy arrived home and unloaded the supplies he had bought at the hardware store and made sure they were neat and organized on shelves and in cupboards. He took his cooler into the kitchen and labeled each of the sandwiches for the next seven days. He wiped out the cooler and put it back in his van before returning to the kitchen to wash his hands. A quick glance at the sides of the van made him smile. *You put the signs away. Good job, Buddy.* He sighed. *Routines. Just like Pappy taught me.* He started toward the computer in his game room, but decided he needed his secure computer and was about to open the kitchen door when a text message pinged on his phone.

He smiled as he read it: I'll come collect on our bet.

What does he mean by that? I don't owe him anything. Their bet about meeting the Chief or new lead detective had completely slipped Buddy's mind.

He returned a text: OK. @7. Don't count chickens...

Buddy knew Albert would understand the message. Every time Albert had been sure he'd win a bet, Buddy had trounced him in their videogames.

Buddy moved quickly now. He had some research to do to find out if there was a report in Maryville about the little packet he'd left on the cruiser. He wanted to have time to heat up a can of soup for his supper and organize the questions he wanted to try and get Albert to answer without giving away anything himself.

Buddy went through his routine entering the shed and waited for his eyes to adjust before turning on this computer. *All that work to teach myself how to hack into computers and to find files that others thought were well hidden just might pay off.* He began the search by looking up the license plate he'd noted on the cruiser. Then he'd search for the duty rosters. *Well, that was easier than I thought.* He wrote down the officer's name and the shift sergeant that headed the team that shift. *They better figure out how to close that back door or they'll be getting folks who run malware or ransomware—then they'll be sorry.* Buddy hacked into computers to help with his plan—not to do damage. *Maybe I should start leaving the name of my plan as a calling card.* He sat back in his chair. *Yeah, maybe I'll do that.* He had named his project: "Something in Common" or SIC. He started to chuckle, then laugh, and then his maniacal laugh overtook him.

At the Station

Quinn sent a text to the chief from her secure phone as soon as they had a signal. "Headed in. New info on Summers."

"See me on return."

"10-4."

Quinn put her phone away and tried to relax into the passenger seat. The knot in her hair pushed against her neck. She reached back and loosened her hair.

"Any thoughts to share, George?"

"Pretty much try to line things up in my head before I speak, but I have to say those prints were the strangest I've ever seen."

"Agreed. I'll start a board when we get back. How do you usually handle a board in the department?"

"Seriously?" George glanced over at her. "Listen, Quinn. Chief Nelson was a by the book police chief. I liked him personally and respected him. From day one to the last, I never understood why he hired Albright." He looked at Quinn. "Not nice to speak ill of the dead."

She gave him a slight nod of her head hoping he'd continue.

"Albright wasn't from here, hell, he wasn't even from Tennessee. He was a control freak of the first order and, in my opinion, we could have solved some cases that never got solved if he hadn't had the need to be in control." George let out a long sigh.

"George, I'm very aware that I am not only new to being lead detective here, I'm younger than every other detective. Already told you I prefer to work on a team and I would like it if we could do that. No apologies needed for your opinions—not on Albright or a case. I just ask that if you have a problem with how I operate that you come tell me. We may have to agree to disagree, but I will always listen and hope for the same courtesy."

"Wouldn't have said what I just did if I hadn't already figured that out." There was a lightness now in his tone. He chuckled. "I'm a detective, remember?" She could see the smile on his face. "Done with the past. I suggest we set up a board that is available to all of the detective squad and see what we can do as a team."

"Any empty rooms that we can use and secure?"

"No one ever uses the conference room across the hall from your office. Maybe the Chief will give you permission…"

"On it. I'll let you know before the end of shift."

George pulled into the back of the station and stopped by the back door.

"I can walk from your parking space, Detective."

"Yes, ma'am, no doubt. But you'll get to the Chief sooner, and us to building a board, if I let you out here. Besides I need to stop at the back for gas." He smiled. "Welcome aboard, Quinn."

She nodded and stepped out of the car. "I'll text as soon as I have an answer."

She moved quickly to her office, took off her parka, changed from her boots to her shoes, and sent an e-message to the chief. "In house."

"Come down."

Quinn took a deep breath, picked up her Yeti, and took a long swig of water. She stopped at the restroom, ran her fingers through her hair, and washed her hands. She was in the Chief's office in less than three minutes.

Establishing Routines

"Sounds like you did the right thing, Quinn." Jill Hansen had listened as Quinn described the scene and the actions she had taken. "But you didn't need me to tell you that."

"Chief...Jill," Quinn quickly remembered the chief's request to use first names. "In Immigration Enforcement, I always found we did our best work as a team. Each person has their expertise and if you're lucky, some have breadth and depth. I want to approach this situation as a team."

"But?"

"No, real 'but'—more a need to know that you're agreeable to that approach."

"In Atlanta I dealt with some massive cases that would have been impossible to solve if we had not been a team. You would not be sitting across from me if I didn't believe you could lead a team—so go do it. Text or e-message me if you need anything from me. Otherwise, I'll count on your daily reports to keep me current. I'd guess you've already figured out I have a full-time job working on the organizational side of this police force."

"I look forward to learning from you."

Jill raised her eyebrows. "Looking to take over my job?"

"No way. My only interest in organizational matters is to make sure that they function so we can do our work."

Jill laughed. "Good. That's my goal. Now let's see what we can do to make it all happen."

"Yes, ma'am."

"I told you..."

Quinn interrupted. "I said 'ma'am' out of respect—not out of obligation." Quinn winked at her. "Welcome back to small time life in the Smoky Mountains." Quinn stood, shook hands with the Chief, then stopped. "Sorry, Jill, one more thing. See any problems with using the conference room across from my office to set up a board to work this case?"

"None that I can see. Got word that it could be a problem?"

"George Marshall told me it was 'hardly ever used.'" She put air quotes around George's words.

"I'll look into how space is allocated, but in the meantime go ahead. I think it's better to keep a board in a secure space that doesn't put people in direct contact with evidence."

"Me, too. Thanks." Quinn turned.

"And if you think we need to change the locks to limit access, let me know."

Quinn stood still for a minute. "Sure." She dragged the word out. *Does the Chief know there's a problem?* "Have a nice evening, Chief."

As she walked down the hall, Quinn typed a text to George Marshall: "Meet in five?" She looked up from her phone and just avoided bumping into the shift sergeant ending his day.

"Headed home?" His voice was light and pleasant.

"No, but I hope you are."

"Yes, ma'am. We just finished the hand-off and I'm headed out."

"Good for you, Sergeant. Good for you."

"And what about you? When will you head home? Heard you were here pretty early."

Quinn tried not to show surprise as she realized the night shift sergeant would likely have told him she stopped in. She smiled. "Before too long. Thanks for your concern. Have some work to do first. You get some rest." Quinn stopped outside her office.

"Count on it." The sergeant kept walking.

Quinn opened her office door and heard footsteps behind her. She turned to see George standing in the doorway.

"Any idea where to find a key to the conference room?" She pointed across the hall.

He pulled a keychain out of his pocket. "Didn't say it wasn't accessible, just said it was hardly ever used."

"So you did. Who else has a key?"

"Hmmm...all the detectives and who knows who else."

"Give me a minute." She stepped in her office, picked up the phone and called the Chief. "Need the locks changed, please."

"10-4." The Chief hung up.

"Okay, let's go see what we've got across the hall."

Marshall opened the door and the mustiness flew on the air through the doorway.

"Whew. It must have been a very long time." Quinn covered her mouth when she coughed.

"Like I told you..."

Quinn flipped the light switch and looked around. There was a chalk board with a combination cork board that reminded her of her high school days. "Any white boards around the building?"

"Yep. We have three in our office. Two have some notes on cases we're working, but one is portable and not being used at the moment."

"Create any problems if we move it here?"

"Ha! It'll give us some room to move."

Quinn made a mental note to do a reconnaissance on the allocation of space the detectives had assigned to them.

"When was the last time this place was dusted?" She looked around the room.

"Your guess is as good as mine."

"Tell you what. If you'll go get the white board, I'll find something to use to dust the table and chairs. Who knows—might even find some air freshener."

"Hold on." George took his phone out. "Hey! Marshall here. Got anybody who could come give the old conference room on first floor a lick and a promise?" He listened. "Ten minutes is great. Thanks. Owe you one." He turned to Quinn and shrugged.

"Good work. That a number you can share?"

George Marshall laughed. "Always make sure you know how the Chief operates and who the custodians are. That'll keep you functioning in the job."

"Good advice." She smiled at him. "The number?"

He gave it to her. "They're all good folks. Doesn't matter who answers."

"Thanks. Thanks for making it happen."

"I'll go get the white board. Then maybe we can brainstorm in your office while they clean. That'll help me organize my thoughts for how you want to lay out our board."

It was not lost on Quinn that he said: "our." Back in her office, she sat at her desk and began to make notes on what they knew about the scene at the Summers' residence.

Chapter 8

*It is beneath human dignity to lose one's individuality and become
a mere cog in the machine.*
Ghandi

The Bet

Buddy was gasping for air with tears running down his face from his own maniacal laugh. He heard the ping of a text on his phone.

His eyes went wide when he read it: "At your door."

He saw on the clock it was seven p.m. He sent a reply: "In the john. Five mins."

He logged out of his computer wondering where the time had gone. *What was I thinking? I know better.* He turned off the lights in the shed, let his eyes adjust, opened the door, closed and locked it, and walked quickly to the back door. He opened and closed it softly, locked it, and quickly washed his hands. He turned on the hall light and then the living room light from his phone. *Shoot, didn't have time to set up my beer.* He opened the front door.

"Hey, Buddy. Not nice to leave a friend out in the cold. Worried about paying the debt?"

"Ha. We'll see who pays." Buddy moved into the kitchen. "Beer?"

"Sure. Surprised you don't have them ready." Albert stopped himself. He knew Buddy didn't like to be teased.

"Something I ate isn't agreeing with me." He made a show of washing his hands before he got Albert's beer. "I'm sticking to water tonight." He popped the top on the beer and handed it to Albert.

"Here's mud in your eye!" Albert lifted his beer and took a swig. "Now, about that bet."

"Let's go play. I'm not feeling so bad I can't beat you in the game of your choice."

"Whoa, Buddy. I may end up losing everything you're about to pay me, but I want my winnings up front."

Buddy stared at him.

Albert stopped himself. He never thought Buddy was very quick at word games. *Hmmm...maybe I should challenge him to a game of...* "Sorry, I should have told you which bet I won."

"That'll be the day."

"Hey, it was only last night that you bet me. Forgotten already?" Albert was surprised at how dark Buddy's eyes appeared. He'd never encountered anything close to anger in Buddy before, but this look was unlike anything he'd ever seen. "Hey, lighten up. You made a bet for me to try and meet the new Chief or the new lead detective. I thought I'd lose, but guess what?"

Buddy's eyes changed as if someone had turned on a light switch. "Oh, yeah. Lots on my mind today." He slapped Albert on the back and nodded toward his game room. "Come on, tell me. I'm all about a debt being paid." *Might have an opening to find out what Albert knows.*

Albert was surprised by the backslap. Buddy had never touched him before—not even to shake hands. They sat down in their chairs at the monitors.

Albert looked at Buddy. "Ready?"

Buddy nodded.

Albert's eyes were wide. "I met the new lead detective at a crime scene."

"Wow! Where?" Buddy was excited. He wanted to get as much out of Albert as he could.

"Out off of Route 54. Why does it matter where?"

"No reason."

"Yep, I met Detective Quinn Isaacs in person—eyeball to eyeball."

Buddy turned his chair and extended his hand, palm side out. "Pay up."

"Pay up? You owe me. I met Quinn Isaacs—today. You said you thought I could meet the new lead detective or the chief in three…" Albert's voice trailed off. *I'm the one who is stupid. He bet I could do it and I did.*

Buddy shook his head. "The bet on my part was that you *could* meet the detective or the Chief. You're the one who thought you couldn't, so I win."

Albert sat there staring at Buddy. "Yeah, yeah. Finally dawned on me." *How come I thought he wasn't quick with words? He tricked me. And what's wrong with me that I didn't try to avoid meeting either one so I could win?* "Fair enough. Fair enough. You win. Next time I'll be listening to your words a lot more carefully." He reached for his wallet.

"Aw, let's split the bet. It really wasn't a fair bet." Buddy was trying to figure out how to get Albert to cool off so he could ask his questions. "I wasn't too smart in setting up a bet where you could have won by just avoiding any opportunity to meet the new Chief or lead detective. So tell me, what's he like?"

"Who?"

"The lead detective? Quinn? Was that the name? Sounds like a movie star."

"She's a she."

"I know the new chief's a woman. I asked about the lead detective."

"She's a she, too. Quinn is a woman."

Buddy sat back in his chair and a small frown crept across his face. *Well, well. A woman. Two women at the top. I thought we had stupid before…* Buddy turned to Albert. "What did you just say?"

"You must be feeling worse than you think, Buddy. I said, 'She's one smart cookie.'"

"Oh, she is, is she? Then guess I need to meet her. Never met a smart woman in my life."

"How many women have you met in your life besides your grandma?" Albert wished he could take the words back as soon as they left his mouth. He knew Buddy grew up with just his pappy and it wasn't his fault—at least he didn't think it was. Besides he liked Dr. Wilkie—Buddy's pappy had been their high school science and math teacher.

Buddy's eyes turned the menacing dark Albert had seen earlier.

Albert stood. "Look, Buddy, I'm tired. I was out at the Summers' house all day and it was cold and I haven't had a hot meal yet today. So, I'll just run along and we'll catch up next week."

Buddy hopped up. "Hey, man. Sorry. Just off a bit today. I can heat up some soup. What do you say?"

Albert shrugged. "Nah, I'll run along. Thanks for the invite. I'll see you next week." Albert was out the door.

Buddy locked the front door and used his phone to turn off the living room light. He watched Albert's car drive away—the taillights bright against the dark, cold sky.

At the Summers' place? Hmmm...

End of the Day

"Thoughts?" Quinn stood back from the crime board in the conference room that now smelled like lemon drops—fresher than it had probably been in years.

"Mostly I'm thinking we'll know a whole lot more when the Alpha team gets a report to us."

"Agreed..." There was a knock on the door. Quinn turned and walked toward it. She opened the door and a young man in a coveralls stood there.

"Is Detective Isaacs here?"

"I'm Quinn Isaacs." She read his name on the badge clipped to his shirt. "How can I help you, Mr. Frost?"

"Jake. It's Jake Frost, ma'am. I'm here to change the lock. Chief said to do it right away and give you two keys and give one to her office."

"Thanks, Jake. Give me just a minute." She turned to see that George had already turned the white board around so a blank side was facing the door, and it blocked the cork board where they had tacked up the photographs and map. She nodded at George and smiled. "It's all yours, Jake. Detective Marshall and I shouldn't be in your way."

"No, ma'am. I'll have it done in five minutes or less." He set down his toolkit and started to work.

Quinn walked back toward George who had pulled two chairs between the white board and cork board. One was set so Quinn could also see the door.

George pointed toward a photo. "Ma'am, I think this pattern could be important."

Quinn assumed his formal tone was due to Jake's presence. She nodded.

Quinn and George looked at the photographs of the footprints and the measured distance from the back steps to the beginning of the tire tracks they assumed belonged to an ATV.

"Look at the distance." Quinn pointed to the measurement. "Would you have pulled up this close with an ATV?" Her voice was low, almost a whisper.

"Nope. Too noisy. Maybe the individual was a regular visitor—someone expected." George took her cue and spoke softly, too.

"Right. Also, clearly someone who wouldn't want to walk too far. No matter how you managed to..." she pointed to the one foot forward and one backwards.

"How would..." George stopped when Jake interrupted them.

"Ma'am. Lock is changed. Just need you to sign for these two keys. Chief wants a keypad lock, but that'll take more time. Have to order one."

"Thanks, Jake. This will do for now. I'm going to sign for one and ask Detective Marshall to sign for the other. That work for you?"

"Yes, ma'am. You're in charge." He stopped. "Maybe you could initial beside his signature so I can prove I gave it to you?"

"Perfect. Good thinking, Jake."

She turned to George. "You sign and I'll initial." She let him sign for the first key and initialed it and then signed for the second one.

"Really appreciate the speed with which you got to this."

"Sure, ma'am. I've checked the keys and they work. Want to try them while I'm here?"

"I'm sure it's not necessary. Have a good evening, Jake."

"You, too, ma'am." He nodded to George. "You, too."

George gave a slight wave and returned his gaze to the board while Quinn locked the conference room door from the inside. When she turned George had moved the white board against the side wall on the same side as the door.

"Quinn, how would there be one foot forward and one foot backward?"

"I've been trying to figure that out, too. No one would be hopping on one foot on the snow and ice underneath it."

"Agreed." Marshall stared at the pictures. "What if you only had one leg and you had a very sharp pointed stick that would hardly leave a mark..."

"Go on."

"I hate speculating."

"I hate not thinking of as many possibilities to explain something so out of the ordinary. So give me your possibilities."

"I'm still trying to figure out how you could so perfectly pace yourself to have it look like you were going forward, or backward for that matter, at the same time."

"Practice, practice, practice?" Quinn gave a slight chuckle.

"For damn sure." George started to apologize for swearing and let it go.

"How about this? The person is an amputee at some joint forward of the ankle and has an insert built into the back of the boot that supports the ankle."

"Yeah...I can see the insert for support, but why is the boot backward?"

"What if only *this* boot is backward? Maybe he, or she, normally wears the boot forward, or has another boot that is designed with an insert to walk forward."

"Yeah, yeah." George was getting excited. "The backward boot is designed to throw off a trail at a crime scene."

"Ever had any other prints like this, or heard of any in other jurisdictions?"

"Quinn, I can pretty much tell you in my twenty years here we've never had this pattern before. Matter of fact, I've never heard of any in the state and I'm pretty sure I would have." He looked from the pictures to their notes on the board. "It's so unusual should be easy enough to do a search to see if it's out there someplace else."

"Then let's call it a day." She saw the look on George's face. "Something on your mind?"

"Interesting there's no evidence out front."

"Too many people before we knew it was a crime scene."

"True. Yeah, hard to know whether this guy was coming or going." He let out a snort.

Quinn nodded her head. "We should have some new information tomorrow from the Alpha team." She started for the door.

"Quinn, thanks."

"For what?"

"For treating me like an equal."

"Whoa, George. You are far more experienced than I am and we each bring our part to this. I'll make the decisions I have to make as lead detective, but for me that is administrative, not field work. I'm excited to work with you and to start building a team."

"Me, too."

"I'd appreciate it if you talk the other detectives tomorrow to see if there are any cold cases which might connect here."

George grinned. "You bet. We're all here days and rotate taking night calls."

Good to know. "I'll send out a message for us to meet in your office space."

She locked the door and turned to George. "Good work, Detective. See you in the morning."

"Yes, ma'am. You sure will." George extended his hand to shake. She reciprocated.

Quinn watched him walk down the hall for a few seconds before she turned to the lab and her office inside it. *I'll need to get Chuck up to speed tomorrow and see what he might know about this pattern of footprints.* She slipped out of her loafers and into her winter boots while she waited for her computer to start. She wanted to be sure the tone of her e-message to the other detectives was right. *I suspect it won't be long before they have quizzed George about working with me today.*

Home

The bitter wind had whipped up the snow on the trees as she went out the front door of the police station. The officer on the desk was talking with someone at the window and she just gave a cursory wave. She had already notified dispatch that she was gone for the night. She was grateful for no new snow today and a windshield that would be clear as soon as she warmed up her car. *Wonder when my official vehicle will arrive?* She didn't think it would be difficult to have her space moved to the back lot of the station. *I would love to know why Detective Albright wanted to park in front.* As her car warmed up and the defrosters cleared the front and back windows, Quinn backed into her parking space which the captain had pointed out to her from the front door on her first day. She realized she had never actually read the sign because the print was too small to read in her mirror. She stepped out while the car warmed up. She stared at the sign: Lead Detective-Albright. *Wow, why on earth would you signal to the world that a given vehicle was yours?* She shook her head and knew she would have her space moved tomorrow.

The blinking light on her home phone and the note leaning against the vase by the phone caught her eye immediately. She put on her slippers which she had remembered to place by the door. She quickly hung up her coat. As she pushed the button to listen to her messages, she read the note from Mildred, the head of the team who cleaned her home: "Drip in upstairs bathtub. Tightened faucet. Might want to check it." *Okay, I'm not crazy.* "Hey, lovely lady…" Quinn turned her attention to the message on the phone—it was Billy.

As she opened the fridge, Quinn looked at her watch and saw it was already seven-thirty p.m. *A thirteen-hour day. Have I eaten since breakfast?* She remembered she'd had two protein bars. She pulled the glass container with the left-over vegetable-beef soup and put it in the microwave to heat while she looked to see if she had any crackers. She finally found some Club crackers and saw that it was the last pack in the box. "Alexa, put Club crackers on my shopping list." *I have to figure out a better routine around meals. Ha. Around shopping for meals.* She put the soup on the kitchen counter and pushed the button to listen to the message from Billy again: "Remember, you did plenty of detective work in immigration. You've got this." She took her first spoonful of soup and began to relax—not sure if she felt warm from the soup or the encouragement from Billy. *Should I call him? Will I seem too anxious?*

Dishes in the dishwasher and the light off in the kitchen, Quinn decided to take a hot shower and then spend some time in her office going over the day. Settled in at her desk, she turned on her computer and in secure mode started a fresh list of "what I know" from the Summers' case. As she typed, she began to think about the child's shoe and the bones that had been left on the patrol cars on Sunday night. She'd see what the lab techs knew at this point. *Chuck will be in tomorrow. It may be coincidence, but I think we may need to put a rush on those bones. What if they are connected?* She leaned back in her chair and closed her eyes.

Time for a glass of wine. She shut down the computer and went into the great room. She opened the small fridge under the bar and poured a glass of Swanson Pinot Grigio and headed for the stairs to check out the faucet in the bathroom.

At the top of the stairs she looked around at the rooms she rarely entered. Her grandmother had bought the home for her when she was assigned to Round City, close to their home in Knoxville. *Well, Gran, wonder what you'd think of this house today?* It had taken almost a year to have everything done to remodel it: new plumbing, new electric, modern kitchen. *I don't even know the last time I was up here.* She walked into the bathroom shared by the three bedrooms and flipped the light switch. There were a few drops of water on the bottom of the tub. She sat down on the edge of the tub, looked at her watch, and sipped her wine. A drop of water fell from the shower head. She looked at her watch and saw she'd been there for five minutes. *Guess it doesn't matter how often the drops fall, the reality is I need a plumber.* She turned the faucet but found it was tight. She had never needed a plumber so would have to ask someone at work who to get. *Surely George will know someone.*

Back downstairs in her bedroom, she sat in the oversized upholstered chair which faced out the French doors to her back garden; it was her favorite chair for reading. She picked up the collection of short stories that Bella had sent her: "Stories to be Told." She flipped open to the table of contents and found the page number of Bella Anderson's story: *High on a Mountain: Altitude and Drugs.* She tucked her feet under her and began reading. When she finished, she made a note on her phone to send Bella a thank you note and comment on the story. *Short stories are just the right length for nighttime reading and this one was excellent.* She was beginning to realize the benefit of having friends who were not in the town where she was now a detective—especially Billy. Quinn set the empty glass on the bathroom counter and sat on the side of her bed to make one more note on her phone: plumber.

Intrusive Thoughts

Buddy gave up on going back out to the shed when Albert left. He returned to his gaming room and logged in through an incognito screen to play a few games. He wanted to be anonymous with folks he didn't know—who were someplace he had no interest in knowing. *Keep your head down and your brain on.* He shook his head trying to block the thoughts. Pappy had said that to him thousands of times. *Where are you, Pappy? Why won't you tell me?* Over the years since Pappy left, Buddy assumed that some of the things he came upon were messages his pappy was sending. He just didn't understand why Pappy left—just disappeared one day when Buddy was in his early twenties. *I know all these signs are from you. Why did you leave?* He slammed his hands on the keyboard. His ankle hurt and his head felt like a top spinning out of control—his head pounded.

The message box in this particular game, which was something Buddy did not like about the game, flashed on his screen: "Hey, dude. Play!"

Buddy read the note. *Good news for you that I don't know where you are.* He hit the button to resign the game, shut down his computer, and stood up. He turned on the light in his bedroom from his phone and turned off the one in the gaming room. The routine in turning lights on and off didn't really matter—both rooms had blackout curtains. Somehow it made him feel better knowing if any light got past the curtains, there was a pattern to his movements. *Patterns are everything, boy. How many times do I have to tell you that?*

Buddy let out a loud scream: "I know patterns are everything. I've been laying out a pattern for years." He stopped by the door, pounded the back of his head against the door frame, and moaned: "Stop. Stop. Stop." He just wanted the thoughts, the pain, and the questions to stop. He stumbled across the hall and fell on the bed. He still had not eaten the soup he had planned to have. Sleep came quickly and he was weighted down with the darkness.

Chapter 9

Sometimes the place you are used to is not the place you belong.
William Wheeler

The Cottage

Dr. Oscar Wilkie stretched out on the small cot in the cottage deep in the 120 wooded acres he had owned for years. It had always been his refuge. When he finished medical school, he had learned he couldn't work with the pressures of the hours in a hospital, and he didn't handle adults well enough to have a private practice. His mother had been heart-broken. In spite of her considerable wealth, which had put him through college and medical school with no debt, she had lived an isolated and frugal life. As Oscar matured, he realized that he was the cause of her withdrawal from social circles. His extremely high intellect and his complete inability to build friendships with people his own age separated her from a world she had known all her life—before him. When he was a teenager, he was most comfortable with kids half his age or younger; they didn't make the social demands he was incapable of understanding. As he matured, he learned to function with others around his academic interests, but he never interacted with others outside of that arena unless it was absolutely necessary.

When he told his mother he wasn't going to practice medicine, she arranged for him to teach math and science at a small rural school which had three other teachers. She had done some discreet inquiries and learned the other teachers were married women, so she knew they would not make social demands on her son. In the early days, he was able to show up to the school, teach his classes, and go home—to her home. Several years into his teaching career, he bought the acreage with a stone house not too far from the school. The school closed shortly after Buddy graduated.

Years ago he had been approached by a representative of a national phone company who wanted to put a wireless tower in the far corner of his land. They would pay him outright and buy the land, or they would lease it on a fifty-year renewable lease. He opted for the lease. Having the tower on his land suited him just fine. It ensured he had phone signals at his stone house and at the cottage he had built after the school closed. No one knew about the cottage—no one.

He couldn't get settled on the cot tonight. The boy he had found barely alive on this land thirty years ago, in shock from the loss of blood, invaded every thought. Oscar had always followed paths on his land made by larger animals looking for patterns to their habits. He knew he was on a bear trail and was surprised when he came upon the boy. A quick tourniquet made from his scarf stanched the bleeding at the foot. He had thrown the boy over his shoulder and taken him back to his house. He tended his wound, stole antibiotics from the local pharmacy where he helped out—mostly when the pharmacist who owned it had been drunk all weekend.

He never told anyone about finding the boy—or the people with him who were already dead.

"Come on, Buddy, you're going to make it." Oscar looked up at the ceiling remembering the high fevers and hoping the boy would live. He did. The child had no memory of his parents, or where he was from, his name, or even how old he was. Oscar read the papers and could find no evidence of any missing persons. He continued to call the boy Buddy, and kept him hidden in his home where he taught him for the next two years.

Then one day after reading about a terrible car wreck on a back road in the next county, he told his mother that it was a family whose children went to the school where he taught and they had all been killed except for the little boy. Since she had never caught him in a lie, his mother accepted his explanation that he had offered to take in the boy. Oscar's mother treated Buddy like a grandson and paid for his university and left him her house. She had split her estate between her son and grandson—neither had to worry about money.

Now the boy he'd taken in was likely thirty-seven years old and was still called Buddy. Oscar was afraid Buddy was starting to fall apart. He'd taught him about biology, survival, cleanliness, following patterns—all the things he knew were important. He tracked him just like he did the animals in the woods, although it was easier because he had a GPS tracker on Buddy's van.

Oscar was pleased that Buddy continued to go to the stone house every Tuesday and clean it. *Discipline, Buddy, discipline. You learned that well. Why did you go to two different places in Maryville though?* Oscar knew about the hardware store, but he couldn't figure out where he went in the small strip mall. There were several shops there that were possibilities. *What was the quick stop on the back road out of town? It was too quick to be with a woman.* He rolled over on the cot and knew that sleep would not come easy tonight. He just hoped he wouldn't have to make another outing tonight—like he had done on too many nights.

Oscar woke to the alert which notified him Buddy was on the move. He slipped on his coveralls and boots and headed out.

Not Again

Buddy waked from his deep sleep when his phone rang. It was the one he used for plumbing calls.

"Yeah?"

"Hey, mister. This is Jason. Remember me?" The voice was soft but urgent.

"You have the wrong number." Buddy started to click off the phone.

"Don't hang up, mister." There was a pleading in Jason's voice that Buddy recognized.

"What do you need?"

"Tell me again how to make that stick work in the toilet."

Buddy sat up. "Is your ma home?" He realized who the boy was—one of the two at the house last night.

"She's in the room with her door locked. The toilet ain't going down. She'll beat me."

"I'll be there in twenty minutes. Don't turn on the lights. I'll park on the road and walk up. Be really quiet. Okay?"

"Yes, sir. She don't wake up easy."

Buddy suddenly realized he was still dressed. He didn't remember falling asleep on the bed fully dressed—ever. He was in the garage and on his way in two minutes. He remembered what it was to be a boy desperately afraid to avoid trouble.

Buddy pulled the van beyond the house and his headlights reflected on a vehicle parked down the road. He saw no sign of movement in or near the truck. He put his latex gloves on under his winter gloves and got out. As he approached the door, it opened and without a word the boy let him in.

They tiptoed into the small bathroom. Buddy remembered the floor was rotten and he put his fingers to his lips, put his hand up to the boy to stay in the doorway, and used the fingers of his right hand to signal Jason to look at him as he used the plunger, "the stick" the boy had called it. He breathed a sigh of relief when the toilet water went down. He rinsed the plunger in the clean water and put it back by the toilet and moved toward the door.

As he stepped out the front door headed for his truck, hoping the woman would not hear them, he saw a light come on in the house and heard the woman yell.

"Boy, who was that? You let somebody in this house? Get in your room and drop your drawers. You've done done it now."

Buddy could not hear the wailing from Jason or the lock on the outside of the bedroom door being bolted. He didn't need too. He moved as fast as he could on the slippery driveway and got into his van. He sat there shaking—it wasn't from the cold.

He started the van and drove further down the road. He saw the empty truck. Tonight he would wait.

The Wee Hours of the Morning

Buddy pulled into his garage shortly after four a.m. He had waited in the cold of his van for the lights to go out. *Isn't there some way to save these boys?* His heart raced thinking of the abuse they must suffer every day. The lights had gone out as quickly as they had come on, but then he saw them come on again. He thought he heard a door slam, but he could see it wasn't the front door. He waited. Finally, the house light was turned off again. He pulled on his ski cap, went to the house, and found the door was closed but unlocked. *Just like I hoped—the boy was so scared he must have run to his room and she didn't think to lock it.* Buddy took care of business, unlocked the latch he found on the top of the door to the boys' room and snuck out of the house. He was a master at stealth—had been for years. The other truck was gone.

In spite of the heater, he was still shaking when he pulled into his garage. He took the small cooler from the back of the van and went through the kitchen straight out to the shed. He shut the door behind him before turning on the lights. He took a deep breath and let it out slowly. *I can't mess this up.*

He put on a second pair of latex gloves and carefully lifted the sample from the cooler and decided to use the electron microscope. The inheritance had allowed him to buy very high-end equipment. *Maybe this one will be the last. How come some of the women die and some don't?* He opened the other cabinets and saw that his supply of recent materials was really dwindling. *This has to stop.*

I hoped this new lead detective would figure it all out. Never going to happen—a woman!

Dawn Breaks

Quinn pulled up to the security gate at the back of the station shortly after six on Wednesday morning. She didn't get mail at her home and had gone by the post office to check her box and drop off the thank-you note to Bella Anderson. She was thinking about who she could ask about finding a plumber when she decided George would know. At the gate, she rolled down her window.

"Good morning. Any chance of an empty space in the back where I can park?"

The officer looked at her. "Detective Isaacs, right?"

She had her shield in her hand and held it up along with the ID around her neck. "One and the same."

"Thought I recognized you. You know you have a spot in front, right?"

"I do."

"Well, ma'am..." He tried to be discreet as he looked into the car.

Quinn put the other windows down. "I can open the trunk, as well."

He hesitated. "If you don't mind."

"Expect nothing less, officer." She popped the trunk.

He moved to the back and then shut the trunk. "Ma'am, the closest parking space is in the employee lot in the back. I could get someone to pick you up there."

"No need. I'll walk. Thank you, though."

The officer opened the gate and she followed the signs back to the employee lot. Her long legs moved quickly and she was half-way to the back door when George Marshall stepped out of his official car.

"Morning, Detective." She stepped up and was beside him in two steps.

"Morning." He looked around. "Decided to join the rest of us in the back?"

"Employee parking is for everyone, right?"

"What? You parked way back there?"

"Problem with that?"

They were almost at the back door. He pointed to the empty spot next to the one marked: Chief of Police. "That empty one next to Captain Brown should have the sign: 'Lead Detective.' It's been unoccupied for ten years."

"Thanks, George. I'll follow up on that. What brings you in so early?" They entered the back door into a small entry area where employees scanned their identification cards to get into the main part of the building.

George stopped and looked at her. "Just came from what's likely a murder scene."

Quinn stopped. "Likely? Who? Where?"

"On the outskirts of town. White, female, five-feet-seven, skinny as a rail, mother of two boys—they were in the house."

"Who called it in?"

"Oldest boy, Jason. He's twelve."

"Other child?"

"Jeremiah, age ten."

"Strangest thing. We arrived at the house and the boys had the living room light on and were sitting ramrod straight on the sofa with their hands folded in their laps."

"Circumstances?" They were almost to her office.

Detective Marshall turned to the door across the hall, unlocked the conference room door, flipped on the light, and pointed to the board. Quinn turned and followed him in, shut the door, and locked it.

"Okay, what's up?"

"There's a team working the house and child welfare services has the boys. I need to try and track down next of kin, if there's any to be found. Woman's name is Lizzie Andrews." He looked at the board on Mrs. Summers. Then he looked at Quinn.

"Quinn, I think she's going to be on this board."

"Why?"

"No signs of physical assault, but a somewhat freshly used condom was on the floor." He watched her.

"Just like Summers."

"Yep. Can Chuck run both of them? I think we need his expertise."

"He'll be in shortly. Is Dr. Walters on his way in? The body?" Quinn watched George pace.

"I suspect Doc is already here and I called out the techs to sweep the place and check the yard for footprints. They're finishing up preliminaries—should be here anytime now."

"Okay, let's get out of these coats and get to work."

The Morgue

"Morning, Tristan. Thanks for getting here so quickly."

"Sure, Doc. Busy with me gone yesterday? What's up?" Unlike his normal inappropriate jokes, Tristan sounded almost normal.

"Nothing I couldn't handle. Finished stabbing victim and woman who was brought in over the weekend—heart attack. Now ready to get to work?"

"You bet!" Tristan gave the ME his ghoulish smile.

"We had an unusual one Monday, but those remains went to the SBI lab in Knoxville."

"Really?" Tristan clapped his hands together loudly. "What was it? Why?" He emitted his sardonic laugh but stopped abruptly.

"Not our concern this morning. We have a new one." The ME pointed to the table on which a body was draped with a fresh white sheet.

"Okay, let me suit up." Tristan all but flew to his locker. He returned with fresh scrubs, his eye goggles and face mask.

Always amazed at how fast that boy can suit up. Doc Walters put out his hand to slow Tristan down. Tristan stopped at the tape which served as a two-foot mark to keep Tristan from touching the table.

"Recorders on." Both men turned on their recorders and the ME began to speak. "Visual scan of the deceased indicates…" He gave a thorough description of the body and all observable marks.

Tristan took photographs being careful not to cross the line on the floor. He started to lean in and the ME put his hand out.

"I see it. I'll take the picture." Doc took the camera from Tristan and photographed the barely visible gash and small patch of dried blood on the back of her neck. "No broken bones. We'll check for head trauma." The ME turned to hand Tristan the camera and was startled by the look on Tristan's face: eyeballs bulging and a glare that could cut steel.

"Look, Tristan, is it too early for you to do this? You can go clean the cold storage units and I can handle this."

Tristan snapped his head back. "No, I'm good, Doc. Keep going."

Dr. Walters turned back to the body and continued his examination. Tristan tried to lean in.

Doc put his hand out again. "Something about this victim that particularly interests you, Tristan?"

Tristan seemed agitated. Doc was used to his behaviors. *You're not my patient, Tristan, but I'd be willing to be you're on the autism spectrum—seems it's hard for you to understand boundaries.* Doc shook his head.

Updating the Board

Quinn and George, coffee mugs in hand, were laying out the reports from the technicians who had finished up at the Summers' residence.

"Any word from the SBI in Knoxville on Summers?" George's tone was even and unhurried as he sorted through the photos and drawings.

"Not yet. I had a text from Assistant Director Nelson that we should hear from them sometime today."

George whistled. "The SBI boss himself? You know him?"

Quinn continued to sort through papers and photographs as she spoke. "Worked a few cases with him in my former job." She left it at that.

"Helps to have connections in high places."

"Hope they treat all cases with dispatch." She made sure there was a lightness in her tone.

"I'm sure they do. Never had any direct dealings myself."

"You'll like Director Nelson—easy-going and a good team player."

"Really?"

"Really." Quinn kept her eyes on the evidence board, she assumed George's response was from his experience with the formalities of the Director's brother, the late Chief David Nelson.

The photos and drawings of the Summers backyard footprints were spread out on the table.

"Let's each choose our top three photos and drawings. We'll discuss each one and agree which ones go on the board."

"Sounds like a plan." George was studying the information and marveling at the ease with which Quinn was both attentive to the work and their working relationship. *Albright could have learned something from you.*

Quinn walked over to their board and looked at the earlier photographs to see which photo of the footprints had the most detail. She returned to the table and looked carefully at the ones taken after the high-powered lights were set up. She decided on her top three. Then she leaned against the wall reading the written report but glancing up occasionally to get a sense of how George worked. Her secure phone buzzed.

"Isaacs."

"Detective?"

She recognized Chuck's voice. "Morning, Chuck. Everything okay?" She looked at her watch and saw that it was seven-thirty a.m.

"Yes, ma'am. I'm here, are you?"

"I'm here. I'm across the hall in the conference room."

"What?" Chuck's voice conveyed disbelief.

"Come over."

"Be right there."

She held the door open as he stepped out of the lab they shared.

"Come in." She stepped aside and Chuck walked through the door and stopped dead in his tracks.

"Wow. I always thought this room was off-limits to everyone."

Hmmm...Do I want to know that? "This will be our work space for now—for this case."

"Good. I hated that everyone was brought into the lab..." He stopped when he saw George at the white board.

Quinn didn't miss a beat. "We're a team, Chuck. No need to rehash the past, just need to know what we can do going forward to maximize working conditions for all of us. Deal?"

"You bet." Chuck grinned from ear to ear.

George nodded.

"What's this case? What'd I miss?"

Quinn brought him up to date on Ms. Summers' remains being sent to the SBI lab.

"Man, I could have swung by there. Wish I'd known."

"Wish I'd thought to text you." Quinn watched his face when she said it.

"Oh, sorry. No criticism intended."

"None taken. There should be two condoms in your lab. One from the Summers' case and one from a body brought in this morning. Another female. Any problem with expediting them? We expect to have information from the techs at the scene of this second one before too long, but it would help if we know we're looking for the same guy for both murders."

"On it, boss...uh, Detective."

Quinn tried to figure out how to negotiate addressing each other so they could get on with the work. "George, Chuck."

Both men looked at her.

"Unless we are in a formal meeting or in public, could we go with first names...or last? Either is fine with me. You know I'm lead detective; I know I'm lead detective and I would like us to be a team."

Chuck spoke first. "I'm fine either way, too."

"First names are fine with me, too. I've been at the formality a lot longer than you two, so it may take me a while."

"Okay, that's settled. Chuck, can you get on that evidence?"

"On it, Quinn. Later, George."

"Later, Chuck."

Quinn let out a soft laugh when Chuck walked out of the room.

"What's funny?"

"Humans. Well, at least live ones. I just couldn't help wondering how long we'd all be dancing around the changes from one lead detective to another." She smiled at George as she picked up one of the photos.

"Trust me, there was no dancing before. It was more like marching. We'll adapt and we'll be a better department for it. Just give us time."

"10-4. Now, ready to decide on photos and drawings for the board?" She pulled her hair back into a ponytail and knotted it at the base of her neck.

They spent the next half hour looking at detail and discussing their reasoning for the photos they finally put on the board.

Quinn spoke while studying the board. "Mrs. Summers wasn't found until late night on Monday, but the time of death appears to be Sunday night. Did Doc give us an approximate time?"

George stood quietly for a few seconds. "No, he just seemed to think it was important to get the remains to the SBI lab. What are you thinking?"

"Maybe the killer was a frequent visitor who normally came in the front door and exited the back door because he knew the ATV was there. Earlier, I assumed the ATV was the killer's but it may have been the victim's and the killer knew where to find the key."

"Makes sense." George was nodding his head while looking at the footprints. "It would explain why we didn't find another set of prints. Any that might have been out front could have been wiped out by the husband and EMTs when they came to get the body." He continued nodding his head.

"Okay, let's see what the A-Team finds. We'll have electronic access to all of this and can…" Quinn trailed off as she looked around the room. "Guess we'll have to get electronics into this room."

George nodded. "Yep. Guess so." *Betting you'll have it done by end of shift.* "I need coffee. How about I check in with Doc Walters on the new DB?"

Quinn blinked. She hadn't heard DB in a while. She had always preferred it to "dead body."

"Sounds like a plan. Nothing more to do here for now. I'll check with Chuck on the evidence he's working. I also want to revisit the information on the shoe that was left on the officer's car Sunday night."

"You know how to reach me." George opened the door and waited for Quinn to exit. He turned out the lights and she stepped across the hall. He headed to the break room for coffee.

Chapter 10

Great difficulties may be surmounted by patience and perseverance.
Abigail Adams

Work to Do

Quinn sat at her desk, ran through a list of things to be done, and then prioritized them. She sent an e-message to Chief Hansen: "OK to move my parking to back?" Next, she pulled up the budget for the detective bureau and looked for a line item for technology. She let out a long low whistle. The only expenditure in five years out of a hundred-thousand-dollar line item for technology was for the new key pad door lock on the lab where her office was. She picked up her desk phone and dialed the Chief Administrative Officer.

"Brown, here."

"Good morning, Sir. Quinn Isaacs."

"Morning, Quinn. Something I can help with?"

She explained about the Chief giving permission to use the conference room and he listened. "We need access to technology in that room. There appears to be sufficient funds in the detective division budget. I would appreciate your help with protocol on how to utilize those funds."

"Chief Hansen has directed my office and the budget office to expedite anything you need up to twenty-thousand dollars—over that amount you will need to go to the Chief. Officer Gilbert is in charge of technology and he can help you. Anything else you need?" He was brief, but professional.

Quinn was stunned. It took her a moment to respond. "No, Sir. You've been most helpful. Have a nice day." She ended the call and stared at her computer screen. She opened the directory and found the number for Officer Gilbert.

"Gilbert."

"Quinn Isaacs here. Do you have a few minutes?"

"Absolutely, Detective Isaacs. How may I be of service?"

She explained the need for technology access in the conference room and they agreed to meet in thirty minutes. Quinn stood and stretched. *I forgot to ask George about a plumber.* She picked up her mug, walked into the lab, and saw Chuck bent over a microscope and decided not to disturb him. *He'll let me know when he has something.* She turned to walk out and realized she still had on her boots. She slipped in her office and changed to her loafers. Then she headed out to get coffee.

She was almost to the door of the break room when Officer Simmons stepped out.

"Morning, Detective. How are you today?"

"I'm well, Officer Simmons. You?"

"Just fine, ma'am. Catching up on some paperwork today."

"Thanks for your help yesterday at the scene. Really appreciate it."

"Here to serve, ma'am." He held the door for her.

"Oh, Officer, do you happen to know a plumber?" Just then her secure phone rang. She shrugged as she pulled it out of her pocket.

He started to give her Buddy's name.

She mouthed, "Sorry."

"No problem, ma'am." Simmons shut the door.

"Isaacs." She stepped back into the hall as there were other people in the break room and saw no one was in earshot.

"Williams."

"Oh, hey."

"Busy?"

"Just headed to get a cup of coffee and was about to ask one of the young officers if he knew a local plumber."

"Problems?"

"Nothing big—just a drip in my upstairs bathroom. It's driving me a bit crazy."

"Got a distant cousin over there who owns a plumbing company. I'd trust him to be in your home without you there. Want me to call him?"

"Oh, Billy. I'd really appreciate his name and number. I can call him though."

"Nonsense. I'll call him and you just tell me when you want him there."

"Billy, just give me the name and number. I can make the call." She unknotted her hair and ran the fingers of her left hand through it.

Disappointed, but not surprised at her independence, Billy gave her the name and number. "Matthew will do right by you."

"I have no doubt. Now, I think you have some amazing powers of deduction but I don't think you called because you knew I needed a plumber. What's up?"

"Just wanted to let you know we found the kid who stole the car from over there and have notified the owner of the car. The boy's in jail. Your detective was very helpful."

"Detective Marshall?"

"Yeah. Said he knew the family of the stolen car." He chuckled. "Said the boy who left the keys in the car is grounded for life."

"Well, hopefully it won't be that long, but maybe he learned a lesson. What's new in your world?" She watched as two officers came down the hall.

"Just counting the days until Saturday."

"How about we talk about that tonight?" She smiled and hoped it conveyed through the phone.

"What time?"

She laughed. "I'll call you when I get home. Have a good day, Detective."

"You, too, Detective."

She smiled and shook her head as she walked into the break room to get coffee. She slipped her phone into her pocket.

Her mug filled, she greeted the officers sitting at tables and walked out. Chief Hansen was walking toward her in the hall.

"Just stopped by the lab."

Quinn held up her mug. "How are you this morning, Chief?"

"Moving fast to stay ten steps behind."

"Then I won't keep you." Quinn continued walking expecting to pass the Chief.

As the came alongside each other, the Chief stopped. So did Quinn.

"Sign has been moved to the back. Your vehicle is expected Friday. You're free to park there now."

Quinn nodded. "Thank you."

"Needed to be done. Conference room working out?"

"Yes, ma'am."

"Good. I look forward to reading your reports. Have a good day, Detective."

"You as well, ma'am."

The two women walked in opposite directions. *Well, well. Needed to be done. Wonder what's behind that?* She put the code in the door and entered. Chuck was walking toward her.

"Detective..." he stumbled over the word, "Uh...Quinn. The Chief was just here. I didn't know if I should call you or what. She said she'd catch you later." The quiver in his voice was apparent.

"Chuck, pull up a stool." She pointed to the stainless steel tables and walked over to sit down, too.

"What? Did I do something wrong? Did she have a complaint about me?"

"We have a lot on our plates right now and need to focus on each of them, but I think the only way we can is if we clear the air. The Chief likely just wanted to take a walk and all she let me know is that I can now park in the back." Quinn smiled at him.

"In the back. That's good, right?" His face went pale.

"Yes." She watched him carefully. "I will listen to anything you want to share about your working conditions in the past, but you don't have to say anything. What I do need to know is this; if you had your ideal work situation, what would it be?"

Chuck stared at her. "Really? You really want to know?"

"I do." She smiled, hoping to ease his nerves. She would later think she had turned on a tap full force when she reviewed the speed at which things flowed from him.

"I'd like to be able to consult with the techs in the downstairs lab without having to bother you. I'd like two days in a row off once in a while; Wednesday and Thursday are good because most of the stuff happens around here on the weekend. I'd come in if you needed me, though. I need some newer more high-tech equipment, but Detective Albright said..." He trailed off and looked at her.

She just smiled. "Go on."

"These microscopes work fine. They're so old it wastes a lot of time trying to be accurate when the new photographic microscopes would be so much more accurate and faster." He stopped and looked at her again. "That's all."

"Thank you. I need you to do your job with as few encumbrances as possible. Has there been a problem with working with the other techs that you need permission?"

"Nope. Just the way it was done."

"Okay. I'll speak with the techs downstairs and I'll expect from now on you'll each communicate as you need. Just keep me informed."

"Will do." His enthusiasm was exceeded only by a child's joy on Christmas morning.

"I'll verify with Captain Brown, as I'm not an expert on personnel matters, and we'll work out the two days off plan. I'm meeting with Officer Gilbert in a few minutes…" There was a knock on the door to the lab. They both turned to see Officer Gilbert standing there. "Well, obviously I'm meeting with him now. If you know what technology you need, get it ready. Otherwise, I'll let him know we'll be getting him an order. That work?"

"Yes, ma'am." He jumped up to go to the door. "Okay to let him in?"

She laughed. "By all means. And, Chuck. Thanks for your honesty."

"You bet. Thank you." He opened the door and greeted Officer Gilbert.

The "SIC Plan"

Buddy was pacing in his kitchen. He had to finalize his plan. After all these years, he still couldn't figure out what his pappy meant when he said, "We have something in common." *Why wouldn't he ever tell me?* He circled the kitchen and then walked in a straight line from the sink to the kitchen door and back again—then he'd walk in a circle. Then, as quickly as the pacing started, it stopped. He headed out to the shed and once inside turned on his computer. He knew the electron microscope would have finished the analysis and he wanted to see the results. He was getting close. *I thought that lead detective might figure things out. He never did. Now there's some dumb woman as lead detective* and *one as chief.* He leaned forward and put his face in his cupped hands. *They can't even get the new stuff I get to them. How can I trust them to get the old stuff?* He rubbed his eyes with his palms and pushed back hard as the pain in his head shot through him.

The electron micrograph on his screen brought his attention back to the moment and he tried to ignore the pain. He refocused on the screen and a slow smile spread across his face. There it was. *Okay, detective. I've got it. I watched your team pull up and there's time for you to figure it out. You better be working fast. I don't have long.* He leaned back in his chair and like a tire deflating, his head dropped to his chest and he was fast asleep. There'd be no figuring out a plan this morning.

Technology Matters

"Officer Gilbert, Quinn Isaacs." She extended her hand. He shook it. "Let's step across the hall to the conference room."

Gilbert looked from her to Chuck and back again. "Okay. Don't think I knew there was a conference room up here."

Quinn unlocked the door across the hall.

"Hmmm…I always thought this was a storage room."

Quinn pointed to the lettering on the door.

"Well, yeah. Wouldn't be the first time a door was mislabeled or reused. Honestly, I never saw anyone use that door."

"Fair enough. It's now in use and the label on the door is inaccurate. That's for another day." She smiled at him. "We needed a place we could have our crime scene board and not interfere with the lab work. However, we need more than what's in here." She pointed to the boards: white, chalk, and cork.

Gilbert's laugh was infectious. "Welcome to the 1980s, Detective."

"Quinn. Quinn is fine."

"Sure, Quinn! Call me Gil."

Quinn knew many law enforcement officers used last names to address each other, but she didn't understand the undue attention he was giving to his. She gave him a quizzical look.

"Please don't make me show you my ID badge." He held it up and grinned: Horable Gilbert. "Blame my grandmother." His eyes rolled. "Folks just call me, Gil."

"Good enough, Gil." She tried to suppress a smile at his first name.

"Seeing this room makes me wonder how we ever solved any crimes here. Any better across the hall?"

She smiled. "No chalk boards over there."

Gil chuckled. "That's good." His voice shifted. "Please don't use the one here if we're about to put some high-tech equipment in place. That chalk dust is tough on electronics."

They talked for about thirty minutes on how to set up the room—placement of a computer, a screen, and how long it would take to run the wires.

"I've got wires in the ceiling, so it shouldn't take much to get an internet hub in here. I always have two computers set up ready to run in case something goes wrong with one someplace in the building. We can put up a portable screen for now and I'll work on one that we can mount if you're planning to use this long term. You do know it'll get billed to your department, right?"

"I do. What's the sticker shock?"

"What?" He looked at her. "Oh, how much?"

She nodded.

"Computer, screen, labor...all told, roughly five grand. Do you have that much?"

"We're good, Gil. How soon can you start?"

"Finishing up a new computer in the Chief..." he dropped off. "Sorry, I do know better. Have one job ahead of you. We'll get the wires dropped today and the computer up here. I've got an extra wall mount and could put the computer on that—it's an all-in-one unit. Then you wouldn't have to worry about it getting knocked off a smaller table or taking up room on this conference table."

"Sounds perfect. I'll either be in here or across the hall. Safe to assume your techies have security clearances? Hate to have to take down this board."

Gil looked at her with disbelief in his eyes. "You're joking, right?" He watched her face. "They could hack into every computer here; they damn well better have clearances."

"Just doing my due diligence, Officer." She looked back at him with a laser stare.

"No offense intended, ma'am."

"None taken." She headed for the door. "Now if you have time, Chuck needs some equipment, too."

They walked into the lab and Chuck jumped up with a piece of paper in his hand. Quinn looked over it and asked, "That will work for now?"

"Yes, ma'am." Chuck nodded excitedly.

She handed the paper to Gil. "Estimate?"

"Give me ten minutes?"

"No problem. Thanks for your time and the prompt response, Gil. Look to hear from you in ten. Come back anytime." She smiled and extended her hand.

"Pleasures all mine." He smiled back. *I underestimated you, lady. Won't happen again.*

Quinn turned to Chuck when the door shut. "Chuck, I've been meaning to ask you why that lamp comes on at odd times?"

Chuck bit on his bottom lip. "Well," he hesitated, "I have it set to random times so that I don't get so focused that I actually lose concentration. When it turns on or off it's just a little distraction."

"Clever. I was just curious." She nodded at him and turned to walk into her office.

Quinn called the number Billy Williams had given her for his cousin Matthew who was a plumber. He offered to meet her at her home at seven in the morning. She put it on her calendar and had just opened the email from Officer Simmons when there was a tap on her door frame. She saw the words, "plumber" and "Buddy" on the screen as she turned to Gil.

"Quinn," Gil waited for her to acknowledge him. "Hope I wasn't over the line earlier. Just got carried away that we have a lead detective who actually knows why we need technology."

"We're good. Can you help Chuck?"

"No problem. It'll take about three thousand to get him the quality he needs. Of course, we could spend fifty and really make this a class-A lab."

She laughed. "I'm sure we could. However, this week we'll start with the three thousand. I'm still learning the ropes here, so is it safe to assume I'll get invoices to approve?"

"Yep, that's the way it works. The sooner we have them signed the sooner we go to work."

"Electronic signatures?"

"Woohoo, a twenty-first century detective. I'm on it. Later." He stepped back to leave, then leaned back into her office. "Oh, and Quinn, welcome aboard."

"Thanks."

She sat back and took a sip of her now cold coffee. "Ugh." She pushed it to the side.

A Visit to the Morgue

"Meet in the morgue?" The text was from George Marshall.

"Now?"

"Yep"

She walked out to the lab. "Chuck." She waited til he looked up. "I'll be in the morgue with Detective Marshall if you need me."

"Okay, boss." He grinned.

She emptied the cold coffee into the lab sink, rinsed it out, and decided not to think about whatever else might have been in that sink. She also decided not to use it again. Then she stopped walking.

"Something wrong, boss?"

"Quinn." It slipped out of her mouth.

"Right, sorry. Something wrong, Quinn?"

"No, just trying to figure out how my thinking could be so mixed up."

"Something I can help with?"

"No." She chuckled. "Thanks all the same." She headed to the door. *Lab sink, bathroom sink, breakroom sink. All the same—lots of germs and lots of evidence.*

She knocked on the door at the bottom of the stairs and was startled when it was jerked open and Tristan was standing there.

"Detective Isaacs, I believe. Welcome to our dungeon." Tristan wiggled his eyebrows at Quinn and reached out to stroke the top of her hand.

What was he going to do? Stroke my hand? My face? She pulled back a step.

"Tristan." The ME's voice had a harsh edge as he dragged out the name.

"Sorry, Doc." Tristan shrugged at Quinn and rolled his eyes.

Quinn decided not to extend her hand. He had his left hand on the door and his right one behind his back.

"Nice to meet you officially, Tristan."

"Pleasures mine, dear lady."

"Detective, will do nicely, thanks." *Now why did I say that? Not the first odd behavior I've encountered.* She decided to let it go as she saw Dr. Walters' nod. She assumed it was in response to her comment.

"Good morning, Dr. Walters." She nodded. "What do we have?"

The ME used a stainless steel instrument to point to the mark on the back of the neck. "I think she needs to go to Knoxville, too."

Quinn nodded, stepped over to a corner, and took out her secure phone. This time she reached the special-agent-in charge at the State Bureau. As she turned, she noticed Tristan leaning toward her. She moved toward the ME's office.

"Jackson."

"Sir, Quinn Isaacs here."

"Detective Isaacs, I hear. Congratulations. How may I be of service?"

"We have another DB and similar MO to the Summers woman. Checking..."

"Time of Death?"

"Early hours of the morning."

"I'll send a helicopter. Need to get it here ASAP. That work?"

"Yes, sir. Is that really necessary?"

"We'll have a report to you shortly, but I'd say we need to get this one and hope we can find what we need."

"Yes, sir. I don't know where you land a helicopter over here."

"On your roof. Doc will know. Later, Quinn."

"10-4. Thank you, sir." The call was already ended.

Quinn turned to George and the ME. "Get her ready for a copter ride."

Tristan's arms were flapping. He was hyperventilating.

"Tristan. Go clean up the back room." The ME stared at Tristan. "Now."

Tristan's shoulders drooped like a deflated balloon. He headed off looking back over his shoulder at the victim on the table.

Quinn watched him go. *I need to come back and talk to Dr. Walters about how to interpret and manage Tristan.* She turned as she saw Dr. Walters moving toward his office.

As soon as George entered, Dr. Walters closed the door. "They'll be here in about fifteen minutes so I need to get to work. I assume they found something on Summers?"

"Agent Jackson just said we'd have the report shortly. He was insistent about getting the body there ASAP."

"Good. Chemicals can dissipate quickly if the person using them knows what they're doing."

Quinn nodded. "If the person did know, why the marks?"

"Can't control how a body will react to an injection. On some folks, nothing shows. On others you'll get hives, others bruise quickly..." He stopped abruptly. "If you'll excuse me, I'll get things ready. George, can you stay and help me get her up to the helipad?"

"I'll leave you gentlemen to it. Thanks, Doc." She turned to the elevator and then turned to walk to the stairs. "George, if you have time when you finish…"

"I'll stop by." George nodded at her.

The two men moved toward the table with the body of their latest victim—Lizzie Andrews.

Quinn stopped and watched the men, twisted her hair back into a knot, and headed back towards the stairs. *Two or three?*

Chapter 11

Pay attention to what you pay attention to.
Amy Krouse Rosenthal

Let's Call It a Day

The final email of the day read; Quinn turned when she heard the knock on the outside door—a few feet from her office. She started to stand but saw Chuck headed to the door.

"Thanks, Chuck."

"It's George."

"Any reason not to give him the code?" Quinn's question carried the tone of trust she was trying to build with Chuck.

"None I can think of. You're the boss."

That I am. Just wish I knew why the former lead detective was so strict and why he left so abruptly. "Then I'll take care of it, Chuck. Thanks."

"Hey, George. She's in her office." Chuck turned and walked back to the lab table where he was working on the condoms found at the scenes of the two murders—they were hopeful that DNA would lead them to the potential murderer.

"Anything new, Quinn?" George stood in her doorway.

"Detective Marshall, do come in."

George looked at her and wondered what he had done that she shifted to the formal address. "Yes, ma'am."

"Sorry, not much space in here." Quinn pointed to the one chair that fit snugly into the corner of her office behind her own desk chair. "Since

I am about to give you confidential information, just wanted to make this a bit more official than our earlier conversations."

George looked around the small office and saw that it was cleaner than the last time he was here with the former lead detective. *That was what…three years ago?* He liked the coat tree and the bragging wall that had only pictures of Quinn with her family members and her University of Tennessee diplomas. He was quite sure she probably had plenty of accolades from her time in Immigration Enforcement, but apparently didn't need to put that in other people's faces. He liked that.

"Detective?" Quinn wondered what had distracted him.

"Oh, sorry. Yes?"

"The code to this lab is 7734. It's for your use only."

His eyes widened and a smile started across his face. "Understood." Then he started to chuckle.

"Something tickle your funny bone?" Quinn cocked her head.

"Sorry. Did you set up the code?"

"No. Chuck did. He said that Detective Albright told him to choose something he would remember. Why is that funny?"

"May I?" He reached for a pencil and piece of paper from her desk. He wrote the four numbers in block form and then flipped the paper upside down. "Old joke."

Quinn grinned. "Well, well, that's one I didn't know. Good job, Chuck." She turned to George. "I'm glad to know Chuck has a sense of humor." She glanced at the block letters spelling "hELL."

George chuckled. "I love it." His eyes turned serious. "Thanks for the trust, Quinn."

She waved a hand dismissively. "Need to know someone besides me can get to Chuck if he ever needs help." She didn't skip a beat. "Now let's see if we can wrap up this day."

They chatted for several minutes and agreed that they would bring fresh eyes tomorrow. They expected to have the report from the A-team and hopefully the preliminary reports from the SBI on the two DBs they had in their possession.

"Anything else you can think of, George?"

"Nope. Been a long day for you."

"You, too."

"Used to it."

"Me, too. Doesn't mean we shouldn't be satisfied with a twelve-hour day and head home."

"Works for me." He stood. "See you in the morning, Quinn."

"Good night, George. Get some rest. Something tells me this is bigger than we might realize on the surface."

He nodded as he walked toward the door. She heard him chuckle as he turned the door knob.

Quinn took her coat off the rack and stepped into the lab. "Time to call it day, Chuck."

"Yep. I've got a bit more to do here and then I'm gone, too. Have a nice night."

"You, too." Suddenly she remembered that her car was in the back parking lot. She hurried to the door. "George?" She looked down the hall. She was going to take him up on his offer from earlier in the day and get him to drive her out to what people called the "back-forty." *Oh, well, the walk will do me good.*

Home, Food, and Phone Calls

Quinn backed into her garage and closed the overhead door. She never got out of her car until the garage door was closed, and she was confident there were no unexpected visitors following her in. *I can think of one unexpected visitor I wouldn't mind seeing.* At that moment her personal mobile phone rang. She saw the name and smiled, in spite of her disappointment that it wasn't Billy—the visitor she would have welcomed. She'd call him after she ate.

"Hey, Mother. How are you tonight?"

"I'm well, my daughter. How are you?"

"Tired, but loving the challenges of my new job. How was your day?"

"Lovely. Classes start next week, so I'm enjoying these first few un-hurried days of the new year. I won't keep you."

Quinn knew that was the lead into something her mother wanted from her—usually in the form of a personal appearance. "No problem, Mother. Always nice to chat with you." She decided she was not going to open the door for the request that was surely coming.

"Well, dear. I know you're really busy with your new job and all, but I assume they give you time off, right?"

Quinn rolled her eyes. She loved her mother but so often wished she could just relax a little and have a normal conversation. "Of course, Mother. What do you need?"

"Need? Oh, nothing, really. I was just hoping you could come to dinner on Saturday and maybe bring that fine young man, Mr. Williams."

"What's the occasion, Mother?" She knew there would be no idle chit-chat. Her mother would get straight to the point.

"We don't normally have new faculty in the second semester, but we have a Fulbright exchange scholar from Spain. His lovely wife is here, too. They are close to your age and I thought they might just be more comfortable at dinner with another young couple."

Her mother's emphasis on "another young couple" was not lost on Quinn. *So, now you're playing matchmaker, Mother?*

"May I get back with you? I think I can come, but I will need to see if Billy is available to join us." Quinn prayed that they would be far enough along on the current cases that she could get free to go Saturday evening. "I'll also need to check the weather forecast." She paused. "In any event, if I can make it, I'll need to get back right away."

"Oh, Quinn, honey, please spend the night. You can travel back on Sunday after breakfast. Please."

"Thanks for the invitation, Mother. I'll make every effort to be there, and I'll let you know if I'll have a guest or not no later than tomorrow. That work?"

"Perfectly. Thanks, my lovely daughter. Oh, and tell Mr. Williams it's casual dress."

Quinn smiled to herself. *Right, Mother. You might die of shock at what Billy and I would call casual.* "Give my love to Daddy. I'll confirm as soon as I can talk to Billy. Good night, Mother. I love you."

"Sweet dreams, Quinn. I love you, *mi hija.*"

Quinn did love it when her mother used Spanish terms of endearment. The phone call clicked off. Quinn held the phone out, looked at it, and then slipped it in her pocket. She was still standing in the garage.

Her boots by the door, her slippers on, and her coat hung up, Quinn put her service weapon and shield in the gun safe. She opened the refrigerator to decide on a reasonably healthy supper. She ended up pulling out a stool at the kitchen counter. She sat down—she was tired. Her shoulders slumped and she wondered if she could do this job. *Working with the team…*her thoughts wandered. She couldn't figure out what had put her mood in the dumps. She could not remember the last time she'd had a personal pity party—it had been years. She undid her knotted hair and ran her fingers through it and then turned her head from side to side.

*Why do I keep trying to figure out what happened in the past at the Round City Police Department? Why can't I just focus on…*drip, drip, drip. She lifted her head toward the ceiling, then stood and ran upstairs to shut off the tub faucet, hopefully for the last time. *The plumber will be here at seven in the morning. Thank, God.*

She was at the top of the stairs when the doorbell rang. She was not expecting anyone. She saw the porch light had come on with the motion detector and her phone would show who was at the door, but she didn't bother to look. She went down the stairs and straight through the living room to the door. She looked through the peephole as she unlocked the deadbolt.

"Well, well. To what do I owe this pleasure?"

"Going to be that kind of evening?" Billy Williams pulled the storm door back as she unlocked it, lightly grabbed her hand, pulled her to him—and kissed her.

She returned the kiss with a longing not missed on him. She stepped back, cleared her throat, and smiled. She stared over his shoulder at a slow-moving vehicle on the street.

"Where *are* my manners? Do come in." Her southern drawl was dripping like honey. She took his overcoat as he took it off and hung it on the hall tree.

"Had to come over on business; it finished later than I thought and took a chance..."

She took his hand and headed toward the kitchen flipping on the switch which controlled the lamps in the large great room off the kitchen. "If you'll grab that remote, you can turn on the fireplace. Have you eaten?"

"Today? Or lately?" Billy loved to tease.

"Since midday?" Her tone was clipped and purposely formal. She could give as good as she got.

"Should have called and offered to bring something over. I'm sure *you* probably have not eaten."

"You would be right. But, hey, you're a detective." She laughed. "I'm hungry and was going to make a salad. Enough for you on a cold winter's night?"

"Whatever works for you. How can I help?"

"Sit and talk to me about something other than detective work."

Billy pulled out a stool at the kitchen counter and looked at her. "I'd rather help."

She shook her head. "If you insist, then do something useful. I'll have cabernet. Help

yourself."

He had been here before and knew not to open the cabinets directly behind him. They held the formal dishes her mother had bought. He walked over to the cabinets with her everyday glasses and took out a wine glass and beer mug.

He handed her a glad and made a toast. "To pleasant surprises in the middle of the week."

"Oh, you know how this night is going to end?" She lifted her glass and clinked his beer mug.

I know how I would like *this night to end, but I'm a patient man...But if your kiss is any indication, I don't know how much longer I can be patient.* He just smiled and lifted his glass.

"Come on, let's sit in my great room..."

"I invite you into my parlor..."

"Enough! I surrender. No more jokes for the moment." Quinn picked up the tray with the plates and bread. She pointed to her glass with her elbow. "Please."

"Happy to oblige." Billy took their glasses and followed her. They sat at the small game table near the fireplace in her great room. The salad with lettuce, tomatoes, carrots, kalamata olives, cubed ham and tossed with an Italian dressing, was hearty and the loaf of French bread on the cutting board he had taken down tore apart easily.

"Continental style," Quinn held up the torn bread—relieved it wasn't stale.

Billy studied her face. "Bad day at the office?"

"Nope. Bad night at home."

"Ah, maybe the damsel is lonely in the tower of her castle?"

"Not anymore." She lifted her wine glass, winked at him, and sipped the cabernet. "You have saved me from a pity party—which are generally better self-indulged."

"Oh, I don't know. Distraction can be a great antidote to self-pity. Why the mopes?"

"How long do you have?"

"Forever. Or until I get a call to fight crime—whichever comes first."

Quinn laughed. "Thanks, Billy. I needed that. Shall we try again?"

"Try what? Making you laugh?"

"No, the distraction."

To her surprise, he abruptly stood, moved over to her and pulled her to her feet. The kiss and the embrace were promises of things to come she had dreamed about.

"Wow. Thanks. I needed that."

"Pleasure is all mine. Feel better?"

"Getting there. Delighted you stopped by. I was going to call when I finished eating."

"You really are Spanish—eating this late." He gestured to her chair and she sat.

He returned to his.

"Purely circumstantial..."

"What?"

"You commented that I was eating late. It has nothing to do with being Spanish, although I am—well, fifty percent anyway. Speaking of my parents..."

"Oh, were we?" Billy raised his left eyebrow.

"Well, we weren't..."

"I think I need a map to keep up with this conversation. I'm a pretty simple guy and it's late, as you know because I just knocked on your door..."

"Okay, okay. Let's start over. First, thanks for stopping by. You are definitely the antidote I needed. Now...about the rough evening..." She looked at him as he took a bite of bread. "I need to ask, on behalf of my parents, if you'd consider accompanying me to dinner at their home on Saturday. They are..."

"Yes!" He didn't let her finish.

"Wow, I didn't even tell you why."

"No need. If it guarantees I'll get to see you—and I've kinda figured out that you *do* honor your parents' requests—I'm in."

She knew he meant it.

"Hmmm...you know how to get to a woman's heart—please her parents."

"Whatever works." He paused. "Seriously, tell me how to dress and how to behave and I'm with you. In the meantime, tell me how I can help you cheer up from the mopes."

"You already have. I think I was struggling with how to honor my parents and at the same time help them understand that I don't get to control my time like they do."

"That the only thing bothering the new lead detective?"

She hesitated. "No, but maybe we could leave it for our drive on Saturday. It's not pressing, and it does in fact have to do with being a lead detective. So, I'd greatly appreciate perspective from the best lead detective I know."

"Well, I'll just say two things now. Since I might be the only lead detective you know, it may be faint praise."

"Ouch!"

"And, second, just remember that free advice is worth what you pay for it." He laughed. "Lighten up, Quinn. I'm sure you're off to a great start, and there's nothing in this job that you can't learn. Let's eat."

Quinn smiled in the dim glow of the lamps and fire. She liked this man—personally. And she respected him—professionally. "Thanks, Billy. You *are* the perfect antidote for my mopes. It can wait until Saturday."

As they finished eating, his voice was soft and gentle. "What's the dress code? I may need time to prepare."

Quinn started laughing. "Seriously?!" She couldn't stop laughing.

"What? Don't think I can dress right for your parents? I have jeans, a plaid shirt, and cowboy boots." Billy knew her laughter was a letting go of whatever was bothering her. He let her laugh.

She laughed harder. Then she sputtered, caught her breath, and said, "Give me a minute." She sipped her wine. "My mother said, 'the dress is casual.'"

"Well, see. I told you I know how to dress."

"I'm in if you promise to have your phone out to dial 9-1-1 when my mother sees us dressed that way."

"Got it. No jeans. Suit and tie?"

"Jacket, slacks, no tie." Her voice faltered.

He heard the unspoken apology.

"Jacket, slacks, no tie, it is. Let me know what time to pick you up. We could go to K-town early and enjoy the sights."

"Knoxville sights are much more interesting in the spring and summer. I'll confirm a time after I make my mother's day tomorrow when I tell her you can come—after all, she's the one who asked for your presence." She let that hang in the air.

"So, that bribe I gave her at Christmas finally pays off."

Quinn smiled as they cleared the table. She knew Billy loved to joke around and it had proven to be just what she needed. The dishes in the dishwasher, Quinn turned to walk back into the great room.

"As much as I hate to leave a damsel in distress, I have to return to the Valley. Besides, it's late and you have had a long day." He headed toward the front door.

Quinn saw a slow-moving vehicle going in the opposite direction from earlier. "Are the roads icy?"

"Nope, cleared and dry. I'll be safe. I promise—I have a date on Saturday." He watched to see her reaction to the word: date.

She leaned in and kissed him. "Then make sure you're ready for the challenge."

"Challenge." He pulled back and looked into her eyes.

"Oh, you'll manage my parents just fine. Mother is enamored with you. Can't promise her daughter is as easily tamed."

He smiled, pulled her into a passionate kiss, stepped back and out the door as he winked at her. "I welcome the challenge. Good night, Quinn. See you soon." He turned and was down the steps and into his SUV.

Quinn started to shiver and closed the storm door, waved and stepped back to close the front door. She turned toward the living room and leaned back on the door. *Oh, yeah, Billy Williams. You are the perfect antidote for what ails me.*

Out for a Drive

Buddy drove slowly past the address listed for Quinn Isaacs, the new lead detective in town. He had found the address by hacking into the property records for the city. *In this day and age they need better security. Anyone with decent techie skills can find the cops, even with their names not being tied to their property on public access records.* On his third pass down her street, he was wondering how she could live in such an expensive home. *Her husband must be rich for her to live like that.* He turned toward home focused on how he was going to handle the most recent evidence he was going to give the cops. He slammed on his brakes. *Wait. There was no husband listed on the property.* He sat there while he thought about that fact—she lived alone in that big house. *How did I miss that on the property record?* He knew he was too good at details to have ignored that piece. *No wonder my head hurts.*

He pulled into his garage and went through his ritual of putting his plumbing signs on the shelf. He had put them on while he did his surveillance so that anyone who noticed his multiple passes on the street would assume he was looking for a job he was headed to do. He entered the house, went to the sink and washed his hands, turned off the timer on his hall and bedroom lights since it would be obvious if anyone were watching that he'd just come home. He took a can of soup out of the cupboard, put it in a bowl, and heated it in the microwave.

His soup finished and his bowl cleaned and put away, he went through his ritual of going out to his shed. While he waited for his eyes to adjust, he sat down and rubbed his ankle. The pain was always the worst in cold weather. *Pappy never liked it when I said my ankle hurt.* He closed his eyes as he heard the voice of his pappy in his head; "You don't know what pain is, boy. Toughen up." He leaned back in the chair and tried to push the pain out of his mind. Then he remembered he had turned off the kitchen light without resetting the timer for the hall and bedroom to come on. He pulled out his phone and turned them on in order. Then he turned off the hall light but decided to leave the bedroom light on. He stood and walked to the drying cabinet. There were only sixty minutes left on the timer. He tried to remember what material he had put in there. His head and his ankle hurt. Finally, he turned on his computer and looked at his inventory to see what was in the drying machine. He sat back—convinced that if the cops couldn't figure out this evidence, he was going to have to take a whole different tack. *That new lead detective is probably dumb as a rock—like most women—as Pappy used to say.* He winced at the pain in his head.

End of the Day

Quinn stepped out of the shower and wrapped her hair in a towel. She pulled her soft comfortable robe tightly around her and looked in the full-length mirror at the end of her room sized walk-in closet. Even though she had worked out in her home gym this morning, she wondered if she needed to start planning a night workout—just to get rid of the stress. *Maybe I'll try that tomorrow night—fifteen minutes with the new video workout.* She nodded to her reflection in the mirror. *But...Billy Williams, you could be a much better stress reliever...*

Her feet tucked under her in the large leather arm chair in her bedroom, Quinn leaned her head back and reviewed her day. *Wonder why I read in my wing back chair and use this one to think?* She shrugged and started to review the specific crimes they were trying to solve, and the administrative tasks she had accomplished, she decided that she had actually made some progress—especially in building trust with George and Chuck. Chief Hansen was supportive and clearly a sharp cop, and from what Quinn had observed she was a strong leader. Quinn had already learned some things about leadership from the Chief that she had never observed with her boss at Immigration Enforcement—like leading by example.

And the highlight of my day was Billy's visit. She smiled as she thought through the easy banter and the genuine concern for her that came through from him—without him being sloppy in giving the platitudes that too many men she'd encountered in her dating life thought were the "way to a girl's heart." She wanted mutual respect, trust, interesting conversation, and...*what? What do I want in a relationship?* She closed her eyes and smiled as she realized she had already listed what she wanted—along with love and great sex. *And if Billy's attention tonight is any indication...Yep, that'll do it.* She stood, threw her robe across the end of her bed and crawled into it looking forward to a time when she wouldn't be in it by herself.

Chapter 12

The ability to learn is the most inspiring quality a leader can have.
Sheryl Sandberg

Plumber Arrives

Quinn sat at her kitchen counter at six-forty-five a.m. She'd completed a vigorous workout, some target practice with her new virtual reality police simulator program, showered, and dressed. As she waited for Matthew, Billy's distant relative who was a plumber, her eyes looked around her large kitchen. *I may really need to figure out my conflict about wealth: I tell myself I don't need it, but then I live in this house and love that I can afford to buy things like that new virtual reality system.* As she walked to the front door in response to the doorbell, she made a mental note to check the date for her next official range qualifier. *Better add that I like the luxury of seeing who is at the door with my doorbell monitor.*

"Good morning" She smiled as she opened the door. "I'm Quinn. Thanks for coming on such short notice."

"Yes, ma'am. Happy to be of help."

"Have to ask you to humor me. May I see your identification."

Matthew cleared his voice uncomfortably. "Yeah, sure. It's in my truck. Billy told me you'd ask. Sorry." He turned to walk to his truck.

Quinn stopped him. "Don't worry about it. Old habits die hard."

"Given what I've heard about you, I think I'm the one who has to be worried." He grinned sheepishly.

"Billy telling tales out of school, is he?"

"No. Not really. He just said you were a pretty bad-ass cop." He turned white as a sheet. "Please don't tell him I said that."

Quinn cocked her head.

"He'll tell my mom and it won't matter that I'm thirty-five, she'll whoop my behind for saying such a thing to a lady."

"Then it will be our little secret. Come this way." She watched as he stepped out of his boots on the porch and slipped on cloth booties over his socks. She was impressed. She took him to the upstairs bathroom.

She leaned against the wall in the hall and watched him—impressed that he put a piece of canvas on the floor before setting his tool bag on it.

Finally, he turned to her. "Here's the culprit, ma'am. The shower valve has O-rings, you know just like the Challenger shuttle? They wear out over time. How old is this valve?"

"The bathroom was remodeled when I got the house almost ten years ago. Should I have known to have them replaced?"

"Does this shower get used much?"

"Rarely."

He nodded his head. "Well, sad to say, lack of use is just as much a problem as too much. The O-rings can dry out and crack."

"Remedy?"

"Replace the O-rings is simplest. But, honestly, no offense, ma'am, I hope you didn't pay the plumber too much for this work." He turned back to the tub.

"Problem?"

"Not a very high-quality valve."

"Have a good one on that truck of yours?"

He looked over his shoulder. "I carry a good quality mid-range one— that's what most folks are willing to pay for. I can get a top quality one at the plumbing supply that will hold up to lots of use or none at all."

"Then let's put in what you have on the truck, you get what you need to do it right, and we'll replace the one you put in today." She smiled.

Then the smile vanished as she felt a pang of guilt as the wealth demon rose up in her. *Sure, because I can afford it.*

He sat back on his heels. Then he stood and looked at her eyeball to eyeball.

Quinn saw a strong resemblance between him and Billy and admired the confidence in his gaze.

"Uh, ma'am. I'd have to charge you for both the valves and both visits."

"That's fine. Would you be able to use the one you put in today for someone else after removing it to put in the higher quality one?"

"Well, I suppose." He hesitated. "Not in the habit of providing used equipment to folks." He blushed.

"Ever do work for folks who can't afford to have it done?"

"Sure. Of course I do. They choose the lowest end valve I'm willing to put in."

"Then how about you give it to someone who would benefit from having the better model and tell them it was donated. That work?"

"Well, sure. Never done that before, but..." he hesitated again; his gaze averted. "Listen, ma'am, since the bathroom isn't used much, the easiest thing is to just leave the water off up here while I go get the new valve."

"How long will that take?"

"To go get it, come back and install it...two hours give or take. I could just come another day if that's easier for you."

Quinn thought about her time this morning and having to make another appointment anytime soon with him to come back. *Bird in the hand, and all that.* "If it's all the same to you, let's just put in the valve you have on the truck and you get the new one and put it in when we can find a good time."

"Okay, ma'am." *Your money.* "I'm sure there's sure plenty of folks who'd appreciate getting an unused valve." Then he nodded his head and smiled at her. "That'll be fine. Just fine."

She knew the mountain double speak meant he had relaxed. "Good. Then I'll go do some work I need to do in my office downstairs, and when you finish put both valves and both visits on the bill. That way you can just come install the new one when you can work me in." She knew she'd let him be in the house without her if needed and didn't want to worry about him being paid promptly.

Matthew followed her downstairs and went toward the front door. He stopped. "Ma'am, would you prefer I come in the back door?"

"You're fine, Matthew. Just call out when you're finished."

"Sure thing. It will take a little over an hour to do it right."

"Then do it right." She smiled and turned toward her office. The first thing she did was send a text to Chuck: Tks for coming in today. In by 10 or update. Call if u need me.

At eight-fifteen a.m., she heard Matthew call out. "Detective Isaacs?" It startled her. She had not told him she was a detective. *Ahhh…Billy. Of course Billy would have told him.* He was standing in the front hall.

"All done, ma'am."

"Let me get my checkbook."

"No rush. You can send it to me." He chuckled. "I know where to find you."

She laughed lightly. "That you do, but this way it won't get piled up on my 'to do' list." She raised her eyebrows.

"I hear you. Happens to me, too. Thank you, ma'am. When do you want to put in the other valve?"

She looked at her watch. It was Thursday morning. "Any chance you work Saturday mornings?" She walked toward the kitchen where her checkbook was. He followed her.

"Most weeks I end up putting in seven days. Saturday morning is fine. What time works for you?"

"You're the one with a schedule on that day. You tell me." She watched his shoulders relax.

"Then let's both have a second cup of coffee. How about I'm here by eight-thirty and out of your way by ten at the latest. I want to do a good finish job on a tile that popped loose."

"Eight-thirty Saturday it is." She took the bill and wrote the check.

Matthew leaned over the paper and marked "paid" on it, put the check number on the bill, and signed it. He pulled her copy of the bill and tucked his copy on his clipboard.

She extended her hand. "Thanks, Matthew. I appreciate your prompt and professional attention. I'll see you Saturday."

"Yes, ma'am. See you then." He turned and was out the door quickly.

She locked the front door and opened the curtains. A van moved slowly down the street and she noticed it too was a plumber's van—the magnetic signs read: "Plumbing Services."

Guess I'm not the only one needing a plumber today. She walked to the kitchen, took her service weapon out of the gun safe, and pulled on her coat over her suit jacket. She was out the door, into her boots, and down her driveway when the van she'd seen earlier stopped just past her house.

The driver got out and was walking toward the back of the van and her driver's window. Later she would wonder why she reached down and unsnapped her weapon guard. The man waved and leaned over to look in her window as she lowered it.

"May I help you?"

"Just looking for this address. Know where it is?" His eyes studied her carefully. Then he averted his gaze.

She looked at the scribbled house number and the more carefully written street name: 1213 Sunrise. 1213 was one house number off from hers in many neighborhoods, but because she and her neighbors each owned two lots, they jumped by four—her neighbors were 1207 and 1215. There was a city park across the street. She studied his face—his eyes were a penetrating blue.

"Sorry, I think you must have been given an incorrect address. There is no such number on this street. Do you know the name of the person?"

The man shrugged. "Forgot to write that down. Mostly just need addresses in my line of work—wrong number must be why I couldn't find it. Sorry to bother you, ma'am. You have a good day now." He winced—closed his eyes tightly and then opened them again.

Quinn waited for him to return to his van. She memorized the license plate as she reached down and resnapped her gun guard. She made a mental note that the man was roughly six feet tall, fit, and had penetrating blue eyes. *Where have I seen those eyes before?*

Watchful Eye

Buddy drove to the end of the street, turned the corner, pulled over and parked. He pounded his fists on the steering wheel and lowered his head on top of his hands. The headache was excruciating.

The tap on his window startled him.

Quinn Isaacs was standing there. He turned his head and her vehicle was in front of his. He slowly rolled down his window.

"Sir, are you okay?" Quinn's voice was calm.

"Yeah." He sounded almost drunk.

"Do you need me to call an ambulance."

"No, no. I'm fine. Just annoyed that I wrote that address wrong. Means I lost a job and probably a new customer." His words slurred a little less as he talked.

She pulled her badge off the belt of her slacks. "I'm Detective Isaacs with the Round City Police. May I see your license, please?"

Pappy had taught him years ago to keep his license on his visor. He'd said there were too many trigger-happy cops in the world. He reached to the clip that secured it, took it down, and handed it to her.

She read the name on it: Buddy Wilkie.

"Mr. Wilkie, please give me a minute." She walked to her car without thinking about being in her own vehicle—no computer to check his license. She got in her car anyway and called dispatch.

"Detective Isaacs?" The dispatcher was prompt in recognizing the incoming number.

"Yes. I need a license checked and an officer to meet me at the southeast corner of Sunrise and Primrose. Suspected DUI." She gave the dispatcher the license number.

"Officer enroute." A few seconds later she said, "ETA two minutes. License clean."

"10-4." She hung up and got out of the car just as the officer turned the corner. *That was a fast two minutes.*

Officer Simmons left his flashing lights on and stepped out of his vehicle. "Morning, Detective. What's the problem here?"

"This man may be impaired. His speech is slurred and he stopped me in front of my house to ask for directions to an address that doesn't exist. He has been cooperative and a run on his license is clean."

"It's Buddy, ma'am. He's a friend of mine. He's a bit strange at times, but harmless. Since I know him, would you rather I get another officer?"

Quinn remembered the email from Simmons: Plumber...Buddy...

"I assume you can be objective, Officer Simmons. We all encounter people we know in our line of work."

Albert nodded. "Yes, ma'am. Want to handle it or want me too?"

She was interested to see how a local officer in her new employment handled a stop. "Go right ahead. I've got your back."

Albert walked up to the van. Buddy had the window down.

"Morning, Buddy. You doing okay?"

"Yeah. You?" The slurring was still present.

"Fit as a fiddle. Need you to step out of the van for me."

Buddy complied. "Albert, I just have a terrible headache. Sorry to bother the good detective there. She was real nice when I asked for help with this address." He held out the paper.

"No such number, Buddy. Sure you wrote it right?" Albert looked at Buddy. *Where did he get that address?*

Buddy rubbed his eyes. "No." He squinted against the sun that was bright against the clear January sky.

"How about I call an ambulance and have you looked at in the ER?"

"No. I've been getting these headaches for a little while now. This one was just worse. It'll go away. I'll just sit in my van until it does."

"Give me a minute, Buddy. You okay to stand there?"

Buddy leaned against his van and shut his eyes.

Albert walked over to Quinn. "Detective, I've known Buddy since middle school and I've never seen him like this. Yeah, like I said, he's a bit quirky when it comes to dealing with folks, but he's good people. I've never seen him drink more than one beer, and I sometimes wonder if he actually drinks it. His pappy took off a few years ago and his grandma passed away. I'm pretty sure I'm the only friend he has."

Quinn listened. "What's your plan of action, Officer?"

"Well..." he paused, "I was thinking I could give him a breathalyzer just to be on the up and up, and then drive him home, come back and get his van if you could follow me and bring me back to my car."

"Let's start with the breathalyzer."

Quinn knew this was a small community and things like this probably happened frequently—helping out a neighbor as it were. She watched as Officer Simmons administered the test. He walked back to Quinn and showed her: no alcohol measured.

Quinn considered the liability that could be involved in using her personal vehicle. "I'll notify the station that I'm going to drive Mr. Wilkie in your cruiser and you drive his van. Then you can bring me back to my car." She wanted a few more minutes to observe Mr. Wilkie and this would give it to her.

The officer had a slight look of annoyance on his face.

Arghhh...I should have let him tell me how he wanted to handle it. Why did I just take charge?

"I'll go tell Buddy." Simmons walked off and Quinn took out her secure phone.

"Yes, Detective Isaacs."

"Detective Marshall, if he's in."

"Yes ma'am."

"Marshall here."

"Isaacs here."

"Want me to come up to your office? Or meet in the evidence room?"

"I'm not in yet." She filled him in on the situation and told him she'd be in within an hour. "Would you just let Chuck know that I'm running late?"

"Sure. You good with this? I could come out?" He bit his tongue wondering why he questioned her.

"Concerns I should consider?"

"Nope. Sounds like an everyday plan right here in Round City police work."

"See you soon."

"10-4."

She looked up to see Officer Simmons standing back waiting for her to finish.

"Ma'am. Buddy wants to ride with me in the van. Any problem with that?"

"What problems could you foresee with it, Officer?"

He looked at her. *What problems do I foresee?* He hesitated. "Well, ma'am, it's possible he could have a serious health issue and cause problems for me driving, or he could attempt to assault me in a way that I would not expect of a friend." He nodded. "That's all I can think of."

"Good thinking. Now, do *you* think you should have him ride with you?"

"No, ma'am. He needs to be in the back of a cruiser. I'll get him in." Albert walked back to the van and she heard him talking gently to Buddy.

"It'll be okay, Buddy. We'll go straight to your house. Come on now."

Buddy walked with him.

Quinn could see that his gait was slow but appeared okay—no shuffling or awkward steps. She held the back door on the passenger's side open. Buddy got in.

"Address, Officer?"

Albert told her. "I'll lead the way and pull into the garage."

"Fair enough, Officer. Fair enough."

Buddy didn't speak on the three miles to his home. She saw that he had his head leaned against the headrest and his eyes closed. She couldn't see his hands and wondered why she hadn't considered handcuffing him—there were risks even with a divider between the front and back of the cruiser. *Quit overthinking this. He's just a civilian getting aid.* She stopped thinking about it as she pulled into the driveway behind the van. Her eyes blinked. The orderliness to the garage was evident. *He must do meticulous work if he keeps his supplies like that.*

She stepped out of the cruiser as Officer Simmons opened the door for Buddy.

"Come on, pal. Let's get you inside."

Buddy didn't argue.

Quinn let Simmons handle it. She got in the passenger's seat of the cruiser and waited for him. She'd do her own run on Mr. Buddy Wilkie later today.

The driver's door opened and Simmons got in. He had exited by the front door which faced the open field on the other side of the road.

"He'll be fine, ma'am. Never knew Buddy to have headaches before. He told me they'd started a few weeks back. Said this was the worst one yet."

"I hope your friend will get medical attention."

"Doubt it. His pappy was a doctor who ended up teaching high school math and science. So he's never been to any doctor that I know about. He's pretty private."

"Well, I'm sure you'll check on him and make sure he's okay."

"Yes, ma'am. I will, for sure. Thanks for your help."

"Here to serve, Officer. Here to serve."

"Uh, ma'am."

"Yes?"

"Do you mind if I ask you something about being a detective?"

"What's on your mind?"

"Is it more interesting than field work?"

"As you know, my field work was in a different area of law enforcement. I, personally, found the field work in immigration very interesting and it presented many opportunities to learn new aspects of problem solving a case—its own kind of detective work. Are you interested in being a detective?"

"Been thinking about it. Matter of fact, Buddy encouraged me to study for the exam."

"Sounds like a good friend."

"Yes ma'am. In his own way he is."

"Then perhaps you might decide if the problem solving you do as an officer is interesting enough to consider doing a job that is all about solving problems."

"Might need to think on that. Thanks. And, ma'am, I learned something today from you."

"Oh?"

"I should have thought through the possible consequences of taking Buddy home by myself before I presented it to you."

"Then glad I could be of help." She paused. "I owe you an apology, Officer."

"Ma'am?"

"I took charge in telling you that I would drive him in your cruiser. You were in charge and I should have waited on your instructions."

"Wow, Detective. No one has ever apologized to me for making a mistake. Thanks. It's okay though, I knew you were the senior officer there."

"Doesn't make it right. You hadn't asked for my help. Thanks for understanding."

Simmons pulled up behind her vehicle. Before she could get out Simmons said, "And, ma'am. I think I figured out that you must have thought about being in your personal vehicle and it wasn't secure. Not sure I'd have thought of it."

"You just did, though. Good job. Thanks for your work."

"I'll copy you on my report, ma'am. Have a good day."

"Thanks. You, too, Officer Simmons." She got out and into her own car.

Ten minutes later she was through the gate to the back of the police station and parked in the spot now marked: "Lead Detective."

Chapter 13

We are stronger when we listen, and smarter when we share.
Rania Al-Abdullah

Updates

Quinn entered the back of the station and headed straight to the break room to get coffee. *Maybe I'll take over making coffee in the lab.* She shook her head trying to clear it. *That's ridiculous. I don't need one more thing to do.* She almost ran into the Chief as she turned the corner.

"Morning, Chief."

"Good morning, Detective. Out in the field so early in the day?"

"Ended up handling a local stop. Citizen seemed to have some health problems."

"No officer available?"

"Called for one. Ended up assisting the officer with transport. Concern about that, ma'am?"

"None. Just learning the lay of the land."

"Me, too. Thanks for the parking space move."

"Long overdue."

Quinn nodded. "Have a nice day, Chief."

"You, too." The Chief continued down the hallway.

Quinn got coffee, left her money in the box beside the coffee pots, and headed for her office. She pulled out her phone and called George Marshall.

"Marshall here."

"Can you meet in the conference room in twenty minutes?"

"See you then."

"Thanks."

She hung up and put the phone in her pocket. She rolled her eyes as she entered the code into the lab door. *Wonder if I will ever be able to enter that code now without thinking about Chuck's choice of numbers?*

"Morning, Chuck."

He looked up from his lab table. "Morning, Quinn. Come over when you've got a minute."

"Will do." She hung her coat on her coat rack, touched the wood thinking of her grandmother, changed into her loafers, and took her coffee into the lab.

She waited on Chuck to look up. "Thanks for coming in today. What's up?"

"Running the DNA from the condoms. DNA is the same in both. The good news about condoms is that the chances are pretty good the sample isn't contaminated with DNA from someone else." He looked at her. He'd had a female lab partner in college and she didn't seem at all uncomfortable around any type of evidence. He decided Quinn wasn't either.

"Well, if there's some good news today, we may be looking for the same suspect."

"Or we could just be looking for a randy fellow."

Quinn laughed. Chuck wasn't thirty yet. She was surprised he chose that word. "Fair enough, Chuck. Fair enough."

Chuck blushed. "As for the database run, no hits yet, but it can take some time."

"Did it take a long time to get the actual DNA identified?"

"It can take only a few hours to run the sample, but it takes a lot more sophisticated equipment than we have. I had the results this morning. So, now the DNA search is running through databases looking for a match.

We aren't a high priority in the forensic database computer systems, so it could take a while. Just wanted you to know I'm on it."

"I can..." She stopped herself before she said, 'ask the SBI.' *You told him to ask if he needed anything.* "...imagine. Thanks, Chuck. Do we have anything from the A-team search of the Summers' home?"

"Yes. They brought in some things from the crime scene, but the downstairs lab is working on it. Seems pretty routine to me—not likely to yield much. Still trying to figure out the footprints from the Summers' house. That's going to take some real work."

"Any of it need more equipment than we have to do it?"

"Who wouldn't want the latest equipment and software in the business? The truth of the matter is most forensic work just takes time and close attention, and that's dictated by the humans you have to do it."

"Good point. Thanks, Chuck. Let me know when you know more."

"Will do." He turned back to his lab table.

Quinn went back to her office and checked for any new emails or messages since she had last checked at home. Nothing other than routine. Then one from Officer Gilbert caught her eye. She read it quickly before heading across the hall. She wanted to study the crime board.

Ten minutes later George Marshall entered. He didn't speak.

Quinn turned. "Hey. Thanks for your patience today. Somehow things like plumbing don't get fixed if you aren't home."

"I hear you. My wife and I try to juggle those things around whoever can be home or get home."

"May I ask what she does?"

"Carrie bakes, manages, and owns Sweet Creations downtown."

Quinn clapped her hands together. "Oh, my. The best pastries in east Tennessee—maybe the world."

"She'll be thrilled to hear that. Honestly, her days are longer and much more tiring than mine—most of the time."

"I'm happy to know she's the owner and baker for the next time I allow myself an indulgence. In the meantime..."

"Yeah, I know. A conundrum."

"A-Team reports from Summers?"

He held up a folder. "I printed out what I thought was relevant information for the Board. We can go over the full report when you're ready."

Buddy

Buddy rolled over on his sofa and looked around the room. He never laid down on his sofa. *How did I get here?* He touched his head—it didn't seem to be hurting anymore. *Well, maybe a little.* Then he slowly pieced together parts of his earlier morning. *I did talk to that new detective, didn't I?* He sat up and swung his feet over the side of the sofa. The pain started again. He was nauseous and put his head between his knees to try and keep from getting violently sick. The pain in his head was excruciating. He stumbled into his bedroom and collapsed on his bed.

Evidence Board

Quinn pulled out a chair at the conference table and George sat opposite her.

"George, before we start, I want to tell you about the man from this morning."

"Go."

Quinn described Buddy Wilkie, his stop in front of her house, and finding him at the corner. "Do you know him or his father?"

"Wilkie? Nope. Had a chance to run him or the license?"

"I had dispatch run his driver's license—clean, but haven't done the plate on his van. I'll do that to make sure it isn't stolen."

"Seems Simmons would have said something if it wasn't Wilkie's. Got some reason to suspect this is any more than a fellow making an honest mistake?"

"Nothing I can put my finger on—call it gut instinct." She hesitated then said, "I've probably only flipped my gun guard a half a dozen times in ten years—short of an actual action situation. Not sure why I did when he approached my car."

"Good gut instinct counts for a lot in this business. Glad you trusted it."

"If you don't know the name, then I'm less concerned about it. I'll do some checking later today. I suspect you're right about the van. I think Simmons would have said something if he had concerns."

"Let me know if you want me to do anything."

"Thanks. Now to our murders."

"Chuck able to find anything?"

"Same DNA in both condoms. Running DNA through databases now. We'll see. He said that there was nothing else from the Summers' house that was likely to yield anything, but the downstairs lab folks are working on it."

"Well the same fellow might be a break."

"Or as Chuck said, 'we may just have a randy fellow.'"

George burst out laughing. "How does a twenty something-year-old know *that* word?"

"Reads a lot?" Quinn raised her left eyebrow.

"Sure. If you say so. Okay, back to the crimes. Team is finishing up at Andrews' place. Don't think there'll be much there."

"Any footprints?"

George shook his head. "Don't think we're going to be so lucky this time. Back yard was pristine and too many feet in the front. Think we'll be dependent on the condom, and SBI if they find anything."

"Do we have Andrews yet from SBI, or just Summers?"

"Just Summers." He looked at the Board and then at Quinn. "Nothing to report other than the normal autopsy information: TOD, cause: suspected chemical of unknown origin."

"Dr. Walters thought it might be a paralytic but he said they dissipate pretty quickly. Sounds like the best we have is the photographs he took of the likely insertion point on Summers." Quinn looked at the Board. "Let's get that up there. Do we have the photos from Andrews yet?"

George took the photos on both women from the ME out of his folder. Each showed the likely insertion point. There was no other evidence of bruising or assault. He walked to the Board and carefully pinned the photos side-by-side.

Quinn stood and walked over to look at them and the photos of the footprints found in the backyard of the Summers' residence. "George."

"Yes."

"Is there any way we can find out if the Summers owned an ATV? It might help us figure out why we only have what is likely one set, albeit they're unexplainable at this point, of footprints out the back door."

"Ah, that's what foot slogging detectives are for. The locally owned places that sell ATVs are pretty good about sharing information without a warrant. Chain stores less so. We'll start with the husband, he had an ironclad alibi for TOD, but maybe he'll answer the simple question about whether they owned an ATV. I can get one of our other detectives on it."

Quinn stood quietly studying the footprints.

"Uh, Quinn. Sorry. I'm not in charge of the others. Do you want to get one of them?"

She turned her head toward him. "What? No. I want us to be a team. If I need to be the one, then tell me. Otherwise, division of labor solves crimes. Will any of the others have a problem with you asking?"

"Might faint from shock when I tell them what you said, but no, we do it all the time." He stopped. "Well, Albright didn't *know* we did, but how else do you get the work done?"

"True that, George. True that." She turned back to the photos of the footprints and crooked her index finger on her chin. "George, I've decided I want to see all the photographs we have on the footprints. I know we tried to put the most detailed ones up to save space, but we might be missing something. Let's move them over to this wall by themselves. Something tells me they're going to be crucial to this investigation."

"May turn out to be all we have—if they belong to our murderer."

"*If* is such a big word in police work, isn't it?" Quinn's voice was soft and deliberate as she dragged out the short, two-letter word.

"Yes. Yes, it is. So, looks to me like we have some foot slogging and computer searching work to do."

"I agree. Let's divide and try to conquer."

They sat down at the rectangular conference table and Quinn made a note on her tablet. "Try to find a round table." Then they talked through the evidence they currently had, who would follow up on forensic team reports, what computer searches needed to be done, and agreed to touch base by end of the day if nothing surfaced that would change the course of the investigation.

Time Flies

The first thing Quinn did when she got back to the office was call Officer Gilbert and thank him for the email detailing the delivery and installation dates on the tech equipment for the conference room and lab. "While I have you on the phone, do you have time for a question?"

"Sure. What's up?"

"I know you're confident about our computer security, and for that I'm glad you're on the job, but do you have the same confidence about the city government security?"

"Something specific?"

"Mostly just trying to make sure that any searches through public records are going to yield what I need."

"Meaning?"

"Meaning that I don't go off chasing an address only to find out some hacker got in and changed the street number." She felt a bit guilty being evasive, but sometimes it went with the job—she learned that in immigration work.

"Oh, that. Doubtful. First of all, hackers are by nature either malicious or playing what they think are funny games. Odds are one in millions that they'd target a single address. More likely they'd screw up payment records for taxes or voting information. That said, I do talk with the head of computer services for the city with some regularity and without having done a run on his background, he seems pretty knowledgeable. I think the records are safe to check."

"Good to know." *Why was 1213 written on the paper?*

"Not worried about your own address, are you?"

"No. Should I be?" *Maybe that's what's popping in my head.*

"I assume you know that your address is blocked in public access records."

"Have to admit, I haven't done an incognito search to find out, but knew it was practice in Immigration Enforcement, if not policy."

He was laughing. "I love it. A lead detective who can speak techie. You're alright, Detective. You're alright. I think your address is secure. Not that someone can't follow you home." *Why did I say that?* His tone changed. "Need anything else?"

"Not now." She hoped the forced smile on her face came through in her tone as she pulled her hair back into a pony tail and knotted it. "I'm good. Thanks for your time."

"Any time."

"10-4." She hung up. She let out a sigh—*was the plumber actually looking for me?* It was innocent enough to have the wrong address, Simmons knew him, and he was cooperative on the ride to his house. *Must be the dripping faucet upstairs that has me focused on plumbers.*

She decided to see what she could find on Buddy Wilkie. She started a search in public records on Buddy Wilkie even though she knew she should see check to see if there was some way she could help Chuck. She made a note to follow-up on her meeting about working with both labs and Chuck's schedule. She'd make that a priority today. *Can I do investigations and manage a department? That's a big one to figure out.*

Her administrative duties pushed to the front of her brain and she decided to leave Buddy Wilkie for now. She sent a message to Captain Brown to ask for clarification on adjusting an employee's schedule. She picked up the phone and called the ME.

He answered on the first ring.

"Hey, Doc. It's Quinn."

"Hey to you. Any news to share?"

She smiled at the ME's easy ways. "None on our cases other than the one you've already received from the SBI that they suspect a paralytic with Summers, but can't verify same."

"Yeah, figured that would happen. Hoping Andrews proves different."

"Me, too. I won't take up much of your time. Just need to know if you have any concerns about me talking with the downstairs lab folks and Chuck to see if we can figure out a way that they can divide the work and feel comfortable asking for assistance when they need it?"

"Now, missy, that's some welcome news and a breath of fresh air down here in this basement. You go right ahead. Just let me know the new protocol and we'll be right happy to follow it."

"Any suggestions that would help facilitate the conversation?"

"From my time here, we don't normally have too many big cases going at once. I think if you just let them know that they can continue with the responsibilities they have but can share as they need to, it'll go a long way. Simple conversation would give you time to get the lay of the land and learn who is good at what kind of forensic work. Everyone knows that Chuck is the best forensic tech we could hope to have so you won't ever get pushback on him having the tough stuff to deal with. I think the biggest issue has been they've felt isolated. Just an observation."

"Appreciate your observations and thank you for sharing them. I can make decisions, but much prefer being part of a team."

"Generally goes a long way to getting the job done in my experience. Glad you're on board, Quinn. Call if you need anything else."

"Thanks, Doc. I will."

She sat back and looked at the ceiling and felt the knot of hair on her neck. She undid it and shook her head to loosen the strands of hair. Her stomach growled. She looked at her watch. It was almost two-thirty p.m. *Where did the day go?* She took a protein bar out of her desk and decided to leave the search on Buddy Wilkie for her own time. Her email folder open, she started through reports and things she needed to address.

She opened the email from Captain Brown: "Scheduling is totally up to you. If you need help looking at the employee budget you have, let me know."

There was a tap on her doorframe. She looked up.

"Quinn, still no hits on the DNA. I might be getting close to narrowing down info about that kid's shoe though."

She sat up straight and turned to look at him. "And?"

He filled her in on the information he had. "Nothing more definitive, but progress. Oh, and it's looking like the bones on the other cruiser are from a pig—a baby pig."

"Old joke, isn't it?"

"Yeah, I suppose. I haven't been around long enough to remember the days of folks throwing pig's blood on cops, but I've read about it."

She frowned. "Let's hope for better days. Thanks for your work on it. Two things, then you get out of here for today."

"Sure, how can I help?"

"First, I want to talk with you and the other techs, briefly, and make sure y'all know I want you to work together and get the job done. If you need help from me to sort anything out—evidence, equipment to do it, people problems, just tell me and we'll figure it out. Your thoughts?"

"The word is already flying around the station that you don't do business like we've lived with for the past ten years, well eight for me. If you send us a note with a time and a place to meet, I think the others will be glad to hear it directly from you. Shouldn't take long."

"Thanks, Chuck. I appreciate your perspective. Will try to get this done in the next day or two so we can all do our work. Second thing:

as part of the cooperative work environment, I'll look at everyone's schedule, but if you would put a request to me in an email for a schedule you think would give you time to do the work and have a life outside of work, I'll do everything I can to make it happen."

"Sounds good. I appreciate both those things. Okay, then, I'm headed out. You should leave at a decent hour today, too. Got some weather coming in. Good night to be in front of a fire at home."

"Thanks. I might just do that. Good night, Chuck. Thanks for your work."

"10-4."

Maybe I can *manage investigation and leading a team.* She turned back to her computer.

"Isaacs here." She had not bothered to see who was calling.

"Hansen here."

"Chief. How may I help you?" She felt herself sit up a little straighter.

"Any chance of a few minutes of your time to catch up this afternoon before you leave?"

"At your service."

"Then I'll be down in fifteen minutes. Hoping to get everyone out of here that we can before dark. Big storm headed our way."

"So I've heard. Anything special I can have ready to share?"

"No, I'm sure you've got it covered. See you soon."

Quinn stood and headed for the ladies room. She threw the paper towel in the trash after opening the door and wished she had brought her brush down with her. She ran her fingers through her hair. When she got to the office, she pulled out a hair clip and secured her hair; she picked up the phone.

"Marshall here."

"Hey, it's Quinn. Unless there's something pressing downstairs, you and the others wrap it up and call it a day. Big storm headed our way apparently."

"Got some help working on the ATV, but the stores are closing, too. Have a call in to Mr. Summers. No response yet. We'll all wrap up and head out—except for the lucky stiff who has the duty tonight. Of course, he may be in the warmest place in town."

"Ah, yes, backup generator! Maybe I'll stay over."

"Go home, Detective Isaacs. You've been here way too late every night."

"Thanks for your help today. Call if you need me." She felt uncomfortable saying she had a generator at home. *Thanks, Grandmother.*

There was a knock at the door. She stood to open it for the Chief.

"Welcome. My office is a bit cramped. We can sit out here." She pointed to the lab stools.

"Your office is fine."

"Please take my desk chair. I'll take the one in the corner."

"No need." The chief stepped in and sat in the chair in the corner. "Updates."

"Yes, ma'am." Quinn updated her on the two murder cases, the shoe and the bones, and the administrative things she was doing.

"Week two isn't over, Quinn. Plan to blaze a trail through here that leaves scorched earth?"

"Ma'am?"

"Back-handed compliment. Shame on me. I know better."

"Little slow on the uptake sometimes. Do you have concerns?"

"Concerns? Plenty! None about you. If I do, I'll let you know. I'm particularly pleased that you are team building and can operate without having to get permission every ten seconds." She let out a sigh.

Quinn realized that might be *why* the chief chose to come to her office. She needed to get out of her own—and needed support, too.

"Chief, I can be guilty of *not* letting grass grow under my feet. You hired me to do a job and I'll do it to the best of my ability. I'll ask permission if I'm unsure or can't find policy or procedure, but if I foul up and *should* have asked you, please tell me."

"Keep up the good work, Quinn. I need you doing exactly what you're doing. Just don't hesitate to ask for support when you need it—we all do at some point."

"Some way I can help *you*, Jill?"

"You already have. Just keep on keeping on. Now get out of here. You can do whatever you need to do remotely. No need for you to be socked in here with the storm."

Jill stood.

Quinn did, too. "Thanks, Jill. I'm sure the honeymoon will end soon, but so far everyone has been cooperative, and eager to work together."

"Well, we may both find that a change in management style is good for *most* people. Good night, Detective." The chief had the outside door open.

"Good night, Chief."

Quinn walked back in her office, changed into her boots, put on her coat and was relieved that tonight she only had to go out the back door. Her parking space was the third one.

Chapter 14

Curiosity is the wick in the candle of learning.
William Arthur Ward

Cold Hard Facts

Quinn walked in the kitchen and her personal phone buzzed. There was a text: Will monitor snow for clearing your driveway. She smiled. *A crucial consideration for law enforcement folks in these mountains to be able to get out in bad weather.* She had used the same company for ten years to plow for her and they had always kept her driveway and sidewalk cleared. She sent a simple: Thank you.

She touched Billy's number on her recent calls list.

"In out of the cold?" His voice was sincere and the warmth radiated through her.

"I am. And, you sir?"

"Still at the station, but headed home shortly. Things are pretty quiet on this side of the mountains."

"I'm sure you and Chad are relieved about that. Speaking of Chad, how are things with your sheriff?"

"Good. So far he's living up to his pledge to actually have a normal life and have us work as a team. Of course it means one or two folks have had to step up their game."

"Wouldn't be anyone I know, that's for sure. You were already a pretty amazing team. One I'd like to emulate."

"Enough shop talk, Detective. Tell me about my favorite lead detective. Anything new in your world?"

She wanted to tell him about Buddy—not as a detective, but as a friend—someone she'd like to become a very good friend—but she let it go. "Not work related, but for sure about your relative. Now how is it that Matthew is related to you?"

"Second cousin twice removed or some such nonsense. Close enough since we both live in these hills and we know and like each other, but mostly relative when we have family reunions."

She laughed. "Fair enough. Matthew was prompt, courteous, and efficient. Thanks for the recommendation, and I now have his number of speed dial."

"Is mine?" He said it playfully but with sincere hope.

"First one."

"Good."

Just to give him back his normal banter, she chuckled, "You don't think I'd call anyone else if my life was in danger, do you?"

"Ha! Ha! Speaking of whom you might call. Have you looked at this storm?"

"Not yet. Big one?"

"May make roads hard to navigate for a couple of days. We don't usually get a heavy snow like this in January."

"I know. Usually happens when the moisture starts to increase as spring comes in. I haven't called my Mother yet to tell her you said you'd come, so I may just tell her we can't."

"Whoa, don't make it about me. I'll get out my snowmobile and pick you up and we can travel in style."

She loved that he made her laugh. "I think we could just use the snowmobiles down here instead of trying to go to the city. What do you think?"

"I think you'll tell your mother that I said I'd be delighted to see her anytime, and I'll leave it to your judgment about whether one of those times should be Saturday."

"Very gallant of you." She sighed. "If I let the storm start, maybe she'll call me and say the folks from Spain, who probably are not from the Pyrenees, asked for a raincheck."

"Or a snow check." Billy laughed.

"Okay. Okay. I surrender." She laughed. "I'll let you know one way or the other."

"If it's the other, I hope it puts us back to the glass of wine—my place or yours—either one."

"Thanks, Billy. Works for me, too. I'll let you know. Now, get home ahead of the storm and when you see the good folks over there that I know, tell them I said, 'Hey!'"

"Will do. Talk to you soon." He hesitated. "Quinn, thanks for calling. Made my day."

"Mine, too. Talk to you soon." She ended the call.

She opened the freezer and pulled out the vegetable soup she had made with all the fresh vegetables in the summer. She just wished she had another loaf of French bread to go with it. She reached for the last of the Club crackers. *Guess it'll be crackers.* She put the soup in the microwave to defrost.

She strode down the hall to the bedroom and put on sweatpants and a sweatshirt. *Might as well get comfortable.* On her way back, she stopped and turned on the gas fireplace in the large great room that was part of the kitchen. *Wow! I think I might like this storm.*

Twenty minutes later she had her laptop on the table with her bowl of soup and crackers and a cup of hot tea. She'd decided to wait on a glass of wine until she finished her preliminary search. She typed "Buddy Wilkie" in the search engine. *Might as well see what normal things pop up.* Her soup was cooling off as she clicked through pages. No social media set up by a Buddy Wilkie. "Plumbing Services" came up in a generic page, "If you own this business…" bid to get you to use their webservices. Never one to let her curiosity run away with her, Quinn also knew her inquisitive nature and refined search skills would find something if there was anything to find in the same places any normal citizen could look. *His pappy disappeared and his grandma died.* She typed in "Wilkie Obituary Round City TN." A brief obituary appeared on the local funeral home website for Gladys Wilkie, dates of birth and death—a little over thirteen years ago. The only other thing listed was: "Survived by Oscar Wilkie, M.D., son, and Buddy Wilkie, grandson." *No service. Looks like cremation. No mention of a daughter-in-law.*

She pushed her laptop to the center of the table, picked up her spoon, and ate her soup and crackers. *How can anyone have so little information about them in this day and age? I'm making way too much of an innocent mistake.* She was so deep in thought she almost slurped her soup. *Mother would have my head for that.*

As if on cue, her phone rang. *Mother.*

"Hey, Mother. You and Daddy inside and bundled up for the storm?"

"Hello, Quinn. Of course we are, my sweet girl. I know you would call before the evening is over, but I wanted to save you the trouble."

"Mother, it's no trouble to call you. I was just eating my first…" She knew better than to tell her mother she had not had lunch. "spoon of soup. It's vegetable. I think you'd like it."

"I'm sure I would dear. Seems a good night for soup. Anyway, I wanted to know if you had spoken with Mr. Williams yet."

Quinn shook her head. *Maybe that's why I love detective work. Mother is a master at asking a question that tells her what she wants to know at the same time it's a reminder that you had a task to do. And yet there is not one hint of reprimand in it. Hmmm…*

"Yes, Mother, I spoke with Billy and he would be honored…"

"Oh, Quinn. It would be lovely to see him again, but I'm afraid that our other guests are a bit intimidated by the storm and graciously asked if we could reschedule."

"Where are they from in Spain, Mother?"

"Montoro. Do you know it?"

"Yes. Yes, I do. It's in Andalusia. A small quaint village near Seville."

"You always were a brilliant student, my pet."

"A year in Spain during university with the privilege you gave me to travel every inch of the country taught me as much as my geography lessons. However, this isn't about my education. I can certainly understand why they would prefer not to be on the roads in a storm like the one being predicted."

"I offered to send a car for them..."

"Mother, I'm quite sure you graciously accepted their request to reschedule and I look forward to another opportunity to meet them. Maybe you'll bring them to Round City one Sunday afternoon in the spring and show them parts of east Tennessee that most don't know exist. I'd love to host you all for lunch."

"Perhaps, dear. Quinn, please give my sincere apologies to Mr. Williams..."

Quinn interrupted her. "Mother, his name is Billy. He is my friend, and he is enchanted by you. I'm quite sure he'd prefer it if you called him by his first name. If you aren't comfortable with that, his title is detective. Detective Williams." She let that hang in the air. *What is wrong with me?* Quinn was not disrespectful to her mother even when she tired of the formal behaviors that were her mother's life. This time she was.

"Yes, of course, Quinn. Please thank Billy and tell him we look forward to his next visit."

"I will, Mother. Be safe in the storm and give my love to Daddy. I love you."

"And, you, mi hija."

"Buenas noches, mama."

She took her soup bowl to the kitchen, set it in the sink, and poured a glass of Kim Crawford Chardonnay. She decided now was as good a time as any to do some serious thinking about this day. *Maybe it's time to face some cold hard facts about myself.*

Pappy

Oscar Wilkie was getting worried about Buddy. Something had happened to the GPS tracker he had put on Buddy's van. It wasn't sending him a signal and he had no idea where Buddy was. *That boy follows routines. Every day. The only time he isn't home is when he's doing that silly plumbing work he wants to do, buying supplies, or cleaning the old stone house. Where is he?*

Oscar knew the storm that was coming in would have him buried for days. He had no intention of ever having anyone know that his cottage was back here. His solar panels gave him enough power to run his computer, and he had free access to the internet thanks to the deal he made with the phone company for their tower on his land. *Even if there are problems for the tower in this storm, the road in to it doesn't go anywhere near my cabin. I made sure of that.* He looked over at the picture of Buddy when he graduated from high school. Oscar's mother had taken the picture and then had it framed for Oscar. It was the only indication in this cabin that he had a family—in fact that he had any connection to the outside world. He hadn't seen or spoken to Buddy in years. He had no plans to do so now. He just had to make sure Buddy didn't do something foolish.

Bet his ankle is hurting with the storm blowing in. He never could stop complaining when the weather got really cold. How many times did I try to tell him there was no science to support aches and pains related to weather phenomenon. Temperature changes that your body feels, yes. Nothing more. He walked over and put another log on the fire. Then he sat in the big wooden chair he had made from logs he took from the land. He fell asleep—thoughts of Buddy forgotten.

Buddy

Buddy sat up on the side of his bed and put his face in his hands. His head still hurt but not as bad as it had earlier. The house was cold. He didn't know there was a storm coming in. He normally kept the heat at sixty-six. *Pappy, I don't care if it costs money. I'm turning up the heat.* Memories of the cold in the old stone house which depended completely on a wood fireplace ran through his mind. He shivered. He stumbled to the thermostat in the hall and turned it up to sixty-eight. He was headed to the kitchen when the lights came on in the hall and his bedroom. He was trying to figure out how that happened. He had no memory of having them on automatic timers. He stumbled in the brightness of the light, turned and tried to get back to his bed—his headache pounding. He didn't hear his phone ringing.

Round City Police Station

Officer Albert Simmons had come in off the day shift at four p.m. The night duty sergeant knew Simmons was single so had left him a message to stop by.

"Sarge, you wanted to see me?'

"Yes, Simmons. Glad you got my message. Any chance you could stay at the station tonight? With this storm headed our way several of the officers with families called in. Don't need you on the road, but trying to have a few officers in the house in case an emergency arises."

"Sure, no problem, Sarge." He turned to leave.

"Simmons," the sergeant's tone was hesitant.

"Yes, sir." Albert turned back toward him.

"Saw the report on that stop with Detective Isaacs."

"Yes, sir. Dispatch sent me over. It was just Buddy Wilkie with a bad headache. Detective Isaacs helped me get him home. It was all in my report, sir."

"Oh, yeah, that wasn't my question."

"Sorry, Sarge. What's the question?"

"What's she like? Tough broad even though she's a looker?" His lips were crooked with a lecherous grin as he wiggled his eyebrows.

"Sarge, she was very professional. She let me handle the situation and thanked me for my service. That was all."

The sergeant sat up in his chair. "Exactly what I expected. Good work, Simmons. Thanks for staying over."

"Anytime, Sarge. Anything else?"

"Dismissed."

"Good night, Sarge."

"Night."

Albert walked back to the lockers, got out the change of uniform he kept there, his toiletries and robe and headed downstairs to the bunk room. He hoped he could catch Thursday night basketball on the TV in the common room. *Hope nobody starts a movie before the game.* He walked into the common room and smelled the beef stew on the stove.

"Who's the cook?" He was glad he didn't have to cook.

One of the older officers shut the door to the fridge. "Me, what's it to you?"

"If somebody had asked me who, I would have bet it was you! Nobody can create such amazing smells like you do. Beef stew?"

"Okay, Simmons, brown nosing not required. Yep, beef stew. Biscuits almost ready to go in the oven. We'll eat in thirty."

"Hope there aren't too many of us. I'm hungry as a bear."

"Plenty to go around." The cook turned on the oven and finished rolling out his biscuits.

"Thanks. Beef stew and Thursday night basketball. Who can beat it?" Albert headed into the bunk room and toward the bunk in the far corner which he preferred when he stayed in the station. He hung up his heavy coat and jacket ready to slip on if a call came during the night. He hoped his undershirt and uniform shirt would keep him warm down here. He hated sweaters and didn't have one in his locker.

Buddy. I need to call Buddy. He took out his phone and dialed Buddy's number. It went to voice mail. "Hey, Buddy. Just checking on you. Sent you a text earlier and you didn't answer. At least text me and let me know how that headache is. Need anything, just holler." He shrugged and went back to the common area. There were three other officers in the room besides the cook and all exchanged greetings and settled in front of the TV.

End of the Day

Quinn had decided to shower and put on her flannel pajamas on this cold night and do some serious thinking. *I don't know why I'm struggling with the wealth of my family. I snapped at my mother which I have never done. The encounter with Buddy Wilkie has me stumped. And, admit it, Billy Williams has you more than a little interested in having a man in your life.* She took her second glass of wine with her and sat in the leather chair in her bedroom and turned on the fireplace in front of her chair.

Where to begin? She lifted the pencil and paper from the table beside her chair and doodled as she thought. "$ = conveniences." "Whose $?" She looked at both notes. In a few short minutes she was starting to sort out the difference in her and most people her age, especially single women. *Yes, I've worked since the day I left grad school. Unlike others, I left with no debt, thanks to Mother and Daddy, and I have a house paid for—thanks, Grandmother. I have a good pension building from my federal government service, and now my police job.*

She lifted the pencil when she realized she was doodling and was avoiding that fact she had a trust fund—which she now realized she had never touched. *Okay, Quinn. Enough about the money. Yes, you're fortunate not to have a mortgage, but you don't ask your parents for money and you pay for everything you do from your income. The fact that mother gives me gifts of clothes and furnishings is her choice.* She started laughing as she realized her mother would be surprised most of the fancy label clothes hung in the closet only to be pulled out when Quinn went to visit her parents in Knoxville—except for the luxurious robe.

She sipped her wine. *Maybe I could quit being so hard on myself. I am generous to charities—maybe I'll up that from my trust. Yes, that's what I'll do.* She nodded her head and drew a line through the two dollar signs on the paper and put a smiley face by the words: increase charitable giving.

She stretched her legs out in front of her as she reached for her phone. She smiled when she saw it was Billy.

"What a pleasant surprise." She all but cooed.

"Well, progress, I guess."

"Progress?"

"At least you didn't call me, Detective."

She hiccupped as she laughed. "Sorry."

"So glad I can make you laugh. What's so funny?"

"If I tell you the truth, promise you won't stop calling me?"

There was silence.

"Billy?"

"Here's the promise I'll make you. If you ever *don't* tell me the truth, I'll stop calling you."

She waited a second. "Thank you."

"For what?"

"For bringing me back to my senses. I've been off kilter all day for some reason. I was sitting here trying to figure out why. I was rude to my mother when she called tonight and I've never done that before. Now, to a man who thoroughly intrigues me, I challenge him over me telling the truth."

"Quinn, maybe you need to face some cold hard facts."

"And what would they be?" She was surprised that he used the very words she had used to herself earlier in the evening.

"You are smart, curious, two weeks into a major job in a new organization, with people you don't know, and a police department that has lost a chief and gotten a new one in less than a month. And besides that you're beautiful."

She laughed. "What do looks have to do with any of those other things?"

"Nothing. I just wanted to tell you how beautiful you are."

"Thank you, kind sir." She took a sip of wine. She decided to just dive in. "My mother called to cancel Saturday evening. She insisted that I thank, 'Mr. Williams.' I told her your name was Billy, and that if she wanted to use a formal form of address you are Detective Williams."

"Ouch."

"Hmmm...I seem to make you say that with some regularity."

"Nah, I like playing the wounded victim." He chuckled. "So what you said is true. What's wrong with that?"

"Maybe I should tell you *how* I said it." She put the sarcasm in her voice as she repeated it.

"Double ouch. That would have gotten me the switch from my mama."

"Oh, nothing so normal for my mother. If I were still living at home, it would be, 'young lady, I think you need to go to your room and think about an acceptable way to share your concerns with me. Go on now.' Believe me, I would have been in my room in ten seconds."

"Might have depended on where you were in that big house in K-town."

"Nope. I'd have flown." She laughed. "Know something? I like you, Billy Williams. I like that you are smart, funny, a top-notch detective, an easy person to talk to, and good looking to boot."

"Then I'm thrilled to be a member of this mutual admiration society. I really just called to make sure you were ready to weather the storm, but I see I found you in the middle of one that most of us face at this age."

"What's that?"

"Who we are in relationship to our parents. I lost both of mine before I got too far into it, but even in retrospect I have some angst about whether they liked my choice of career, was I a good son, could I have done more, why did they do so much for me, all that stuff."

"Maybe you're right. Maybe I just need to sort out what's underneath my being unsettled today." *Has the nightmare had me unsettled all week?* "Uh, Billy?"

"Yes, ma'am."

"Why did you get into law enforcement?"

"Wanted to stay in the Valley, love helping people, and at some level guess I was enamored of the badge." He paused. "Of course, now I know the realities. Even with that I wouldn't change it. How about you?"

Quinn felt her hear start racing, her hands shook, but she calmed them. "When I was a senior in high school, there was a shooting..."

He could hear the angst. "Oh, Quinn, you don't have to talk about this."

"It's okay, I want to tell you." She recounted the shooting and the death of Eliza and her belief that in some small way she helped the other two girls. She took a deep breath. "Sometimes I have a nightmare and relive it."

"Shh...Quinn. It's okay now. Thank you for trusting me with your story. I was a rookie deputy when that happened. Of course, I was thirty-five miles away from Knoxville, but we all went on alert. I wish I could have been there then and now to comfort you."

"You do, just by listening." She took some shallow breaths. "So, you see I have to be in law enforcement. Maybe at some levels my behavior with my mother today was the nightmare Sunday night and then a week that has been anything but routine. None of it excuses my rudeness, though. Talking to you helps me see it has nothing to do with my mother."

"Even if it does, I have no doubt you'll find a way to make amends with her. Do you want me to come over?"

"I'd love to see you, but this will have to work for tonight."

"Okay, you only need to say the word."

"Thanks, you're sweet. Now about Saturday."

"So, the dinner is off, but wine is on, right?"

"It is if we aren't snow bound."

"Oh, I promise you *I* won't be snowbound. I'll find my way to your door if I have to hike on snowshoes." He laughed.

"Then consider it a date, unless..."

"I know the drill. Unless a case...blah, blah, blah."

"I think we'll have to figure out a code word for work."

"Then we'll think on it. Sleep well, Quinn. Call if you need to talk, or even if you don't."

"Night, Billy. Thanks for the call. Sweet dreams."

"You, too." *You have no idea the dreams I'll have of you, Quinn Isaacs.* He ended the call.

Quinn leaned her head back, closed her eyes and then sat straight up in her chair. She almost knocked over the last of her wine.

It was Buddy's eyes. That's what has me unsettled. Where have I seen those eyes?

Chapter 15

The most difficult thing is the decision to act, the rest is merely tenacity.
Amelia Earhart

The Raging Storm

Friday morning found the northeastern region of the Smoky Mountains blanketed in heavy snow with thick ice on secondary roads which were slowly being serviced by the city and county. Unusually high winds continued and snow was expected to fall the rest of the day—limiting services to more isolated areas. Advisories to stay off the roads, except for emergencies, were on radio, TV, and all matter of internet media. Chief Hansen had notified non-essential personnel to remain in current locations. Her message included a statement to protect family and neighbors and be available should situations warrant assignment based on changing conditions.

Quinn read the message at six a.m. and was impressed that it also included a statement thanking all employees for their service. Her boss at Immigration Enforcement had certainly not been one to thank people. He expected you to do your job, and put up with his inconsistent behavior. *He never understood that every employee should have equal access to his praise, not just those he made his buddies. Chief Hansen is proving to be a much better leader.* She headed for her exercise room and hoped to clear her head and be ready to do some serious computer research and reading.

An hour later, Quinn was dressed to head out in weather if needed. She sat at her desk in her home office and drafted her own email to send to the detectives and forensic techs. First, she called the station.

"Detective Isaacs, how may I direct your call?"

"Detective on duty, please. Thanks."

"Millwood here."

"Detective Millwood, Quinn Isaacs here."

"Morning, Detective. Something you need here at the station?"

"Thanks, no. Just wanted to make sure you're good to stay on since the Chief has asked people to remain in place."

"I'm good. Wife and kids are fine. Need me to do something?"

"No. If things change for you, or something comes up you need assistance, just call me. I can get to the station."

"No need. I'm good. Marshall asked me to follow-up on the ATV on the Summers case. Still haven't heard from the husband. Won't get anywhere today, likely this whole weekend, with the local stores closed." He chuckled.

"Something I missed?" She wondered why he chuckled.

"Sorry. Just made me chuckle that the local stores will be the ones that stay closed. You'd think they would *try* to open—especially the ones with heavy equipment. Not many folks plan ahead. When we have the rare storm like this one, they want snow plows and snow mobiles. Anyway, it just struck me as funny."

She tried to make her voice sound light. "A boring all-nighter can do that to you, too."

"True that, ma'am. True that. Well, y'all be safe. We've got things covered here. Good day for me to get some computer research and reading done."

"Me, too, Detective. Me, too. 10-4." She ended the call. One more read of her email to the detectives and forensic staff and she clicked send.

She reviewed her notes from the public search on Buddy Wilkie and reread the brief obituary for Gladys Wilkie, Buddy's grandmother. She entered Oscar Wilkie in her search engine. The only thing she could find on him was a brief announcement in a now defunct local newspaper from almost forty years ago. "Oscar Wilkie graduates with honors..."

then a similar entry on his completion of medical school. *Simmons said Oscar Wilkie taught math and science at a school. Why doesn't that show up?* She sat back in her chair. *Okay. Enough. Get your curiosity in check and get on with the work at hand. There is nothing that has happened that justifies doing a search in police records.* She made an electronic folder on her computer, entered the document with the information she had on Buddy and Oscar, sparse though it was, and started reading reports from the detectives on all the cases—major, and mostly minor, that were operational at the moment.

"Isaacs." She answered the secure phone lying on her desk.

"Marshall, here."

"Morning, George. Everything okay at your place?"

"Like a crystal palace—fire in the fire place, my wife has bread in the oven, and we're hunkered down. Hope you have a fire going too; although, that's not the reason for my call."

"All's well here. What's up?"

"SBI report came in on Andrews."

"And?"

"Presumed paralytic injection to the neck. Chemical analysis of the liver and kidneys of both victims is still being conducted."

"Were they able to identify the drug?"

"Apparently it was a massive dose compared to the amount generally given for the intended use and she's skinny as a rail to boot. Seems we may have gotten her to the SBI lab in time for them to find something useful. Appears to be rocuronium bromide which stops movement during surgery; regardless, there was enough fentanyl to have caused death."

"How would someone know to use these drugs?"

"The internet?" The sarcasm was evident in his clipped response.

"Right."

"Sorry, didn't mean to sound so terse. The good news—and the bad news—about today's world of technology is that you can find anything."

"Maybe."

"Looking for something you couldn't find?"

"The old saying, 'curiosity killed the cat.'"

"Ah, but the ending is the answer."

"I know. 'Satisfaction brought it back.' My search was unsatisfying."

"Something I can help with?"

"No, thanks all the same. Just a crazy notion I was chasing. Anyway, back to the Andrews case. Fentanyl is obviously available, but how would someone get rocuronium? Since it's a paralytic, isn't that only used in surgeries?"

"Not sure, but there are many ways in this world to get something if you want to go looking for it."

"True that. Anything else significant?"

"Not to the cause of death, but the fear we saw in Ms. Andrews' sons, may be explained by her own apparent history."

"Which suggests?"

"Multiple untreated broken bones as a child, apparent burn marks consistent with cigarette burns, and..."

Quinn interrupted him abruptly. "Do the boys have any evidence of these?"

"Can't know on the bones without an exam and x-rays. Children's Services caseworker has been notified and he will follow-up on it. Officers didn't report any visible bruising or burns, but it's winter and they had on long sleeves and jeans. The most telling thing was in their behavior—the excessive obedient response to questions and rigid body stance."

"Sounds like the officers were very observant."

"Most of ours are pretty good, for sure. As detectives, we know which reports are going to be spot on—even in action packed situations."

"I'm sure I'll learn those, too."

"No doubt, Quinn. If it's all the same to you, I'd rather not provide any bias by telling you the officers who I think do the best job at helping us solve the crimes they go in to stop."

"Fair enough. I'm good with that. Thanks for getting Children's Services to check on the physical well-being of the boys. I haven't heard from Chuck on whether there's a match for the DNA search he's running."

"I'm sure he'll let you know as soon as he knows. I'll just tell you from experience that even though we can get put in the slow lane in the world of computer runs in forensics, it's doubtful there's going to be a match if we don't already have it."

"That's my experience from Immigration Enforcement, too. Doesn't cost a bit more for it to run, right? May be some obscure individual from way back when."

"That tends to work better when you have fingerprints. Those have been collected since the early twentieth century. DNA is too recent at this point."

"Lots of controversy over whether everyone should have to provide it."

"They don't have to provide fingerprints, and I'm betting that's been in the courts for decades. So, requiring DNA—not sure it will happen anytime soon and my non-cop self isn't so sure I ever want it to happen."

"I'm with you. Even though my own prints are own file, my DNA isn't. Anyway, I'll leave that one to the ethicists."

"Other than the SBI report, I don't have anything else new. You?"

"Talked to Millwood and he said he has a call in to Mr. Summers, but no return call."

"The storm will slow things down. So, if you don't mind a little personal advice: relax, read a good book, and see what the day brings."

"I'm always open to advice—doesn't always mean I'll take it, but I'll listen."

"Good for you."

"I have plenty to learn about the Round City Police Department. So my reading will be on pending cases, policies, and procedures. Sound like fun?"

"Like I told you, never wanted to be lead detective—too much admin-istrivia for my blood."

She laughed. "Thanks. I'll mark you off my list of possible folks wanting to unseat me."

"No worries, there. Rumor mill runs fast in most cop shops, and we're no different. Seems folks might actually like the new lead detective. The rest is up to you—you'll either earn their trust and respect—or you won't."

"Do you charge for all this good advice?"

"Just happy to have you on board. Call if you need me. I smell bread coming out of the oven."

"Owww...do you deliver?"

"Not in this weather. But I'll give you a hint. Carrie was so thrilled with your compliment that I suspect you'll find a treat on your desk one of these days."

"Thanks, George. Tell Carrie I look forward to meeting her properly. Talk to you later." She ended the call.

Whose Deal?

"Come on, Buddy. Answer the phone." Albert Simmons muttered to himself as he looked at his watch. It was after four on Friday afternoon and Buddy had not returned a text or answered the phone. Albert was beginning to worry.

"Come on, Simmons. That gal you're trying to reach doesn't want to talk to you. Your deal. Let's go." The officers in the common room, who had stayed over in the storm, had not been needed on the streets, so they were passing time playing poker.

"Yeah, yeah. Hold your horses."

"Who's cooking supper?" One of the officers looked around the group.

"Plenty of beef stew left, right? Let's just eat that." Another re-sponded.

"Works for me." Albert loved beef stew and it wasn't something he'd ever cook for himself. "Tell you what. We ate all the biscuits, so I'll open that box of cornmeal and make cornbread. Deal?" Albert looked around the table at the men.

"That's what we're waiting on you to do—deal the cards!"

"Okay, last hand for me. Then I'll heat up the stew and make cornbread."

"You're on."

The cards were shuffled, dealt, and the plastic chips flew onto the table.

"Dealer takes one."

The laughter ensued and the men played through the hand.

"Can't win 'em all."

"You didn't win any, Simmons. What's got you so distracted?"

"Worried about a friend."

"Still not going to tell us her name?"

"Old high school friend. He wasn't feeling well yesterday, and hasn't answered my calls."

"Probably just sleeping it off."

"Yeah, you're probably right. Okay, I'm out of this game. Supper at five-forty-five sharp."

"Yes, sir."

"Yahoo."

"Go, Albert."

One of the men shuffled the cards and they played another hand. Albert pulled out the large pot of stew and the iron skillet to make cornbread. *As soon as we're released, I'm heading to Buddy's house. Not like him to at least answer my text.*

Clues to Search

Quinn started a search on how someone could get access to rocuronium. After an hour searching and reading everything from drug manufacturers to research articles, she picked up her secure phone.

"Williams."

"Isaacs. This is a work call."

"Happy to help if I can."

"Any experience with deaths caused by a paralytic agent?"

"Planning to murder someone?" His off-the-cuff humor was evident.

"Work, Williams, work."

His voice became serious. "None in our jurisdiction. I attended a workshop at SBI a few years back. I'd have to pull up my notes to speak to specifics, but have some general knowledge. What do you need?"

"Just trying to figure out how someone could get hold of a drug designed to be used as part of surgical procedures."

"I'd feel better discussing this if I refreshed my memory. That said, on the surface there are plenty of ways to get it: theft by employee, theft through robbery of a pharmacy, or pharmaceutical company, or robbing a delivery truck and those are just the easy ones—those ways are sometimes traceable. Distribution by thieves...well, that's tougher."

She sighed. "You have just pointed out why it's shocking to me that Chief Hansen chose me for lead detective."

"Quinn, listen to me. You've done detective work for years—you just weren't called one. You can learn everything you need to know. You have several good detectives over there, and the SBI and FBI at your disposal. More important—what *you* bring to the job, which I'm sure the new chief acted on, is the intellect, curiosity, methodical way of thinking that will get to the answer—you don't have to know everything—that's the fun of discovery."

"Thanks, Billy. I needed to hear that." She let out a sigh.

"Am I safe in betting you've been at this all day?"

"Pretty much. What time is it?"

"Going on six-thirty."

"In the afternoon?" She feigned shock.

"Uh...yeah! Have you eaten?"

"Nope. Guess that would help clear my brain. How about you? How's your day?"

"I took leave. Nothing I could work on from home. So I've been turning wood today."

"Nice. That's a great escape from the day-to-day life of solving crimes."

"Been nicer if you'd been here. Think we can make tomorrow work?"

"I have no idea. Haven't looked out the window or at the weather forecast. What's the probability?"

"Winds dying down, snow fall accumulation significant—depending on where you are, but the snow has stopped falling."

"Then it sounds like *our* time tomorrow will depend on the roads getting cleared."

"Ha! I already have my snowshoes cleaned up and if I start now, I'll be there by this time tomorrow."

She laughed until tears ran down her face. "Let's just wait and see."

"Yeah, I agree. Go get some food, find something that can prove a great distraction, and relax. Talk to you tomorrow."

"Good night, Billy. Thanks for your insight." She held the phone out and looked at it. *Two detectives today have told me to relax.* She leaned back in her chair and stretched her arms over her head. *Can I separate personal and professional? Billy's a colleague in another jurisdiction, but...*a vivid image of her mother and father popped in her head—each of them in their academic gowns with the hoods around their necks that represented their doctoral degrees. *How many years have they had separate, but intertwined professions? Most of my life.* She smiled as she reached for some eggs, cheese, ham, spinach and mushrooms. This was a night for an omelet. *Mother and Daddy have made it work their entire careers.* She set the ingredients aside and took out her phone.

"Hola, mi hija. Como estas?"

"Bien, gracias. How are you, Daddy?"

"All is well here in our comfortable home. Wish you were here to ride out the storm with us. How are things there? Have power?"

"Yes, Daddy. Thanks to Grandmother..." She stopped herself before she said something sarcastic. "Is Mother available?"

"She's right here beside me. Love you."

"Love you, too, Daddy."

"Hello lovely daughter. I take it you are doing well in spite of the storm. Are you at home?"

"Yes, I am. Listen, Mother, I called to make sure you are both okay, but also to apologize."

"Whatever for, Quinn?"

"For my rudeness yesterday. I know that you're amazing at dealing with a situation and moving on, but that doesn't change my obligation to own up to my bad behavior. I know you were being respectful in speaking about Billy in the formal use of his name last night, and you weren't talking about him as a detective, but as my friend. I was out of line and I'm sorry."

"Apology accepted. Now, tell me what you are doing in this storm."

"Although I'm at home, it's still a work day for me and I know you understand how that is. Thanks to technology, I was able to catch up on all the reports that are part of cases in my department, and I'm working my way through policy and procedure manuals."

"Well, dear girl, you were always good at detail, and also able to capture the big picture. I've always admired those skills in you."

"You can do that, too." Quinn thought of how competent her mother was.

"No, not like you. One of the great things about our profession is that I can teach Spanish grammar and linguistics because I love the minutiae, and your father can teach literature which presents the big picture of the people and culture—he grew up steeped in it. It's ideal for a married couple in the same profession, don't you think?"

Quinn nodded her head. *So that's how you've done it all these years. I never thought about it.* "Ideal, Mother. I must admit I never really thought about how you could work in the same department and be together so much more than most couples are."

"Small department helps, big university helps, loving each other helps most of all."

"I know, Mother. I've been happy for as long as I can remember that I know my parents love each other—not everyone gets to say that. I have a better appreciation for what that means when you share a profession. Thanks."

"Thank you. Now have you eaten?"

Quinn knew that meant they were probably at the dinner table. "About to make a spinach omelet. Thanks for the chat. Tell Daddy I said goodnight. Stay safe. Love you, Mother."

"I love you, mi hija." The call ended.

And most of all, Mother, you and Daddy both do best in a predictable life where the routines are established. It doesn't work for me. I like the unpredictable nature of my profession. I think I knew it the day of the shooting.

Answer the Phone

"Good cornbread, Simmons."

"Yeah, he can even reheat stew without burning it."

"Yeah, yeah," Albert laughed. "Just glad I didn't have to make it from scratch."

"So are we," bellowed one of the other officers.

They all stood and took their dishes to the dishwasher, and one of the other officers washed the empty stew pot and the mixing bowl from the cornbread.

Albert saw that it was six-forty-five p.m. and he still hadn't heard from Buddy. He took out his phone and tried again. No answer. "Hey, guys, I'm going up to see, Sarge. Call on my phone if you need me."

"Brown-nosing are ya?"

"Bucking for a promotion?"

He waved them off and ran up the stairs. The shift sergeant was standing in the hall area behind the desk in the main lobby. Albert was pleased to see that it was a different sergeant from the one yesterday afternoon. *This one's a pretty good sergeant.*

"Sarge, got a minute?"

"Sure, Simmons. What's up?" He walked over to Albert out of earshot of the desk officer.

Albert told him about the stop that he'd been called to yesterday that had involved his friend, Buddy. "Sarge, Buddy is a little on the weird side, always was, but I never saw him like that. He said his head was hurting something awful."

The sergeant was nodding. "Want me to send an officer around for a wellness check?"

"Well, Sarge, I don't think Buddy will come to the door for anyone but me."

"What will you do if he doesn't come to the door?"

"I'll call for back up and force entry."

"How about a compromise. I'll have the sector duty officer meet you there. You do the door knock. If there's no answer then you can call it in and...how many hours has it been?"

"Something over thirty."

"You know we don't normally enter without cause for forty-eight hours with adults, but since you know this man has no relatives and was in crisis, I'll authorize it. Just check in before you break down a door or window."

"Absolutely, Sarge. Thanks." He gave the Sergeant Buddy's name and address and went back to the common room to put on his boots, get his jacket and overcoat, and his sidearm. The other officers were absorbed in a movie as he slipped out. His phone buzzed just as he got to the back door. He pulled it out hoping it was a text from Buddy.

It was from the sergeant: Evans on way. Use official vehicle. Do it by the book.

"10-4." Albert keyed into his phone. He scanned his badge at the garage where unassigned vehicles were serviced and ready to go.

The garage mechanic on duty saw him come in. "Sarge said you need a car."

"Right. Got the address?"

"Yep. Sign here."

Albert signed. "Thanks for having it warmed up." He extended his hand to shake.

"Don't get used to it." The man chuckled and slapped Albert on the shoulder. "Be safe out there."

"10-4." Albert was in the car. The police lot was cleared and navigable. He was checked out through the gate within two minutes. The roads were passable, but not with any speed. It took him more than thirty minutes to get to Buddy's house—normally less than fifteen minutes from the station.

The sector officer was parked on the street. She stepped out of her cruiser.

Albert pulled into the driveway and noted that the house was totally dark. He got out and was glad it was someone he'd worked with before. "Hey, Evans."

"What's going on here, Simmons?"

Albert filled her in as they walked toward the front door. He knocked, rang the doorbell, and there was no answer.

Evans was scanning the outside of the house. "Is there any chance a window or door is unlocked."

"None. Buddy's good people, but he's pretty compulsive about most things; his privacy is number one."

"You say you brought him home yesterday morning, right?"

"Yes."

"How did you enter?"

"I was driving his van and pulled it into the garage. Detective Isaacs had Buddy in my squad car."

Evans hesitated. "Really? Detective Isaacs. I hear she's a pretty tough cop."

"Not really. Maybe by the book, but...yeah, maybe tough in a good way."

"Got the hots for her, Simmons?" Evans elbowed him.

Albert ignored her. He had no interest in the detective other than as a potential boss someday. "Let's find out about Buddy." His tone was flat and final.

"How did you leave yesterday? Through the garage?"

Albert jerked his head and, with the lights from his headlights, she could see the surprised look on his face. "How did you leave yesterday?" She said each word slowly and deliberately.

"Through this door." He stood there for a second. "Maybe Buddy's head hurt so bad he didn't lock it."

Evans pulled her weapon and so did Simmons. He held his to his side and turned the door knob and pushed lightly. The door opened. He stepped back and pulled out his phone.

"Dispatch, Officer Simmons, how may I direct your call?"

"Sarge."

"10-4."

Albert quickly told the sergeant the situation. He held the phone out so Evans could hear. The sergeant authorized the entry.

He ended the call, pushed the door open, and stepped in. Evans was right behind him.

"Buddy. Hey, Buddy, it's Albert. You doing okay? How's the headache." He flipped on the lamp that he knew was beside the sofa. Albert knew Buddy would freak out about their wet boots on his floor.

He pointed toward the kitchen. Evans nodded. "Buddy, It's Albert. I'm coming into the kitchen—just checking on you, my friend." He made a point of stamping his feet hard on the wooden floors.

The kitchen was empty and immaculate.

Evans whispered, "A single guy lives here?"

Albert nodded.

"Might nominate him for man of the year."

Albert glared at her. He wasn't use to this kind of banter.

"Buddy, I'm coming down the hall." He reached to turn on the hall light just as it came on. He jumped back into the archway of the living room and held his hand out for Evans to stay back.

"Buddy, that you?" Silence. Absolute silence. Then the bedroom light came on.

"Hey, Buddy. Come on. Stop playing games. I'm coming down the hall to check on you." He knew Buddy would be mad when he found out another cop was with him, but he had to declare it. "Listen, I have another police officer with me. We both have weapons. We aren't planning to use them—just want to protect you. Got it, Buddy?" Silence. No sound except the breathing of the two officers.

Albert nodded his head down the hall. He stomped his feet and led with his weapon. Even though Buddy was his friend, he wasn't about to be surprised by him, or anyone else, with a gun.

He turned into the doorway and almost tripped over Buddy on the floor. He instantly bent over him and checked for a pulse. He shook his head.

Evans had her phone out and called for a detective and a wagon.

Buddy's body was rigid and as cold as it was outside.

Albert sat back on his heels and a tear ran down his face. *I should have come yesterday.*

Part II
Follow the Clues

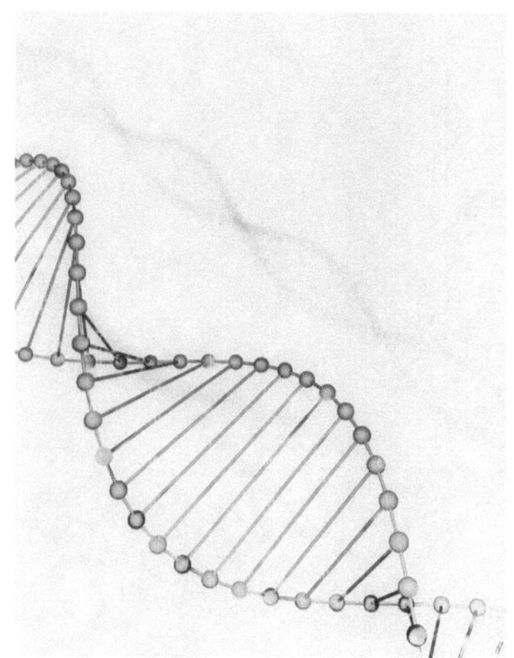

Chapter 16

Leadership is not about necessarily being the loudest voice in the room.
Jacinda Ardern

Gathering in the Storm

Flashing lights from two police vehicles lit the dark street which ended just before a large field. Detective Millwood pulled up to Buddy's house at the same time the morgue van arrived.

Simmons and Evans were standing on the porch.

"Officers."

"Detective." Simmons nodded. "Evans met me here at the scene and entered the house with me on authorization of the shift sergeant."

"What have we got?"

"Resident is deceased on the floor entering his bedroom."

"Any reason to suspect foul play?"

"No sir. I know the deceased—personal friend since middle school. His pappy disappeared more than a decade ago and not sure when his grandma died. I don't know of any other family—or friends for that matter." He inhaled and a small cloud filled the air as his warm breath reached the cold of the night. "I responded to a backup call for Detective Isaacs yesterday morning. It was Buddy and he complained of a bad headache. I hadn't heard from Buddy since bringing him home yesterday morning even after multiple texts and phone calls. I knew it wasn't like him. Sir, he is...was...a bit strange, but he would've sent me a text, even if he didn't want me to come over." He explained getting permission to officially check on Buddy, as well as, the steps he and Officer Evans had followed entering the house. He gave a very detailed account of their actions and stood back.

"Officer Evans, anything you'd like to add?"

"No, sir."

"Okay, thanks." Millwood nodded to her.

Tristan from the ME's office walked up. The others recognized the second man as a forensic tech from the downstairs lab.

"Got a body for us?" Tristan's bluntness caused the others to cringe, but they were all aware of his unusual behaviors.

"Need you to verify and do your thing. Make sure you notify me before you move the body. The remains are to the left down the hall." Millwood was direct and left no question about what he expected, at least to anyone but Tristan; who had a tendency to interrupt.

"Including turning it over?" Tristan's sardonic grin was well-known by everyone in the police force.

Millwood rolled his eyes, thought about this young man's odd behaviors, and made a decision. "Yes, I want to be present for any movement of the remains."

The two men stepped out of their boots on the porch and put on booties over their socks.

Millwood relaxed a bit. *Okay, he's strange but he knows protocol.*

"Sir, I'd like to stay, if it's okay." Simmons had waited until the others had entered the house.

Millwood looked at Albert. "Sure. Until we have reason to suspect anything other than natural causes, I think it's fine for you to be here for your friend. Just ask you to wait on the porch or in your vehicle for a few minutes." He turned to Officer Evans. "Stay warm. Get in your vehicle."

She headed for her car. Albert stayed on the porch.

Millwood stepped into the living room and took off his boots and put covers on his socks. He headed for the bedroom. The floors were wet from the entry by the two officers. *Yuck. I hate wet socks.*

Satisfied that the morgue techs were handling things appropriately, he walked through the game room and then back down the hall into the kitchen. *This guy was either the homemaker of the year, or paid a bunch to have someone keep this place clean. Looks like a laboratory.* He looked out the back door and noticed how dark it was even with the moonlight. He flipped the switch by the door, but no light came on. *Looks like a tunnel or something off the back porch.* He opened the back door. He saw the arbor and the plants covered in snow. *It's a tunnel, of sorts.* In the quiet, he thought he heard a pinging noise, but couldn't tell where it was coming from. He went back to the front of the house and wasn't surprised Simmons was standing outside the front door.

"Simmons, ever been out back of this house?"

"No, sir. When I come over, we usually go straight to the game room. We like to play video games and try to beat each other."

"How often you see this man?"

"Depends on my schedule, sir, but usually on Monday nights. Sometimes we play on Friday nights, but that's not every week."

"Any idea how long he's lived here?"

"This was his grandma's house. I don't think he moved in until after she died, but not real sure. We didn't see a lot of each other when he was away at university or the first few years after. Like I said, his pappy disappeared years back and that left him alone out in the country. He told me he never liked living in the country..." He shrugged. "So he moved in here."

Millwood made a few notes on the small pad he carried in his pocket. "Got it. Thanks." He closed the door and went back to the bedroom and watched the techs.

The young man with Tristan stood. "Detective, based on body temperature and lividity, the victim has been dead for at least eighteen hours, but not likely as much as thirty-six—still in rigor."

Millwood made notes. "Any evidence of trauma?"

The forensic tech shook his head. "None that is evident. I'm satisfied that we can get the gurney and remove the remains to the morgue. Doc was notified when we were. I suspect he'll be there by the time we arrive."

Millwood noticed that Tristan actually stood back and let the forensic tech do the talking. "Need help with the gurney?"

"No, thanks. We can manage it." The tech and Tristan headed for the door to get the gurney.

Millwood looked at the remains of Buddy Wilkie. He took out his secure phone and called Quinn.

"Isaacs."

"Millwood, ma'am. Normally I wouldn't bother you, but since Officer Simmons indicated you were on the stop with Buddy Wilkie yesterday morning, thought it best to let you know that I am on scene at Wilkie's house. He is deceased."

"Under what conditions, Detective?"

"Appears to be natural causes. Been gone eighteen hours more or less. Forensic team about to transport to the morgue."

She looked at her watch. It was eight p.m. "Who found him?"

"Officers Simmons and Evans. Seems Simmons is a friend of his, and came to check on him after no response to texts and phone calls."

"Did he go as a friend or as an officer?"

"Officer, ma'am."

"I have the address. I'm on my way."

"Really not…" Millwood stopped himself. She was his new boss. It wasn't his place to tell her what to do. "Yes, ma'am. Do you want us to wait to move the remains?"

"Please. I'll be there in less than fifteen minutes."

"Roads in town are mostly drivable—but not dry surfaces. Be careful."

"Thanks for the warning. On my way." She had her sidearm on, her coat on over her jacket, and was in her boots in less than two minutes. As the garage door opened, she looked out and realized she had not even heard her driveway being cleared. *Can't beat reliable services.* She had purposely backed into her garage, as she usually did in winter weather. *Might need to get in the habit of backing in. Never needed it in immigration, but in this job…probably.*

Twelve minutes later she pulled up to the house amid flashing lights of the officers' cruisers and morgue van. She grabbed the small bag which had booties and gloves in it, and put a pair of each in her pocket. An officer got out of one of the cruisers as she walked up.

"Officer."

"Detective. I'm Jessica Evans, ma'am."

"Pleased to meet you." Quinn kept walking. Both women stepped up onto the porch.

"Detective Isaacs, I didn't know you'd been called." Simmons straightened up.

"Sorry for your loss, Officer Simmons." The front door opened and Millwood stepped back for her to enter. The empty gurney was sitting in the living room.

"Detective, thanks for your call." She didn't mind that Simmons and Evans knew she'd been called; she just didn't think it was necessary to justify her presence in response to Simmons.

"Remains are this way." Millwood waited while she stepped out of her boots and put on booties. "Floor's wet, ma'am."

"Thanks for the warning. I'll try to step around the wet spots."

"Wish I'd thought of it myself." He grimaced.

Quinn looked around the living room and turned down the hall in the direction Millwood pointed. She noted that the furnishings were very fine quality, but sparse. The house appeared immaculate. She saw the foot sticking out into the hall and pulled on gloves. She bent down and touched the ankle and lower leg. In several cases in her previous job, she had dealt with victims of death. Even through her latex gloves she could feel the body was cold. She wasn't sure why she had the need to touch the corpse. She stood as she peeled off the gloves and turned them into themselves before putting them in her pocket.

"Good with the techs moving the remains?" Millwood watched her face.

"Yes." She nodded. "Thanks for calling me. Could we talk in the other room while they take him out?"

"Yes, ma'am." Millwood walked toward the kitchen where the Tristan and the forensic tech were waiting.

Quinn had not seen them when she entered. She was right behind Millwood and stopped when she saw Tristan—then she heard him.

"We've got this. Come on, techie." His voice was much too loud for the room.

Quinn looked at him as she stepped into the room. His eyes were darting all over the place. She stepped to the side so he could pass her. She watched the gurney move down the hall.

"What's on your mind, ma'am?"

"I told Detective Marshall yesterday that there was something about the deceased that put me on guard."

"Anything you could put your finger on?"

"Not really..." *Except his eyes—just like Tristan's eyes...* "Excuse me one moment, Detective." She walked down the hall. Her long legs made the short distance in a few strides. The remains were on the gurney. Tristan turned in response to her footfalls.

"Ma'am. We've got this." He stared at her and his grin spread across his face.

She looked him squarely in the eyes. "Good work, gentlemen. Just wanted to verify that Dr. Walters was expecting the remains."

The tech spoke up. "Yes, ma'am. He's waiting on us."

"Good. Thanks for your work." She turned and went back to the kitchen where she and Millwood waited for them to take the remains out of the house.

"Detective," Millwood started.

"Please, call me Quinn or Isaacs. I'm good with titles when we need them, but first or last, whichever works for you."

"Got it. I'm Kevin. Care to share what took you down that hallway?"

"Eyes. It was Wilkie's eyes that caught my attention, and I remembered that I had met Tristan earlier in the week and found his eyes unusual, too."

"Ha. His eyes are the least unusual thing about him."

"Fair enough." *She wasn't convinced Tristan's looked like Buddy's, but both were an unusual shade of blue. Or was it blue-gray?*

"Quinn, I'd like you to look at…"

"Detective Millwood?" Simmons called from the door.

"Give me a minute." Kevin stepped to the front room. "Yes, Simmons."

"Sir, unless you need me, I'm going to return to the station."

"Sure. You could just go home. I know you stayed at the station last night, but I can let the sergeant know I sent you home."

"No need. I'm good staying there."

"Okay. Sorry, again, for your loss. Would you ask Evans to hang around a bit longer. I'll talk to her shortly."

"Yes, sir."

"Get some rest, Officer." Kevin walked back into the kitchen and saw Quinn looking at the two phones he had put in evidence bags sitting on the kitchen counter.

Quinn looked. "Simmons going to be okay?"

"Yeah, he's a pretty good cop—lives alone. I'm sure this was a shock for him. He stayed at the station last night and said he will tonight."

"I heard that. Probably good to be around other people at a time like this."

"Fair point. Hadn't thought of it that way. Anyway, I bagged the phones so we can see if we can find out next of kin and anything else that might be helpful. In the meantime, I'd like you to take a look out back with me."

"Sure. Concerns?"

"Probably nothing, just feel better if I verify." He opened the door and was about to step out in to the snow on the porch when he remembered he didn't have on his boots. "Forgot I wasn't in my boots. Take a look and listen."

Quinn stepped into the door frame and let her eyes adjust to the dark. She leaned back in and turned off the kitchen light.

"The porch light needs a bulb. I tried that switch."

"Actually, I wanted to see this without any light." They both got quiet. "Do you hear a pinging noise? Or wait, is it a hum?"

Millwood spoke quietly. "I heard a ping—not a hum. This tunnel is unusual." He reached in his pocket. "Okay if I use my pocket light and see what's what?"

"By all means. I've got you covered." *I thought I heard a ping and a hum.* She listened again as she unhooked that guard on her service weapon.

"Think I'll go get my boots. I don't think we need to worry about the foot traffic in the house."

"Good idea." Quinn followed him to get her boots.

Boots on, they returned to the back porch. Millwood turned on the small high-powered flash light and whistled. "This is quite a tunnel. Who does that just to get out to a shed?" He carefully navigated the steps which had less snow than the porch as they were protected by all the vines on the tunnel. The sound of the pinging got louder as Millwood approached the shed.

Quinn stood on the porch. She still heard the ping, but not a hum.

"Sound is coming from in here. The door handle is no ordinary door handle—it's security grade."

"Step back, Detective. Let's get this place secure and a team out here. Don't want that pinging to turn out to be a bomb."

Kevin was back on the porch in a few long strides. "I agree."

One Step at a Time

"Dispatch, Detective Isaacs, how may I direct your call?"

"Is Sergeant Clark in the station?"

"Yes, ma'am. Putting you through."

"Clark."

"Quinn Isaacs, here." She told him the situation and asked for his team. "I promise I won't make a habit of calling you on every case, but this one is unusual enough I need your expertise."

"Here to serve, ma'am. You say you have concerns there might be a bomb in that outbuilding?"

"No way to know. Not sure why there would be a bomb that sounds like this, but when you see the setup, you'll understand the concern. I'm pretty sure you'll want your high-grade lights for this scene."

"I've deployed my team. Be there shortly. You and Millwood stay out front."

The team was in their well-equipped van and on the road within two minutes. Clark expected nothing less of his team.

Quinn, Kevin, and Jessica Evans moved their vehicles across the street out of the way.

"Ma'am, do you want me to put up tape around the front?"

"Let's wait. Could be the timer on his dryer pinging." Something told her it wasn't, but now she wished she'd thought of that earlier and checked to see if there was a washer and dryer in the house.

"Yes, ma'am. I understand."

The large equipment van and Sergeant Clark's SUV pulled into the driveway. The team exited.

Quinn stepped forward.

Clark turned to his four-person team. "Check the perimeter and see if there's any way in to this outbuilding other than through the house."

Quinn had told him that from the inside there didn't appear to be any way into the shed. She was impressed that he didn't give them any other direction. Two took off to the left and two to the right.

"Either of you able to give me the cadence of the noise?"

Quinn didn't play her piano much anymore, but she understood the question. She tapped the fingers of one hand on the palm of the other.

Kevin nodded. "Yes, that's it—exactly."

"Any good at pitch, Detective Isaacs?" It was clear Clark wasn't joking.

"Not without a piano."

"Fair enough."

"When my team gets back, we'll sweep the house for good measure." The two who had gone left reappeared from the right side. The other two were coming around the corner from the left. Each time had clearly done a complete 360° surveillance.

"Report."

"Completely fenced. Vine covered brick and wood and a stand of trees."

"From wall on southside, there's an archway +/- twenty feet in."

"No motion sensors activating any light source."

"Snow was pristine and no evidence of anyone outside of house."

"No gate from wall to back or sides of property."

"Anything else?" Clark waited two seconds.

"No, sir." Only one team member spoke.

Quinn was not only taking in everything that was reported, she was making mental notes about how they worked as a team: total efficiency and attention to detail.

"Boots on, sweep the house."

One of the team stepped into the van and exited with four towels. Quinn watched them each take one and step on them on the porch and then dry the tops of their boots.

"Sergeant." Quinn waited until the team entered the house. "I was impressed with the results your team reported from the Summers' house, but you are to be commended on the efficiency of your team."

"Thank you, ma'am. Takes lots of training as a team and each member being responsible for his/her own role on the team—and each other's."

"It would appear they know that."

The front door opened. The member who had spoken earlier exited.

"Sir, the house shows no signs of forced entry or a struggle. The garage is a magazine set for how to organize and maintain your equipment and supplies for a business."

"What kind of business?"

"Plumbing, based on the signs on the van and the shelves. Washer and dryer are in the garage and as pristine as everything else."

"Continue."

"Tunnel from back door to the outbuilding is a glorified arbor made of steel and covered in vines thick enough that even without leaves you can't see into or out of it. Sound is a regular beat and consistent with a timer alert on a piece of equipment."

"Doesn't mean it is." Clark's tone was clipped and wary.

"Sir, no sir. Door handle is definitely security grade, but breachable without blowing the door out."

"Noted."

"Had to jump off deck to survey sides of buildings. Windows appear to have been painted black from the inside. No way to see inside."

Quinn wondered if Clark was responsible for this level of military precision or if he chose his team because they all had military training. *Be interesting to find out.* She tucked away the thought.

"Suit up. Let's get that door open and see what we have."

For the first time since she came on board and met the A-team, she realized that they did both security and forensic work. *Guess that comes with being a small department.* She made another mental note to talk to George Marshall and get a better understanding of how different teams worked in the department.

"Detective Isaacs, any questions or concerns?"

"Appreciate the effort to enter without destruction. I want to know what's in that building."

"The team will alert us when it's safe for us to enter—assuming it is."

The team members checked their own protective gear and the other person that was apparently their two-person team.

"Sir, ready to deploy."

"Permission granted."

The four-person team ran up the steps, dried their boots again, and went into the house in lock-step.

Quinn had entered houses suspected of harboring illegal immigrants, but she had never been part of such a precision team.

Clark watched his team head into the house. He turned to Quinn. "Now we wait, ma'am."

She nodded.

Chapter 17

Truth is never to be found in simplicity.
Isaac Newton

The Shed

Time seemed to stand still. Quinn knew the feeling from long surveillance details in her immigration work. She pulled her hair into a knot. Neither she nor any of the others said a word. All four were standing out in the street. Heads turned when light poured out of the front door as it opened.

Clark put his hand up. "Wait here, please." He moved quickly to the porch. The officer stepped off the bottom step and spoke to him. Clark turned and waved the others forward.

"We need to do a search for keys. There are many locked cabinets in the shed and a locked chest freezer—rather not force them open unless needed."

Quinn turned to Officer Evans. "Remain out front and do not let anyone on the premises. I'll call for additional officers to cover the side street." Her phone was already in her hand.

Clark sent his officers to check the bedroom, kitchen, and garage for keys. She put her phone in her pocket.

Quinn turned to Clark and Millwood. "Additional officers enroute to cover the side street." She looked around the living room more carefully now. There was a beige sofa, two brown leather arm chairs, a wooden coffee table, and an upholstered foot stool at the end of one chair. There were end tables for the sofa, which she noticed were not identical to the coffee table in design or wood, but somehow seemed to match—each had a lamp. She could tell it was all expensive furniture and well kept.

"Something catch your attention, Detective Isaacs?" Clark stood in the arched doorway between the living room and kitchen off of which the hall extended.

She shook her head. "Sorry, looking for anything that seems unusual or out of the ordinary for how most folks live."

"Ma'am, if I may say so, this whole house is pretty out of the ordinary. Nothing on the walls, clean as a whistle except for what we've tracked in, and I'm willing to bet that the cupboards, closets, and dresser will be neat too." Millwood looked at her and then Clark.

"Sir," one member of the A-team stepped up. "These keys were on a hook at the back of a shelf by the back door."

"Look like they'll open what you've seen?"

"Not the cabinets or freezer, sir, but one might open the desk. Maybe the keys are in there."

"Is the pinging from one of those cabinets?" Quinn's question was direct.

Clark nodded to the woman standing beside him.

"Ma'am, the ping is from a timer on the cabinet and built into the equipment. I might say that the cabinets appear to be custom made—very custom made."

"Sargent, I would like to have a look before they are opened." Quinn's voice was flat.

"Your show, Detective Isaacs."

Quinn followed Clark out to the shed. He stepped back and let her enter first. Millwood stayed in the house with three of the A-team members.

Clark let out a low whistle. "What *is* this place? If it weren't so pristine, I might think it was the laboratory of a mad scientist."

Quinn did not miss a beat. "It might be, Sargent." She walked in the center of the space and carefully looked at each cabinet, the microscopes, the computer and the very old freezer—It was inconsistent with everything else in the space except for the old wooden desk. Her eyes took in the black out drapes on the two windows. She pointed to them.

Clark reached with a gloved hand and pulled back one of the drapes. "Drapes and black paint."

Quinn nodded. "That makes sure no one can see in." She turned to the officer and looked at the name in black ink on the patch on her protective suit. "Officer DeLoach..."

"Yes, ma'am." She held out the ring which had five keys on it.

"Ma'am," Clark interrupted, "may I suggest we step out and let De-Loach open the desk? She's suited up."

"Could you give us a minute, Officer?"

Officer Ruth DeLoach stepped out without saying a word.

"Sargent, I was going to ask the officer to step out so we could talk. She likely assumed I wanted the keys. What I wanted to ask is whether we have access to bomb sniffing dogs?"

"We can call the SBI. They have a handler in Maryville who could be here fastest if they don't have anything else at the moment."

"Do you observe anything that makes you concerned this is more than it appears?"

"What does it appear to be to you, ma'am?"

Quinn looked around the shed. "On the surface, it isn't totally inconsistent with a man whose home is so clean you could eat off the floors—before we walked all over them. That said, I am no expert on any kind of explosive device, and will accept your assessment of the best course of action."

"I have no idea what we're going to find in here. I've never seen anything like these cabinets; I'd guess they're custom built and built for this space, not brought in from somewhere else. They appear to be firmly attached to the walls. The old freezer has me stymied because it is inconsistent with the rest of the equipment." The ping from the cabinet continued in the background. "On the surface, that ping appears consistent with a timer like an oven." He watched her face. Her eyes looked at each item in the room.

Quinn focused on the Sargent. "If we bring in the SBI, and there isn't a bomb, we've lost nothing but time. Any reason to rush?"

"Given that the man has been deceased for almost a day at this point, I'm guessing it's been pinging for a while."

"Then let me make a call before we do anything else." She took out her secure phone.

The phone barely rang once. "Jackson here."

"Quinn Isaacs, sir."

"Evening. How may I be of service?"

Quinn filled him in on the situation. "I think a bomb sniffing dog is all we'll need for the moment. Once we know if it's safe to open these cabinets, I may find something I'm not expecting."

"What might that be?"

"I have no idea. The deceased has a reputation for being…well, eccentric. He has a plumbing business and I promise you his garage is as clean and neat as his home. I suspect there is a spreadsheet on this computer for every single item. Based on a report from one of our officer's, a personal friend of the deceased, he has no known family. Making sure of that is my first mission as soon as I make sure this place isn't going to blow up and take half the town with it."

"Hope that means you're outside."

She didn't respond. "Appreciate the help with the dog. I'll keep you informed."

"I'll text ETA."

"10-4." She turned to Clark.

"Dog is being sent. We'll have ETA shortly. I suggest we all wait out front."

Clark was out the door of the shed and all headed toward the living room and out the front door.

Quinn stepped aside and sent a text on her secure phone to the chief. Quinn's phone rang. *She must be a speed reader.* "Isaacs."

"Sit rep." The chief didn't waste words.

Quinn gave her a situation report in detail including that a text had just arrived that the bomb sniffing dog would arrive within the hour—depending on the roads. Quinn knew you could drive it in twenty minutes in good weather. She assumed the chief knew that, too.

"Yes, ma'am. If there is any evidence of explosives, I'll contact you before we do anything." She listened to the chief. "Yes, ma'am. 10-4."

She walked back over to Detective Millwood and Sargent Clark who were on the porch. The others were all gathered inside the A-team van. She updated the two men and shrugged. "So, we wait."

Clark spoke first. "I'll have my team do a thorough check of the house once we have clearance on the shed. Might turn up something that would give us a clue about any family."

Kevin Millwood leaned his head to one side. "I have two phones in evidence. We'll get what we can once we have a warrant. Judge won't be keen if there's no crime, but maybe not so hard-hearted to have someone buried without next of kin."

"Judge is doing his or her job, Kevin. Just like thee and me." Clark's tone held no rancor.

"Yep, that's what we do. This situation has me doing a lot of thinking, though."

"Me, too."

They both turned when Quinn spoke.

"I dealt with one situation of a subordinate with Obsessive-Compulsive Disorder—she couldn't handle the chaos of our work."

"Think this guy was OCD?" Kevin looked from Clark to Quinn.

"Way out of my league." Clark looked straight ahead as he spoke. "It's hard not to speculate, isn't it?"

Quinn nodded. "Speculating doesn't always prove beneficial and can prove risky. It may be splitting hairs, but I find the more possibilities you can raise to explain an unusual situation, the less likely you are to miss something because you take that unusual situation at face value."

Clark decided to see what her response to challenging her would be. "I thought detectives were supposed to follow the evidence. Our job is to bring you the evidence—your team's job is to figure it out."

"Well, Sargent, I'd say we're in the middle of some pretty unusual evidence at the moment. It just doesn't seem plausible to me that everything here is as perfect as it might appear."

"Fair enough, Detective Isaacs. Fair enough." The headlights coming down the side street caused him to turn. "Looks like backup is here."

Quinn called all the officers together and brought everyone up to date. They huddled in idle chitchat at the van. Twenty minutes later, the SBI K-9 unit arrived and everyone stood back while Quinn and Steve talked to the agents.

"Let's go see what you have, Detective." The SBI agent moved quickly toward the porch.

The Cabinets

Clark's lead officer, DeLoach, took the two SBI agents and the dog into the house and out to the shed. Quinn heard the SBI agent call the dog Millie.

The others stood outside waiting—none of them wanted to miss anything. The darkness, cold, and stillness added to the palpable tension which comes with wondering if you might be blown from here to kingdom come.

Quinn looked up at the glittering stars. *Here's to all of us seeing tomorrow.*

Officer DeLoach came out the door and the SBI agents and Millie followed.

Sid Brown, the lead SBI agent stepped over to Quinn. "Ma'am, no evidence of a bomb. It's safe to open that cabinet."

Quinn nodded. The flashing lights of the police vehicles made it look like there was a halo over her head. "Thank you, Agent."

"Ma'am, as you know, the dog sniffs chemicals, and although there were none with bomb making properties, she hit on a cabinet that is part of the desk. I suspect you'll find chemicals used in whatever is being examined under those high-powered microscopes."

"Thanks to both of you—and to Millie. Safe travels home."

"Good luck. Hope this is no more than a scientist doing his research."

"Me, too, Agent. Me, too."

The agents and Millie were in their SUV and headed out.

Quinn sent a text to Agent-in-Charge Jackson at the SBI: No danger. Thanks.

She stepped forward. "Let's go see if we can get into those cabinets."

Waiting at the door, Quinn turned to DeLoach. "Officer, see if one of those keys opens the desk. We'll see if it gives us keys to the cabinets."

DeLoach entered the shed and the second key she tried opened the center desk drawer. The drawer only opened about three inches. The officer tried to open the side drawer. It wouldn't move. She reached under the top of the desk inside the center drawer. "Voila!" She looked up at Quinn and Clark.

Clark nodded.

"There's a lever here. I suspect it will open this side drawer." She pulled on it and heard a latch release. The side drawer opened easily when she pulled on it. Inside was a set of keys. She removed them.

Quinn looked around the room. "Let's start with the one that is pinging. Officer, if you will."

Quinn, Millwood, and Clark watched as DeLoach found the key that unlocked the cabinet. The pinging stopped immediately. DeLoach stepped back and held the door open. "Ma'am, it would appear we're going to have a long night ahead of us."

The others stepped up and saw what DeLoach had seen. Each looked from one to the other.

"I'd like to get Chuck here so that we can make sure we handle all this with the utmost care. He will know what we need to do. In the meantime, let's open the other cabinets and the freezer. Detective Millwood, would you please have the officers establish a perimeter around the house with tape. By then I will have Chuck on his way."

Quinn, Clark, and DeLoach stood in silence looking at the contents of the cabinet.

Clark shook his head. "Honestly, I've never seen anything like this— the construction or the contents."

"Me, either. It had to have been custom built. Wonder what the temperature range is on it. What would it take to figure out how to construct all this?"

"I have no idea. Any thoughts DeLoach?"

"No, sir, except to say I never ceased to be amazed at what we can find in the most mundane places."

Clark cleared his throat as Millwood reentered the shed. Quinn's back was to him.

"My team can sweep the house, Quinn."

Quinn looked at him in surprise. She had met Steve Clark informally at a restaurant months ago, but he had only addressed her formally since she joined the force. "Thanks, Steve. This is Detective Millwood's scene. I'll leave it to him and your team to decide the best way to go forward. I'm available for whatever you need."

Millwood stood up a little straighter. "Ma'am."

Quinn turned around. "Yes?"

"Perimeter is being secured."

"Thanks. Your scene, Detective."

He didn't hesitate. "Let's open these other cabinets and then lay out a course of action."

"I'll be inside the house." Quinn walked toward the door and pulled out her secure phone.

"Chief, Isaacs here. There was no evidence of a bomb, but the contents and design of the cabinet that was beeping warranted making this a potential crime scene."

"Go on."

Quinn told her what was in the cabinet. "I'll call our lead forensic tech. I want to make sure this is handled the best way possible not to damage any evidence. Then I'll head to the station and be available for whatever is needed."

"These folks are used to long nights. I suggest you consider a good night's sleep being on your list so you are ready for whatever we need to do to follow this through."

"Yes, ma'am, I understand. However, no disrespect intended, but I will support my team. Sleep can come later."

"I expected nothing less, Quinn. I, however, am going to bed. Call if you need me immediately, otherwise, I will read any updates in the morning."

"Yes, ma'am. Good night."

"10-4." Quinn turned as she heard her name spoken.

"Yes?"

"I think you're going to want to see the contents of the freezer and each of these cabinets."

"I'll be there in just a minute. Thanks." She opened her contact list and called Chuck. "Yes, that's the address. See you soon. Thanks, Chuck."

She ended the call and smiled. She had heard the professionalism and the excitement in Chuck's voice. She put her phone in her pocket, stretched her arms above her head, lowered them, and walked out to the shed.

"Start here." Millwood pointed to the freezer.

Quinn walked over and lifted the lid. She looked left to right at each of the baskets and saw that there was more below them. She turned back to the others.

"Chuck is on his way. Thoughts, Detective Millwood?"

"A-team will search the house, attic, and see if they can find a way under the house. We can't rule out a burial ground in the backyard tonight, but we need to see what we have in the house and then have forensics figure out what we have here. Then we'll sort out what we need to do in the yard."

"Sergeant?" Quinn turned to Clark.

"Millwood and I discussed it and I recommend leaving DeLoach here with him and the rest of us take the house. Close quarters here to begin with and when Chuck arrives, well, three's company."

Quinn nodded. She walked around the room and looked in each of the cabinets. The material was neatly stored, labeled with numbers and letters written in a very precise script. *Wonder if these numbers represent dates. They sure look like it.*

"Sounds like you have a solid plan. Once you hear Chuck's take on it, we'll make a determination on calling in the SBI."

"Ma'am, with all this, we'll need the SBI." Millwood had spoken quickly. He stopped.

"I think we'll be in agreement on that. Right now, we'll regroup once Chuck has seen it all. I'm headed to the station. Regular updates, please."

"Yes, ma'am."

Quinn walked toward the door, stopped, and turned around. "Thanks to each you for your professionalism and attention to detail. I am honored to be a member of your team."

"Likewise, ma'am."

"Thanks, Detective."

"We'll do this right."

She walked out of the shed, into the house and out the front door to speak to the officers on perimeter duty.

Restless Night

Oscar Wilkie brought up the video footage from the drone which he had flown this evening to Buddy's house—his mother's home—the home of his childhood. He carefully studied each image of the video. He had gladly paid the money to get the highest rated professional drone that didn't require registration—one which could easily cover the five miles from his isolated cabin to Buddy's home. Tonight he knew not to fly it too low for fear of detection; the hum from a drone was unmistakable. He hoped the flashing lights from the police cars blocked the lights on his little spy machine.

The footage moved across his computer screen and it was impossible to tell how many people there were because he didn't dare come in too close.

Buddy, what's going on? How did you lose my GPS tracker on your van? Why are the cops at your house?

He continued to stare at the screen. *Two police cars. Maybe one of the neighbors down the street called the cops. Why? Buddy doesn't speed. He keeps to himself. He doesn't bother anyone.* Then he sat up straight. *Maybe it's Albert playing a trick on Buddy. They were always playing tricks in school.* He nodded his head. *Yeah, I bet that's it. Hmmm…wonder if Albert found the GPS tracker. Do those cop cars have a way to detect them?*

Oscar stopped the video and did a computer search on GPS detection. *So, there's an app to detect GPS trackers. Wonder if the cops use them?* He sat back. None of it made sense. *Did Buddy find it? Nah, it must have fallen off on a rough road.*

He decided he'd fly his drone tomorrow and see what things looked like in the daylight. *That boy was always too smart and too curious for his own good.* He shut down his computer and went to bed. He couldn't sleep. Something was happening and he couldn't figure out what it was.

Chapter 18

Not everything is as it seems, and not everything that seems is.
Jose Saramago

Round City Police Station

Quinn was cleared at the gate and turned to park in her assigned spot. There was a brand-new mid-size black SUV in her space. *The chief said my official car would be here today. It is.* She drove to the back-forty lot and started the walk to the station. Images of the cabinets in Buddy's shed ran through her mind. She was so engrossed she almost ran into someone at the back door to the station.

"Sorry, I was engrossed…"

"I can see that. What's got your attention?" George smiled as he scanned his ID.

Quinn scanned hers and stepped inside. "Looks like we may have a pretty big case on our hands. Wait, what are you doing here?"

"Millwood and I always trade off days when there's bad weather."

"He's on scene. You'll want a briefing. Let me make a hall stop and get some coffee, then I'll meet you in the conference room. Something tells me we may have a connection to the two murders."

They continued down the hall. "On a more mundane matter, I see your new wheels are here. If you need help taking your personal vehicle home and coming back for this one, happy to help out."

She stopped and turned to him. "I'll take you up on it. My head is so wrapped up in what's going on it never occurred to me I have that little challenge."

"I'm quite sure you would have figured it out. Just thought I'd offer."

"We might manage that little task yet tonight as I'm pretty sure you're going to want to see the scene." She stopped outside the restroom. "See you shortly."

"10-4."

Quinn loosened the knot in her hair, took a paper towel, and dried her hair from the snow. *Do I know how often I shake my hair out? Does it bother anyone?* She walked to the break room and got coffee; the room was as empty as she had expected. She was about to put the code in the lab door when George walked up. He reached in front of her and put in the code and opened the door for her. Then he turned to unlock the door to the conference room.

"Chuck in on the new case yet?"

"On scene. I'll be with you in just a minute." She walked into her office, hung up her coat, and put on her loafers hoping her feet would warm up—they were freezing. She walked across the hall with her coffee and heard George give a low whistle.

"Look at this, would you? Real technology so detectives can do their jobs." He turned to look at her. "I assume this is your doing?"

"Teamwork—the best kind."

"Did Gilbert faint and fall over that you opened the purse strings?"

"I think he was more surprised I knew enough about technology to be dangerous."

"Whatever it takes. Wow. Great setup. So, what's up?" He looked from the front wall to the back. "Hey, the chalk board's gone, too."

"Not good for computers."

George raised his right eyebrow. "Not tech savvy, eh?"

She shook her head. "Straight from the mouth of Officer Gilbert."

Quinn filled him in on Simmons finding Buddy Wilkie and the subsequent find in his shed. She told him she had Clark and his A-team there and the perimeter taped off.

"What makes you think there's a connection to these murders?"

"Not sure. May be nothing at all. Just don't want to leave one stone unturned."

"Sounds like we have a mountain to move, not stones."

"Could be." Quinn got quiet. "Do you want to go see the scene?"

"I'll text Millwood and see if he wants me there."

"Good idea. I should have thought of that."

"He hasn't had the pleasure of working with you yet. He might feel he has to let me come if you reach out. This way he'll tell me straight up."

She nodded and stared at the Board. "I have some computer work I want to do. Let me know what you two decide."

She pulled out the keyboard from the new setup Gilbert had installed. This room would work well for them to handle complex cases as a team.

"Quinn, before you get into that, Millwood wants to stay on, but wants me to come over. So, what do you say we take your car home and I drop you back off here?"

She realized he had a point. That task would be done and then she could focus on the research she wanted to do.

"Meet you at the back door in two minutes." She walked across the hall and was out the back door as George pulled up.

"I can walk to my car."

"I'm sure you can. I don't know your address, so hop in, give me your address and I'll drive you to the back-forty."

She got in, leaned back on the seat, and sighed. "Thanks, George. Glad we're on the same team."

"Me, too."

Twenty minutes later, he dropped her at the front door of the station. "Thanks, George. I really appreciate it."

"Oh, in case I forget to tell you. The garage duty mechanic will have your keys. You'll have to sign for them."

"10-4." She smiled and entered the station.

"Evening, Officer Jamison."

"Evening, Detective. Cold out?"

"That it is. The snow has stopped and the roads are being cleared. All good signs for fighting crime."

"Yes, ma'am."

"Here's to a slow night, Jamison."

"We can hope." His smile was pleasant.

"Good to be in the house. Have a good evening." She headed for her office.

"You, too."

She was out of her coat, into her loafers, and back across the hall on the computer in five minutes. Her coffee was cold. She pushed it one side and logged in. *Now Buddy Wilkie, I'm on solid ground to see if there is anything out there that will address my gut feeling about you.*

The notes on her pad read:

No criminal record

No fingerprints on file

Find out who is on birth certificate*

Plumbing license #T434719

House transfer from Gladys Wilkie to Buddy Wilkie

Trust from Gladys Wilkie to Buddy Wilkie

Trust from Gladys Wilkie to Oscar Wilkie – Buddy's birth father? *

She sat back in her chair after she added the two asterisks to remind her to focus on this piece and see if they were father and son—biologically or by adoption. *Got to have some coffee.* She walked to the lounge. As she walked, she ran through the list in her head. *Trusts—almost always means there's money.* She knew about trusts: one from her grandmother, and the one that her parents already had established which she would receive on their deaths. *Think I'll start with Gladys Wilkie and see if I can figure out the source of that money. She wouldn't be the first millionaire to live below her means.*

Even though it was close to time for the late-night shift change, she knew there would only be a few officers as the shift sergeant would switch officers on the streets with the ones staying in the station. Coffee cup in hand, she headed back. Her mind stayed focused on the pieces of this puzzle. *Simmons said Buddy's daddy had disappeared some years back; what's on the birth certificate for Buddy Wilkie—need to figure out if Buddy is a nickname. Need to check driver's license for DOB. Did they find a wallet?* She unlocked the door and entered the conference room.

Buddy's House

George Marshall, senior detective but not lead detective, walked up to the officer at the driveway.

"Evening, Evans. All quiet?"

"Yes, Detective. Weird, but quiet."

"Weird? In what way?"

"Maybe eerie is a better word. Not sure if it's having this big snow-covered field behind us…it's like a big mirror reflecting the moon. Sorry, sir. Nothing I can put my finger on."

"Think of anything. Speak up." He walked toward the house. The front door was unlocked, but he knocked anyway.

One of the A-team members opened the door. "Evening, sir."

"Evening. Detective Millwood is out back I believe?"

"Yes, sir. This way." The man pointed to the back door.

Marshall looked around the kitchen. *Carrie is pretty serious about cleanliness in the kitchen, but this is like a laboratory.* He looked at the frames around the windows and doors and there was no evidence of dust. *Who was this guy?* He put on a pair of latex gloves. As he opened the back door, he ran his finger along the top of the door frame. There was no dust. *Who was this guy?* He saw there was no light on the porch or anywhere outside. He took out his pocket light just as the door of the shed opened. Someone stepped out—the light from the shed put the face in shadow.

"Evening, George."

"Evening, Steve. Caught an interesting one, did we?"

"You don't know the half of it. Sure glad Chuck came. We need to make sure we handle all this evidence the right way. My team's pretty careful, but...well, you'll see for yourself. I'm headed in to see what my team's found inside."

"10-4." George stepped into the shed. This time his whistle was drawn out and loud.

"Yeah, right?" Millwood nodded.

"What is this place? A laboratory? Mad scientist? Serious scientist?"

"Call it whatever you like. Just wanted you to see this. It's going to take days to remove and get the forensic team working on it."

"Chuck." George nodded a greeting to the forensic tech. "Do we have what we need to handle this?"

"Not likely. Got some new equipment, thanks to Detective Isaacs, but some of this is so old we're going to need a forensic anthropologist."

George moved over to the freezer which Millwood had opened. He carefully studied each basket. He turned when Millwood pointed to the first cabinet.

"Here's our best theory. The material in the freezer was moved to this cabinet which is a high quality, slow drying oven of sorts—has its own built in drain system. The skull in there must have been dry as there was a ping from the timer we heard—that's what led to calling in a bomb sniffing dog from SBI."

George nodded. "I'm guessing there was no bomb?"

"Obviously." Millwood and George were used to bantering.

"And the next cabinet?"

"It appears to be airtight if the seal around is any indication, but it has this small fan in the top that just seems to keep air circulating."

"Chuck, look like anything you saw in college? Or at SBI?" George looked at Chuck.

"Nope. I'm astounded by how sophisticated it is."

Millwood opened the next cabinet.

"Any idea what the numbers and letters mean?"

"Could be a fancy way of dating them, but who knows. We're still trying to get into the computer, but it's pretty well protected, so we're going to need a warrant."

George glanced at the computer. "Detective Isaacs is waiting on an assessment to start that ball rolling."

"Well, I think it's time. Just wanted you to see everything and make sure it didn't just look like a scientist interested in old bones." Millwood shook his head as he spoke.

"What do you think?"

"I think I have no idea, but the only way to get answers is to get into that computer and his phones." Millwood pointed to the evidence bag on the table.

"Your call." George looked at him.

Millwood took out his secure phone and called Quinn.

"Detective Isaacs, I think we may find this man was just a scientist doing some research, but with human remains, I think we have evidence that can support a warrant."

"I'm on it, Detective Millwood. This evidence isn't going anywhere. So, I suggest you make sure the shed and house are secure and we have at least two officers who can monitor the perimeter. Clark can decide if he releases his team, and the rest of you come in and let's make a plan. Then I want you all to get some sleep. This is not going to be ordinary, no matter what it is."

"Yes, ma'am. I'll alert the team."

"10-4." Quinn opened a secure mail message and informed the chief. Then she called Peggy O'Haire, the District Attorney.

"O'Haire. This better be good." It was almost eleven p.m.

"Isaacs here. Wouldn't call otherwise."

Peggy listened, and when Quinn finished, she said, "To be clear, you opened these cabinets because you had reason to suspect a bomb was inside and therefore a crime had been committed?"

"Absolutely." Quinn hoped she could defend the ping on a locked metal cabinet in that setup as reason to suspect a crime.

"The warrant is for two phones and a single computer? That's what you want to get into?"

"Yes—for now."

"What does that mean? You think there's more?"

"There are two computers in his gaming room, but one of our first officers on scene has known the deceased since middle school and played video games with him almost weekly."

"Which officer?"

"Simmons."

"Don't know him. Reliable?"

"From all I can tell. Two weeks here isn't a lot of time to have my own judgment. I will say that Clark and Marshall both say he's a good cop."

"Good enough for me. Sounds like the computers belong to the deceased, so I'll put all three computers. Judges don't like us to come back and ask for more. You sure there's nothing else?"

"Peggy, this guy could be a legitimate scientist and the material in the freezer and cabinets could be purchased legally for research. We just can't know without getting into the computer. That said, our officer said he has no known living next of kin. Can you put his birth certificate on the warrant?"

"I'll add the birth certificate. Relax. Remember I'm on your side. All this will get easier to navigate. Have to say though, nothing like jumping into a can of worms your second week on the job."

"Seems that way. Although I've seen dead bodies with…"

"Enough, Detective. There's a reason I'm a DA. I only have to look at the pictures of those kinds of things." Peggy laughed.

"Sorry to wake you."

"No problem. I may not reach a judge tonight, so it may be morning or later. I suggest you folks get some sleep. Sounds like you're going to have a long weekend, and heck, even a long week ahead."

"Thanks, Peggy. You made this easy. Sometimes I feel like I know enough about procedures and protocols to be dangerous."

"Quinn, you're smart, have a good rep in law enforcement, and the job you have now isn't a whole lot different from what you did—well, except now you have to make the big decisions."

"Yeah, I get that. Thanks, again, Peggy. I'll look to hear from you."

"You'll be the first to know. Good night."

The finality in her tone told Quinn that Peggy might not wake a sleeping judge. *And should she anyway? We have no evidence the death is other than natural causes. It's the environment in which the death happened that's in question—and finding next of kin.*

Conference Room

Quinn sent a new message to Chief Hansen outlining the justification for the warrant and what the DA had told her. *She said wake her if it was urgent. She said she expected me to do my job, and ask for help if I need it. Nothing urgent. Well, if I screwed up, hopefully I'm still in the honeymoon phase of the job.* She sat back and sipped her coffee. *How much did I learn by living through that school shooting?*

There was a knock on the door of the conference room as a key unlocked it. She knew it would be George—and hopefully Clark, Millwood, and Chuck. She logged out of her secure email and stood. She shook hands with each of the men. "Thanks for your work and for coming in." She saw evidence bags carried by Kevin, Chuck, and Steve.

George spoke up. "I asked the shift sergeant to have someone get us a pot of coffee and five cups. It will be up from the common room soon."

Another lesson learned. "Thanks, George. I appreciate it."

They gathered around the conference table and each looked up at the new combination cork and whiteboard had been placed on the empty wall. Quinn had started a skeletal outline with her notes from a search on Buddy Wilkie.

"Like what you've done with the place, Quinn." Millwood nodded approvingly.

"Officer Gilbert made it happen. Let's see if we can put it to good use. What's in the evidence bags?"

Millwood set the bag with the two phones on the table. "Once we can get into them, I suspect one is personal and one is business. That might give us some direction."

"DA is working on a warrant."

"Computer, too?"

Quinn nodded. "Computers—all three."

All four men nodded.

Sergeant Clark set his evidence bag on the table. "My team found this in a false board in the bedroom closet. Nothing there but this." He set the bag on the table.

Quinn looked at Chuck.

"Ma'am...Quinn." He set an evidence bag on the table.

"Steve, do you have pictures from the scene where this was found?"

"They're printing as we speak. I'll go get them when the coffee gets here. We thought you would want to see this."

A knock on the door caused all of them to turn their heads. George stood up and opened it. An officer stood outside the door with a rolling cart. "Your order, sir." He made a mock bow to George.

"Good work, Officer. I'll take it from here. And, thanks to the folks downstairs who made this happen."

"Here to serve." The officer turned and walked away.

Quinn noticed that Steve slipped out the door and that the officer delivering the cart never even tried to look in. *Duty bound. Don't nose around in things that aren't yours to know.* She'd have to get the officer's name from George.

"Cookies!" Chuck was excited. "Warm cookies. Wooho..." He caught himself and looked at Quinn.

"I like cookies, too." She smiled at the excitement of this young man over such a simple thing in a deadly serious environment. She reached for a paper plate, took a cookie, and refilled her coffee.

There was a knock on the door. George opened it to let Steve back in carrying a folder. He walked to the cork board and put the photos up. Quinn walked over to look while the others got their coffee and cookies and sat down. The photos were clear and crisp. An obviously astute A-team member had seen the small lock that had been drilled into a board. When it was lifted, on an equally obscure hinge, there was a metal box beneath it.

"It was in there?" She pointed.

"Yes, ma'am. This picture shows how it was placed in there." He put it on the board.

She studied the photos and finally walked to the table and sat down. She saw the others were looking at the photos, too. *Of course they were on scene, so they saw it in situ.* She took a sip of coffee, cleared her throat, and looked around the table.

"Gentlemen, based on these two pieces of evidence and the shed, we will consider this house a crime scene."

They all nodded.

"Chuck, is there a match?"

Chuck looked from the evidence bag Steve had brought in, and the one he had.

"On cursory inspection, ma'am, I'd say that the evidence found at the home of the deceased and the one left on top of the officer's cruiser on Sunday night are a pair: a very old pair of shoes which belonged to a child."

Chapter 19

The way to right wrongs is to turn the light of truth upon them.
Ida B. Wells

The Hour is Late

It was shortly after midnight when Quinn drove her official SUV into her three-car garage. After the team made a plan, they headed home for the rest which would be needed in the days to come. She was restless and her mind kept turning over what they knew, and struggling with all they didn't know. Her sidearm stored, she saw her home phone blinking as she walked to the hall closet. She pulled out her two phones and saw text messages on her personal phone. She glanced at them as she started the messages on her home phone. The three texts were from Billy.

7:05 p.m.: Hope U R warm and cozy by a fire.

9:00 p.m.: Important case? No response earlier.

11:00 p.m.: Please let me know UR OK.

She smiled. It was nice to have someone care that you were home and safe. The first message on her home phone was from the plumber reminding her he would be there at eight-thirty Saturday morning. *Arghhh...THIS morning!* The second was a hang-up. *Telemarketer no doubt.* The last one was from Billy. "Hey, I know it's almost midnight but you haven't answered my texts, and I'm at least smart enough not to call your secure phone, but would you please let me know you're OK. I happen to be very fond of you and I don't care what time of the day or night it is. Text or call."

She poured a glass of Kim Crawford Sauvignon Blanc and walked to her bedroom. Seated in her reading chair, she tucked her feet under her and dialed Billy's number.

"Thank, God. And, thank you for calling. Everything okay?"

"Now it is." The sigh carried the warm feeling she had just hearing his voice. "I haven't had time to even look at my phone. Thanks for checking on me. It means a lot."

"To me, too. Anything you can talk about."

Quinn leaned her head back on her chair, closed her eyes and decided that he was, after all, another law enforcement officer. "It would take the rest of the night to tell you…"

"I have nothing but time."

"Are you at home or the station?"

"Home. I took the day off, remember?"

"What?" She sat up and almost spilled her wine. "Is this still Friday?"

"Well, technically it's very, very early on Saturday, but for most of us mere mortals we call it Friday night."

She was laughing. "Billy Williams, you are so good for what ails me."

"Tough night, I take it. Listen Quinn, you don't have to tell me anything, and we both know we won't step over the line of confidentiality. But if you want to talk something through, I'm here. If you just need a friend…" *What I hope will become a very good friend.* "I'm a good listener."

"You are! Best of all you make me laugh."

"Then see, I'm good for something."

"I have your distant cousin coming at eight-thirty to finish the plumbing problem. I'm going to leave him here since I have a nine a.m. meeting with my team. Any problem with that?"

"None, except work isn't what I hoped you and I would be doing today."

"You didn't work today, remember." The lilt in her voice was light.

"Which day?"

"Okay, okay. I give. You win. If my early read is anywhere near what we've got, this is going to be a big case—and not just because I'm new at the job. I'm waiting on the autopsy report and a warrant. Then we can make a plan. That's the meeting."

"You've got good people there and I'm sure you'll provide the leadership they've been dreaming about after ten years with...well, let's just say word travels and people I know to be mighty fine cops and detectives have been hamstrung by over-control."

"I'm learning that." She grew very quiet.

"I'm thrilled to hear your voice, but I really hope we can still get together in the afternoon, so get some rest and call me when you can after your meeting. I'll be right here."

"Thanks, Billy. Thanks for caring that I'm home and safe and the reassurance that dawn will bring new insights."

"It will. By the way, I said I'd be right here, but I could be over there. If you need me, call—or even if you don't need me you can call."

She was laughing again. "Thanks. I will. Good night."

"Good night, lovely lady." He ended the call.

She lifted her wine glass. "To you, Billy." Then she sat quietly and drank her wine as she ran through all that they had uncovered this night. She desperately wanted a shower, but in the end, she changed into warm pajamas and crawled into bed. She was asleep in minutes.

Billy lay on his side in his bed thirty minutes from Round City and wished he was face to face with Quinn. *May take some navigating to sort out our jobs, but I am more than a little infatuated with you, Detective Quinn Isaacs. Sleep well.* He fell asleep thinking of her.

The Sun Rises and the Snow is Melting

As often happens with freak storms in the Smoky Mountains, the sun was brilliant on Saturday morning and the roads would soon start to thaw under the layer of snow left from clearing. Quinn was showered and dressed by seven-thirty and amazed at how soundly she'd slept. *Billy's voice was a great soother before sleep, but his actual presence would have been...* She snapped out of her reverie. The meeting this morning was critical, and she wanted to be ready to walk out the door when Matthew got here to finish up the plumbing in the upstairs bathroom.

She had her sidearm in her holster and her coat on the kitchen island when the doorbell rang.

"Morning, Matthew."

"Good morning to you." He already had his boots off and booties on since her front porch had no snow.

"Come in out of the cold."

"Thanks."

"While we're here at the door. I have to go to the station, so would you please lock the door on your way out? All you need to do is push this button with the lock symbol on it."

"Familiar with them. Have one myself. It will take me about an hour and a half...maybe a little longer, but you've already paid me, so we're good to go."

"There's an envelope on the table." She pointed toward a small table to the left of the door. "Thanks for your good work and your flexibility. I'm leaving now. Have a great Saturday."

"Yes, ma'am. You, too. Go fight crime so our fair city is safe."

"That's the goal, Matthew. That's the goal."

She was out the back door and headed to the station and through the gate to the back in less than ten minutes now that the roads were slushy and not frigid ice. *I often wonder what everyday people like Matthew think when stories break about cases they could not even imagine happening.*

The gate guard nodded as she held up her ID and his eyes looked through her car.

"Everything good, Detective Isaacs?"

"Sun is shining, and we get to serve our community. What could be better?"

"Fishing?" He smiled.

She laughed. "Not a fan myself, but hear it's a great sport. Hope you get to do some soon. Have a nice day."

As she opened the outer door to the lab and her office, she was overwhelmed by the smell of coffee—good smelling coffee.

"Morning." Chuck held up his mug.

"Did *you* make that coffee?" She regretted putting so much emphasis on "you."

"Are you kidding? You know how bad my coffee is. George had the officers downstairs include us in their morning wake up. Hot coffee and muffins await in the conference room. George said to tell you he's in there."

It was eight-forty-five a.m. when Quinn knocked on the door and opened it with her key.

George Marshall was in the process of standing up to answer the door when he heard the key. He stood, but stayed at the table. "Morning, Quinn."

"Good morning to you. I hear you are a savior this morning."

"Nah, it was the folks in the common room. They make real coffee. It's better than what we get in the break room."

"And it's better than..." the knock on the door caused her to turn back and open it.

George chuckled. "Enough said."

Chuck walked in.

Quinn was about to close the door when Steve and Kevin appeared. "At your service, come on in." She smiled and made a point of opening the door wide and pretending to bow.

"Morning everyone."

"Morning."

"Haven't heard anyone say 'good' morning." Steve chimed in.

"What's stopping you?" George stared at him.

"Same thing stopping everyone else—it's Saturday and we're here."

Quinn could hear they were simply sparring by the tone of their banter. She could also see in their demeanor they were all ready to engage in where ever this case might lead them.

Steve held out the coffee pot. "Anyone?"

Quinn put her mug under it. "Gladly. Thanks."

The rest filled their mugs, Kevin and Chuck grabbed a muffin and they were all at the table at eight-fifty a.m. It wasn't lost on Quinn that they were early.

"Hope you all had a chance to get some sleep. My goal today is to update the board with what we know and any new information from the ME..." Her secure phone rang.

"Isaacs."

"O'Haire. You've got your warrant. Should be in your secure folder in the next few minutes. Good luck."

"Thanks, Madam District Attorney. In case no one's told you lately, you rock."

"Go get 'em, Quinn." The call ended.

Kevin Millwood's face lit up. "Warrant?"

Quinn nodded. "Now, I can do a search for a birth certificate and we can get into those computers and phones. I need direction on whether we have the geeks to do that or need outside support. I've already mentioned we should have the ME report soon, I hope. What else do we need to add to getting those two things addressed?"

"Ma'am...Quinn." Chuck looked around the table.

George patted him on the back. "You'll get used to it, Chuck. She really does have a name."

"Quinn, I thought about this most of the night—even in my sleep. We can get a forensic tech from SBI without having to get anyone else, but I think this is so unusual we should have someone from SBI look at it before we move anything."

Heads around the table nodded. Quinn looked at each of the men.

"I'm okay with that. I can call the Agent-in-Charge and see what we can make happen. Kevin, you're lead on this case, any concerns?" She was pretty sure she saw a trace of a smile on each of their faces. *I hate that they weren't treated as professionals—they are smart and conscientious men.*

"It's way bigger than anything we've ever dealt with. I think the apparent age of some of the evidence may be more than we have the skills to manage—no offense, Chuck."

Chuck jumped right in. "I agree. We have some new equipment, but nothing like what this is likely to take. I say bring them in."

They all turned at a knock on the door. Quinn was closest and stood to open it.

"Good morning, Chief Hansen."

All four of the men stood immediately.

"Relax. Don't let me interrupt. Thought I could learn something if I hear your discussion." She took the chair that Kevin Millwood pulled out for her. It was the only vacant one.

Quinn was glad she had included the meeting in her last message to the chief last night.

She looked at Kevin. "Detective Millwood, how would you like to lay this out?"

"Well, Detective, I..."

"Excuse me." All eyes turned to the chief. "I did not come here to speak, but I'm reasonably sure each of us knows our jobs and the chain of command. You'll spend more time stumbling over your titles than getting the work done. I know who each of you are—you know who I am. Just get on with it."

Quinn couldn't stop her smile. *I bet these guys are wondering what has happened here. Two women saying the same thing. We know what we do and who we are. Let's do the work!*

Kevin nodded at the Chief. He stood up and walked to their board. "The main evidence we have in hand of something very unusual is the child's pair of shoes. We still need to tie the shoe from the squad car to this one. Do we have agreement that we need to bring in a forensic anthropologist and SBI agents to review the scene before we move anything?"

All heads nodded assent.

"Then Chuck, you get on those shoes and see what links you can find. Steve, once we know what the SBI has to say, you can decide if we need any of your team to move it. George, will you follow up with the ME on the deceased. Quinn, if you'll contact the SBI so we know when we might have them available, and see if you can find a birth certificate. I'll get with the geeks to see what we can do about getting into these two phones."

Quinn nodded. *He's a detective because he's logical, can follow a path, and just needed to have the chance to do it.* She saw a slight nod from the Chief.

Steve spoke up. "Kevin, sounds like a good plan. Regroup time?"

"Eleven give everyone time to get things moving?"

They all nodded.

"Good, then unless you get notification from me to regroup sooner, we'll be here at eleven."

Everyone stood. The Chief shook hands and exchanged a comment with each of the men as they exited. "Got a minute?" she said as Quinn moved toward the door.

"Of course."

The Chief walked over to the metal cart and took a paper cup and poured some coffee. "I've been smelling this since I walked in the door. I..."

"Oh, ma'am, I am so sorry I didn't offer."

"I was about to say, I didn't want to break the momentum. I can get my own coffee, but thanks. Now, I'd like a debrief from you of what happened at the Wilkie home and how you assess where we are at the moment. You can keep it brief. I've read your reports. I know you need to get on with contacting Special Agent Jackson."

The two women sat. Quinn ran through the events which occurred prior to her arrival and complimented the officers. She gave a much more complete description of what they had found than she did in the report. The chief never interrupted her.

"Lastly, I think everyone involved is clear about their roles and have handled them appropriately." She hesitated.

"But?"

"But…I don't think they've been allowed to use their knowledge and talents as a team."

"Looks to me like Millwood was more than capable of being lead on this case. Good for you for giving him the reins to do so." She stood.

Quinn stood as well. "Thank you, Chief. You set a good example." She smiled.

"Let's get this case figured out." She shook Quinn's hand and walked out the door and closed it behind her.

Quinn picked up her coffee cup and took a sip as she pulled out her secure phone.

The Fire is Out

Oscar Wilkie woke to a very cold stone floor and the reality that his wood burning stove had gone out. *I guess I fell asleep after all.* He looked around the room and saw that he only had four pieces of cordwood inside. *Gotta bring in some wood today.* He restoked the fire and filled the old-fashion coffee pot with water, put the basket with coffee grounds in the pot, and put it on the wood burning stove to boil.

Buddy, what's going on at your house? I've left you alone 'cause you're better off without me. Not proud of the man I am. He sat down in the one chair he had and sipped the boiling hot coffee. Although he'd always been a brilliant scientist, he knew he couldn't interact with adults. That's when he left Buddy—when Buddy became an adult. *I'm an old man, now.*

I was almost forty when I found you. The years are starting to tell. It had been just over thirty years ago that he'd found Buddy in the woods. *I did my best to teach you right from wrong. Mother always loved that you were smart like me, but you might have handled people better if I hadn't ended up your pappy.* He sipped the hot coffee and was startled as a tear ran down his face. He'd never been able to express any kind of emotion. *I'm tired, Buddy. It's all been more than I expected. Not sure I could have done anything differently...*

Oscar refilled his coffee mug and walked over to his drone. *Let's go see what we can see.*

Chapter 20

See all human behavior as one of two things: either love, or a call for love.
Marianne Williamson

Teamwork

"Jackson." The phone was answered on the first ring Quinn heard.

"Sorry to bother you on a Saturday, sir."

"Every day is a work day in law enforcement, isn't it? How are you, Quinn?"

"I'm well, sir. Hope you are. Thanks for your help with the dog team. Thankfully there was no bomb. However, we could not have been prepared for what we found."

Special-Agent-in-Charge at the State Bureau of Investigation listened as Quinn spoke for almost ten minutes.

"So you see, sir, we need your help."

"When is your team meeting again?"

"Eleven."

"We'll be there by noon. That'll give you time to review what your team has learned this morning. See you then." He ended the call.

Quinn held her phone out and shook her head. *Great, thank you, SAC Jackson.* Then she smiled thinking of the work he did with the team when they worked with Sheriff Oliver over in the Valley, and she was representing immigration. It was a good decision to call him.

She used her secure phone and called Billy.

"Good morning."

"And to you, Quinn. Did Matthew show up on time?"

"Spot on and already with his boots off and socks covered. That's not why I called."

"What's up?"

"Are you in the middle of something heavy duty in your own shop?"

"Nothing out of the ordinary—after months of extraordinary."

"I know that's the truth. Appreciated being involved—given that we have the job to fight crime. Now I need to know if you are available to be an expert consultant on a case which, by the way, may go someplace we have not yet begun to fathom."

"For how long? Just need to know to clear with the sheriff."

"Initial meeting with our team, SBI, and you at noon."

"Sure you need me with that horsepower?"

"We need your very analytical brain and extensive lead detective observation skills."

"I'm off until Monday, so I'll clear it with the sheriff. Any chance it might spill over into our jurisdiction?"

"No idea…" She considered the location of the Summers' home. "It's possible it could involve the DB whose property runs along the boundary between us."

"So you're suggesting someone could have gained access or egress from our side of the line?"

"I have no proof of anything, but we're working on ATV tracks that likely crossed over into your territory."

"Then Monday may not be a problem either. Back with you shortly. Thanks, Quinn."

"Thank you." She ended the call.

She stood up and stretched as she looked at the pictures of her parents and grandmother on the wall. *Why do I think the two murders are connected to Buddy Wilkie? Did I just say that so Sheriff Oliver would approve Billy working with us?* She shrugged and walked into the lab. Chuck was hovering over one of his new pieces of equipment and she could see the child's shoe. She walked up to the table but didn't speak.

Without looking up, Chuck said, "The fibers in the shoes match, although the one that was left on top of the officer's car, which I've labeled #1, is less stable than the one found in the floor."

"Does that make sense?"

"It could. Depends on how long #1 was in a different environment than #2, the right shoe, and what the environmental conditions were."

"Could it have been through the machines in the shed?"

"Possible. It's going to take some work to figure out the settings and purpose of all that." Now he looked up at her. "What isn't different is the scuff marks at the heel where the two shoes rubbed together when the child walked. They match almost perfectly. Want to see?"

"Absolutely." She went to the other side of the table as Chuck put the two small shoes side by side under the large magnifier. *Even I who know little to nothing about forensic testing, can see the match in the scuff marks.* "They sure appear to be a match."

"I have pictures I'll bring to the meeting."

Quinn stood up. "Was there a wallet found by the A-team?"

"Yeah, haven't gotten to it. They brought in a few personal effects." He looked up at her. "Hope that was okay. The A-team didn't enter the shed and nothing was removed, but they looked for anything that could help us identify him..."

"If Kevin okayed it, works for me."

"His idea. I didn't look at anything once I saw the second shoe. Let's see what's in them. Looking for something in particular?"

"Yes, I want to run the driver's license."

"Oh my gosh. I should have looked immediately to see if we had that." He moved quickly to the evidence bags." He held up a bag. "This says the driver's license was found in the van. The wallet was on the deceased." He took it out with gloved hands. I can give you a photo of the license. Will that work?"

"Perfectly. Chuck, calm down. The man is deceased. We're trying to figure out what's going on, not find a relative to approve treatment at the hospital." She smiled at him. "While you do that, I'm going to get some ice tea from the machine in the break room. Want something?"

"Sounds good. I like mine unsweet." He let out a sigh.

"Done. Back shortly." *I wonder if authoritarian leaders ever think about the stress they create for people…which can lead to mistakes.*

The Morgue

Last night, Tristan had been pacing when Doc Walters entered the morgue just before midnight.

"Been here long?" The ME had addressed the question to the forensic tech.

"Little over an hour. Was worried about you, Doc."

"Wasn't easy to get through one of the side country roads. Took longer than I expected and the phone signal out there isn't the best. Sorry to keep you waiting."

"No problem, Doc." Tristan had hopped from foot to foot.

The forensic tech gave his report describing the scene where they had found Buddy Wilkie.

"But Doc…" Tristan had tried to interrupt several times and Doc Walters held his hand up.

Doc Walters wasn't bothered by Tristan's eccentric facial and voice behaviors—for him they were overshadowed by Tristan's high level of intelligence and keen skills of observation. The ME asked a couple of questions of the tech. Then he turned to Tristan.

"Okay, what's got you in a tizzy?"

After listening to Tristan's monologue, Doc nodded. "Okay. Suit up. Bring the camera. Let's see what we've got here."

"I'll head over to the lab, Doc. Call when you need me."

"You on all night?"

"Luck of the draw." The forensic tech headed for the door.

"Thanks. I'll call in a bit, I'm sure."

Tristan had changed into scrubs and was back with the camera. He stood behind the line which Doc had long ago taped down as the boundary for Tristan unless he gave him permission to move in closer—it kept the photographs consistent and ensured that Tristan didn't reach out and touch something on a body that Doc didn't want touched. He did sometimes wonder about Tristan's impulse control.

"Hey, Doc. Think our TOD on scene was accurate?"

Doc looked at him. Tristan knew time of death was one of the first things done. He let it go. "TOD is approximately six p.m. Thursday. You know the remains were found Friday evening. Now get your pictures." Doc knew Tristan would capture the minute details.

Tristan had followed the red tape on the floor and took pictures at all angles. "Think I got everything from the line, Doc. Want me to come in closer?"

"Not yet. We'll take closeups as I collect samples." Doc had continued his routine and weighed and recorded vital organs and the brain. He had closely monitored Tristan taking pictures of each element of the autopsy. He looked closely at the scar on the left ankle. *Wonder what this man encountered as a young boy. That scar is pale but it was deep. Bear?* He reached over and took the camera from Tristan.

"What is it, Doc?" Tristan's voice rose as he spoke.

"Just hand me the camera, Tristan." He took pictures from several angles and handed the camera back to Tristan. He saw Tristan scroll back threw the electronic images. *Guess his curiosity is something that intrigues me.*

It was almost six a.m. when he stopped. Doc yawned. "Okay, Tristan, time for a break. I'm going to have some coffee and see what I can scrounge to eat."

"I can go see what's in the break room." Tristan was all but jumping up and down.

"Be back in less than fifteen. Okay?"

"You bet, Doc. Want anything?"

"No, I'm good." He walked toward his office. *I just need a break and some time to think.*

Tristan took off.

Doc was satisfied he had a preliminary cause of death and he didn't suspect foul play. Doc knew he needed the analyses that would make sure there was no evidence of chemicals contributing to the COD, but he thought this was pretty straight forward. He hoped that getting family history would help him figure out the unusual death of such a young man.

Fifteen minutes later he was studying his computer screen, drinking his coffee, and eating a protein bar when he heard the outside door open.

"What's the COD, Doc?" Tristan's voice roared through the morgue.

"Patience, Tristan. We'll get there." Doc was not going to give Tristan, or anyone else, a cause of death until he was as accurate as possible. He also wanted to talk to the detective in charge to make sure he had more than the report from the forensic tech and Tristan.

The remains sutured and in the refrigerated unit in the morgue, Doc Walters was ready to do some chemical analyses of his own. He'd already sent some things to the downstairs lab.

"Okay, Tristan. I think I'm good here. Thanks for your help. You can head out. Have a good rest of the day."

"I can stay, Doc…"

"Tristan, time for you to go. Thanks for your help."

"Okay, Doc, but…"

"Get some rest."

"10-4." Tristan loved using police terminology. He took off his scrubs and headed to the door. His hand on the push bar, he turned back. "Doc, I can stay."

"Message received. Later, Tristan." Doc turned to his microscope. He enjoyed the opportunity to do some of the more scientific aspects of the work even though most was done in the labs. He wanted to get a preliminary report to the detective in charge as soon as he could. He was at his computer when George Marshall walked in. The ME looked up at the clock. It was nine-twenty-five.

"Morning, Doc."

"Morning, George. You lead on this case?"

"No, Kevin is. Just my assignment to see where you are on COD."

"Have a seat? Coffee?"

"Don't mind if I do." He lifted the pot on the small table in the ME's office and poured it into a paper cup. "What's the word?"

The Drone

Oscar picked up the drone and inserted a new battery. He had three battery charging stations because of the limited watts his solar panels provided. *Gladys, what would you think of spending money on all these gadgets?* He had always called his mother by her first name—she gave up trying to get him to call her "mother" by the time he was four. *Now little drone, I have a mission for you. Let's go see what's happening at Buddy's house.*

He put on his coat and boots and took the controller and drone outside. He knew the coordinates for Buddy's house by heart and headed the drone there. The speed wasn't great, but the five miles quickly disappeared. Oscar decided to see what he could see from high up so as not to be detected.

There were more police cars around Buddy's house than he saw last night. The lights were no longer flashing. He lowered the drone and hoped if it were spotted that the police would think it was some kid playing around. *As trigger happy as you folks can be, sure hope you don't shoot it down.* He dropped the drone lower. Then he saw the yellow tape surrounding Buddy's house. *What have you done, boy?* Just as he was about to pull the drone up, he saw a cop pointing at the drone. *Time to head home, but you're going to take the long way round. Don't want them tracking you back here.*

He headed the drone west from the house. He knew this was a good tactic since the small street in front of Buddy's house ended at his driveway—a dead-end street. Gladys had bought the land on all sides of her home that didn't already belong to someone else—she liked her privacy. Now all that land was in Buddy's name. Oscar took the drone down low so it was just above the trees and couldn't be seen by the cops. *Maybe I'll just set you down and come get you later.* He watched the video screen and soon saw a perfect opportunity. *I forgot about that old spring house on the pond.* He smiled and dropped the drone onto the roof of the spring house in the curve of the eave. Oscar knew he could use his other two drones until a little time had passed and it was safe to get this one. No one would ever know.

The Geeks

Detective Kevin Millwood entered the room where the technology geeks worked. They ran the station technology and loved the chance to get into lawfully authorized hacking of phones and computers. He was glad he had grabbed his coat because this room was like a refrigerator.

"Morning, Gil. Drew the snow duty, eh?"

Officer Gilbert, head of technology, looked up from his computer. "Nah, it was my weekend to work. We find it easier in this shop to work the weekend and stay in the station. What's on your mind?"

Kevin held up the evidence bag with the two phones. "Need the special touch of someone in your shop."

"Got a..."

Kevin held up the piece of paper that Quinn had printed out when the warrant came in. "And, it's in your secure file."

"Hmmm...must have just come in."

"I'm sure. Now...you got someone who can get us into these?"

"Only the best." Gil rubbed his hands together. "Me."

"Yeah, yeah. Prove it and you might get to play with some computers in a pretty fascinating case."

"Promise?"

"No promises, but I'll try to give you first dibs."

"That must mean some big guns are coming to town. Okay, now the big question. Is the owner of these phones under arrest in our station?"

"Nope. He's in our morgue."

"That works. Want to take a walk?"

"Sure."

Gil picked up the evidence bag and nodded to Kevin. "Let's go."

They entered the morgue and Doc looked up from his computer.

"Hey, Kevin. Heard you were lead on this case. Was hoping to talk to you today."

"I'm here and we can talk, but Gil here needs to talk to you first."

"Not really, except to show you the warrant and see if you'll let me use the DB's finger?"

Doc looked at the warrant. "What did he do? I didn't know this was a criminal case."

Kevin looked at both men. "Don't know that it is yet. Need to get in the phone and see if we can find next of kin, as a starter."

"You sure these phones belong to him?" Gil watched Kevin's face.

"Both were in his pocket, we've dusted for prints, so as soon as we get the ones from Doc, we'll verify."

"How about we start there?" Gil's voice had an edge.

"Been a long night, Gil. You're right. Doc, do you have prints?"

"That was done hours ago. Don't know if anyone has done a run on them since we know the name of the deceased. I didn't suggest to the tech we needed anything more than to record them."

Kevin nodded. "What we don't know is if there are any next of kin. One of our officers knows him—said his daddy took off years ago and the grandmother is deceased. Hoping these phones will help us find a relative."

Both men nodded.

"Sorry I was terse there, Kevin." Gil extended his hand. "Had a geek's nightmare with some data we were running for Chuck. Let's see what we have here."

Both phones had a finger print ID. Gil took Buddy's index finger and nothing happened.

"Can you get a read from a…" Kevin was interrupted by Gil.

"Yep, like the old TV show: 'dead or alive.' Just have to figure out which finger. Most folks use the index finger of the hand they use to write. Sometimes folks get cutesy and use a ring finger. Little fingers don't work as well for most folks."

"Why is that?" Doc sounded genuinely interested.

"You have to roll your finger to get the print registered when you get the phone and most folks find it harder to do with their pinky finger."

Gil tried the index finger with no luck. Then he moved to the middle finger. "Voila! One open." Gil put down Buddy's hand and quickly touched the face of the phone.

"Now what?" Doc watched Gil's fingers move across the screen of the phone.

"Need to change the settings so the phone doesn't close on me while I get the other one."

"Makes sense." Doc hesitated. "Just give me bodies. I know what to do with them."

Kevin, who had been watching, chuckled. "Guess we all try to settle where we know what we do best."

They watched as Gil took the other phone and none were surprised when the middle finger opened this one, too. Gil adjusted the settings. "Okay, headed to my office so I can get these on a charger and see what we've got. Coming, Kevin?"

"Yes, but what if you need a fingerprint to open an app?"

"Cross that bridge when I get to it." He pointed to the corpse. "Not going anywhere, is he?"

Doc pointed to the refrigerated cabinet. "Back in the drawer."

Kevin and Gil nodded and headed for the stairs.

"Thanks, Doc. Assume George got down here."

"That he did."

"Appreciate you coming in the middle of the night. Okay if I give you a call to touch base?"

"Figured you must have something more than is obvious here."

"Working on it, Doc. Working on it." The familiar repetitive statement of the mountains slipped out easily for Kevin.

"So you need next of kin?" Gil was already at the top step of the stairs.

"That's a good place to start. I need to know anything and everything you can find on either one of these phones that might help us make a positive ID, and also figure out what this man did for a living."

"Nothing at the house to indicate occupation?" The two men were about to enter Gil's office.

"Some pretty good evidence..." He stopped.

"Guessing that slow down suggests you just made a connection."

"Need me?" Kevin turned to head down the hall.

"Nope, I'll get you a report..."

"Can you be in that fancy conference room you set up so nicely—thanks by the way, at eleven with whatever you've got?"

"10-4." Gil walked in his office and Kevin headed for his and looked at his watch: ten-twelve a.m.

Chapter 21

We do not have to become heroes overnight. Just a step at a time meeting each thing as it comes up, seeing it as not as dreadful as it appears, discovering that we have the strength to stare it down.
Eleanor Roosevelt

Who Were You?

Once again Quinn was determined to figure out who Buddy Wilkie was. She knew most people did not have extensive files in law enforcement records, but most adults had some information out there in the ether: driver's license registration, traffic tickets, auto accident reports, property appraiser's records, voter's records, bank records—something. She had not done a search in the records she could access as a detective because her early searches were based on her uncomfortable feeling that there was more to this man than met the eye—his very strange eyes. Given some time before the eleven meeting, she was going to search any record that didn't require a warrant, and one that did—*who gave birth to you Buddy Wilkie and when?* She set her focus on the screen and started her search.

Kevin Millwood walked into his cubicle. *Were you a plumber, Buddy Wilkie? What don't we know about you.* Kevin sat back. *Hell, what* do *we know about you—not much.* He keyed in his password on his computer and started with plumbing licenses. *Why didn't I think to ask in the meeting if anyone knew if he really was a plumber. The stuff in that shed was* not *about plumbing.*

Officer Gilbert started his search of the phone #1. There were only a few calls in the "recents" list on the phone and only two numbers. One number was called only once and the others were all to the same number. He entered it in a search engine that would identify the owner and saw that the number belonged to Albert Simmons. *Officer Albert Simmons, I believe.* His eyes searched the screen. *Kevin said Wilkie was friends with one of our officers. Not mine to investigate, just mine to give the information.* He entered the information in his notes for his report. The other number in phone #1 was an unassigned number. *Must have been a misdial.* He looked carefully to see if it was similar to the number for Simmons. *Off by one number. It was the last number entered in the phone.* He wrote down the time and date for his report. Next, he opened the contacts list. *Not one listing. Not even Simmons. Might explain the misdialed call.* Gil shook his head as if to clear the cobwebs. He'd never seen such a clean phone. He opened the texts. *Multiple texts from Simmons on Thursday and Friday.* He wrote the information in his log for his report and took screenshots of the text messages.

Let's see what your other phone offers. He opened the "recents" list on phone #2. *Several calls in recent* weeks. *Let's see what the most recent yield.* The most recent was early Tuesday morning—before that was Monday night from the same number. He scanned the numbers as he entered the number to search for ownership. While that search was running, he made a note that there were two calls from that number—both incoming. The information popped up on his screen: *L. Andrews, hmm...why do I recognize that name?* He wrote down the address. The number prior to the Andrews was a single call on Sunday night—incoming. His search gave the name: *Summers.* Now he was sure he had seen that name. *They were on the board in the conference room when we installed the new tech equipment.* He didn't believe in coincidences. He noted the full name and address. He searched the two other numbers and noted the information. *This guy either didn't get many calls or he cleared his calls regularly. No problem.* It would take a warrant to get the cell provider to give them the history. *Quinn will get a warrant.* Of that, he was certain.

Kevin called the ME a second time. Kevin appreciated the thoroughness of the ME's work and the information he gave when he called him earlier. He had told him they would talk again after the meeting with the SBI.

"Doc, Millwood here."

"What's up, Kevin? Already had your meeting?"

"Nope. Running down a clue. Would you give me an assessment on the hands of Wilkie?"

"Meaning like calluses?"

"Anything that might indicate what kind of work he did."

"Everything suggests the man was fit, good muscle tone, and I'd say strong hands that did some manual labor. Appears to be right-handed and yes, there are heavy calluses which are mostly on the joint where the index finger meets the hand."

"Suggest anything to you?"

"Held heavy tools that required leverage against that joint."

"Like a pipe wrench?"

"Could be. What are you thinking?"

"Has a plumber's license. Trying to figure out legitimacy of that as his line of work."

"I'd say it's possible. Can't be 100%."

"Anything else explain your observations?"

"Not off-hand, but doubt my assessment would hold up in court without corroboration."

"Won't need it in court. Thanks, Doc." *If he's guilty of crimes, he won't be tried for them.*

"Here to serve."

"Glad for it. 10-4."

"10-4."

Kevin sat back in his chair. "So, maybe you did some legitimate work, Mr. Wilkie. Wonder what made you choose plumbing? He looked at his watch and saw it was ten-forty-five. He headed up to the conference room to make sure the room was set up and figure out if they had room for SBI agents and Detective Williams from the Valley Sheriff's Office. *Glad she invited Billy—he knows these mountains, too.*

Eleven A.M. Meeting

Kevin was headed to ask Quinn to unlock the door as she walked out of the lab.

"Just about to ask for entrance." He pointed at the conference room.

"Asked to have an extra key made for you. It will be here momentarily and you can sign for it. Then you don't need me or George for these meetings."

"Thanks. Appreciate it. I realize there may be more than one case posted in there."

"Or not." Quinn said quietly.

"Beg your pardon?" He looked at Quinn.

"Headed down the hall. Back before eleven."

Kevin tucked away what he thought she said, but knew he needed to focus on being ready for this meeting and the next one. He brought in folding chairs since he wasn't sure how many agents would come from the SBI. A quick count of his own team had him at six if Gil came. He took out his phone.

"Gilbert."

"Millwood. Are you able to come to the meeting?"

"I wouldn't miss it for the world."

"Sounds ominous."

"Headed your way." The phone went silent.

He held out his phone and looked at it. "Well, 10-4 to you, too."

A knock on the door and a key turning told him it was either George or Quinn. He ignored it and stayed focused on running through his plan for the meeting.

"Need help?" George looked around the room.

"Nope. Got your coffee?"

George held up a cup. "Need some yourself?"

Kevin held up his. "Think I need to order some for the SBI folks?"

"There are officers in the common room. Chief hasn't released them yet. I can call down; they'll take care of us. Beats the coffee from the break room, and that's better than the coffee from the jail."

George made the call as he walked to the door. Chuck and Steve entered, Gil and Quinn were right behind them. They were all here.

Seated and ready to go, Kevin started.

"To bring everyone up to date, each of us at the nine o'clock meeting had a task. Gil is here as he opened the phones and hopefully has some information for us. Quinn contacted SAC Jackson and he will have a team here at noon and Billy Williams from the Valley is coming over. Might have some trespassing on his territory in this. Any questions?"

He saw all heads shaking to indicate "no." "Okay then. Quinn anything to add?"

"Let's figure this out."

Kevin didn't hesitate. "Chuck, what do we know about the shoes?"

Chuck ran them through what he had found, showed them the pictures, and put them on the board.

"Got those in an electronic file?" Gil asked Chuck.

"Yep. Want me to pull them up on that screen?" He looked at Kevin.

"By all means. Need help from the resident geek or..." Kevin let it drop. Chuck was already logging into the computer.

In moments, pictures on the screen were bigger than life. Chuck zoomed out to normal size on the picture so they could see by the ruler measurement these were a child's shoes.

George spoke first. "Those scuff marks are a match, looks like to me."

"Me, too." Kevin was nodding his head.

"Close as you might get—even if the aging on the shoes looks different." Gil was looking at Chuck. "Any idea why one looks older?"

They spent the next few minutes reviewing what was known about where the shoes were found and possible explanations for the condition of each.

"Any more on the shoes?" Kevin looked at Chuck.

"Not at this time."

"What do you have, George? ME finish the autopsy?"

"Preliminary COD is a brain aneurysm. ME is hopeful we'll find next of kin so he can see if there is a family history. He said that brain aneurysms are more common in folks over forty and more common in women. If this man's age is late thirties, he's young for it."

"That might explain..." Quinn stopped. She was caught up in the COD and didn't realize she had interrupted George. "Sorry, George."

"No apologies needed. Might explain what?"

"When I first met him..." She explained her observation of his stop in front of her house, her subsequent stop around the corner and the assistance from Officer Simmons and Buddy's complaint of a headache. "I was so concerned by the look in his eyes when he approached my vehicle that I released my gun guard. An aneurysm would explain why he had such a strange look in his eyes, and why he had a headache."

"Let's verify that with the Doc." Kevin said as he made a note.

"Simmons was in on the stop?" Gil asked.

Quinn nodded. "Sent as backup. Turned out he knew him."

"There were only two numbers on the personal phone." He proceeded to tell them what he had found on phone #1. The looks around the table showed they all knew that Simmons would have to be interviewed. Kevin made a note.

"Let's wrap back around to George for a minute. Anything else from the ME?"

"He's running some toxicology which will take some time, but he doesn't think there were any chemicals involved. Just need to verify. That's all for the moment."

"Gil, you told us what was in phone #1. How about phone #2?"

Gil had been staring at the board which had the information on the two dead women. "Summers" and "Andrews." He stood and walked over to it. "Anyone know if either of these women called for a plumber?"

All eyes looked at the pictures on the Board. Quinn stood up and walked across the room. "Do we know? George you were on scene with the Andrews' boys, right?"

George shook his head. "There was no mention of a plumber. Why do you think there's a connection, Gil?"

"Three numbers were on that phone—all incoming. The first one was from a 'Summers' at..." he gave the address.

Now George stood up. "And the second?"

"Andrews." Gil gave the address.

"One and the same." George barely whispered it. He looked at Quinn.

Quinn turned to Chuck. "Any hits on the DNA in those condoms?"

"No, ma'am." The tenor in the room had shifted dramatically. Formality returned and the seriousness of the implications was paramount.

Quinn was all business. "Kevin, I would ask that we allow Chuck to leave and get with Doc Walters so we can get DNA going on Wilkie. Steve, we'll need the reports on any evidence besides the condoms found at the Summers' and Andrews' residences."

Chuck was on his feet. "This will take some time, but I'm on it." The door shut quietly behind him.

"George, do you know if the ME is still here?" Quinn was tapping on the board just beneath the picture of Lizzie Andrews.

"Was as of forty minutes ago. Chuck will go straight down there, I'm sure."

Steve raised his hand and quickly lowered it. "Old habits die hard." He gave Quinn a quick smile. "There wasn't much evidence to be gathered at either scene, but we haven't released either location. I suggest we go back and dust the beds for prints." He looked at Kevin who nodded.

George spoke quickly and with some hint of agitation. "Get your team on it."

Steve ignored him and sent a text to one of his team members to verify they had prints from bedrooms of the two women or to go look for them.

Quinn spoke quietly. "George is lead on the women and Kevin on Wilkie. It seems we have at least an initial link. So, coordinating these and covering all bases is critical. For now, let's turn back to the initial warrant on the phones and computers."

"Whoa, what? You have a warrant on some computers?" Gil was all but out of his seat. "Kevin, you didn't..."

Kevin nodded. "Let's not get ahead of ourselves. Yes, there are computers to be accessed, but we'll discuss that in the meeting with the SBI at noon. Can you be here, Gil?"

"Wouldn't miss it for the world."

"Okay, I'll just tell you the run I did and then we'll make a plan for the next meeting and take a break if we have time." He told them what he had found looking for the plumbing business and other identifying information on Wilkie. "Slim pickings, really."

Quinn added the information she had found. "I found his plumbing license, too. If we go back for a warrant, I want his utilities included." It was all placed on the board with the information on Buddy Wilkie.

"Anybody have anything else?" He looked around the table. "Then let's lay out our plan for walking through this with the SBI."

At eleven-forty-three a.m. Quinn stood as the knock on the door. They heard a key opening it. Quinn knew it would be the Chief.

They all stood.

"Be seated. Would appreciate a brief overview of where you are. Had a call to inform me Assistant Director Nelson will be with the SBI team." She sat in the chair Chuck had vacated.

Kevin took a quick breath and ran through their plan.

The Chief stood and held her hand out for them to stay seated. "I'll meet with Assistant Director Nelson and see if he wishes to join you." She walked out of the room.

Quinn was not surprised he was coming. After all, although they were born in the Valley, for him and his late brother—this was their hometown.

The SBI is Coming to Town

Millwood asked to speak to Quinn in her office.

She immediately realized he needed to calm his nerves. He was a detective with a number of years under his belt, but George was the senior detective and Kevin had likely not had a case that brought in the SBI.

"Kevin I've worked with AD Nelson before and he knows his primary role is administrative, but this is home. It matters to him."

"And the former chief was his brother."

"That, too. I suspect he is coming to assure us that we have the full backing of the SBI and whatever resources we need to solve whatever is going on here. You'll be fine leading this investigation. I do not intend to take over—it's your case."

"Yeah, but you and George already had the two women."

"Then work with George as you see fit. I'm here for whatever you need, but we're a team and it will take all of us to figure out the answers to a puzzle that has only just started to unravel. We haven't even touched the shed."

"I know." The confidence from earlier in the day had left Kevin's voice.

"Come on, let's go solve this puzzle. Remember, we're still looking for a killer, as far as we know. It could turn out to be Wilkie, but we're not making that leap. We'll follow..."

"The evidence." Kevin nodded and sounded more assured.

"Exactly. If you'll excuse me, I'll step down the hall and then meet you in the conference room."

"Yes, ma'am."

Quinn let his response go. Formality was comfort right now. She understood that. She took her secure phone out of her pocket and looked at the text. "Det. Williams in lobby." She went to the front to get Billy.

"Detective Williams, thanks for coming." She extended her hand.

Billy took her hand to shake and at the same time gently stroked his fingers on the back of it—a signal of more than a professional greeting. "Thanks for the invitation."

Quinn tried to ignore the feeling running through her from the gesture. She looked straight ahead.

They started down the hall.

"Big case you have here?" Billy was smiling—he felt the heat in the exchange.

"Time will tell. Please ask any questions in the meeting that come to mind."

"Like whether this squelches our afternoon date?" His voice was low and sexy.

"Detective! Business only, please." She gently bumped shoulders with him.

It's Noon

Introductions had been made and the six Round City Police members offered the chairs at the table to two SBI agents, AD Nelson, and Billy Williams. Quinn and Kevin joined them. George, Chuck, Gil, and Steve pulled up folding chairs at the far wall behind them so they could see the screen and the boards. It wasn't lost on any of them that the chief had simply walked AD Nelson to the door and left.

Quinn was relieved that the two SBI agents, Sandy Reynolds and Ed Franklin, who she knew was a forensic expert, were the agents SAC Jackson had chosen. She had worked with Sandy on a case in the Valley and knew that Ed had helped with the forensics when Billy's car was forced off the road last fall.

"Thanks for your time to help us solve this unusual case. Detective Millwood is lead on this investigation, so he'll run the show. Feel free to get up and help yourself to something to drink and the sandwiches and chips." Quinn turned to Kevin. "It's all yours."

"Let's get started." Kevin Millwood's voice came across with confidence. "Director Nelson, sir, thank you for coming. Is there anything you would like to say or share?"

"As I told your Chief, this is my hometown. God willing, I will return here to live when I retire. I would appreciate being allowed to hear the facts you have at the moment, and I want to assure you we will provide all the support and resources we can to help you get to the bottom of this. We serve, of course, at your invitation."

"Thank you, sir. You're welcome to stay. We need all the help we can get."

Quinn smiled as Kevin walked to the white board and pointed to the elements of the case with pertinent facts and known connections. She recognized his handwriting.

Eugenia Summers – Died Sun. night, found late Monday, body in custody of SBI

Condom found at bedside – DNA running- no hits

Call from her home phone to Buddy Wilkie Sunday evening

Lizzie Andrews – Died Mon. night, reported early hours Tues., body in custody of SBI

Condom found at bedside – DNA running – no hits

Two calls from her home phone to Buddy Wilkie Monday night – hours apart

Buddy Wilkie – Died Thursday night, found Friday night. Body in morgue.

Warrant in hand for phones and computers in shed and house

Shed on property contains cabinets with human bones,

ages undetermined

Child's shoes, age undetermined, estimated thirty-plus years-
One left on cruiser Sun. night. One found in house of Wilkie
Fri. night

"These, ladies and gentlemen, are the basic known facts. Given the nature of the findings in the shed, we need your assistance to determine next steps. Phones and the shoe are the only thing removed from the house. Nothing was removed from the shed. Before we take you to the Wilkie house, questions?"

Quinn watched as one-by-one they finished off the food. *Law officers are the same everywhere.* She smiled as she made a note to send a thank-you to the officers who prepared it.

An hour discussion ensued with questions addressed where the facts were known. Notes were taken for follow-up. As voices quieted, Kevin looked at each person.

"Anything else?" There were no comments or questions. "Agents, Detective…" Kevin paused and nodded toward Billy. "I know you came for a meeting, but if you have time to visit the Wilkie house while you're here, we would like to take you there. If we need to schedule another time…" He saw the agents and Billy shake their heads. He also watched Director Nelson leave the room. "Okay then, the space is small in the shed. George can escort you there. Chuck is working on evidence but is available. Steve will also go. His team will retrieve the computers and bring them back here. I believe if we can meet at four, earlier if you call and say so, we can come up with a plan to move forward. Then I suggest we all get some rest. Buddy Wilkie is not leaving our morgue until we release him—and at the moment we don't even know if there will be anyone to claim his remains."

"I've arranged for a van, so we can all ride together." George folded up his chair and put it against the wall as he spoke. "We'll meet at the end of the hall in ten. Steve, would you show our guests the restrooms?"

"On it." They all walked out the door.

Gil stayed back. "Kevin, I'd like to be the one to remove the computers. Okay if I go in my own vehicle? I have straps to secure them. I can use Steve's folks, but prefer to transport them myself."

"Sure. Apologies for not asking." Kevin took out his phone and informed George and Steve.

Gil waved it off as he left.

Quinn looked at Kevin in the now empty room. "Good job, Detective. Not only were you prepared, you led the team well, and we'll have a solid plan."

Kevin let out a long exhale. "Quinn, I can't believe I did it. You know that we were never..."

"I know. New day. New chief in town. She expects us to do our job; let's do it."

He extended his hand and she shook it. "Thanks. Thanks for giving me the chance."

She smiled and waited til he walked out the door. She turned out the lights and locked the door.

Once in her office, Quinn sent an email to Jake in maintenance and asked for the code lock to be installed as soon as it arrived. Keys were easily lost and she needed access to be secure, but available to the team. *And the code will* not *be 7734!* Her next message was to the officers in the common room downstairs to thank them for the coffee and food. She leaned back in her chair, shut her eyes, and remembered Billy watching her whenever he wasn't looking at facts on the Board or documents. *I think I'm going to like this job. And, I* know *I like Billy Williams—more and more.*

Chapter 22

Every individual matters. Every individual has a role to play. Every individual makes a difference.
Jane Goodall

Buddy's House

"Steve, you take the agents and Detective Williams to the shed. I'll keep Officer DeLoach with us, if that's okay." George was moving everyone into the living room.

Steve didn't hesitate. "DeLoach was lead earlier. She knows the layout of the place."

"Thanks. Holler if you need me."

Steve took Billy, Sandy and Ed, the two SBI agents, and headed through the kitchen. "Chuck has seen all this and really wants your input."

George Marshall turned to Gil and Officer DeLoach. "Come on. I'll show you the room where the two computers are; Simmons said he and Wilkie played video games almost weekly."

Gil sat down at one of the computers. "George, any problem for you if I try to open these before we disconnect them?"

"You're the geek. Have at it." George nodded to Gil.

Officer DeLoach stood back and watched.

As head of technology, but also a police officer, Gil knew the importance of doing this by the book—he already had latex gloves on. He turned on the first computer. "Both are relatively new computers and top of the line models. Probably going to require fingerprint access."

"Can you get around that?" George looked over Gil's shoulder.

"You mean without the fingerprint?"

"Yeah?"

"Not easily. This is a laptop. I'll take it to the morgue and get his fingerprint to open it."

"You can do that?" Ruth DeLoach put her hand to her mouth. "Sorry, sir."

"Learn something new, did you?" George chuckled.

"Old computer at my house." She gave a wan smile.

"Relax. Mine, too."

Gil turned on the second computer. "Interesting, this one only requires a password—no fingerprint."

"Must be the one Simmons used. He might know the password."

"Amazingly lucid thought, George. His name might *be* the password." Gil went back to the keyboard. He typed in "Simmons." Nothing happened. He typed in "Albert." The computer opened.

"Way to go, Gil." George patted him on the back.

"Disappointing. Probably means there's nothing here but gaming programs." Gil was moving from screen to screen on the laptop. "Okay, I'll shut these down, disconnect them and take all the cables and cords." He turned off both laptops and turned to DeLoach.

"Let's put them in this padded case. We'll leave them in the house until it's decided if we're going to try and get into the other one in the shed here or take it to the station."

"Yes, sir. I can put them in the living room until we're ready to leave."

"Fair enough." Gil put each laptop between the pads in the case, stored the cables and power cords, shut, and locked the case. He started to lift the case.

DeLoach leaned in. "Got them, sir."

Gil didn't resist. He knew this team handled evidence all the time.

"George?" Steve called from the back door.

"Coming." George headed for the kitchen.

"Agents want to talk to you in the shed."

"Be right there." George headed out. "DeLoach, please show Officer Gilbert the rest of the house. Might be something he needs to check out about the technology."

"Yes, Detective."

Steve followed George out to the shed.

Ruth and Gil walked into the living room.

Gil looked around. "Ever see a house this pristine?"

Ruth shook her head. "Not even my own. Come look at the garage."

"Good idea. I wanted to see what internet service he has coming in here."

They walked through the kitchen. Gil looked around. "Seriously? *Who* lives like this?"

"Someone with OCD or a parent stricter than an Army drill sergeant."

"Wouldn't know about either." Gil was shaking his head. He whistled as he entered the garage. "Good Lord, can you eat off the floors out here, too?"

"Probably everywhere but where the van parks." Ruth pointed to the tread marks made from the slush on the roads. "I doubt if this guy was two inches off either way every time he parked."

"Never seen anything like it—or this garage. Too bad the guy's dead. I'd hire him to clean my garage." Gil slowly looked from orderly shelf to orderly shelf.

"This is nothing. The only thing in his fridge are sandwiches from some deli and each one has a successive day in the week written in magic marker."

"You mean like: Monday eat this one?"

"Well, it doesn't say to eat the sandwich, but the remaining ones are Friday, Saturday, Sunday, Monday."

Gil stood in the middle of the garage. "So, he buys them on Tuesday?"

"That's my best interpretation. Where he buys them will be the question—not from any of our local places that I can tell."

"Eat sandwiches out that much, DeLoach?"

"More times than I'd like. But, we're not here to talk about sand-wiches, or my dietary shortcomings. Can you find where the internet comes into the house?"

Gil moved around the outer wall and peered behind the well-organized things on each shelf. "Bingo. In these old houses, the utilities are almost always on the outside wall away from the garage door."

"Makes sense." Ruth moved in.

"I'll make a note of the provider, but need some pictures to verify."

"Done." She took out the pocket camera and took shots from all angles.

"This isn't part of identifying him, so we'll just file it unless, or until, Detective Isaacs decides to try and get a warrant. It'll save me a trip if we need anything from the provider."

"10-4."

The Shed

"Detective," SBI Agent Sandy Reynolds pointed to the computer. "Is this computer included in the warrant?"

"Yes, ma'am." George saw Billy Williams standing in the far corner watching.

"Any luck with the ones inside?" Sandy was all business.

"One was an easy password bypass and, on the surface, appears to only be used for gaming. The other one will require the DB's fingerprint to open. Laptops make that easy."

She nodded. "According to Ed, we're going to need a forensic an-thropologist on all of this." She pointed from the freezer to each of the cabinets. "Safe assumption you don't have one?"

"That would be an affirmative; part of why we called SBI."

"And the other part?" Ed looked at him.

"Need your expertise and resources. You can see that this shed alone is a big job. With the unfolding of the connections to the female DBs already in your shop...well, Ed, it's going to take teamwork."

Agent Ed Franklin leaned against the freezer and glanced at Billy who had not spoken since they entered. "No doubt. I suggest that we get a joint team for removal and divide the spoils based on whose got the equipment to handle it."

George didn't hesitate. "Well, can't disagree, but this is Kevin's case. We'll run it all by him when we meet at four. That work for you?"

Sandy looked at her watch. "I think we can let Kevin know we'll be back there and ready by three-thirty. In the meantime, let's get your geek out here to see what he thinks about this computer."

George called Gil. When Gil stepped out the back door, he pulled out his pocket light. "This guy was something else. Who does this much work to get vines growing over an arbor to block out the world?"

"Someone who doesn't want to be observed?" Sandy said from the doorway.

"Fair enough." Gil entered the shed and the others stepped to the side. "Whoa, don't think the explanation earlier set me up for the reality." He looked at the open doors to each of the cabinets. He shook his head. "Do I want to know what's in the freezer?"

Ed lifted the lid.

Gil looked in. "Glad I work with computers. So, what's your plan for this one?"

"The warrant covers three computers—which apparently includes this one. Can you open it here, or do we need to get it into your shop?"

Gil sat down. This one did not have a fingerprint ID. *With the setup of everything else in this shed, this guy was probably not a typical computer user. Likely there's more than one password.* He turned it on and the screen showed a box for a password. He sat for several seconds before he looked up.

"Listen, folks. I could sit here for days and try the usual patterns people use for passwords on everyday home computers. Something tells me this guy was anything but typical. If I try too many things, I could end up locking us out and taking even more time to get in. The best thing is to take it back to the station. I have equipment that can help us. If we can get into his laptop once I can get his fingerprint on it, we might be able to find the easiest way into this one."

Sandy looked at George. "We're the guests here. Your call."

"We're wasting time. Gil, get this one packed up, and get it back to the station. We've got round the clock patrols on the house—none of this is going anywhere. The rest of this can wait until a decision is made about a plan to figure out what all there is."

George opened the shed door and saw Ruth DeLoach on the back porch. "Hey, I was about to come get you. Can you help Gil get this back to the station? I'll take our guests back." "10-4." She stood to the side while the others came out of the shed.

George stood in the doorway. "Be right there, folks. Then we'll head back. Gil and DeLoach can bring these computers in."

He turned to Gil. "Need anything?"

Gil was moving carefully around the wires and computer.

"Looking for a booby trap?"

Gil looked at each wire, the base of the computer, and the top of the desk. "Just want to make sure there's nothing here that's going to erase this thing if I move it."

"Didn't know you could erase it just by moving it."

"Just by moving it, you can't. But folks have some pretty fancy ways of protecting their data." He looked up. "I think we're good. Only wires are power, and what I believe is a cable to a backup, though it appears to be in this drawer…"

"Wait." George all but snapped it.

Gil pulled his hand back sharply hitting his elbow on the arm of the chair. "Is *this* booby-trapped?"

"No." George chuckled. "Sorry about that. However, it does have a catch at the top. You have to reach in and release it to get the drawer all the way open."

"Got it." The latch released. Gil shook his arm to relieve the pain in his elbow and pulled the drawer all the way out. Mounted to the inside back of the drawer was an external drive. "One more device to explore." He grinned like a child with a new toy.

"We all get our kicks in different ways. DeLoach is here. Guess you want this door shut. It's cold as a witch's thorax in here."

"Yeah, yeah. Send her in. Let's get this baby wrapped up before it freezes to death."

Ruth stuck her head in the door. "Ready with your padded case. Let's do this."

No Rest for the Weary

Quinn and Kevin revisited the board on the two women. Quinn studied the photos of the women even though they were already emblazoned in her brain. "We need to go through the report on the women and see what the A-Team collected besides the condoms. DNA still hasn't made a hit."

She turned to Kevin. "Is it safe to assume the A-team dusted for prints at the Summers' residence?"

"I'm sure they did once you found those footprints, but that doesn't mean things weren't smudged or wiped away by the perpetrator, the husband when he found her, or the EMTs who moved her. No one thought it was a crime at the time she was moved."

"True." Quinn dragged out the word as she knotted her hair. *Almost a week since she died. I have a feeling we're going to be a while before we know the real COD, if we ever do. And maybe longer before we know if we have our killer.*

"Quinn?" Kevin said her name louder.

"Sorry, I was trying to put together pieces in my head. What's up?"

"I said they may have collected them and not run them. It's only been a few days and we've only just suspected there was a connection between the women and possibly Wilkie."

"True. Am I missing your point?"

"Not a TV show—things take time and just because we've collected evidence doesn't mean it was run. Really no reason to do so."

"Thanks for the perspective. I'm learning."

Kevin started to speak then looked at his phone. "Text from George. The agents and Detective Williams are on their way back in with George and Steve. Meeting moved up to three-thirty. Work for you?"

"Sure. I want to go take one more look at Wilkie's driver's license. Sure would like to know what he presented to get it issued."

"That depends on when he got it. If he took driver's ed in school, it doesn't require any documentation from him like utilities, etc. as the parent or parents would have signed and provided proof of residence."

"Good point. But, what about his birth certificate?"

"Don't know for sure, but I assume since they have DOB on school records, they just verify with that."

Quinn decided to wait until they all met to share the news that there was no birth certificate, at least in Tennessee on Buddy Wilkie; she had searched on name and date of birth listed on his driver's license. We just need to get enough justification for me to go back to the DA for a warrant to get into anything and everything of his.

She started toward the door. "I'll be here at three-thirty."

She walked down the hall to the ladies room. *George told me the other day that detective work was a lot of slogging. I know that. Why can't I accept we won't have answers instantly?* As she splashed water on her face, she tried not to get any on her jacket or the turtleneck she had on underneath it. *Times like this I'm glad I don't wear makeup.* She dried her hands and headed out the door, and almost bumped into someone walking down the hall.

"Oh, excuse me." She looked up.

"My pleasure—almost." He whispered in her ear as he leaned over like he was helping her with something.

Quinn laughed. "Work, Detective. This is work."

"Whew. Don't I know it." They walked toward her office. "Can't say as I've seen anything like that shed—even in some of the gruesome stuff I read in college or things I saw in SBI and FBI trainings. Been thinking about all this."

"Really? And what do you think?" Quinn smiled at him.

"I think we should each write down what we think you have going on here, put it in a locked box, and see who comes closest."

Quinn feigned horror. "You would make a game of this?"

"Sometimes the only way to get through the day, Detective Isaacs—the only way." His voice was steady and without a hint of sarcasm.

She entered the code to go into her office.

Billy followed her. "Like what you've done with the place."

"I haven't done anything."

"The coat tree lends a homey touch and the diplomas and photos strike just the right chord."

"Musician, are you?" She closed her office door. "Have a seat."

"I'd rather do something else."

"Control yourself, Detective. There's time for that later."

"Promise?"

She wiggled her eyebrows and turned to open the door.

Chuck was about to knock again. "Sorry, Quinn." He saw Billy and switched to her title: "Detective."

"Thanks, Chuck. Detective Williams and I go back a ways—worked some cases with him in the Valley."

"Oh, sure. Then it's okay to call you Quinn?"

She laughed. "Yes. What's up?"

"I'm working on Wilkie's DNA. Do you need me in the meeting at four?"

"No, and it's going to be at three-thirty now, but it's just a planning session. If something comes up, I'll come get you. We *definitely* need that DNA. How long?"

"Wee hours of the morning if we're lucky. Maybe longer. Doc had samples I can use, but just hadn't sent them up to be run."

"Then keep at it."

"Thanks, Quinn. See you later, Detective."

"Billy works. See you later, Chuck." He saw the smile on Chuck's face. Quinn left the door open.

Billy gently closed it. He brushed his lips against her cheek in a light kiss and moved to sit down. She pulled him back to her and gave him a long kiss on the lips. "Stay tuned."

"All channels." He raised his eyebrows. "Now, Detective Isaacs, what is with all the title stumbling going on in this place? I never knew that Chief Nelson was that strict."

"I don't think he was, although he was always by the book. I think the challenge was for these people to navigate around…"

"Albright." Billy whispered. He didn't want her to say it aloud in case the walls had ears.

She nodded.

"Only had a few interactions with him. The chief was usually the liaison. Now I see why."

"Billy, I need your assessment of what you've seen and heard so far in this quagmire."

"Were you expecting the connection from Wilkie to the women?"

"Not on the evidence we had before this morning, but gut—yeah. The thing is…I'm not so sure this is as clear cut as it appears."

"They rarely are. What pleases me, as a detective for many years, is knowing you won't take the easy way out. You have a dead suspect. Two dead women who had each called him, presumably for plumbing services, the night they died. Signed, sealed, and delivered."

"Not that simple for me. We didn't address it earlier, but I want you and the SBI folks to look at the footprints we found at the Summers place. There weren't any at Andrews place, but the only entrance used by anyone was the front door and that sidewalk was wet, but no snow or mud for footprints. She had two sons who likely had to clean off every snowflake—I suspect we'll find out they have been pretty badly abused." Her voice dropped. "No, not simple."

Billy looked at his watch. "Then let's go talk to these folks from the SBI and your team and make a plan. Good plans, as you know, generally lead to good results."

"Thanks, Billy. I needed a friend by my side—and a colleague who has experience and objectivity."

"Whoa…I'll have objectivity about the case. Not sure I can be as definite about keeping objectivity about my feelings for you."

She kissed him again, but lightly this time. *Now I'm really glad I don't wear makeup.*

"Later. We have much to discuss." She opened her office door and walked out toward the conference room. Billy followed her.

Chapter 23

Comfort can be dangerous. Comfort provides a floor but also a ceiling.
Trevor Noah

Something in Common

Always one to analyze situations, Oscar Wilkie, sat at the spartan table in his small dark cabin heated only by the wood stove. He made notes on a piece of paper. The heading was "something in common." *Buddy, how many times did I tell you we had something in common. Why didn't you ever ask me what it was?* He looked over at the two pairs of boots by the door. They were heavy leather boots with thick soles and solid heels custom made for him. They were identical except for one feature—the toe of one boot faced backwards when he had it on. He reached down and rubbed the stump of his foot long calloused from walking on it after losing the front of his foot when he was a teenager. He was still fairly nimble walking around in his heavy woolen socks, something he had never done in front of Buddy. It wasn't until he moved out here full-time that he quit worrying about someone other than the shoemaker knowing about his foot. He had long ago mastered walking in the boots—no matter which pair he wore.

His notes were scribbled, doodling almost, while he made a plan to find out what happened at Buddy's house and retrieve his drone. *I should have used one of the smaller drones. When can I go get the one on the spring house?*

Several minutes later he looked down and saw he had completed two distinct drawings. One was the wall around Buddy's house—the house

291

where he himself grew up. The other was a body lying flat with arms at the side. Underneath it he wrote: Buddy Wilkie. *Where are you, Buddy? What's going on?* Absently he scratched the side of his left ankle. *Yes, Buddy, we've always had something in common.*

Just the Facts

The team was gathered in the conference room which was their base for what might be unrelated cases, but the phone numbers on Buddy Wilkie's phone made it seem highly probable it was not all coincidence.

Kevin stepped over to the white board where he had listed the links to the three bodies: the two women with credible evidence they were murdered and Buddy Wilkie with a COD from the ME of a brain aneurysm. "Ladies and gentlemen…"

The quiet talk among them stopped. "Our goal this afternoon is to lay out a plan and then get started on it. That may require some of us to continue working through the weekend, and others will get what's left of their well-deserved weekend."

"Alright!"

"Let's do it."

Kevin let them finish their comments. He understood the stress of trying to piece together a case. "We'll begin with an update from George on the Wilkie house."

"Gil is working on getting what we think is Wilkie's main laptop open, and then he'll work on opening the desktop from the shed. The second laptop appeared to be a gaming computer only. Gil will spend more time on it, though. The discussion at the shed, which involved our colleagues from the Valley and SBI, provided a consensus for identifying who could best handle what evidence, get it assigned, picked up, and analyses started. Think that covers it."

Kevin had drawn a line off to the side of Wilkie's name. He wrote:

Item(s)   Team

"Quinn?" Kevin looked directly at her.

"Chuck is working on getting the DNA from the samples he received from the ME. Once he has them, he will run them through the system and target them for cross-match with DNA from the condoms found in the bedrooms of each of the women." She looked around the table. "Without a warrant, the only thing I've found on Buddy Wilkie is that there is no birth certificate…"

Sandy interrupted. "I thought earlier we established that he and his father inherited the estate of Gladys Wilkie."

Quinn responded, "Oscar Wilkie and Buddy Wilkie did inherit and were listed in the very brief obituary as the son and grandson of Gladys Wilkie. However, there is no birth certificate in the state for Buddy Wilkie, or any male child in the county close on the date of birth on Wilkie's driver's license. Unless we find something in his computers to verify who he is, we should be able to broaden the scope of the warrant."

Billy nodded. "DA O'Haire will do all she can to get you what you need."

"She's been very helpful already." Quinn glanced back at Sandy. "Thoughts, Agent?"

"Things aren't always as they seem?"

"That may be an understatement in this matter." Quinn turned to Kevin. "If you would move over to the board with the two women, I'd like to draw everyone's attention to the footprints from the Summers' residence. Have any of you seen anything like this before?"

Ed stood up and looked closely at the prints. "One legged man?"

"Good question, Agent. We have no idea. None of us could figure out how, in the snow, someone could maneuver on one leg."

"In all my years doing forensics at SBI, I've never seen anything like it." He looked closely at the photos. "May I have digital copies of the photos?"

Quinn nodded to Kevin.

"Absolutely. Steve, could you take care of ?" Kevin wrote on the board:

Digital photos of footprints to SBI - Steve

"Sure thing."

"Anything else, Quinn?"

"That's all I have at this time."

Sergeant Steve Clark raised his hand.

Kevin nodded. "No need for formalities, Steve. Speak up."

"Old habits really die hard. Thanks, Kevin. We collected prints from the door knobs and headboard on the beds of the two women. They are in the downstairs lab, but don't know if they've been run. Might be worth it to see if there's a hit there. Anyone know if Mr. Summers has prints on file?"

"He had an airtight alibi for the night of his wife's murder, so he was not charged with any crime, nor was he a suspect. There was nothing on file related to him when I checked." George sat back in his chair.

"If there happen to be prints of more than one person, and we don't get a hit, we can revisit Mr. Summers." Kevin wrote on the board as he spoke.

> Run fingerprints from Summers residence. Marshall
> Andrews residence. Marshall

"Anything else?"

"We should interview your officer who was Wilkie's friend." All eyes turned and looked at SBI agent, Sandy Davis.

Quinn quickly assessed this was her hit to take—she should have brought it up earlier. "You are absolutely right, Sandy. My error for not bringing it up sooner. I suggest you and George conduct it."

Heads nodded in agreement.

"I can see if he's still in the common room." George looked at Quinn.

She nodded. "Once Kevin gives us our marching orders, that sounds like a good plan—if Sandy has the time today."

Kevin wrote on the board:

> Interview Officer Simmons – SBI Agent Davis and Marshall

Steve spoke up. "I'm not sure having one officer in the front of the Wilkie house, and one checking the perimeter is sufficient. I can send one of my team over to focus on the shed. Did I miss something on how we're going to handle the material in there?"

Kevin made a note on the board about security around the house:

Secure shed and surveillance – A-Team

"It's my understanding that a forensic anthropologist is going to be needed. Is that right, Ed?" Kevin waited for his response.

"Absolutely. All of it is old, just like those shoes best I can tell on first observation. Did Chuck have a date on the shoes?"

Quinn nodded. "He found the brand was made until about twenty years ago, but the particular style was closer to thirty. I don't know if he found a starting date for when the style was made. We don't have the equipment to do the analyses necessary to determine the age of the material in the shed, though."

Ed knew his role as an SBI agent. He looked around the table at the local team. "Anything you have strong feelings about trying to examine yourselves?"

Quinn looked at the detectives and Steve Clark. The three men shook their heads. "I'd like to talk with Chuck, but I think it's a safe bet you are much better equipped to figure out what we have than we are at this time."

"Happy to have Chuck come spend some time in Knoxville and work through it with us. That possible?"

Quinn looked at Kevin and George. "Can we handle what we have with him away?" As senior detective, George spoke up. "Aside from this being pretty major, we don't have anything else that is out of the ordinary at the moment. Be good for Chuck to work with these guys, seems to me."

Kevin wrote on the board:

Pickup of materials in Wilkie shed - Sgt. Clark and agents from SBI

Analysis of materials in Wilkie shed - SBI with RCP Tech, Chuck

Kevin stepped back from the board and looked at the group. "Quinn, the warrant only covered the phones and computers. We'll need one to remove the material in the shed, right?"

Quinn nodded. "Please put the computers and phones Gil is searching on the board."

Kevin wrote:

> Warrant based search of computers/phone
>
> Wilkie's residence – Gilbert

Quinn nodded. "Thanks to all of you for your work. I'll leave it to each of you to set the timeline for your assignment. Sandy, Ed, thank you for your support and that of SBI. If you need anything at all, let me know." She stood. "Unless you need me for something else at this time, I need to go update Chief Hansen and talk to the DA. I'll touch base with Chuck to see how much time he needs. Detective Williams, may I speak with you?"

Billy nodded. "Kevin, I know the Summers' residence is in your jurisdiction. If you need our help in any way, or if it becomes apparent any of it happened on our side, I'm just a phone call away. Thanks for letting me sit in on this. I'll be interested to know where it all leads." He followed Quinn out of the conference room.

Where to Next?

Quinn stepped down the hallway and Billy followed. "I need to check with Chuck and then update the Chief. Then I need to talk to Peggy O'Haire about a warrant. Do you have time to hang around?"

"I do. I was expecting the company of a lovely lady this afternoon, but the wine will keep and the food won't spoil."

She whispered, "I think I remember someone willing to put on snowshoes and walk here. Did I miss something?" She put one hand on her hip and cocked her head.

"Ouch. Foiled by my own words. Anything open in this town where I could pick up some food?"

"Not sure. The 'stay off the streets order' may have been lifted, but doesn't always mean anything will open." She shook her head at him. "What a pathetic look. You won't starve. Here's the code to my house lock." She held up two fingers twice, then one, then three.

"Even I, a lowly detective, can remember those numbers."

"Good job. Help yourself to whatever you want to eat or drink. The fireplace remote should be on the coffee table. I'll be there as soon as I can. I need to pick your brain."

"Ouch, again. I thought this was just an alternative date location."

"It could be. If you play your cards right."

"On it. Dealer takes two." He winked at her and headed for the front door. "Thank Chief Hansen for inviting me to sit in on this."

"Absolutely." Quinn shook her head and put the code in the lab door. She walked toward Chuck who was hovered over one of his new high-tech microscopes. *At least I assume it's a microscope.*

"Need me, Quinn?"

"Need to know how much time you need Wilkie's DNA before you could head to Knoxville to work with the SBI folks on the material from the shed?"

"Really? You want me to go work on it with them?"

"Really. By the time I get a warrant to remove the material in the shed, it may be Monday anyway."

"I'm pretty close to having the DNA mapped. Then I need to start the run. Guess we're thinking it'll match the DNA in the condoms?"

"No one in the room was speculating. It will be what it will be."

"Right." He hesitated. "Uh, Quinn?"

"Yes?"

"When I went to see the ME about getting samples for DNA...well, Tristan was there."

Quinn waited on him to continue.

"He gets really hyper and, well, his voice is really sing-song. He wanted to know what we were doing. Wanted to know if he could help."

"What did you say?"

"I didn't say anything. I think I'm always stunned at how strange he is. Anyway, Doc stopped him—told him he should go get a degree in forensics if that's the job he wanted. I mean he was nice about it, but I can see he knows how to keep Tristan in line."

Quinn nodded. "Sorry it caused you some angst. If you need anything, let me know. Keep up the good work."

"Nope, I'm good."

"Okay, I need to see if I can get a warrant and then update the Chief. I'll check back with you."

"Yes, ma'am." His response was perfunctory as he was back at his equipment.

Quinn entered her office. She pulled out her secure phone to call the DA.

"O'Haire."

"Peggy, it's Quinn."

"What's up?"

She filled her in on the SBI team and the work they had done today. "We need to move the contents of the shed to the SBI lab in Knoxville. It's going to take a forensic anthropologist to figure out what we have and the age of the material."

"So, let me be clear. How does this material tie back to the fact that the two women who are deceased happened to have called the same plumber the night they died, and he is now in your morgue?"

"Good question. I don't know. What I do know is that the child's shoe left on the roof of one of our officer's vehicles is a mate to the one found in the home of Mr. Wilkie." She took a breath. "And, Peggy, what I have referred to as material in this discussion includes a skull which appears to be a child. We have not touched or removed anything in any of the metal cabinets or the freezer, but it is obvious we have human remains."

Peggy tapped on the phone with her nail. "The owner is deceased, there is no known next of kin..."

"I agree, no known, but there could be. I can't find a birth certificate for a Buddy Wilkie or any other name close to it that matches with the birthdate on his driver's license."

"Then I better add adoption records to the list. Send me a written request with any and everything you can think of you need and I'll try to get hold of a judge. It's almost six on Saturday night, on a day when most folks never left their homes. You know I may not…"

"I understand. We have the house under surveillance and one of our A-team members specifically on the shed."

"Okay, okay. Since you're new, I'll save you the DA lecture."

"Thanks, Peggy. I'm willing to learn, so feel free to lecture me anytime."

"Yeah, yeah, that's what they all say." She laughed. "We're good, Quinn. I'll be back in touch."

Quinn let out a long slow sigh. *Do I have any clue what I'm doing?* The information for the warrant request completed, she had just hit send on the secure server when she heard the knock on her door. She stood and was about to say, "Come in, Chuck." She saw it was the Chief. She stepped back.

"Ma'am. I was just about to reach out to you with an update."

Jill Hansen stood in the doorway.

"Come in, come in." Quinn pointed to the chair.

"I'll stand if it's all the same to you."

"Sure. Yes, ma'am." Quinn spent the next twenty minutes updating the Chief on what they knew, what their plan was, and her talk with the DA.

"Good job. Elliott Nelson told me I didn't know how lucky I was to have hired you."

Quinn felt the heat rise in her face. "Thank you, ma'am. I hope I can prove worthy of the praise."

Jill nodded. "So far, so good. Sounds like the team has a solid plan. Once they interview Officer Simmons, seems like a good night for everyone else to get some sleep. Even if the DA gets a warrant. It will keep until tomorrow or even Monday. Let's get everyone rested and brain-cells a chance to rekindle. Doesn't appear anyone is in imminent danger, right?"

"Not that we can tell. Thanks for your support, Chief."

"Thanks for your leadership."

"Detective Millwood's lead on this."

"My point exactly." The chief turned and walked out.

My point exactly? A slow smile crossed Quinn's face. *Leadership isn't about doing the work yourself. How many times did I think that in Immigration with our boss? Leadership is about getting a team to use their individual strengths and talents to address the issue at hand—working together. Hmmm…I think I'm going to like this job.* She stood just as there was a knock at the outer lab door.

"I've got it, Chuck." She saw Kevin standing there. "Come in." She turned and pointed to her door.

"Thanks." Kevin walked in and sat down.

"Good job, Kevin. Solid plan, warrant is being requested, Chuck thinks he'll have a DNA sequence by tomorrow at the latest. Hope you feel good about the progress."

"Quinn. The Chief came in and told me she heard I was doing a good job. The *Chief*!"

"She did because you are. Was Simmons still in the station?"

"Yes. Sandy and George took him to our offices since no one else is here. Hopefully he'll just see it as a quiet place, and not feel that he's being interrogated."

"Any reason to think he has anything to do with any of this?"

"No." His answer was swift.

"Okay, then let's see how it plays out. Major goal is to see if we can find out anything about next of kin and anything he knows about Wilkie's habits."

"George is good at this. Don't know about the SBI agent."

"She's good, too. I worked with her over in the Valley. Be good if we can get some direction. Now, tell me your plans for the rest of the weekend?"

"Since we need to wait on the warrant, I'm going to head home. Steve sent a member of his team to cover the shed at Wilkie's and he set up a rotation schedule. The duty sergeant has a rotation on officers covering the front and perimeter of the house."

"Good work. I thought of one thing I'd like to add to the list."

"Sure. What's that?"

"I think we need to work with Family Services and have a talk with the Andrews brothers."

"Yeah, good point. Sorry I didn't think of it."

"As the Chief said to me, it doesn't appear we have anyone in imminent danger, so let's get rested and clear our heads. Lots of work headed our way."

"Thanks, Quinn. Thanks for everything. Really glad you came on board."

"Thanks, Kevin. So, am I. Let me know anytime you need anything from me. Now go home and get some rest."

"You, too."

"Headed that way momentarily."

Warm Fire

Quinn backed her work SUV into her garage and closed the door. She was about to open the kitchen door when she felt the door knob turn. Her reflex was to unsnap her gun guard—she caught herself before she did.

"What an unexpected pleasure. A gentleman to welcome me home."

Billy reached out and took her hand as she stepped out of her boots and into the kitchen.

She stepped into her slippers, took off her weapon and shield and put them in the gun safe. She was about to turn as she pulled off her coat and realized he was lifting it off her shoulders. She kissed him lightly on the lips. "I could get very used to this."

"The pleasure is all mine." He leaned in and gave her a long, slow kiss.

Quinn stepped back. "Whoa, that's pretty heady stuff after the day I've had. I need something..."

"To drink?" He handed her a glass of sauvignon blanc. He picked up his glass and clinked with hers.

"You're drinking wine? I thought all the male cops in the Valley drank beer."

"Do both. Problem with that?"

She shook her head. "None whatsoever. What do I smell?"

"Took the liberty of taking you up on your offer and rummaged through your freezer. Found a container labeled 'chicken soup.' I can actually defrost and reheat soup." He smiled.

"So you found out I cheat and make frozen biscuits, too."

"How'd you figure that out?"

"The smell is divine—I'm a detective, remember?"

He pulled her into a tight embrace. "So you are, lovely lady. So you are. Go get comfortable, I'll have food on the island shortly."

"No offense, but let's eat on the table in the great room." She flipped on the light in the large great room off the kitchen. "I'll start the fire."

"Your wish is my command. Now go."

Quinn leaned back in her chair as they finished the soup and biscuits. "Thanks, Billy. That was just what I needed tonight—comfort food."

"Thought you might. I'll clean up the dishes and then tell me how I can help."

She stood with him. "Many hands make light work, right? Let's get this done, I'll make some tea—do you want coffee?"

"Tea sounds perfect."

Ten minutes later the kitchen was cleaned up, they had mugs of tea, and were sitting on the sofa in front of the fireplace.

Quinn let out a long breath. "Billy, first of all...thanks for coming over. It helped me to have a familiar face and someone I know I can trust listening in on this. Secondly, but no less importantly, it was nice to come home and have you at the door."

Billy sat drinking his tea and watching her.

"I need to hear what you think of what you heard and observed today."

As he went through his observations from the first meeting to the planning session, she listened attentively. "I think your leadership skills are excellent and you never once preempted your detective. Wish I was that good."

"You're too kind."

"I mean it, Quinn. You're a natural. Most detectives wouldn't necessarily see the work you did in immigration anything close to detective work, but it was all detective work—it seems to me."

She nodded. "In its own way, that's true."

"I also think you've had quite a while to see what you felt you were missing in your former boss and as a very smart person, you must have been thinking about what a good leader could and should be. Am I close?"

"Yes, but you know something else? I learned so many things about leadership from watching Chad lead your team as sheriff. He was a good listener and has a good mind for organization and problem solving—it shows."

"So do you."

"Thanks. I appreciate the feedback and the compliment. Chief Hansen was right, there is no one in apparent imminent danger from what we know at this point, so it's a good night to clear our heads and be ready for the new day."

"I agree."

"I don't have a lathe to go turn wood."

"Don't need one. I have one you can use anytime you want." He set his mug on the table beside the sofa and leaned close to her. "Besides, I can think of something far more interesting than turning wood." He kissed her gently—then passion took over.

She returned the kiss as she undid the knot in her hair. She moved closer to him as she pulled his head to hers.

Chapter 24

If the risk is fully aligned with your purpose and mission,
then it's worth considering.
Peter Diamandis

Under Cover of Night

Quinn's secure phone rang on the end table by the sofa. She pulled back from Billy and reached for it. *Seriously?*

"Isaacs."

"Boss, just arrested an old man at Buddy Wilkie's residence. He says he's Oscar Wilkie. Want one of us to take it; or you want to come in?" Kevin Millwood sounded out of breath.

"Has anyone talked to him yet?"

"No, ma'am."

"On my way. Let's meet and make a plan. Be there in less than fifteen minutes."

"10-4."

She turned to see Billy's face with a long frown. She leaned over and kissed him. "It's going to take a while to figure out if it's a blessing or a curse that we share the same profession."

She took his hand as she stood. "Want to come? They caught Oscar Wilkie on Buddy Wilkie's property."

"Oh, hel..heck yeah. Is it okay?"

"I brought you in as a consultant. You still are as far as I'm concerned."

"Think anyone would question that if there was a video of us five minutes ago?"

She stopped at her gun safe and turned to look at him. "Detective Williams, I may not be forty yet, but I've lived long enough to know that men have worked with friends and even lovers forever. The day either of us loses objectivity on the job; we'll talk about it."

"Yes, ma'am." He winked at her. "Can't blame a guy for being a neanderthal."

"True. I'm pretty sure you're trainable, though." She winked back. She turned to get her weapon and realized she hadn't seen his. "Where's your service weapon?"

"Five more minutes and you would have found it." He turned around and pointed to the small of his back.

"Let's go, wise guy."

"I'll admit I hope to return and pick up where we left off, but just in case you're night is longer than you need me, I'll drive too."

"Trust me, I'll need you. However, point taken. See you at the station."

He stepped into the garage. "I locked your front door. Guess I'll know if I'm welcome again if the code doesn't change." His trademark sarcasm was delivered with humor.

"Guess we'll find out. Now, go." She stepped into her department SUV and turned on the lights so he could see down the driveway to get to his car on the concrete pad close to the street.

Billy was standing in the front talking to the duty officer when Quinn came in from the back entrance.

"Detective, thanks for joining us." She nodded to the duty officer to let him in.

"Detective Isaacs, thanks for the invitation." He walked beside her to the conference room. Kevin and George were already inside.

"Sorry you had to come in, boss." George nodded to Quinn and Billy. "Still on this side of the mountain, Billy? Didn't know you had..." He stopped. "Sorry, that's a little personal. Glad you could join us."

Quinn and Billy filled paper cups with coffee and sat down.

"Thanks for the call, Kevin. Tell me what happened."

"The A-team member assigned to the shed at Buddy Wilkie's house, reported an intruder in the back wall to the left of the shed. Officer Evans was on perimeter patrol and made the corner just as the intruder opened a wooden door in the wall."

"A wooden door?" Quinn furrowed her eyebrows. "Did any of you see a wooden door? All I saw was a wall, reported as brick by the A-team, and covered with vines and a stand of trees."

"The door was well camouflaged by the vines, but it was obvious this man knew exactly what he was looking for. He was midway into the yard when Evans came from the back and the A-team member came off the back porch."

"Any identification?" Billy said.

Kevin and George shook their heads. "Nothing. Seems he didn't hesitate to say he was 'Oscar Wilkie' when the officer asked him who he was. Then he muttered something about being the pappy of the boy who lived there."

"Officer Evans relieved him of the Bowie knife he used to cut through the vines. He didn't resist."

"What do we know about the man?" Quinn looked from one to the other of her detectives.

"Apparently he has a medical degree, but never practiced medicine." Kevin looked across the table. "George, you've lived here longer than any of us; know anything about his family?"

"Only the details we've uncovered. I'd never heard of the family and given the house is pretty well surrounded by vacant land; I'd say they didn't want to be known. Any idea the size of the trust these two men inherited?"

Quinn looked around the table. "That can be hard to unearth. If the interview with him..."

"Interview?" Kevin seemed startled. "You mean interrogation?"

"On what grounds, Kevin?" Quinn's voice was calm and even.

"Trespassing, if nothing else. Don't you think he knows what's in that shed?"

"I have no idea whether he knows or not. I also have no idea whether he is legally the father of Buddy Wilkie. If he is, and Buddy has no other heirs…well, absent a will, I assume the property belongs to Oscar Wilkie now."

Kevin slumped in his chair. "Sorry, Quinn. Guess I'm tired and even willing to admit a little spooked by all this."

"If we're honest, Kevin, I suspect we're all a little spooked. Too many loose threads, a setup like none of us has ever seen before, and five dead people in our small community in less than a week—at least three of them possibly connected."

"Quinn, I've already told Kevin, but when Sandy and I interviewed Albert Simmons, he seemed to be clear that Oscar Wilkie was Buddy's father. Seems Albert and Buddy went to middle and high school at a small rural school that doesn't exist anymore. Wilkie taught them math and science. He said, and I quote, 'Dr. Wilkie was always strict, and a little strange.'"

Quinn didn't miss a beat. "Have we asked Simmons to identify Oscar Wilkie?"

Kevin looked at her. "No. I called you right away when he was brought in."

"Quinn," George said, "I doubt we have anyone else close enough in age to do a lineup."

"Fair enough. If we can't get a definitive ID, we'll do a picture lineup with Simmons after the interview."

George smiled and nodded. *You're always thinking, aren't you, Quinn.*

"Ma'am," Kevin said, "I'd like you and George to do the interview. With your permission, Detective Williams and I can observe through the one-way glass."

Quinn looked at Kevin and then George. *You do realize I have never interviewed anyone in the role of a detective, don't you?* "You're in charge of this case. I accept your assignment. George, you up for it?"

"Can I play good cop to your bad cop?" George grinned at her.

"Next time. I need to learn from a pro."

The tension lifted in the room, and Kevin visibly relaxed. "Up for observing, Billy?"

"Wouldn't miss it for the world."

Forensic Work

Chuck entered the DNA sequence from Buddy Wilkie to start the run looking for a match to yield a DNA fingerprint. Since the DNA from the condoms was in their system, as well as the larger data base they could search, he hoped it would be a quick match—it wasn't. He walked over to get a cup of coffee and saw the light on in the conference room. *I thought the team had gone home for the night.* His coffee mug filled, he walked across the hall and knocked on the door.

Kevin nodded to George to open it.

"Come in, Chuck."

The others spoke and Chuck nodded. "Sorry to interrupt. I thought y'all were gone for the night." He turned to walk away.

"Chuck." Quinn looked up at him. "Any progress on the DNA?"

"Have the sequence from Wilkie. Running it now to see if there's a match in the system. Given it wasn't an instant hit, it could take time. Still no hits on the DNA in the condom."

"Okay, thanks. Are you done for the night?" Quinn said.

"If you need me, I can stay. Okay to ask what's up?"

"Oscar Wilkie, assumed to be Buddy's father, is in holding."

"Wow! No kidding?" He looked at Quinn. "Sorry. Of course you're not kidding."

She smiled. "No kidding. George and I are about to interview him. May be able to get a voluntary DNA sample."

"I'll be right here ready to help with that, for sure. Wow! Something other than domestic violence and bar fights." He pulled out a chair and sat.

They all started laughing. Kevin walked over and slapped Chuck on the back. "Just what the doctor ordered, Chuck. Thanks for the levity. Now, let's get our team down to holding and see what Mr. Wilkie has to say for himself."

"I'd like five minutes with George if that's okay with everyone." Quinn looked around the table.

"You're the boss." Kevin walked toward the door. Chuck and Billy followed him.

As the door closed, Quinn looked at George. "To be sure, I've interviewed and even interrogated illegal immigrants, and the mules who move them. However, I would never pretend that I'm in your league. Tell me how you want to run this interview, please."

She and George talked for several minutes and came up with a plan. George told her the importance of giving the Miranda warning in case Wilkie gave them anything they ended up having to use in criminal charges.

"Questions, Quinn?"

"I'll try to follow your lead."

"If I get a little loud and pushy, just want you to know I'm generally in control. Just sometimes need to establish who's in charge."

"And I'll do my best not to react—I don't know how I'll do as the damsel in distress. I can be loud and pushy myself."

George laughed. "I have no doubt you can hold your own. We're clear on what we're trying to establish here, so let's go do it."

Interview

Chuck entered the code in the lab door. "I'll be right here if you need me to do a DNA swab."

"Thanks, Chuck. I'll let you know either way. This way, Billy." Kevin and Billy headed out.

Chuck turned around and exited the lab and headed to the restroom. He didn't realize he'd left his secure phone on his lab table.

George and Quinn entered the holding area and George introduced Quinn to the matron on duty. "This is our new lead detective, Quinn Isaacs. Not sure if you've met."

"We haven't. Nice to meet you, ma'am."

"Likewise." Quinn extended her hand to shake. "Appreciate your help tonight."

"Room three..." She pointed to a door on the right, "... has the best one way, so I've set up the other two gentlemen in the observation room. Shall I get your guy?"

George said, "Please. Detective Isaacs is going to be first up."

The matron nodded and soon returned with Oscar Wilkie his hands cuffed, linked to ankle chains. Both detectives saw his boots and looked at each other.

"This way." Quinn pointed down the hall. George followed. She opened the door. "Have a seat over there." She pointed to the chair backed to the wall, and took out the pocket recorder George had given her. She had not yet seen the cameras in this room, but George had assured they were present and running. Kevin would have made sure of it.

Quinn totally ignored the one-way mirror behind which Billy and Kevin were observing the interview. "This interview is being recorded." She gave the date and time. "I am Detective Isaacs of the Round City Police, and this is..."

"Detective Marshall of the Round City Police."

"Please state your name, address, and date of birth."

"Oscar Wilkie, no fixed address..." He gave his date of birth.

Hmmm...makes him seventy. He looks a lot older.

"Oscar Wilkie, you have the right to..." She watched at his impassive face as she recited the Miranda warning. "Do you understand your rights and responsibilities?"

"I do. Not sure I need them for going to my boy's house."

They were not prepared to tell him his "boy" was deceased.

"Dr. Wilkie, do you wish to have an attorney present?"

For the first time he looked at her. Quinn assumed he was surprised by the use of his medical degree title.

"No, thanks."

"Dr. Wilkie, you have stated you have no fixed address. Where did you sleep last night?"

"In the woods."

"In what form of shelter?"

"Didn't say I had any shelter."

"Did you?"

"Sufficient to keep from freezing."

"What materials made up that shelter?" Quinn's voice was conversational and showed some curiosity.

"Stone and wood—that's what you find in these hills."

"So, it was a building?"

"Didn't say that."

"So it wasn't a building?"

"Didn't say that either."

Quinn decided to shift topics.

"Dr. Wilkie. Your son, Buddy...isn't that his name?"

"You seem like a smart lady. I'm going to assume you already know his name is Buddy."

"Is that his birth name?"

"That's the name I gave him, otherwise I wouldn't call him Buddy."

"So you gave him the name, Buddy, at birth?"

"Didn't say that."

"So you didn't name him at birth?"

"Didn't say that either."

"Are you Buddy's biological father?"

"Didn't say that."

"So, you're not his biological father?"

"Didn't say that either."

"Dr. Wilkie, you are obviously an intelligent man. Since you know there are police officers at your son's home, you know we have concerns for his well-being."

"I don't know that at all."

She smiled at him. "We do."

He looked away toward the wall.

"Do you know Buddy's whereabouts at the present time?"

"I haven't seen my son in many years."

"How many years?"

"Thirteen, give or take."

"Your choice or his?"

"Mine."

"Why?"

"Best for him."

"Why?"

Oscar didn't answer.

"Dr. Wilkie, we're very concerned about your son, Anything you can do to help us understand him would be helpful."

Oscar didn't speak.

George slid his chair closer to the table and leaned his elbows on his knees. His voice was deep and stern.

"Dr. Wilkie, with all due respect, a man of your intellect and education is capable of speaking." He nodded to Quinn, an agreement they had made. "Your son is..."

"Detective," Quinn's voice was pleading. "Under these circumstances?" She pointed to the handcuffs.

"Uncuff him then."

"Makes no difference." Oscar's voice was a whisper.

Quinn moved closer. "What makes no difference, Dr. Wilkie?"

"Whatever you have to tell me about my son...he's under arrest...he's dead...whatever it is won't change a thing."

"Then why did you go to his house?" Quinn's voice remained soft and calm but loud enough to be recorded. She knew how important the recording might become.

"I went because you have it surrounded by police cars, and I had to see if he was in trouble."

"Has he ever been in trouble, Dr. Wilkie?"

"Depends on what you call trouble."

"How do you define trouble?"

"Breaking the law."

"Has Buddy ever broken the law, Dr. Wilkie?"

"Not that I know about."

"Have you ever broken the law, Dr. Wilkie?"

"Yes."

"When?"

"Tonight...and ..." He stopped abruptly.

"How did you break the law tonight?"

"I trespassed on private property without permission."

"Why didn't you just go to the police at the front of Buddy's home and tell them who you were? You could have told them you wanted to check on your son."

Quinn and George saw a tear roll down his face.

"Because of the other times I broke the law."

"Dr. Wilkie, are you willing to voluntarily submit to a DNA sample?"

"You can do that?" His eyes grew wide and he stared at Quinn.

"With your permission—or we can ask a judge to order you to provide one."

"How do you obtain it?"

Quinn thought the scientist was speaking, not the father.

"A saliva sample."

"Fascinating. Fascinating, indeed." His eyes stared off into the distance.

"Will you give us a DNA sample?"

"Can I see the report on it?"

Quinn looked at George. George shrugged.

"If we can legally provide it to you, I promise you we will." Quinn said it with anticipation of solving a crime and some sympathy for a man who seemed to have avoided people as much as he could in his life.

Fingerprints

Chuck walked out the back door of the station to get some fresh air after being in the lab for hours. He hadn't thought to bring his jacket so he did a quick walk to the maintenance garage to see who was working.

"Hey Chuck, what brings you out here at this hour?"

"Fresh air. How you doing, Fred?"

"Drew the short straw. Pretty quiet tonight. Pull up a stool."

"Don't have long, might be needed on a case, but thought I'd stop in out of the cold and say hey!"

"Well, it's good to see you. Think you'll ever get anything like a regular schedule?"

"Maybe. Our new lead detective is okay."

"She's a looker."

"Hadn't noticed."

"Not interested in older women, Chuck. I hear she's single."

"She's my *boss*, Fred. Cool it."

Fred laughed. "Fair enough. Fair enough. Well, if you ever get a regular schedule maybe we can play some pool."

"You're on. I think you owe me from the last game."

"No, man, you owe me."

Chuck stood up and shook hands with Fred. "Always good to see you, man. See you at the pool hall."

"You're on. Later."

Chuck entered the lab and walked over to the computer to see how the run was going on Wilkie's DNA. He glanced over and saw his secure phone at the edge of his computer screen. *Oh, man, I know better than to go off without my phone. How did I manage to do that?* Then he saw he had two messages.

The first was from the downstairs lab—the second from the matron. He listened to the one from the matron first.

"DNA swab needed in Room three. STAT." He looked at the time stamp. *Whew, it was only two minutes ago.* He sent a secure text. "On way." He walked over to the cabinet where the supplies were stored and got what he needed to do a saliva swab.

The hour was late and he was tired. He completely forgot about the unheard message from the downstairs lab.

Chapter 25

There is no deeper desire than the desire of being revealed.
Kahlil Gibran

Some Questions Answered

"Entering the room with Detective Issacs…"

"Marshall."

"Please state your name for the record."

"Oscar Wilkie."

"This is Chuck Stone. Dr. Wilkie, Mr. Stone is our forensic tech and he will do the swab for your DNA."

Oscar cooperated with Chuck and the whole procedure was completed in a matter of minutes. Chuck was out of the room and quiet settled over it.

"I knew this was coming."

"What's that, sir?"

"The DNA sequencing. It was in its infancy when I last worked. How long does it take?"

"Establishing your DNA sequence can be done fairly quickly, although sometimes it takes longer than others. Once your sequence is determined, it can be compared against databases to compare identities and relationships." Quinn watched his eyes, even though he was not looking at her or George.

"You want to know if I'm Buddy's biological father, right?"

"We do."

"Didn't need the DNA for that. I would have answered that question."

Quinn smiled at him when he looked at her. "I didn't ask the right question, did I?"

"No, ma'am."

I know I'm not qualified to make a diagnosis but, I'm willing to bet if we get a judge to order one, he's on the autism spectrum. Precise language matters.

"Fair enough, Dr. Wilkie. Please tell me who the biological father of Buddy Wilkie is."

"I don't know." Oscar said it quietly and simply.

"Is he the child of your wife?"

"Never married."

"Girlfriend?"

"Never had one."

"Then how, Dr. Wilkie, is Buddy your son."

"I found him."

"You found him?" Her voice was calm as she pulled her hair back and knotted it.

George watched her pull her hair back. *She's getting really serious now.*

"Saved his life. Found them too late to save the rest of them."

"Dr. Wilkie, may I take off your hand cuffs."

"Makes no difference." He lifted his hands from his lap and quietly put them down again.

"Is this one of the ways you broke the law?"

He nodded his head.

George leaned forward again. "Dr. Wilkie, would you like some water?"

"Sure. Thanks."

Quinn nodded. They had agreed if there was a time when George thought Oscar might be more responsive to a man, she'd leave the room on the offer of water.

"Detective Marshall, I'll go get it." She stood. She mouthed to George to ask if he wanted water. He shook his head. "Detective Isaacs leaving room three at eight-forty-nine p.m."

She walked out the door. As soon as it shut, she saw the observation room door shut. Billy was in the hall.

He whispered. "Okay?"

"Will be." She started toward the matron's desk.

"Need water?" The matron said.

"Please. Detective?" Quinn turned to Billy.

"Please. And, matron, may we use this room." He pointed to the one behind her desk.

"By all means."

Once they had the water and were in the room, Quinn turned to Billy.

"How did you know about this room?"

"Been over here before. Drink up." He took the cap off one of the water bottles and handed it to her.

She sipped it and stared into space.

"Surprised?" Billy watched her carefully.

"No. Yes. I don't know. Something hasn't been right about this from the beginning. I feel like I've bungled things because I don't know enough to be lead detective."

"Want my opinion?"

"Unbiased?"

"On the job—always."

"Then shoot...well, not literally." She gave him a wan smile.

"You are a natural. Someone who had been doing this for a while might have ripped him apart with his non-answer answers. You walked him right back to them. More importantly, you made a connection with a man who is clearly not easily capable of connecting with others."

"You saw that?"

"So did the camera. I suspect Chief Hansen will know she can't afford you when she sees that tape."

"Stop it, Billy." She shook her head.

"Don't panic. I'm moving next to you." He moved over, put his arms around her gently and whispered in her ear. "Detective Quinn Isaacs, you get an A+ for that interview and when you get back, I suspect you're going to figure out what's going on here."

"Speaking of…I need to get back." She hugged him and stepped back. "Thanks, Billy. I needed that."

"Most of us do. We just don't generally get it from someone who also has a personal interest in us." He smiled at her and winked. "Now go find out what he knows."

Quinn knocked on the door. "Detective Isaacs reentering at eight-fifty-three." She handed the water bottle with the lid twisted but not open to Oscar Wilkie.

"Never had a plastic bottle with water." His voice was flat and matter of fact.

"Would you like me to take the lid off?" Quinn had not let go of the bottle.

"Please."

She did, handed him the bottle, and sat down.

George shook his head—it was the agreed upon signal that Oscar had said nothing.

Quinn gave him a minute to take a drink.

"Plastic isn't good for the planet."

"No, sir. It isn't. Hopefully we'll find alternatives that are both envi-ronmentally safe, and healthy for humans in situations like this."

"Could be."

"Dr. Wilkie, where did you find Buddy?"

"In the woods. I hike every day, always did. I like animals better than people. His foot had been mauled by a bear and he was bleeding out. The rest of his family already had."

"The rest of his family?"

"Well, I'm guessing it was his family. A woman, a man, another boy, and a girl."

"What year was it?"

"Not sure I remember. Didn't want to. It was right on thirty years ago, though."

"Did you report this to the authorities?"

He shook his head and took another sip of water.

"Is that a no, Dr. Wilkie."

"No, I didn't tell anyone. Not even my mama."

"How did you save Buddy's life?"

"You already figured out I went to medical school. Mama insisted. I was a good student, but never very good with people."

They let him talk.

"Mama had moved into the house Buddy owns when I was little. Folks in her social class weren't very understanding about how different I was. Guess I broke her heart."

He took another sip.

"Mama didn't even know I had Buddy for the first two years. I nursed him back to health, taught him at home and finally took him to the small school where my mama got me a job. Nobody ever questioned me about him."

"Did you adopt him?"

"Not legally. Just kept him. Boy had no one else—not like his folks would come back for him."

"What did you do with their remains?"

"Put them in the freezer."

Oscar was looking at the table. George and Quinn looked at each other.

"In the freezer at Buddy's?" Quinn's voice was soft and gentle.

"What? No. At the house where I raised Buddy?"

"Where is that?"

He gave them the turn off from the county road and told them how far it was to reach it. George knew Kevin would have someone out looking for that house within minutes.

"Do you still own that house?"

"Yes."

"Do you live there?"

"No."

"Does anyone?"

"No. Buddy goes every Tuesday to clean it like I taught him. He always did what he was told—I think."

"Why did you leave him, Dr. Wilkie?"

"My mama died, and I'm no good with adults. You can see that, can't you? He needed to find his way."

"Does he work?"

"Oh, he had a plumbing business, but he didn't need money. Mama left us both a great deal of money. I think he did the plumbing so he could have sex with women who lived by themselves. That's why I tracked him."

Now what? "You tracked him?"

"Yep, had a GPS on his van til a few days ago. It disappeared. Don't know if Buddy found it or it dropped off on a bumpy road."

Quinn thought about the boots on Oscar's feet.

"Dr. Wilkie, did you ever follow Buddy to his plumbing jobs?"

"Every time."

George wiggled his finger. It was the signal they had agreed if either of them decided they needed to end the interview and regroup.

"Dr. Wilkie, I'm going to end this interview for now. It is late and this has been difficult for you. We'll talk again tomorrow."

"Whatever you want." Oscar never looked up. He twirled the bottle of water around and around in his hands.

"This concludes the interview with Detective Isaacs…"

"Detective Marshall…"

"I'm Oscar Wilkie."

"It's nine-ten p.m."

"I'll walk Dr. Wilkie back." George opened the door and escorted Oscar to the matron.

Quinn met Kevin and Billy in the hall and they headed back to the conference room.

Quinn was pacing when George walked in. "This is one hell of a night." He was about to sit down when there was a knock on the door. He opened it. "Oh, it's you. Come on in, Chuck."

"Quinn, I have to see you right now."

"Can it wait?"

"No."

She stood and walked across the hall to the lab with Chuck.

"What's so urgent?"

"I got a call from the downstairs lab and they have a match on one of the fingerprints from the headboard at both Summers and Andrews."

"Do we know who?"

"Yes, ma'am."

"Then who?"

He told her. She pulled out the stool and said, "Say that one more time?"

"I couldn't believe it either." Chuck was pacing back and forth.

"Any hits on the DNA?"

"None. Not for either Wilkie."

"Well, it seems we have someone else's DNA we need. Let's go across the hall."

Next Steps

"Gentlemen, I'd like to regroup on what we know at this moment. Then I'll ask Chuck to share the latest findings."

"Detective Isaacs," George surprised all of them with his formality. "Quinn...I just want to say, before we start, that for all the training and experience I've had, the interviews and interrogations I've observed and watched in trainings, I've never seen anyone handle an interview as well as you did."

Quinn let out a long sigh. "You are too kind, George. We had a plan when we went in and all I did was try to read the man."

"Well, you did it masterfully." Kevin was all but clapping.

"Thanks for the votes of confidence. Now we still have two murders to solve."

"And maybe even more deaths."

Chuck looked at George. "More?"

Billy spoke for the first time. "If I were a betting person, and I'm not. Dr. Wilkie's story of finding this family after they were mauled is probably true. It will give the forensic anthropologist a place to start. Even if their family members aren't in the legal system, they may be in one of the systems where folks are looking for family members. Five family members disappearing without a trace has to have someone wondering what happened to them."

"Astute observation, Billy. What's got you chomping at the bit, Chuck."

"Well, George, I wasn't in on the interview. Recap, please."

Quinn filled in the details. "Questions?"

"Nope."

"None."

"What now?"

"Well, we'll see if those remains are still in a freezer wherever that house is. Kevin, I assume you sent folks looking?"

"Yes, ma'am. He gave pretty explicit directions. That's a pretty rural area though and the road might still have snow."

"I think it can wait until tomorrow if it does." Quinn smiled at him.

"True. Overnight after thirty years isn't going to matter."

Quinn watched the others. "I'm guessing, and it's purely a guess, the remains are in the shed at Buddy Wilkie's house."

"Makes sense." Kevin stopped. "Buddy Wilkie was trying to find out who he was and who those bones belonged to, wasn't he?"

"We may never know." Quinn said. "However, I think it's a pretty good angle to follow."

"But what about the women? Chuck, you said there's no DNA hit with either Wilkie and the DNA in the condoms."

"Right, George." Chuck turned to look at Quinn. "Do you want me to tell them about the fingerprints?"

"This isn't a guessing contest, Chuck. We're all tired, it's late, and you have new evidence. Please share it."

"Well, the downstairs lab ran the fingerprints gathered at the Summers and Andrews homes. There was a hit in the system to one found on the headboard in each house."

"Spill it, Chuck. Who was it?"

Chuck told them.

"Really?"

"No kidding?"

"Wow, what do we do now, Quinn?"

"I go and call the Chief. No evidence and no information can leave this room. Clear?"

"Clear."

"Of course not."

Billy watched all of them. *Glad this isn't in my shop.*

"I'll be back shortly."

Quinn walked to her office and picked up her Yeti cup which had water from early morning. She took her secure phone and dialed the Chief.

"Hansen."

"Isaacs." She filled the chief in on the interview with Oscar Wilkie, the fact that neither Wilkie fit the DNA for the condoms, and the information about the fingerprints.

"Chief, I know the fingerprints don't mean the individual is guilty of murdering the two women. However, he is the only living potential suspect, and I believe we have to bring him in for questioning. We also need his DNA."

"You know, as well as I do, we are allowed to collect DNA without a warrant from a suspect, though it's better if we have one. In this case, I think we have no choice. Your plan is acceptable to me. Keep me updated."

"Yes, ma'am." The line went dead. *How long have I been on this job? Two weeks and a lifetime—since Eliza died.* She decided to walk down the hall to the restroom and wash her face before she went back in the conference room.

As refreshed as she was likely to feel tonight, she took out her key and opened the conference room door.

"Detective Williams, may I speak to you?"

Billy stood up and walked to the door. He closed it behind him. "Yes, ma'am."

"I may be here for hours to come. You are welcome to go to my house. If you need to go home, I understand."

"I'll be stretched out on your sofa. See you whenever." He leaned in and whispered. "You've got this."

She put her palm gently on his shoulder. "Thanks, Billy." She put the key in the lock, opened the door, and remained in the doorway. "Billy, do you have any last thoughts for us before you leave?"

Billy stuck his head in the door. "Good team you've got here, folks. Thanks for letting me learn from you tonight. I'm sure you'll solve all of this. Good night."

"Night, Billy, thanks."

"Later, Detective."

"See you, Billy."

Quinn nodded. "Thanks for your time and expertise. Hope we can repay the favor. Good night."

"10-4." He winked at her when he was outside the door.

Making a Plan

"The Chief has authorized us to bring in the only living suspect we have on the murder of these two women. He is to be picked up by at least two of our officers, more if I hear reasoning for it. George, since you were in charge of the murder, do you have a recommendation?"

"Yes, ma'am. I want in on it and I'll take four officers. We'll want to cover any back exit. Do you want him interrogated tonight?"

"Your call, but as far as I'm concerned, he can sit in a cell, or sleep tonight for all I care. If you want to do it tonight, I would like to observe. So take a minute to think about it. Anyone else have thoughts?"

"George, I think you should let him stew tonight. We all know this guy and he'll be much more likely to trip himself up if he has to figure out what he's going to say."

"Maybe, Kevin, or he'll rehearse a great alibi."

"He won't be able to keep from tripping himself up. Who could?"

"Likely true. I just thought of something though. Does he have access to the chemicals that were used on these women? Well, on Andrews—the one we can prove?"

Kevin stared at George. "Man, you're tired. First of all, anyone can get anything in today's world—you know that. And, he's probably got direct access, at least to some of it. Do we know if any of the chemicals at Wilkie's shed were any of the ones found in Andrews?"

Quinn said, "We don't. We're waiting on the warrant to remove everything. It's the challenge of having potential evidence at the residence of a deceased person and no one else to give permission."

George perked up. "Can't Dr. Wilkie?"

"DA O'Haire is on the warrant, let's just do this by the book. Right now we have two potential suspects in the murder of these women: one's deceased and in our morgue—he's not going anywhere. One is either in our station or at home and about to be arrested as soon as Detective Marshall has a plan."

"I'm on it. We'll arrest him and let him stew tonight."

"Let me know when he's in holding. Then I want all of you to go home and sleep."

"Go home, Quinn. We can cover this." Kevin's eyes looked like a pleading puppy.

"We're a team. We'll all go home as soon as the suspect is in a cell."

George stood. "On it, boss."

They all stood. Quinn turned out the lights as they left and followed Chuck into the lab.

"Good work, Chuck. Now you go home, too."

"Have a little more to do. Then I will. Thanks for making me part of the team, Quinn. Means a lot."

"To me, too."

She sat up straight when her secure phone rang. "Isaacs."

Chapter 26

*Ultimately, we have just one moral duty: to regain large areas
of peace within ourselves.*
Etty Hillesum

Oscar Wilkie

"Matron here. Ma'am, the Wilkie fellow says he wants to talk to you—he has a confession to make."

"Be there momentarily." Quinn took a long slow breath. She knew George was off trying to make an arrest, and Kevin had made clear he was with George. *Should I wait? I'm the lead detective. Guess it's my call.*

She dialed the number for the duty sergeant. "Sergeant, I need someone to sit in on an interview with me. Suggestions?"

"Only got one person in the common room tonight and she's a rookie."

"Okay, thanks."

"Do you..." the line went dead.

Rookie or ask Sarge to sit in? Neither? She heard a knock on the outer door. She jumped up to see who it was.

"Kevin, I thought you went with George."

"Came to let you know we decided against it when we had a chance to talk on the way to the detective bullpen."

"Okay, sure. Your call. Hope you're up for an interview."

"What? Who?"

"Oscar Wilkie had matron call. He wants to talk to me—to make a confession."

"Well, let's go!" Kevin was immediately alert. He held the door open.

They stepped off the elevator and the matron indicated Room two across the hall from room three. "I'll bring him down."

"Thanks all the same. I'll walk him down, Detective. I'll meet you in the room." She nodded to Kevin.

"Yes, ma'am."

Five minutes later they were seated in the room, introductions made and the recording started. Wilkie acknowledged he knew his rights. He never looked at Kevin.

"Detective Isaacs, I was never good with people—well, a little better with children than adults, but I'm smart enough to know there's a time in your life when adults have suspicions when a single man is with children all the time. That's why I kept Buddy."

Please don't tell me you abused him. She silently held her breath.

"He listened. He never talked back to me. He did everything I taught him to do. Problem is, I think I also taught him not to trust people."

"Most parents wonder if they did all the right things raising their children." Quinn's voice was soft and reassuring.

"I always knew he wasn't really mine. When he finally had the strength and I taught him how to walk on that ankle, I told my mama his family was all killed in a car wreck I saw in the paper. Told her he already went to my school and we knew he didn't have a family. She accepted it—and she accepted him. I didn't know the law, but I suspected I should have reported the deaths and tried to adopt Buddy. Time just went on, no one was looking for him or the family, and it just got harder. I broke the law, right?"

"Yes, sir. You did. It's illegal to conceal a death."

"Buddy started acting really strange in the last few months. I tracked him with a GPS signal to make sure he didn't get hurt."

Quinn hated to interrupt him but felt she had to ask.

"How could you track a GPS signal if you don't have a home?"

"Didn't say I don't have a home."

Right, I didn't ask you if you had a home. She nodded.

"Got a stone shack in the middle of lots of acres and leased the rights to a wireless company years ago to put a tower in the middle of my land. I have the best internet around and solar power for electricity."

Quinn was not surprised. The man was intelligent.

"I used to tell Buddy we had something in common, but he never asked me what. I never told him. I'm not going to get to tell him, am I?"

Quinn didn't answer.

"So, that's my confession. I knew I should have reported the bodies and tried to adopt Buddy."

Quinn looked at him—his gray hair and beard long and wild, his penetrating blue eyes carried intellect and pain, his weathered skin the map of years of living off the earth.

"What did you have in common with Buddy, Dr. Wilkie?"

"Being mauled by a bear—only I lost my foot close to the ankle. You already knew that though, didn't you?"

"I suspected it."

"That's why I wanted you to know the truth. I can tell you're smart and you seem fair. You found my footprints Sunday night, didn't you?"

"Where did you expect us to find your footprints?"

"That woman out off Route 54. I knew Buddy answered a plumbing call. I always worry that he'll have sex with someone and have a kid he doesn't know how to raise."

"How could you have stopped that?"

"I paid five women over the years to give the baby away or move away."

Quinn looked at him. *I hope the disbelief doesn't show on my face.* She glanced at Kevin Millwood. He was as stoic as a statue. "Did you ever kill anyone, Dr. Wilkie?"

"No, ma'am. I may not have been able to practice medicine, but I've always believed in saving lives."

"Did any of the women ever come back to you for more money?"

"No. They couldn't have found me anyway. I always made sure I knew where they moved and that was part of why I followed Buddy. He never knew. I paid the women every few years to raise the child. I'll see they're still paid til the child is twenty-one."

"Are any of the children grown?"

He sat quietly for a few seconds. "The oldest will be twenty before too long."

"Do you know any of the children?"

"No."

"Thanks for the information. Now, where were these footprints Sunday night at the house off of Route 54?"

"In the back yard. I wore my other pair of boots. One goes forward..." he hesitated.

"and?"

"The other goes backwards. I worked for years to be able to walk in them. It was a game for me."

"Did you go in the house off Route 54?"

"Yes. I wanted to make sure Buddy got out without any problems. I think the woman wanted to have sex with him, but he left pretty quickly. I was about to leave..." He stopped.

"But what, Dr. Wilkie?"

"Guess that's another crime. I was trespassing. The front door wasn't locked and I had gone in. It's the closest I ever came to running into Buddy. I didn't realize he'd come back in. I turned off the lights in the house so he wouldn't see me." He paused. "Well, guess you'll have me on not reporting the dead bodies from Buddy's family anyway. Buddy left and another man drove up before I could get out. My truck was down the road in the front, so I took the key to the ATV off the kitchen wall and that's when you would have seen my footprints."

No wonder we didn't see any footprints in front. Three men Sunday night and who knows how many when the husband found the body and called 9-1-1.

"That's all, ma'am."

"Did Buddy know about the remains in the freezer?"

"I don't know for sure. I've never been back to the house we lived in together. I just know he goes and cleans it."

"If he did find them, do you think he would be trying to find out who they are?"

"Might be. He studied biology at university—guess I made him. I suppose most folks come to a time in their life when they wonder where they belong."

"Perhaps so, Dr. Wilkie."

"Ma'am. Is Buddy in trouble?"

"No, Dr. Wilkie, I'm sorry to inform you, your son died Thursday night."

Wilkie sat quietly looking at the floor. "Do you know how?"

"Yes, sir. He had a brain aneurysm."

"Dr. Wilkie, I need to speak with Detective Millwood for a moment. Will you excuse us?"

The two detectives logged off the recording and started into the hall when they heard a loud and screeching voice. "You're never gonna believe me. Take your hands off of me." They slipped into the viewing room for Room Three. To their surprise, George walked in with his suspect and another officer.

"Well, we're going to have watch the recording of this interview." Quinn knew her voice couldn't be heard, but she whispered anyway. "What do you think about taking Dr. Wilkie to Buddy's home to see if he verifies the bones in the shed?"

"Why not? Nothing to lose. Tonight or tomorrow?"

"Let's do it tomorrow. We both need sleep and so does Dr. Wilkie. Shall we?"

They reentered and logged into the recording. "Dr. Wilkie, it's quite late and I would like you to try and get some sleep. Tomorrow I'm going to arrange for you to be taken to Buddy's home. Detective Millwood and I will meet you there."

They saw a single tear run down his face. "Sure. Sure. Least I can do for the boy is to pay respects to the last place he was."

Quinn had to tamp down the sadness she felt.

"I only wanted good for the boy. Honest. I only wanted good." Oscar lowered his head.

"Detective Millwood will walk you back to the matron. Try to get some sleep, Dr. Wilkie."

They signed off the recording, the two men left and Quinn sat staring at the wall. Finally she stood, turned out the light and walked across the hall to the observation room for Room three.

"I know my rights. Stop talking. You think I work here and don't know my rights?" the abnormally high-pitched voice was worse than nails on a chalkboard. *Maybe it's just amplified by the speaker.*

Quinn watched as George maneuvered through the interrogation—she appreciated the professionalism he displayed. Her eyes focused on the female: Officer Evans. Quinn saw George nod to Evans.

"Everyone who knows you here is aware of your incredible talents and knows how intelligent you are. Was it part of your plan to see if we were smart enough to figure out the murders?"

The man looked at her. "You don't know anything about my plan."

"No, but I would love to hear about it. We spend our entire working lives trying to protect people and…" she leaned in "…how many times do we end up protecting people too stupid to get in out of the rain?"

"Yeah, and worse yet, women." He glared at her.

"I hear you—we can be a pain. Don't you agree, Detective Marshall?"

"Most of the ones I know are." George guffawed.

"I think you wanted to see if we would figure out how clever you are. Shoot! Having sex with women who willingly open their doors—who could blame you? But you were much more clever than that. I bet that's why you left the condoms. Am I right?"

"Who does she think she is? She can't figure out my plan, George. I can call you George, right, Detective?" He dragged out the title.

"Sure. I always say, 'call me anything but late to dinner and payday.'" George chuckled.

"Good one, George. Do you think I killed those women, George?"

Well, we might be closer to knowing the truth when we get your DNA sequence they're running right now. But then again, we may only know your DNA is in a condom and your finger print on a bedpost.

"Did you?"

"Let's see if you know how they were killed? The dumb ole doc we have for an ME couldn't figure it out."

"True. What are you going to do when you have to have part-time help?"

"What's wrong with part-time help?" His voice screeched like an owl.

"Not a thing. Just don't get as much time out of him. Anyway, that's a discussion for another day. Let's see how I do in solving a murder. Want me to try?"

"Give it your best shot, George."

George sat back on his chair, put the heel of one boot over the rung and leaned forward on his elbow on his knee. He put his hand under his chin. "Your hypodermic was a top grade sharp. Almost undetectable. The fentanyl was enough to kill a horse, but the paralytic...that was the puzzler."

The man slapped his knee. "I knew it, I knew it. I knew you'd never find the rocuronium. It dissipates too fast and you didn't find the women soon enough." His laugh was worse than nails on a chalkboard.

"Well, Tristan, that's where you're wrong. See we *did* find the rocuronium, and I just got word we found the hypodermics in your car." George shook his head. "You're under arrest for the murders of Eugenia Summers and Lizzie Andrews."

George glared at Tristan and turned to the officer. "Get him out of here, Officer Evans."

Officer Evans deliberately jerked Tristan to his feet. She acted like he tried to resist her.

George stayed in his chair. Quinn came in and joined him.

"Good work, Detective Marshall."

"It was too easy. I just hope to hell I didn't mess this up."

"We've done our jobs. Now it's up to the DA." She told him briefly about the confession from Dr. Wilkie. "DA O'Haire can decide about charges on the failure to report the dead family, and what I guess could be trespassing on entering houses his son was in. I would like us to follow-up on the Andrews boys."

George nodded. "Their social worker will let me know what he finds out."

"Good. Now I'm going home and you need to do the same. Thank you for your good work. Tomorrow Kevin and I are going to have Dr. Wilkie taken to Buddy's house and we'll meet him there. Seems the remains might be those of Buddy's family. You're welcome to meet us there."

"I'll read about it in the paper—if it's all the same to you."

"It is, George. It is. Get some rest." She saw it was two minutes after midnight on Sunday. "See you Monday."

"Welcome aboard, Quinn. Welcome aboard."

She walked slowly back to her office. *Tristan's eyes. What makes me focus on them?* She entered the code to the lab. The light in Chuck's area was still on.

"Hey! I thought I told you to go home a long time ago."

"You did. Had to try and figure this out. Come look—you won't believe this."

Quinn walked over to the lab table and looked at the computer screen. "It all looks geek to me."

Chuck turned to look at her. "Quinn, you *are* tired. You mean Greek?"

"Nope, geek. What are all those hieroglyphics and numbers?"

"DNA patterns and relationships."

"So do we have new information?"

"You might want to sit down for this one." He pulled out the stool next to him.

"And?"

Chuck pointed to the DNA patterns and the results. "Quinn, it appears the DNA on Tristan Doyle is a match with Buddy Wilkie."

Quinn sat up straight and stared at the screen. "What? How? Do you know the relationship?"

He nodded his head. "Appears that Tristan is Buddy Wilkie's son."

The oldest will soon be twenty. Oscar Wilkie's words rang in Quinn's ears. *Did I see a resemblance in their eyes? Is that what made me focus on them?*

She extended her hand and shook Chuck's. "Thanks for your work, Chuck. Persistence matters."

"Yep, it does. And, with that I am headed home. See you Monday, Quinn. I hope you're taking tomorrow...today off—well, what's left of Sunday." He pointed to his watch.

"Most of it. You, too, Chuck. Take the day. The rest of this will wait." She stood and walked to her office.

Chuck put on his coat, turned out all the lights in the lab, and knocked on her doorframe as he walked by. "Night, Quinn."

"Night..." She looked past him. "Chuck, it's dark in the lab."

"Good sleuthing...Detective."

"I thought the lamp in the corner always stayed on at night."

"Old regime—new lead detective in town, haven't you heard?" The outside door to the lab closed behind him.

So I've heard. She closed her eyes, unknotted her hair, and was grateful she never turned on her overhead lights. The lamp on her desk was sufficient for the moment.

In the Final Analysis

Quinn sent a message to the Chief, and arranged to have Dr. Wilkie at Buddy's home at one p.m. Sunday afternoon. She sent a note to Kevin of the time and gave him the news about Tristan and Buddy. She sent an email to the DA on Wilkie and Doyle, to George to update him, and finally sent a text to the ME: "Sorry to be the one to inform you, but Tristan Doyle was arrested tonight on charges of murder in the cases of Eugenia Summers and Lizzie Andrews." She had debated calling him and decided against it.

She backed into her garage, took off her boots, and looked up to see Billy Williams standing in the open doorway to the kitchen.

"I could get used to this—twice in one day."

He put out his arms, pulled her into the kitchen and a strong embrace. He pointed to the gun safe. "Got room in there for mine, too?"

"Is that legal?"

"We'll ask a lawyer on Monday. If not, I'll bring my own safe from now on and get an extra one at my place for you."

"Sounds promising."

"Does this late hour mean you made substantial progress?"

She took his hand and walked to the sofa in front of the fireplace. "In ways I could not have imagined." She told him about the Wilkies, the interview with Tristan Doyle and the DNA connection.

He whistled. "Tristan is Buddy's son? Wow!"

She nodded her head and stared blankly into space.

They were each watching the fire. Quinn had a glass of Kim Crawford sauvignon blanc and Billy had a Chimay Blue beer. He held it up. "Learned about this one from Harold."

"Your county manager?"

"One in the same."

"I have a feeling I'm going to think about the Wilkies for a very long time. I'd give anything to have a conversation with Buddy Wilkie—to find out if he was trying to get us to do an investigation by leaving the shoe and bones on police cars."

"Was that the first evidence?"

"I don't know, but things over the last few days tell me we'll likely never know. Still have work to do to wrap this one up. I hope to learn if anyone else saw a possible connection to Tristan and Buddy—like I did with their eyes. Yeah, a lot to do yet, but we'll figure it all out...I think."

"I have no doubt."

She looked deeply into Billy's eyes. "My life was very different last year."

"Yes, and so was the Round City Police Department; for sure the detective bureau was—you are so much smarter, and so much better looking than the last lead detective."

"Flattery will get you everywhere."

Billy wiggled his eyebrows.

"In the final analysis, Detective Billy Williams, we did our jobs to the best of our abilities—under the circumstances we had dealt to us. It is one a.m. and I am happy to be with you." She smiled a very tired smile at him. "I think, no, I know... I'd be happier with you elsewhere." She stood and took his hand and headed toward her bedroom.

She turned playfully and kissed him. "Did you hear? There's a new lead detective in Round City?"

"I heard. I'm pretty sure the best is yet to come."

Author's Note

My undergraduate and part of my graduate work was in special education. I was one of the first teachers of students with learning disabilities in the country. I also had a concentration in students with emotional disabilities. Over the span of my career, I worked with students in K-12 who were diagnosed on the autism spectrum, as was my grandson. The range of intellectual ability and social awareness of individuals diagnosed with autism is as varied as behavior in the population of people. The most frequently defining characteristics revolve around the ability to read, interpret, and respond to social cues. Several of the characters in this book are socially challenged and have behaviors consistent with the autism spectrum.

My purpose for including these behaviors is the hope that readers who are not familiar with individuals with autism will consider that not all who act differently are criminals; sadly, sometimes those who act differently can also be criminals. Of course, we all know that many individuals who appear to be "normal" in their behavior can also be criminals. Thank you for reading my work. I welcome your feedback.

JEJLetters@gmail.com

About the Author

Jacque Jacobs is author of the cozy mystery series, *Love is a Cabin*. *High on a Mountain,* her debut novel and the first in the six book series, has received the Gold Award from Literary Titans (2023), was a finalist in the Florida Writers Association Royal Palm Literary Awards (2022), a finalist in the American Writers Awards (2022), and received five Five-Star ratings from Readers Choice.

Like most authors, Jacque loves her characters and couldn't imagine leaving them out in the cold. This new series, *Detective Quinn Isaacs,* is set in the same Smoky Mountains and includes some of the original characters from the series. Crime and solving it is much more central to this series and some of it is complex and at times a bit convoluted—to keep the reader guessing.

Jacque is President of the Laura (Riding) Jackson Foundation of Indian River County whose mission is: *To serve as the literary hub of Indian River County, Fl.* She is a member of the American Association of University Women, Vero Friends of the Atlantic Classical Orchestra, Florida Writers Association, and the North Carolina Writers Network. She treasures time with family and friends.

Email: JEJLetters@gmail.com
Website: https://www.LoveIsACabin.com